PRAISE FOR
THE WISTERIA SOCIETY OF LADY SCOUNDRELS

"Holton is having as much fun as the English language will permit—the prose shifts constantly from silly to sublime and back, sometimes in the course of a single sentence. And somehow in all the melodrama and jokes and hilariously mangled literary references, there are moments of emotion that cut to the quick—the way a profound traumatic experience can overcome you years later." —*The New York Times Book Review*

"This melds the Victorian wit of Sherlock Holmes with the brash adventuring of Indiana Jones. . . . A sprightly feminist tale that offers everything from an atmospheric Gothic abbey to secret societies."

—*Entertainment Weekly*

"*The Wisteria Society of Lady Scoundrels* is easily the most delightfully bonkers historical fantasy romance of 2021! Featuring lady pirates in flying houses and gentleman assassins with far too many names, I enjoyed every absorbing moment."

—Jen DeLuca, author of *Well Played*

"The most charming, clever, and laugh-out-loud funny book I've read all year—it is impossible to read *The Wisteria Society of Lady Scoundrels* and not fall in love with its lady pirates, flying houses, and swoonworthy romance. India Holton's utterly delightful debut is pure joy from start to finish." —Martha Waters, author of *To Have and to Hoax*

"India's debut is charming, clever, action-packed, with masterful bantering-while-dueling choreography: it reminds me of *The Princess Bride*, except swoonier and more fantastical. It's an instant beloved favorite." —Sarah Hogle, author of *You Deserve Each Other*

"With a piratical heroine who would rather be reading and a hero whose many disguises hide a (slightly tarnished) heart of gold, *The Wisteria Society of Lady Scoundrels* is the perfect diversion for a rainy afternoon with a cup of tea. What fun!"

—Manda Collins, author of *A Lady's Guide to Mischief and Mayhem*

"Holton's writing is gorgeous and lyrical, her dialogue clever and witty, and her characters lovable and unforgettable. The story contains so many enthralling elements—lady scoundrels and spells, pirates and explosions, romance and flying-house thievery!"

—Raquel Vasquez Gilliland, author of
Sia Martinez and the Moonlit Beginning of Everything

"If books are truly a portable magic, then *The Wisteria Society of Lady Scoundrels* is a satchel full of powerful spells and glittering fairy dust."

—Lynn Painter, author of *Better Than the Movies*

"With secret identities, secret doors, and secret histories to spare, this high-octane layer-cake of escapism hits the spot." —*Publishers Weekly*

"In this joyride of a debut, Holton draws us into a madcap world of courtly corsairs, murderous matrons, and pity-inspiring henchmen. . . . As if the Parasol Protectorate series met *The Princess Bride* and a corseted *Lara Croft: Tomb Raider.*" —*Kirkus Reviews*

"A tongue-in-cheek swashbuckling adventure." —*Library Journal*

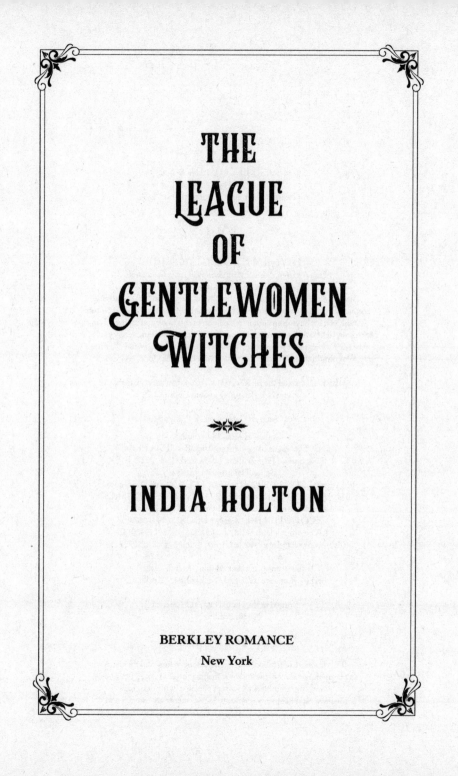

THE LEAGUE OF GENTLEWOMEN WITCHES

INDIA HOLTON

BERKLEY ROMANCE

New York

BERKLEY ROMANCE
Published by Berkley
An imprint of Penguin Random House LLC
penguinrandomhouse.com

Library of Congress Cataloging-in-Publication Data

Names: Holton, India, author.
Title: The league of gentlewomen witches / India Holton.
Description: First Edition. | New York: Jove, 2022. |
Series: Dangerous damsels
Identifiers: LCCN 2021042014 (print) | LCCN 2021042015 (ebook) |
ISBN 9780593200186 (trade paperback) | ISBN 9780593200193 (ebook)
Classification: LCC PR9639.4.H66 L43 2022 (print) |
LCC PR9639.4.H66 (ebook) | DDC 823/.92—dc23
LC record available at https://lccn.loc.gov/2021042014
LC ebook record available at https://lccn.loc.gov/2021042015

Jove trade paperback edition / March 2022
Berkley Romance trade paperback edition / April 2023

Printed in the United States of America
8th Printing

Book design by Laura Corless

For all the wild wind girls

TABLE OF SIGNIFICANT CHARACTERS

- In Order of Appearance -

Charlotte Pettifer . . . a bibliophile

Alexander O'Riley . . . a pirate of low morals but attractively high cheekbones

London traffic . . . difficult

Miss Plim . . . generally speaking, a fly in everyone's ointment

Mrs. Pettifer . . . our heroine's mother

Woollery . . . a quick-witted butler

Miss Gloughenbury . . . a rival

Mrs. Chuke . . . a bearer of interesting news

Miss Dearlove . . . a tremulous lady's maid

Ned Lightbourne . . . a charming rogue

Constantinopla Brown . . . a young woman

Various museum staff

Cecilia Bassingthwaite . . . a pirate of scandalous repute

Assorted pirates

Sundry witches

Mr. Pettifer . . . our heroine's father

Eugenia Cuttle-Plim . . . a sour-mouthed cousin

Doctor Anne Smith . . . decidedly arch

Mr. Smith . . . an unexpected husband

Tom Eames . . . in the wrong place at the wrong time

TABLE OF SIGNIFICANT CHARACTERS

Lady Armitage . . . a persistent nemesis and matrimoniophile

Bixby . . . an impeccable butler

Detective Inspector Creeve . . . nasally gifted

Mrs. Rotunder . . . an extravagantly hatted pirate

Hooper . . . champion fisherman

Mr. & Mrs. Smith . . . caught in a storm

An informative chambermaid

Several tourists

Mr. Rotunder . . . a gentleman and assorted furniture

Vicar Dickersley . . . twice-kidnapped, once-shy

Mrs. Ogden . . . an innocent bystander

THE
LEAGUE
OF
GENTLEWOMEN
WITCHES

Charlotte could listen no more in silence. For several minutes now a young man at the teahouse counter had been abusing a waiter with language that pierced her soul. She had tried to behave as the other customers and look away—after all, who did not understand the pain of being disappointed in one's hopes for a warm currant scone? But finally her patience broke, and she simply had to speak by such means as were within her reach—namely, a volume of Dickens she had been reading over tea and sandwiches.

Rising from her chair, she cast *Great Expectations* at the young man's head and then settled down once more to her luncheon.

The young man roared. Clutching his head, eyes blazing, he glared around the cafeteria. "Who did that?!"

Charlotte raised one delicate, lace-gloved hand.

"He did," she said, pointing to a dark-haired gentleman at a nearby table.

Several ladies gasped. Her chosen scapegoat, however, gave no reaction. Charlotte was unsurprised. She had seen him enter the teahouse earlier and noted at a glance how everything about him was rich, from his long black overcoat to his gold-handled briefcase. She could not imagine him paying attention to anyone he might consider lesser than himself. Indeed, he read his newspaper and drank his coffee as if she had not even spoken.

The angry young man had heard her well enough, however. He stormed across to snatch the gentleman's newspaper and fling it dramatically to the ground. The moment was rather spoiled by paper sheets fluttering about, one covering his face and thereby muting his tirade, but he pulled it away, scrunching it within a fist.

"What do you think you're doing?" he demanded, brandishing his knuckles along with the rumpled paper.

The gentleman blinked composedly. "I beg your pardon?"

"You threw a book at me! Stand up, mister, and face justice!"

"Don't be ridiculous," the gentleman replied, unmoved. Charlotte noted that his voice was rich too, with a slight accent woven through like gold thread. "Compensate me for my newspaper then return to whatever gutter from which you crawled. You are disturbing the peace."

"I'll give you disturbing!" The young man grasped the coat lapels of the older and hauled him from his chair.

"Goodness me," Charlotte murmured, leaning back as the men stumbled against her table. Screams arose from the other patrons, but Charlotte did not indulge in shock. Her teacup was rattling in its saucer. Her sandwiches almost leaped off their plate. If she sat around gasping, luncheon would be entirely spoiled.

With a sigh, she stood, laying her napkin on the table. She took a last sip of tea while the men knocked over chairs with their furious wrestling. She wrapped her sandwiches in the napkin, rescued her purse from the table moments before the men crashed onto it, then left the teahouse, picking up the gentleman's briefcase as she went.

A tiny bell tinkled as she opened the door and stepped out. A breeze plucked at her strawberry blonde coiffure but was unable to disrupt it. Charlotte paused, squinting against the lambent afternoon light, and considered her route ahead.

St. James's Street was busy as usual with a bright drift of ladies going about their regular business, shopping and sightseeing and generally making a promenade of themselves. A woman dressed simply in gray, with only one feather on her hat and the smallest bustle possible without being indecent, would stand out most regrettably amongst them. But there was no choice. She closed the shop door just as a teapot smashed against it. From within the premises came a lady's anguished cry, and then a man shouted: "Where is my briefcase?!" Charlotte straightened her modest hat, hung her purse from the crook of her elbow, and proceeded along the street.

She had not gone far when the tinkle of a doorbell shook through her consciousness. Without glancing back, she began to lengthen her stride. She managed to cover several yards of St. James's Street within moments and, nodding to acknowledge a police constable who veered in his path to make way for her, turned onto King Street.

Almost at once she found herself stalled by a half dozen ladies laughing together as they moved at a rate that barely qualified as strolling. Charlotte managed to tap her foot impatiently even as she edged forward behind them.

"Stop, thief!" arose a shout from St. James's Street, the force of its anger making it clearly audible despite the distance. Charlotte attempted to circumnavigate the ladies without success. Really, people had no consideration for others these days. How was one supposed to effect a robbery when dawdlers blocked the footpath in this disgraceful manner? They left her no option but to cast off all decorum and step out amongst the wagons on the road.

A driver hollered at her to immediately evacuate his intended route (or at least words to that effect). As she looked back, Charlotte saw the gentleman from the teahouse enter King Street, his coat billowing as he strode toward her. Realizing that she would not be able to outpace him, she muttered under her breath.

All of a sudden, the wagon's horses whinnied and reared, forcing their vehicle to a shuddering stop in the center of the road. Pumpkins flew from the back, bursting open on the cobblestones and causing ladies to scream as orange mush splattered over their gowns. A phaeton coming up behind narrowly avoided collision, and as its driver rose from his seat to shout abuse at the wagoner, various pedestrians rushed to join in.

Within seconds, the street was blocked.

Charlotte walked away from the tumult, her heels clicking delicately against the paving. Noticing Almack's public assembly house farther along, she began to aim for it.

A policeman's whistle pierced the clamor of the crowd, and Charlotte winced. Pain from the noise ricocheted along her nerves. If only she could leave London with all its cacophony and retire to Hampshire, birthplace of Jane Austen, where green peace whispered wild yet gentle poetry to one's heart. It was never to be—duty forced her presence in London, noble duty (and the fact there was not much of value to steal in the countryside)—yet still she dreamed. And occasionally took brief jaunts by train because, truly, there was nothing like leaving home for real comfort.

Thus imagining oak trees and country lanes while behind her the brawl intensified, Charlotte made her way without further impediment toward Almack's. Its door stood open, a delivery boy's bicycle leaning on the wall beside it, and the warm interior shadows promised respite from London's inconveniences—as well as a back door through which she could slip unnoticed by policemen, pumpkin carters, and aggravated briefcase owners. She was almost there when she saw the child.

A mere scrap of humanity, he huddled within torn and filthy clothes, his small hand extended pathetically. Charlotte looked at him and then at Almack's door. She came to a decisive stop.

"Hello," she said in the stiff tones of someone unused to conversing with children. "Are you hungry?"

The urchin nodded. Charlotte offered him her wrapped sandwiches but he hesitated, his eyes growing wide and fearful as he glanced over her shoulder. Suddenly, he snatched the food and ran.

Charlotte watched him go. Two cucumber sandwiches would not sustain a boy for long, but no doubt he could sell the linen napkin to good effect. She almost smiled at the thought. Then she drew herself up to her fullest height, lifted her chin, and turned to look at the gentleman now looming over her.

"Good afternoon," she said, tightening her grip on his briefcase.

In reply, he caught her arm lest she follow the example of the urchin. His expression tumbled through surprise and uncertainty before landing on the hard ground of displeasure; his dark blue eyes smoldered. For the first time, Charlotte noticed he wore high leather boots, strapped and buckled, scarred from interesting use—boots to make a woman's heart tremble, either in trepidation or delight, depending on her education. A silver hook hung from his left ear; a ruby ring encircled one thumb, and what she had taken for a beard was mere unshaven stubble. Altogether it led to a conclusion Charlotte was appalled not to have reached earlier.

"Pirate," she said in disgust.

"Thief," he retorted. "Give me back my briefcase."

How rude! Not even the suggestion of a please! But what else could one expect from a barbarian who probably flew around in some brick cottage thinking himself a great man just because he could get it up? Pirates really were the lowest of the low, even if—or possibly because— they could go higher than everyone else in their magic-raised battle- houses. Such an unsubtle use of enchantment was a crime against civilization, even before one counted in the piracy. Charlotte allowed her irritation to show, although frowning on the street was dreadfully unladylike.

"Possession is nine-tenths of the law, sir. Kindly unhand me and I will not summon a police officer to charge you with molestation."

He surprised her by laughing. "I see you are a wit as well as a thief. And an unlikely philanthropist too. If you hadn't stopped for the boy, you might have gotten away."

"I still shall."

"I don't think so. You may be clever, but I could have you on the ground in an instant."

"You could," Charlotte agreed placidly. "However, you may like to note that my shoe is pressed against your foot. If I am so inclined, I can release a poisoned dart from its heel which will penetrate boot and skin to paralyze you within moments."

He raised an eyebrow. "Ingenious. So you too are a pirate, I take it?"

Charlotte gasped, trying to tug her arm from his grip. "I most cer- tainly am not, sir, and I demand an apology for the insult!"

He shrugged.

Charlotte waited, but apparently that was the extent of his reply. She drew a tight breath, determined to remain calm. What would Jane Austen's fiercest heroine, Elizabeth Bennet, do in this situation?

"I consider myself a reasonable woman," she said. "I take pride in not being prejudiced. Although your behavior is disgraceful, and I shall surely have bruises on my arm, I do appreciate this has been a difficult afternoon for you. Therefore, I give you permission to withdraw."

"How kind," he said wryly, although he did ease his grip on her arm. "I am going nowhere, however, without my briefcase."

"But it is for the orphans," she said, her tone suggesting horror that he would deprive the poor, wretched creatures of whatever small comfort his briefcase might afford them.

"The orphans, indeed? And you're taking it to them right now?"

"Don't be ridiculous. It's afternoon. No well-mannered lady does business in the afternoon. I'm taking it home, selling its contents, and adding the income to my estate. It will support my general affluence and prestige, which in turn will lend weight to my opinion about the sad plight of orphans."

"I see. So by contributing to your personal wealth I am helping the poor?"

"Exactly."

He grinned. "You sure you're not a pirate?"

"Certainly not! I am the *opposite* of a pirate. I am a good person. I only steal from the rich."

"And those who would be rich if they'd just put their minds to it?"

"Yes." She paused, frowning. "No. That is—" She broke off, muttering.

"I beg your pardon?" the man asked, then flinched as a pumpkin flew past his head, narrowly missing him before exploding against the wall of Almack's. Wet pulp splashed his coat, although by good fortune (and some reversal of the laws of physics) none touched Charlotte.

The man regarded her steadily for a long moment. Then with his free hand he pulled back her sleeve to reveal a delicate gold bracelet set with tiny jeweled bee charms.

"I thought so. I've heard of women like you. What is your name?"

Charlotte tried again to escape his grip, without success. "Very well," she relented. "I am Miss Anne Smith. And whom do I have the misfortune of addressing?"

"Captain Alex O'Riley, madam. Which, may I add, is *my* real name."

So he was Irish, as suggested by his mild accent. An Irish pirate in London, Charlotte could only imagine the unbridled poetry he was leaving in his wake. "I cannot say I am pleased to meet you, Mr. O'Riley. But if you leave me your card, I'm sure I'll acknowledge the acquaintance should we happen to encounter each other again at some public ball or soiree."

"Or," he countered, "I could just knock you unconscious, take back my briefcase, and kiss you before I leave."

He smiled wickedly. Charlotte almost gasped for the second time in twenty-one years. Her outrage was so great, she struggled to summon a witty retort. Elizabeth Bennet, consulted urgently, could only suggest that his arrogance, his conceit, and his selfish disdain of the feelings of others, were such as to bypass her disapprobation and move straight to dislike! But Charlotte did not have time to express all that before he spoke again.

"Forgive me," he said without the slightest evidence of remorse. "I'm not usually quite so rough. But what else can a pirate do when he meets a lady of the Wicken League?"

He gave her a smug, challenging look.

"I have no idea what you mean," Charlotte replied.

"No?" He tipped his head to one side as if he might see her better crooked. "I once knew a lady with a similar bracelet featuring bees."

"It is a common symbol."

"For her it showed she belonged to a covert league of women skilled in the cunning arts. That is to say, although I believe it must never be said—" Glancing around to be sure no one could hear him, he leaned so close Charlotte could see the sparks of mockery in his eyes. "*Witchcraft.*"

Charlotte considered this for a moment, then discarding Elizabeth Bennet in favor of Lydia, she stomped down hard on his foot.

Purple smoke burst from her heel. Bother—wrong shoes! The churl might sicken if he breathed in that smoke, but since it was some six feet below his mouth and nose, the risk of even that was minimal. She herself was in more danger, being shorter than him. Luckily, surprise had caused him to weaken his grip, and Charlotte yanked free, bashed him in the gut then under the chin with his own briefcase, and made a run for it.

"Stop!" he shouted, but did not follow, on account of being hunched over, clutching at his stomach. Charlotte knew, however, that he'd soon recover and catch up to her. Escaping on foot was going to be impossible. Almost without thinking, she grabbed hold of the delivery boy's bicycle and clambered on as quickly as her skirts would allow.

The machine wobbled as she began to ride it across the cobblestones. She spoke rushed words under her breath. A lady hurried out of her way, a cry could be heard from what she guessed was the delivery boy, and she went on urgently muttering, muttering, until all at once the bicycle lifted from the footpath into the sunlit air.

Alex grinned through his pain as he watched the witch take flight. Pedestrians were gasping and pointing at the sight of a woman on an airborne bicycle—or perhaps because her lace drawers were made visible by the billowing of her skirts. She really was rather magnificent, he conceded, with her rich strawberry blonde hair and her eyes like tornado weather, not to mention her delightful willingness to maim or kill him. Her manner, though, reminded Alex a little too much of his childhood nurse. The thought of kissing her, mingled with the recollection of Nanny smacking his bottom, made a man more flustered than he wanted to be on a public street.

Besides, Alex disliked witches on general principle. While he'd only ever known one before, that had been one more than enough.

Even the memory of her made him wince, and he hastily transformed the expression into a brooding scowl, in case someone was watching.

The Wisteria Society, leaders of the pirate community, considered witchcraft déclassé, and Alex tended to agree with them, although he preferred *devious, destructive,* and other alliterative words he could not think up just at that moment. Although the Wicken League employed the same magical incantation as pirates, they chose to do so subtly. Alex found this suspicious. What kind of person preferred to trifle with minor things—pumpkins, people, bicycles—when they could fly actual buildings? And why do it secretly, when infamy was possible?

On the other hand, he also agreed with the witches when they called pirates unjustifiably arrogant. He himself was entirely justified in his arrogance, but some pirates he knew could benefit from the Wicken League's assessment. Not that such a thing would ever happen, since the two societies took such mutual pleasure from hating each other that they never willingly met. Alex would not have chased the woman today had he realized she belonged to the League. He might be a nefarious privateer, but he did not generally ask for trouble.

Mind you, the witch was the one heading for trouble now. Flying a bicycle over a crowded street was rather inconducive to the League's precious secrecy, and when her fellow witches learned about it, she was going to be in more danger than she ever would have been with him.

At the thought, he smiled and waved up to her. Losing his briefcase was a nuisance, for he'd come up to Town for a spot of blackmailing, maybe a swindle or two, and her robbery had mucked that up. But mostly he just felt glad to see her go. Never mind that he could still smell her enticingly puritanical scent of plain soap, nor that his—er, his *foot* was throbbing from her impact on him. Alex respected women enough to know when to keep the hell away from them.

But goodness, those certainly were very pretty drawers.

Charlotte frowned as she pedaled upward. All her life she had been bound by one rule. Well, that is to say, several dozen rules, such as never put the milk in before the tea, never slouch on the sofa, and always brush one's hair a hundred times before bed. But beneath the petty requirements that governed women's existence, there was one particular to the circumstances of a witch.

Never do magic in public.

Oh, she might fling a book and make it seem that she'd used her hand to do so. She might stop a wagon, toss its produce to create a diversion. But obvious magic—that was strictly forbidden. Not only might she be burned alive if caught, but she endangered the entire League. Just because no one had encountered a witch hunter in more than a century didn't mean they weren't out there, stalking the streets and haunting the nightmares of decent, law-breaking witches. Charlotte had been raised better than to break a rule, take a risk.

And certainly Elizabeth Bennet would never do it.

Yet here she was, riding a bicycle above a busy London street at noon while a crowd of pedestrians stared up at her in horrified amazement.

Stupid, Charlotte castigated herself. Some man grabs your arm, smiles at you like he's slowly unlacing your brain, and you panic and throw twenty-one years of scrupulous caution to the winds—literally. The briefcase's contents had better prove worth it.

Her hat feather fluttered in the breeze as if from memory. Her skirts billowed around her knees. Charlotte pedaled hard to gain height. If she could just surmount the rooftops, she'd be away free. Unable to resist an anxious glance down at the street, she saw Captain O'Riley waving cheerfully to her. There was something in his hand—

Bother! He'd stolen her purse.

"Odious churl!" she shouted, and shook the briefcase at him. He laughed. The bicycle wavered perilously, and as Charlotte tried to grip its handlebars with both hands, the briefcase's latch snapped. Before she could do anything, it tipped open.

And shredded blank paper floated down on the crowd.

2

MISS PLIM DISAPPROVES—THE PAST AND THE FUTURE—
A DULL TALE IN WHICH NOTHING UNUSUAL HAPPENED—
NEWS!—AN ACROBATIC BUTLER—
MORE NEWS!—THE RACE IS ON

It is a truth seldom acknowledged that a single woman in possession of a good fortune is not especially in want of a husband. Miss Judith Plim, socially advantaged and possessing several fortunes (although legally they belonged to other people), had always felt a man would add nothing to her happiness. As she grew older and the world offered no opportunity for her to test this theory, she became so determined in it that she assumed the same must be true for any woman.

"Just consider poor Hadassah Greig," she said to her sister, Mrs. Pettifer, as they sipped tea at a lace-covered table in the Pettifer drawing room. "Marriage has ruined her health. Why, she's only been a bride three weeks and is practically bedridden!"

"Hm," Mrs. Pettifer replied. She flicked over a page in the magazine she had open on her lap.

Miss Plim eyed her narrowly through a small, round pair of spectacles. "Are you listening to me, Delphine?"

"Of course not, dear." Mrs. Pettifer held out her hand without looking up from the magazine and, with a low mutter, transported a biscuit from a nearby plate to her fingers. "But don't let that stop you from going on."

Miss Plim pursed her lips in lieu of employing the witches' incantation to propel Mrs. Pettifer out the nearest window. Magic was not to be used for fun. Miss Plim was very clear on that—so clear, indeed, that she had made it the unofficial motto of the Wicken League by dint of sheer nagging. She was a stickler. Not for anything in particular, per se—but, rather, for everything. If there was stickling to be done, Miss Plim was the woman for the job. And nothing called for stickling more than witchcraft.

"What are you reading in that rag that could be more important than the willful self-ruin of independent women?" she demanded of her sister.

"An account of the Belfast riots," Mrs. Pettifer said.

"Huh."

(This was, it must be said, an awfully brief statement on the Irish situation from a woman who had recently used witchcraft to campaign against "that atrocious liberal" Gladstone, driving him so to distraction by subtly moving the pencil tray on his desk and the potted fern on his windowsill that he actually proposed Home Rule for the Irish and got himself laughed out of office.)

"Several people have been killed," Mrs. Pettifer reported. "It's quite shocking."

Miss Plim pecked irritably at her tea. "Something more shocking happened yesterday."

"Indeed?" Mrs. Pettifer flicked over another page. "You smiled at someone?"

"No. I was in Twining's and that Darlington woman walked in. She acknowledged me politely with a nod."

At this, Mrs. Pettifer finally looked up, her velvety eyes growing wide. "Not Miss Darlington, the pirate?"

"Indeed," Miss Plim intoned.

"How atrocious! What did you do?"

"Arranged for a canister of tea to fall on her head, of course. What else could I do?"

"Nothing," Mrs. Pettifer agreed. "And how did she respond?"

"Brace yourself, sister."

"I am braced, sister. Tell me."

"She laughed!"

Mrs. Pettifer, despite the bracing, gasped.

"This never would have happened a few months ago," Miss Plim said, shaking her head as she recollected the offensive scene. The knot of black hair upon her crown reverberated with an attitude of disapproval all its own. "Apparently the woman has got herself married to some *man,* and it's caused her to develop a sense of humor." These last three words were spoken as if they tasted of raw lemon rind. "Married, in her advanced years, and moreover when she is independently wealthy! Women should only became wives if they have nothing better to do. Granted, Darlington is a pirate, therefore prone to stupid behavior. But altogether this modern trend for romance is quite ridiculous."

"Hm," Mrs. Pettifer said, trying not to glance at the dozen red roses her husband had given her yesterday. They stood in a vase just behind her older sister's head, making the thin, gray-clad woman appear to be wreathed with folly. If only she knew how Mrs. Pettifer had expressed gratitude to Mr. Pettifer for those roses . . .

All at once Mrs. Pettifer was obliged to repurpose the magazine as a fan.

"I blame education," Miss Plim was saying, oblivious to her sister's blushes. "The female brain is weakened with all those ramblings from male philosophers and foolish examples from kings." With a click of her tongue, she damned the entire compass of pedagogical arts, selected a tiny salmon sandwich from the tiered plate before her, then muttered a few words to engage the teapot in refilling her cup while she herself cut the sandwich into quarters. "At least our Charlotte seems established as an old maid."

"*My* Charlotte," Mrs. Pettifer amended, since the girl in question was her daughter.

"Don't talk nonsense, Delphine." Miss Plim lifted the sandwich to her lips then lowered it again with an expression of vague revulsion. "You know that, as the Prophesized One, Charlotte belongs to the entire Wicken League." In other words, herself. She was after all, as its leader, the very embodiment of the League. (Or the archetype. Or whatever noun necessary to justify Charlotte being in her control.)

Mrs. Pettifer gave a sigh as complex as her tightly curled coiffure. "Don't mention that prophecy. I still maintain Lettice just wanted to predict smaller bustles and higher hemlines."

"Balderdash. I heard her—"

"You dictated to her."

"—and she *clearly said* the true heir of Beryl Black would come, bringing in a new era of greatness. Then she pointed at you. Seven months later, Charlotte was born."

Mrs. Pettifer recalled the scene with distaste. It had quite ruined her wedding day. The fact Lettice had died later that night only served to further inspire general belief in her prediction—mostly because the League witches knew a warning not to ask questions when they saw one in the form of a knife having accidentally fallen into the back of an elderly woman while she slept.

Then again, scandal would have erupted had Charlotte *not* been prophesized somehow. Witches disliked seeing people go about their lives in random fashion; it was altogether untidy. Why, only yesterday

Mrs. Pettifer herself had been predicted by various cards, crystals, and passing clouds to spend the week playing tennis, buying that charming pink hat in Harrod's, and alas, having afternoon tea with Judith.

"Lettice could at least have waited until I was on my honeymoon to announce her prophecy," she said with a bitter look at her sister.

Miss Plim would have shrugged had that not been unladylike (and rather difficult to do when one's posture is even stiffer than an Englishman's upper lip). "There was no time to waste. Rumor had it Margaret Cuttle was about to pay a medium to predict her granddaughter was the One. Can you imagine anything so unscrupulous?"

Mrs. Pettifer thought of Lettice's body in its blood-soaked bed, and decided changing the subject was advisable. "If you feared Charlotte marrying," she said, "why did you insist on her receiving such a thorough education?"

"The risk was necessary. Even if she weren't the Prophesized One, Charlotte is a Plim, and therefore needed to be educated with her heritage in mind."

Plim women had been witches for almost two hundred years, although this did not equate to a blood inheritance of magic. Their power came from a Latin incantation Beryl Black had found in an old seawashed bottle while digging a grave for her husband on the island where he'd shipwrecked them. (He asked her what the bottle was; she told him to go back to sleep.) After Beryl realized the incantation could move any object, regardless of weight, she used it to fly a local's hut back to England, where she shared her tale with the ladies in her book club. Thus the Wicken League was born. (And a subgroup of lesser importance, comprising ladies whose book club contributions had involved drinking too much wine and reading aloud lurid scenes from penny-dreadful novels; they degraded the art of witchery into the crude practice of flying houses and declared themselves the Wisteria Society. The Wicken League had another name for them, too impolite to record here.)

17

One of the first witches was Andromeda Plim, who ~~betrayed Beryl to the authorities~~ arranged for her darling friend's early retirement. Once Beryl was ~~safely tried and hanged~~ ensconced in the countryside, Andromeda took over her leadership role, and a Plim had ruled the League ever since. So it was an inheritance that involved blood, just not *Plim* blood.

Charlotte's role as the next leader could not be left in the soft hands of Mrs. Pettifer, who believed in such nonsense as "love" and "quality of life." Miss Plim had instead installed a strict regime of intellectual advancement and psychological repression that would have left boarding school headmistresses weak at the knees. And the results had proven as excellent as her crystal ball predicted they would. At nine, Charlotte had poured a perfect cup of tea while sitting in a different room from the tea service. At nineteen, she had stolen the earrings from Princess Beatrice's earlobes without anyone noticing. She was the apex of Plimmishness. Put a glass or plate down in front of her and she would be utterly incapable of not moving it, even by the merest part of an inch. One day she would take charge of the Wicken League, fulfilling the prophecy and allowing Miss Plim to retire—i.e., stay on ruling from behind the scenes until she was at last dragged away to her grave.

"I should like to see Lottie happy," Mrs. Pettifer said with another sigh.

"You would," Miss Plim muttered sourly. She reached for a new sandwich but withdrew her hand empty. "Caviar. Really, Delphine, what is with this nautical theme? Do you not have any good, sensible Marmite?"

Just then came a banging of the front door, and footsteps hurried across the entrance hall. The ladies glimpsed a gray-clad figure dashing past the drawing room.

"Charlotte?" Miss Plim called, her voice as sharp as a hook. "Is that you?"

The momentary silence seemed to wince.

"Charlotte," Mrs. Pettifer repeated in a wistful maternal tone, which is far worse than sharpness, for it can be ignored only at the cost of crippling guilt. "Your aunt is visiting. Come and say hello."

A woman stepped into the doorway, bright-faced and breathing a little too fast for good manners. "My word!" Miss Plim ejaculated with astonishment. "You look as if you've emerged from a hurricane."

Charlotte touched the one loose strand of hair fallen from beneath her hat. The hat itself was tilted; a few creases marred her skirt. "I took an unfamiliar route home," she explained, "and found myself rushing. Hello, Aunt Judith. Good afternoon, Mama."

"Won't you join us for tea?" Mrs. Pettifer asked.

Charlotte hesitated, and the ladies watched her blink as she tried to contrive a good excuse. But failing to do so, she came to sit at the table with that particularly exquisite graciousness, which screams reluctance. "What have you been up to?" her mother asked, passing her a teacup.

"Up to?" The cup shook in Charlotte's hand. She set it down firmly and smiled. "Nothing. That is to say, plodding along as normal, feet on the ground, quite boring, really."

"Did you go to St. James's as you planned?" Miss Plim inquired.

"Briefly," Charlotte said—and then unaccountably flushed. "I mean, only for a moment. Just in and out. Saw no one special, talked to no one, please pass the milk."

Mrs. Pettifer eyed her daughter with concern as she incantated the small silver jug across the table. "Are you quite the thing, dear?"

Charlotte smiled again. "Yes. Of course. How was your own morning?"

"I have been busy planning tonight's dinner party and making sure Cook ordered plenty of pumpkins for the soup Lady Montague especially loves."

Suddenly, Mrs. Pettifer and Miss Plim gasped in unison. Miss

19

Plim dropped the sandwich she was about to not eat; Mrs. Pettifer laid a hand against her lace-swathed bosom.

"Is something the matter?" Charlotte asked as she anxiously returned their stares.

"I think you are the one to tell us that," Miss Plim said.

"Dear," Mrs. Pettifer whispered, "you have just poured the milk into your cup—before the tea!"

Charlotte looked into her cup and blanched. "I beg your pardon," she said. "It has been a difficult—which is to say, a boring morning that has quite dulled my senses."

"Ahem."

The three ladies looked up to see the imperious form of Woollery, the Pettifer butler, possessing the doorway. "Miss Gloughenbury," he announced.

Miss Plim and Mrs. Pettifer exchanged a glance. Although neither spoke, the former's pained smile and the latter's leaping eyebrows provided eloquence enough. A middle-aged woman sailed past Woollery in a magnificence of lace, ruffles, stripes, and beads. She carried a small white poodle also dressed to within what would have been an inch of its life were it not actually dead and taxidermied.

"Darlings, how lovely to see you," the woman declared. Her voice was so cultured, every vowel had its own bustle and feathered hat. Her face was a rictus varnished with the sort of glossy health obtainable only from jars.

The three ladies murmured in response.

"Although I fear I cannot entirely see you with all this light." She raised a gloved hand to shield her eyes. "How brave you are to keep your drawing room curtains open. Alas, my own complexion is too refined for me to risk doing such a thing."

"You do use adjectives in the most charmingly obverse way, Maud dear," Miss Plim replied.

"Darling! And you—"

"Won't you have this seat, Miss Gloughenbury?" Charlotte said, standing. "I must be getting on."

"Do stay," Miss Gloughenbury said, and Charlotte was obliged to stop halfway to the door or else be rude. "You will want to hear what I have to tell your mother and aunt."

"Oh?" Charlotte smiled in mild inquiry.

"Yes, I rushed here straight from St. James's to share it!"

"Why, Charlotte was on St. James's Street just this very hour," Mrs. Pettifer said delightedly.

"Darling girl!" Miss Gloughenbury stretched her smile to show fretfulness. "How could you? I say, how ever could you do it?"

"Um," Charlotte said.

"Surely everyone knows St. James's Street is not the place for nice ladies after noon. Hm? Hm?" She looked about the company for agreement, although showed no actual interest in the results. "All those gentleman's clubs corrupt the feminine soul."

"Nonsense," Miss Plim interjected. In fact, she agreed about the unsuitability of St. James's Street for lady pedestrians, but Miss Gloughenbury might have said Plims were equal to queens and she'd have declared it nonsense. The two ladies had been in dispute ever since attending a soiree in the same dress (that is, not together in the same dress, which would have represented a whole different kind of rivalry, but each in a copy of the other's) and for the past several years had only refrained from maiming each other by instead using charities in a proxy war of spiteful generosity and benevolence. That it had inadvertently led to lives being saved, and each lady being awarded medals, was a consequence neither regarded, except to ensure their next donation was even more medal-worthy than the other's had been.

Miss Plim produced from a secret pocket a red-handled device from which she extracted a tiny broom and proceeded to sweep imaginary crumbs from the tea table. This both calmed her feelings and gave her an excuse not to look at Miss Gloughenbury. "I believe a modern, independent woman should go wherever she pleases," she lied.

"Including into the air?" Miss Gloughenbury asked.

Miss Plim's broom flicked a teaspoon from the table. "Well of course not that. One cannot condone piratic behavior."

"Exactly, darling. Which is why I came at once to tell you—"

Suddenly Charlotte coughed. Miss Plim looked up in time to see a bronze statuette on the mantelpiece behind Miss Gloughenbury become liberated from its position and speed toward the lady's head. Only a heroic dash by Woollery, who grabbed the statuette mid-flight, prevented the lady from being brained.

"I do beg your pardon," Charlotte said.

"That's all right, dear," Mrs. Pettifer replied, smiling at her daughter. "Who amongst us hasn't accidentally coughed the incantation?"

"As I was saying," Miss Gloughenbury continued, patting her dog peevishly. "I was on my way to the haberdashers to steal a new ribbon for Barker here when my passage was diverted by a terrible traffic accident on King Street. Pumpkins broken all over the road."

Mrs. Pettifer ejected from her chair in shock. "Egads, that is indeed terrible! Pumpkins? Are you certain?"

"I'm sure even Miss Gloughenbury can identify pumpkins," Miss Plim said, although the compliment was so tinged with doubt as to make it clearly, but deniably, an insult.

Miss Gloughenbury deigned to ignore this. "I am afraid the news gets worse, Delphine. A rather formidable looking pirate chap could be seen nearby, talking to—"

Again Charlotte coughed. Woollery rushed across the room and, thanks to a nimble leap, caught a large ornamental wreath that was wheeling from the wall toward Miss Gloughenbury's back.

"It seems you could do with a pastille, darling," the lady murmured.

"Forgive me, Miss Gloughenbury," Charlotte replied. "Won't you sit down and have some tea? Perhaps tell us where you bought that lovely hat?"

"In a moment, dear, after I have finished sharing my news. Where was I?"

"I cannot recall," Miss Plim said, "but I have a suggestion as to where you might go."

Miss Gloughenbury's smile tightened to such a degree there was some danger of her face snapping back in on itself. No doubt on the morrow several impoverished factory workers would have their rent paid for them and Miss Plim would be scrambling to devise an even more beneficent counterassault.

"A pirate was talking to . . ." Mrs. Pettifer prompted.

"Ah yes. Talking to a policeman, can you believe it? Apparently a bicycle had been stolen in the middle of the kerfuffle, and this pirate was being interviewed as a witness."

"Was he arrested?" Charlotte asked casually.

"One can only hope, darling. But I have not yet told you the most shocking information of all! That bicycle took flight over the street, as seen by dozens of people, and being operated by none other than—"

Charlotte cleared her throat, and immediately Woollery leaped onto a sofa behind Miss Gloughenbury, arms outstretched, to catch a plummeting lightshade before it connected forcibly with her head.

"Really, Woollery," Mrs. Pettifer murmured. "This is not the time to be doing housework. Please go at once to inform Cook about the ghastly pumpkin situation."

"Yes, madam," Woollery said. Casting a stern glance at Charlotte, he departed the drawing room.

"As I was saying," the lady went on, "this aerobatic bicycle was ridden by none other than the notorious pirate Cecilia Bassingthwaite!"

"Really?" Charlotte said with astonishment.

"Why are you surprised?" Miss Plim asked. "I myself have not heard anything more believable lately. That woman is so scandalous, even the Wisteria Society fears her."

"I heard she stole one of their houses and crashed it," Mrs. Pettifer said.

"I heard she tried to kill the queen at the Jubilee Banquet," Miss Gloughenbury added.

"Well, even pirates have their good moments," Miss Plim said, nudging her sandwich with a fork. "But she is still a reprehensible scoundrel. Charlotte, I hope you take Miss Bassingthwaite as an example of what never to be!"

"Yes, Aunt Judith," Charlotte said. Returning to the tea table, she sat down and smoothed the uncreased tablecloth. "I have never seen Miss Bassingthwaite before. What does she look like?"

"I believe she is a redhead," Miss Gloughenbury said.

"That sounds typical for a pirate," Miss Plim remarked. "No witch would possess such indecent hair."

"Charlotte has red hair," Mrs. Pettifer pointed out.

"Blonde," Miss Plim corrected.

"Strawberry blonde," Mrs. Pettifer persisted.

Miss Plim reached across the table to snatch the tumbled lock of Charlotte's hair and hold it out, causing Charlotte to wince despite such a facial expression being uncouth.

"Blonde. As the Prophesized One, Charlotte of course has *entirely proper* hair."

Mrs. Pettifer opened her mouth to argue further—

"Ahem."

Everyone turned to see Woollery once again at the door. "Mrs. Chuke," he announced.

"Darlings!"

A woman strode into the room, her orange silk bustle nearly knocking down Woollery in the process. "I have the most astonishing news!"

Charlotte sighed, pinching the bridge of her nose.

"Listen to this!" Mrs. Chuke commanded so loudly, even the neighbors could have listened were they at home. "I was just in St. James's and heard all about it!"

A vase began to lift from the mantlepiece, its cargo of flowers trembling.

"The British Museum has opened an exhibition on Beryl Black!"

The vase dropped back down with a clink. The assembled ladies murmured excitedly amongst themselves.

"But wait, there's more! Dearlove!" Mrs. Chuke snapped her fingers, and her maid, a pallid young woman with plain brown hair and a plain brown dress, hurried through the doorway, trying to walk and curtsy at the same time. Mrs. Chuke snatched a brochure from her hand and she stepped back, blending in with the furniture. "'For a limited time only!'" Mrs. Chuke read aloud from the brochure. "'Visit now and see the mysterious amulet once belonging to Beryl Black!'"

"Mysterious amulet?" Mrs. Pettifer echoed with gratifying excitement.

"It was only recently discovered," Mrs. Chuke explained. "Apparently it is etched with Strange Markings of an Accidental Nature."

Miss Dearlove hurried forward again and whispered in her mistress's ear.

"Occidental Nature," Mrs. Chuke said. She waved the brochure at them, but when Miss Gloughenbury went to take it, whipped it away behind her back. "I do believe this may be the pendant Beryl made by melting down the bottle in which she found the incantation. It disappeared the night she left for her retirement in the countryside."

Miss Plim and Mrs. Pettifer exchanged a glance. They knew Andromeda Plim had stolen that pendant from Beryl, then promptly lost it by being so foolish as to put it in a safe place where no one could find it—including, as it turned out, her.

"If it is," Mrs. Chuke continued, "then this is a tremendous discovery. After all, the original bottle had the spell inside it and the great power of the sea surrounding it, was molten in fire, and then cooled in a setting of gold. I've heard it said the power of those forces combined was such that a person wielding the amulet could pull pirate houses out of the sky, uproot forests, even summon buildings from a distance."

"It's just a myth," Charlotte said.

"It's in the British Museum," Mrs. Chuke countered, flapping the brochure.

Never before had a moment of silence sounded so loud.

"Imagine being able to weed one's yard without effort," Miss Gloughenbury said dreamily.

"Or bring a bank to oneself," Mrs. Pettifer said with a smile. "Grand larceny from the convenience of one's own doorstep!"

"Imagine being the downfall of those revolting Wisteria Society ladies—literally!" Miss Plim added through a mouthful of oyster savory.

Everyone sighed.

"The museum's Grenville Library has been remodeled for the special purpose," Mrs. Chuke reported, "and extraordinary security measures are in place."

The ladies laughed. Even Woollery smirked.

"Well, now." Miss Gloughenbury tucked her taxidermied dog under her arm so as to more easily straighten her gloves. "This has been lovely, darlings, but I must be on my way. I've suddenly recollected another engagement I have with my—er, my hat maker."

Miss Plim pushed back her chair and rose. "I too must go. Thank you for tea, Delphine, but I have an urgent dentist appointment that quite slipped my mind."

The two ladies raced each other to the door as fast as decorum and heavy dresses would allow.

"Heavens, is that the time?" Mrs. Pettifer said, although there was no clock in the room for her to have consulted. She rose, shedding biscuit crumbs from her flounced skirt. "Excuse me, Mrs. Chuke, but I—er, I have to see a woman about a pumpkin."

"Not at all," Mrs. Chuke replied, backing from the room even as she spoke. "I only called in to share the information, and now must hurry along myself before, before . . ." She blinked at the window as if seeking inspiration. "Yes, before night falls."

With a swish of skirts and a clatter of heels, the ladies departed, and a moment later could be seen hastening along the street behind Misses Gloughenbury and Plim toward Bloomsbury, where in addition to the British Museum there was no doubt a dentist, a pumpkin supplier, a hatter, and several more hours of daylight.

Charlotte sat for a moment in thoughtful stillness, then leaned back in her chair, propped her feet up on another chair, and selected a custard tart from the tea table.

"Will madam be staying at home this afternoon?" Woollery asked from the doorway.

They exchanged a look. Neither smiled, although only at the cost of some effort.

"I believe I might go out in a short while," Charlotte said.

"Can I bring you anything for your purpose?"

"Yes, please. Tell Bagshot I need a new purse. And you might bring me my black embroidered boots, a parasol, three screwdrivers of assorted widths, and a gun."

"Pistol or rifle, madam?"

"Pistol, please. I have a feeling things are going to become rather piratic."

"How exciting, madam," Woollery said without intonation.

"I hope so, Woollery, for I dearly love a laugh." And taking a small bite of custard tart, Charlotte frowned pleasantly into the middle distance.

❈ 3 ❈

A LADIES' MAN—THE EFFECT OF MARRIAGE ON RESPIRATORY RATES—
BEST-LAID PLANS—THE WITCH IS BACK—TWO FOES MEET—
AN UNAMUSING DESTRUCTION—THE TOOLS OF WITCHCRAFT

Alex often thought that there was nothing so bad as meeting with one's friends. He seemed so forlorn with them; especially lately, when they were happy to an almost sickening degree. Alex did not believe in happiness. He believed in temporary self-delusion and gin.

But as he entered the British Museum, he caught sight of Ned Lightbourne leaning against a wall on the west side of the entrance hall, looking bored, and his heart took him over to the man before his feet even knew what they were doing. That was how it was with him and Ned—that instinct for each other, despite everything. Alex didn't like it, but apparently was doomed to an enduring fellowship, a brotherly kind of love, damn it.

As he traversed the hall, his boots smacking against the polished stone floor, he noticed several ladies watching him. Their heads turned beneath elegant hats as they tracked his calm, powerful stride. Their mouths edged into indiscreet smiles. He heard several whispers and felt hot gazes slide up and down his body. One woman even began to approach, but Alex veered away, having no time for conversation despite her pretty golden curls. (As a matter of fact she was a museum employee, wanting to inform him that he needed a ticket to enter. But as she drew near, it became clear to her he was a pirate, and she wisely decided not to pursue both the entry fee and the scary man with a passel of weapons beneath his long black coat.)

Alex did not mind the attention. In fact, after a miserable youth being kicked around—and smashed around, and thrown various distances—he liked now being an object of desire. He was always happy to dance with a lady, or do a great deal more, even if her motive was just to scandalize society by being seen in his company. He would oblige any who wanted to play with fire. It was never heartfelt—after all, no one engaged with a dangerous pirate for the sake of his personality—and yet Alex had no complaints. Women were decidedly enjoyable.

But a good robbery was even better.

Any woman he came across today would be no more than an obstacle between him and his goal, the Black Beryl amulet. And Alex intended to obtain his goal. He could not lose, because he would not lose. He'd learned the hard way that attitude was everything.

"How ya?" he said as he approached Ned.

The blond man glanced up with an expression that seemed all the more deadly because he was attending to his fingernails with a serrated dagger. But Alex only grinned in response. It was hard to take Ned's deadly looks seriously after having sat through his poetry-laden ramblings about the joys of love on the night before his wedding. Alex had been able to clean three guns and sharpen a sword before Ned was done recounting the qualities of his bride.

"Congratulations," he said. "Four months married, and yet you're still breathing."

"I can assure you I'm rendered breathless a lot of the time," Ned replied. He sheathed the knife casually in a pocket of his embroidered black coat. Alex noticed that he was dressed piratically in tight trousers and a hideous waistcoat, and it pleased him that his oldest friend hadn't been transformed, not even for the better, by wedlock.

"Where is your wife?" he asked, looking around for the woman who had become his newest friend, thus bringing the total to two.

Ned gestured vaguely at a doorway nearby. "In there."

"Is that the Black Beryl exhibition? I assume she's assessing how to steal the amulet?"

Ned gave a brief, facetious laugh. "No, she's ogling all the old books."

"And she made you stay here out of her way?" Alex tried not to smirk.

"Actually, I'm on guard in case someone manages to take the amulet and escape. I'll stop them and relieve them of their burden."

"Ah, you're a true pirate for sure, Lightbourne. Always go with the laziest plan."

"Of course. You're here for the amulet too, I imagine."

Alex shrugged. "Maybe." In fact he vowed to never rest until that amulet, and the power it contained, belonged to him.

"Good luck. The exhibition's only been open two days and already at least a third of the Wisteria Society are here, gossiping, trading gunpowder recipes, and sizing each other up for assassination. There are also several other women who I assume are either very enthusiastic historians or witches."

"Witches," Alex echoed dourly, and Ned raised an eyebrow.

"Still holding a grudge after all these years?"

"What can I say, I'm Irish. My grandchildren will inherit that grudge, and theirs after them."

"Then you might not want to go into the exhibition, for everyone's sake."

Alex said nothing in a manner as pointed as any of the seven blades sheathed about his person. Ned laughed.

"I hope you at least have a quick getaway planned."

"My house is just down the road. Yours?"

"The maid has taken it off to do some shopping. It's fine, I expect to be here for a while. Woe betide anyone who decides to steal the amulet before Cecilia's finished looking through the library."

Alex was about to reply when he saw something out of the corner of his eye that froze every word inside him.

The briefcase thief had just walked in.

She paused at the entrance, an elegant figure in gray, her hair bound smoothly beneath the merest excuse of a hat. As Alex watched, she removed a pair of dark sunglasses and coolly looked around the hall. She was even more attractive than he remembered—and for the past two days since their encounter, he'd done a lot of remembering. And restless sighing. And wandering along St. James's Street in case he glimpsed her again (so as to demand his briefcase back, of course, and not to gaze admiringly at her smoky eyes or the slow, promising curves of her body). But upon actually seeing her now, he immediately ducked into Ned's shadow.

Not hiding, not at all; he was a big, scary pirate. He just didn't fancy being noticed in this moment.

The woman pocketed her sunglasses and began to stride toward the ticket counter. Alex's pulse quickened as he realized she was carrying his briefcase.

"You're drooling," Ned commented with amusement.

Alex ignored him. What shoes did she wear today? he wondered. What terrible thing would they do if she employed them against him? And how could he arrange a demonstration?

"You'll want to be careful," Ned said. "That's a witch."

"You know her?" Alex asked, not looking away from the woman.

She had come to the end of the short queue in front of the counter and was waiting in much the same way a stick of dynamite waits.

"I know of her. She's Charlotte Pettifer, niece of Judith Plim who leads the Wicken League."

Alex raised an eyebrow in surprise. "I didn't know they had a leader. Can you imagine someone trying to do that in the Wisteria Society?"

Ned snorted laughter. "I've heard witches are less volatile than pirates."

They both regarded Charlotte Pettifer for a moment, then exchanged a wry glance.

"I suggest you run," Ned said.

Alex frowned. "Have you ever known me to run? However, I may just walk with alacrity into the exhibition room. See you later?"

"If you survive."

Charlotte was quite certain that the person, be it gentleman or lady, who has patience for a queue must be intolerably stupid. And yet it was also considered vulgar to move ahead more quickly by smacking one's purse against those in front, so she merely tapped her foot as she waited for a girl to convince the ticket agent she was indeed over the age of eighteen and any minute now her fiancé would arrive and confirm this.

"I am Constantinopla Brown," the girl declared in a pompous tone. And when the ticket agent only blinked: "I have chatted with Her Majesty the Queen in Her Majesty's bedroom, and therefore *obviously* can be trusted in your silly little museum."

"I had breakfast with the Russian empress this morning," the agent responded with a smirk. "She advised me not to sell tickets to lying schoolgirls."

"Now see here—!"

"For heaven's sake," Charlotte said, leaning past the person ahead of her to frown at the ticket agent. "She's obviously either an overindulged aristocrat or a pirate. Both possibilities suggest you should let her in if you wish to avoid a commotion."

"Very well," the agent relented and gave the girl a ticket. She exited the queue triumphantly and waved the ticket at Charlotte.

"I owe you!"

Charlotte looked at her blankly. "I cannot imagine any instance in which a sixteen-year-old girl might assist me."

"Oh, but I'm only sixteen chronologically speaking," the girl replied, then trotted off on a pair of snazzy yellow shoes that were at least one size too small for her. Charlotte watched with disapproval. Over the past two days she had seen the number of pirates and witches visiting the museum increase as word spread about Beryl's amulet. In fact, some hours it was impossible to actually see the displayed items beyond all the ruffled dresses and madly decorated hats. At least everyone had been well-behaved. Thus far, the only damage done had been to egos as the two societies engaged in conversational combat while scouting the room and assessing the guarded, glass-domed amulet.

But it was also fair to say that if manners got any sharper someone was going to end up needing emergency surgery.

As she looked away from the girl, her gaze happened to meet that of a pale-haired gentleman loitering beside a brochure stand. He was staring at her with an expression so icily intent, Charlotte shivered. His dull suit and shabby brown overcoat suggested he was no pirate; what else might explain the way he kept staring, even after she stared back, as if he wanted to peel off her clothes and skin to scratch at her heart for evidence of—

"Fire! Fire! Evacuate the museum! Fire!"

Charlotte blinked, her thoughts scattering. A young man dashed through the hall, arms flailing as he screamed his warning. The patrons looked at him blandly. This was the sixth false fire alarm since the exhibition had opened, and nobody was fooled. The young man reached the front doors without effect and, blushing in embarrassment, turned around and trudged back to the Grenville Library.

In the meanwhile, the queue had moved forward. Charlotte glanced again toward the brochure stand, but the pale-haired man had vanished. No doubt he had just been an ordinary citizen, transfixed by the elegance of her hat. She purchased a ticket and made her way toward the library.

Over the past two days, she had prepared a cunning plan to obtain the amulet. *Her* amulet. As Beryl's true heir, according to Wicken prophecy, she was clearly also beneficiary to Beryl's possessions—and while old maps and pearl necklaces did not interest her, an amulet with the power to break magic, break buildings, and subdue even Aunt Judith, certainly did. Just thinking of it almost brought a smile to her face. With such power, no one could prevent her from ~~sitting in a quiet corner to read~~ ruling the League uncontested.

So she had stood before glass cabinets, gazing at rows of books while surreptitiously loosening screws in the cabinet door frames. She had located all the light switches. The most significant pirate threat, Miss Darlington, was attending an urgent consultation with her long-suffering doctor after Charlotte delivered to her house a box labeled "measles." And several witches whom Charlotte considered rivals had been lured across town by a supposed sale on rug cleaners ("guaranteed to get tea and blood out of your carpets!"). Charlotte needed no crystal ball to assure her of success.

"Excuse me."

She looked up to see a handsome blond man smiling at her so

charmingly her inner Lizzie Bennet swooned dead away. Instead Fanny Price arose, tut-tutting.

"Can I help you?" she asked plimly (which was even more snootish than primly).

"I noticed a lady drop her handkerchief," he said, "but I'm unsure if it would be polite for me to approach her. Would you be so kind as to do so instead?"

Charlotte eyed the handkerchief he held out. It was a delicate, lace-trimmed thing with pink Asiatic lilies embroidered on it, the sort of confection carried by a lady who had no intention of using it to actually clean anything. "Very well," she said, taking it gingerly. "What lady?"

"She's in the Black Beryl exhibition now. Pale blue dress, red-gold hair in a pure and bright mythic braid. Would you please tell her I think she's beautiful?"

"Good heavens. Can't you do that yourself?"

He blinked his long eyelashes coyly. "I'm ever so shy. Do you mind?"

Charlotte hesitated. Fanny Price advised her not to think well of this man who was no doubt sporting with some innocent woman's feelings. But another part of her would have everybody marry if they could, and was imprudent enough to help the fellow toward that possible aim.

"Not at all," she said.

He tried to offer thanks, but she was already escaping the conversation before he could *smile* at her again.

Entering the Grenville Library, Charlotte paused on the threshold, taking a deep breath as she tried to assimilate the noise and vehement colors of the crowded room. Almost everything in her wanted to escape to some quieter library where the only sound came from the turning of pages, but determined ambition propelled her forward. She noticed her mother flirting with one of the museum guards, and Mrs.

Chuke directing her lady's maid to pick the pocket of a second guard, and half a dozen other familiar faces amongst those crowded around what was presumably the amulet display. Charlotte could not see it past their voluminous dresses, but she could *feel* its magic tugging on her witchy instincts.

At last she located the red-haired woman in pale blue, inspecting a book open on display and possessing such an air of effortless poise and femininity that Charlotte immediately both hated and fell a little in love with her. Here was a woman fit for a romantic story!

And here was Charlotte, tasked with being a servant in that story.

Swallowing down an emotion for which she had no literary reference, she strode over and extended her arm, handkerchief dangling from her fingers. The woman turned to regard the lacy cloth with wariness, as if it might be a weapon, and then with gentle confusion. Her gaze flickered up to Charlotte's face, and one elegant eyebrow lifted in a question.

"I beg your pardon," Charlotte said belatedly. "I believe this is yours?"

Looking again at the handkerchief, the woman's gray eyes began to soften. "It isn't mine, but I did see such a one in a store window this morning and was admiring it. Where did you get it?"

"A gentleman in the entrance hall said he saw you drop it, and he asked me to bring it to you." Charlotte gestured with the handkerchief toward the doorway at the same moment the woman reached out to take it. An awkward dance of hands followed; finally, the woman smiled and carefully removed the handkerchief from Charlotte's grip.

"Thank you."

"He also asked me to convey that he found you beautiful."

The woman laughed. A blush suffused her lovely face. "Let me guess—blond fellow, ridiculous sense of fashion?"

"Yes."

"That's my husband. He's such a rogue." She tucked the handkerchief into her bodice, near her heart. "I noticed you here yesterday also. Have you come up with a plan for acquiring the amulet yet?"

Charlotte's eyes widened. "Are you calling me a pirate?"

"Certainly not. I would never offend you in such a way."

"Thank you."

"I, however, am a pirate; therefore my curiosity is professional."

Charlotte looked more carefully at the woman. Red hair, easy self-assurance, interesting pockets in her dress. "By any chance are you Miss Cecilia Bassingthwaite?"

The woman smiled again effortlessly. "My husband keeps trying to introduce me as Mrs. Lightbourne, but yes, I am Cecilia Bassingthwaite. May I beg the honor of your name?"

"Charlotte Pettifer." She held out a gloved hand and Cecilia shook it. For the merest moment, their grips shifted in what may have been called, by uncharitable observers, a wrestle for dominance, although the pleasant expression on both faces did not waver. As they lowered their hands again, they smiled at each other with ladylike sweetness.

Guns have been cocked less terrifyingly.

"Charlotte Pettifer," Cecilia repeated. "The same Charlotte Pettifer who flew a bicycle over St. James's earlier this week?"

Charlotte narrowed her eyes. "That is a provocative question."

"I certainly hope so, or I'd have to give up piracy and become a reasonable woman."

"Are you going to report me?"

Cecilia gasped with what appeared to be genuine horror. "Egads, no. We may be beyond the era of mass witch trials, but I am aware the death penalty remains for witchcraft. It would be most ill-mannered of me to send you to the gallows."

"While I am pleased indeed to hear that, I feel obliged to mention your duty to the century-old feud between the Wisteria Society and the Wicken League. For example, look over there—Mrs. Chuke is attempting to maneuver a marble bust onto the head of that poor, frail, elderly lady."

"That poor, frail, elderly lady is Bloodhound Bess," Cecilia said. "I am fairly sure her hat will be specially constructed to—and yes, there you go."

Both women winced as the bust bounced off Bloodhound Bess's large purple hat and shattered against a wall. It was followed by a dart that failed to impale Mrs. Chuke only by the prompt intervention of her maid, Miss Dearlove, who leaped in front of her, flicking a miniature metal parasol out from a red-handled device to shield the woman.

A museum employee dashed over, crying, "No! Not Melpomene!" He fell to his knees before the marble shards.

"Tragic," Charlotte murmured.

"What was that tool your associate used?" Cecilia asked with quiet but keen interest.

Charlotte hesitated, but could see no harm in telling her. "We call it our witch army broom, or besom. It has several functions, although we primarily use it as a broom."

"For flying?"

"For tidying."

Indeed, at that moment a stiff woman in an even stiffer black dress held out her own besom and, with a flick of her wrist, caused a thin broom to appear from its interior. She marched over and began sweeping the shards of the marble bust with such vigor, the employee scuttled fearfully aside. As he watched her work, another witch slipped behind him and, whispering the incantation, directed his wallet to float from his jacket pocket into hers.

"Teamwork. How fascinating," Cecilia murmured, as if she had just witnessed fairies dancing through the chamber. "What a shame that, due to the feud, it would be more trouble than it's worth to invite you to afternoon tea. Otherwise I'd certainly be eager to have a conversation with you about that device, the elevation of bicycles, and other interesting topics."

"Alas, I myself am fated to be the next leader of the Wicken League," Charlotte replied. "Therefore I ought not be talking to you even now. Otherwise I'd ask your opinion of Erasmus's *The Praise of Folly,* which you have been perusing. But I'm afraid I'm required to despise you. And as I see my Aunt Plim nearby, I must bid you good—"

She stopped, her heart thudding as she realized Miss Plim was in conversation with a certain tall, dark-haired gentleman whose briefcase she currently held in her hand. Even as she stared at them, Miss Plim's mouth puckered with disapproval at something Captain O'Riley told her. She looked past him to Charlotte, and her brow furrowed above her little round spectacles.

"Oh dear," Cecilia murmured. "I perceive you may be in trouble."

"Not at all," Charlotte replied with a perfectly calm facade. "That is my aunt's regular expression of pleasure."

"And that is Alex O'Riley she's talking to. Just as I know you were on that bicycle yesterday, I also know he was the reason why."

"Miss Bassingthwaite, I must venture to say you are far too clever for anyone else's good."

"Yes," Cecilia replied complacently. "So I have been told before. In this case, it is merely that my housemaid happened to witness the scene. But I do understand about aunts. And I know Alex. He's not malicious, but he is—well, a man. Goodness knows they cannot be relied upon for rational behavior."

"That is true." Charlotte hesitated, biting her lip. "I think I'd better . . ."

"Run away to America?" Cecilia suggested.

Miss Plim lifted two fingers and flicked them brusquely, summoning Charlotte to her side.

"Unfortunately," Charlotte said with a sigh, "I doubt it would be far away enough."

And tightening her grip on the briefcase, she went to face her fate.

✳ 4 ✳

OUR HEROINE IS HANDSOME, CLEVER, AND RICH—
HOWEVER, SO TOO IS OUR HERO—FIRE!—
MR. DARCY IS NOT DISTURBING—CHARLOTTE FLEES—
NOT EXACTLY PEMBERLEY—THE MYSTERY OF MALE ANATOMY—
SOMETHING IN THE AIR

Charlotte Pettifer had lived twenty-one years in the world with a great deal to distress and vex her, but Alex O'Riley was the worst of all. How vile of the man to make trouble simply because she absconded with his briefcase . . . and caused him to be assaulted . . . and, um, assaulted him herself. No doubt he thought he could get away with such behavior because he was a male with a big sword, several knives, and dark-rimmed blue eyes that could only be described as beauti—

Charlotte pressed her lips together in an effort to stop herself from gasping at her own train of thought. She could not afford to let Captain O'Riley rattle her again, especially not in sight of two dozen witches and pirates, primary amongst whom was her Aunt Judith. Getting rattled in front of Aunt Judith would lead to Disappointment. And every instinct in Charlotte's body had been trained at an elite level against Disappointing Aunt Judith.

Besides, Charlotte was better than him. Smarter, as evidenced by the briefcase in her possession. Tidier in dress and mind. He was not even wearing a tie today! Why, she could see part of his chest through the open upper buttons of his shirt . . . could glimpse dark ink thereon . . .

Goodness, but electrical lighting made a room hot!

Charlotte straightened her shoulders, lifted her chin, and marched up to Alex O'Riley (and, er, Miss Plim).

"Hello, Aunt," she said in a tone that communicated no interest whatsoever in the pirate's conversation—or the pirate himself, for that matter.

Out of the corner of her eye, she saw him smirk.

"Hello, Charlotte," Miss Plim said. Her syllables tapped like a sharp fingernail against Charlotte's composure. "Captain O'Riley has just been telling me the most interesting tale about you."

"You shouldn't listen to him, Aunt. He's a pirate."

"Nonsense, dear. I would not be caught dead talking to a pirate."

"But Aunt, have you not noticed his earring? Boots? The extensive collection of weaponry about his person?"

Miss Plim sniffed. "A lady does not look at a man's person, Charlotte. Besides, if he is a pirate, which I doubt, I'm sure he can't help it."

Charlotte's eyes slipped momentarily out of focus as she tried to process this. Perhaps Miss Plim equated piracy to an unfortunate infectious disease? Charlotte could certainly agree with her there. "In any case, whatever he told you is a lie."

"I see." Miss Plim glanced at Alex. He shrugged, and Charlotte knew if she looked upon his face she would find a crooked smile there. Just as well she had no intention of looking. She would rather perish than do so!

He flashed his crooked smile back at her and Charlotte turned quickly away, furious that her eyes had so thoroughly ignored her brain.

"So," Miss Plim said, "to be clear: at St. James's the other day, you did not save a tea shop waiter from cruel verbal abuse, thus earning the admiration of this—this gentleman of undetermined occupation, as well as the pride of your entire family?"

"Er . . ." Charlotte blinked, bemused. "Well, perhaps I might have done that."

Miss Plim stretched her lips into what might have been called a smile by someone without the benefit of wit or a thesaurus. "You are being modest, dear."

"You know me, Aunt," Charlotte said with a brisk nod. "I don't like to draw attention to myself."

Alex did not laugh, but Charlotte sensed how carefully he was not doing so, and she scowled again. Arrogant creature! (The captain, that is—certainly not Charlotte, of course.) Words tumbled in a whisper from her tongue before she could stop them. A moment later Beryl's gold spyglass leaped off a wall display and flung itself across the room toward Alex's head.

He caught it without looking.

"I commend your humility," Miss Plim said, not noticing the inclusion of weaponry into their conversation.

"Thank you, Aunt," Charlotte replied, surprised by such a positive remark.

"Indeed," Alex murmured. "Miss Pettifer seems like an exceedingly humble girl."

Charlotte counted at least three different insults in that single compliment. The churl! She pressed the toe of her elegant, embroidered boot against his much rougher one, and had the pleasure of noticing his body stiffen with what was undoubtedly fear.

"Nevertheless," Aunt Plim continued, "it was gracious of the captain to tell me about it, and a well-behaved lady would be gracious about such graciousness in return."

"And not accuse them of being a pirate," Alex added.

Miss Plim nodded. "Exactly."

"But you are a pirate," Charlotte pointed out.

"That is no cause to accuse him of it," Miss Plim said.

Charlotte took a deep, calming breath. "Thank you for correcting me, Aunt. By the way, did you know about the new orphanage opening today on"—she pulled a name randomly from her imagination—"Knightley Street?"

"New orphanage?" If Miss Plim's ears could have pricked up, they would have. Her knot of hair did seem to spring more erect.

"Indeed, it is so new they have no benefactors yet, and I hear the children are quite starved and cold."

Miss Plim snapped her head around to stare at Miss Gloughenbury, who was standing beside the amulet display, clutching her velvet-clad dog and trying to convince the guard she was a reputable antiques dealer and merely wanted to inspect the goldmark on the piece, after which she would give it back, of course, absolutely.

"Does anyone else know about this orphanage?" Miss Plim asked offhandedly.

"No one," Charlotte said.

Miss Plim stepped back, gathering up her stiff gray skirts. "Good heavens, look at the time," she said, not even pretending to seek out a clock. "I am going to be late for my dental appointment."

"Oh dear." Charlotte gestured toward the exit. "You had better dash!"

No sooner had she thus advised than Miss Plim was hastening across the gallery, keeping an eye on Miss Gloughenbury as she went.

"That woman is more ruthless than a nun who's just seen a student with dirty fingernails," Alex O'Riley muttered.

Charlotte almost nodded in agreement, but caught herself in time. She turned to glare at him. "I don't know what you are playing at—"

"Playing at?" he echoed, his voice all innocence despite the darkness in his eyes. He idly flipped the spyglass around his hand as he looked at her.

"—but I can assure you I am not discomposed."

The spyglass went still. His mouth slid into a smile that would have made a lesser woman blush. "And I can assure you, Miss Pettifer, that if at some point I do choose to play with you, you'll end up thanking me profusely for how discomposed I make you feel."

Charlotte gasped. She did not actually know what he meant, but the suggestion in his sultry eyes was enough to warrant a significant inhalation of breath. "And *I* can assure *you,* sir, that I am not here to play. I am here on business. And the next thing I throw at your head will not be blunt."

"You are reassuring," he said.

To which the only reasonable reply was to stomp on his foot.

Unfortunately, he moved it away a moment before impact, and her boot came down hard on polished stone. Charlotte winced as a metal dart in the boot's sole crumpled, pressing back against her own foot. Only excellent craftsmanship, thick leather, and a durable silk stocking saved her from collapsing with an inconvenient paralysis.

"Oh dear," the pirate said languidly. "It looks like you are in some disc—" He smiled. "—omfort. Allow me to lighten your burden by taking that briefcase from you."

She snatched it behind her back. Inside were documents vital to her plan for getting the amulet. "Never! And furthermore—"

"Fire! Fire!"

The frantic call echoed through the exhibition room. Charlotte sighed. Alex rolled his eyes.

"You'd think people might try to be more original," he said.

"Or at least learn faster," Charlotte added.

They glanced at each other, realizing they had inadvertently stumbled into agreement. Luckily, at that moment a flame leaped from a nearby wooden model displaying Beryl Black's wedding gown.

"Fire!" several ladies screamed, rushing back in horror.

"Fire!" the guards shouted.

There ensued a general trampling, pushing, writhing, and wailing, as the crowd attempted to converge upon the amulet. A guard pulled a hitherto unnoticed lever in the display plinth, and as a panel in the floor opened, the plinth sank immediately from sight. Pirates and witches stumbled over empty ground to collide in a tangle of fury, weaponry, and preposterous hats.

Charlotte shrugged her mouth in reluctant admiration of this security measure. But seeing the same expression on Alex's face, she hastily scowled instead. Anger flaring, she turned on her heel and snapped words at the burning dress. It obediently tipped to the floor.

Charlotte took her besom from a pocket and pushed the minuscule button on its handle. The extendible broom shot out. Walking calmly over to the burning heap of satin, she began to beat it with the broom, albeit one-handedly, her other in firm possession of the briefcase. To her aggravation, Alex joined in, pulling Beryl's black flag from a wall and applying it to the flames. Within moments, they had the fire out.

"Hm," Charlotte said brusquely, in lieu of thanking the gentleman for his assistance.

"Hm," he replied in an equally abrupt tone, tossing the flag onto the charred dress.

"Everyone out!" shouted the museum guard.

Without looking at each other, they followed the crowd out of the exhibition room. Its door slammed shut behind them.

The rest of the day was spent in conjecturing how soon the Pettifer ladies would return to the museum, and determining whom they should invite to dinner when they had the amulet in their possession. At least, Mrs. Pettifer was thus occupied. Charlotte, sitting very straight and very quiet on the sofa, read *Pride and Prejudice* and murmured agreement every now and again. She was not going through the book page-by-page but skipping to her favorite scenes, seeking mental balm so the memories of the day troubled her less. Mr. Darcy— now, there was a man worth thinking about! Dignified, tidy, well-shaven, just exactly the sort Charlotte liked. He would not threaten to kiss a lady, nor smile at her in a way that made her rather wish he would . . .

"Heavens, what is it dear?" Mrs. Pettifer asked as Charlotte jolted up from the sofa. "Surely you approve of Mrs. Claybooth as a guest? It's hardly her fault she married a butcher."

"I beg your pardon, Mama," Charlotte murmured, sitting again and smoothing her skirts. "I thought I saw a mouse, but it was just a shadow."

A quarter of an hour followed in assuring Mrs. Pettifer no rodent of any kind existed in the sitting room, after which the good lady settled again to her planning. But then Mr. Pettifer, consulted as head of the household, declared there should be no dinner at all. A busy man, he had no interest in witchcraft and even less in entertaining witches. He considered them, as a species, altogether unlikable (with the exception of his good wife . . . and Shirley too, of course. No, wait— *Charlotte*). He would absolutely not have witches to dine!

By evening, fourteen names were on the invitation list.

"What about that handsome fellow you were chatting with at the museum?" Mrs. Pettifer asked Charlotte in the kind of mild tone that sets off alarms in a daughter's head.

Charlotte looked up warily from Mr. Darcy's second proposal scene. "What about him?" she asked.

"He seemed nice enough. We should invite him."

"He is a pirate, Mama."

Mrs. Pettifer waved this concern away. "I'm sure he just needs a woman's influence to help him settle down and take a proper job, perhaps as an artist or a slightly melancholy poet. And my rune stones predicted just this morning that you would meet an eligible gentleman, Lottie dear."

Charlotte would have rolled her eyes were they not widened in horror. Over her (or at least someone's) dead body would that diabolical man set foot in Pettifer House!

"I do not think so, Mama," she murmured, and attempted her book once again.

But Mrs. Pettifer possessed the determination of a mother whose daughter was not so much on the verge of old maidenhood as about to tumble right off it into a space devoid of future grandbabies. "Our other guests would be most entertained by his looks—I mean, his books—I mean, he seemed an educated man, judging by his—er—broad shoulders. He must have carried many encyclopedias over the years to make him so muscled. You yourself like reading and thinking. Surely you would enjoy having a conversation with him?"

Charlotte frowned sidelong at her mother, not liking the way she'd said the word *conversation*.

"Mr. Pettifer, don't you agree?" Mrs. Pettifer called across the sitting room to her husband. "A tête-à-tête or two with an erudite gentleman is just what our Charlotte needs?"

Mr. Pettifer snapped his newspaper as a reminder to his wife that he was actually trying to read the thing. "Charlotte is old enough to make her own decisions," he said. (And since her dowry was in an account earning him good interest, he did not mind if she *never* spoke with gentlemen, regardless of their education.)

"I am entirely content, Mama," Charlotte insisted.

"What you are is shy and tenderhearted," Mrs. Pettifer replied, ignoring the fierce scowl Charlotte was giving her. "You need to take a few risks, start a new cycle in life, reach for the sky . . . Oh dear, Lottie, shall I bring you a drink of water?"

"No, no," Charlotte said when she was able to breathe again. "However, I might just go for a stroll to get some fresh air."

Donning sunglasses against the mellow autumnal light, she fled the house. But clamoring pedestrians and the clatter of horse-drawn carriages along the street only served to irritate her nerves further. Soon she found herself longing to run—and run—and not stop until she was in the countryside, where Jane Austen assured her one day was exactly like another, and no blue-eyed pirates with prodigiously long swords could be found.

At this reminder of Captain O'Riley, a strange electrical sensation leaped in her stomach (or at least a zone of her body one must discreetly refer to as the stomach). She muttered without thinking, and a man walking past found himself suddenly jumping to catch his hat, which had shot off his head as if propelled by a small and highly targeted tornado.

Life had been so peaceful before that bothersome pirate barged his way into it! So routine. So exceedingly tedious—no, wait, *tranquil* was the word she meant. And now here she was striding through Soho at an hour usually reserved for attending to her blackmail correspondence. Charlotte vowed that as soon as she had possession of the amulet she would buy a train ticket for Hertfordshire. If adventures would befall a young lady in her own city, she must escape them abroad!

Having reached this pleasant decision, she lifted her chin to face the future with better spirit—and promptly lowered her eyebrows in a frown. She'd unconsciously walked back to the British Museum, where an odd sight confronted her. Several houses were cluttering the footpath—for pirates did not like to walk if they could fly, and set their houses down at maximum inconvenience to everyone else, and then complain about receiving a parking ticket—but amongst the elegant abodes an old cottage squatted. Charlotte removed her sunglasses to stare at it.

Whereas the others were pirates' houses, this was a *piratic house*. Its stones looked like they had been dragged out of a marshland and scraped of old, murky ghosts before being cobbled together into walls and chimneys. Moss stubbled its steep slate roof and grew between many of the stones. This was a building that really needed to take two aspirin and have a good night's sleep. Charlotte wanted nothing more than to give it a scrub down and hang curtains in the bare, white-framed windows. But scorch marks across the front and a broken chimney suggested the house had faced worse than Plimmish disapproval and had responded to it with ferocity. Altogether it brought to mind an ancient raptor (for example, a falcon of millennial age), and Charlotte shuddered again as she recollected the popular notion that a pirate's house reflected their character. What kind of loutish woman lived here?

Just then, movement in a window caught her eye. Someone was standing behind the mullioned glass, buttoning their shirt. A glimpse of naked chest, ridged with muscles and marked with a swoop of black ink, made Charlotte catch her breath. Although she couldn't see a face, she knew instinctively this was Alex O'Riley. The knowledge seemed to sing through her blood and nerves, causing more of those electrical sensations that made her wish to take an urgent holiday to Rosings Park. She averted her eyes.

He finished buttoning the shirt and proceeded to tuck it into his trousers. Charlotte realized her eyes had once again disobeyed a direct order, and she closed them firmly. But her vision fought back, flashing an afterimage of bare skin in the darkness behind her eyelids.

She had never seen such a thing before, except in cold marble. Years ago, she'd consulted the natural science books in Pettifer House library, only to discover certain pages had been torn out. It did not seem dignified to pursue the matter through a public library; besides, classical statues provided enough information to convince her men's physical specificities were all a storm in a teacup.

Why, therefore, her pulse should be racing now, and in places where one's heart was not located, she could not understand.

Suddenly the man paused in his shirt-tucking. He began raising his head, and as long black eyelashes and a crooked smile were slowly revealed, Charlotte understood that he was aware of being watched, and that any second now he was going to see her.

The smile curved, and she realized he already *had* seen her.

Despite the several layers of her clothing, she felt naked right down to her hot-blushing soul. Turning abruptly, she marched home, intent upon taking up a copy of *Mansfield Park* and submitting herself to a stern talking-to from Fanny Price.

So focused was she on this course that she failed to notice the pale-haired gentleman following her from a distance, his nose making sharp little noises as he sniffed the air in her wake.

✳ 5 ✳

The season, the scene, the air of the following morning were all unfavorable to tenderness and sentiment. Charlotte frowned irritably as she marched yet again toward the museum. Miss Plim had conscripted Mrs. Pettifer to help her find the Knightley Street Orphanage by means of walking, consulting maps, or hitting City Planning Department employees around the head with a parasol, so determined was she to track the orphans down and bloody well feed them before that Gloughenbury woman could. Responsibility for stealing the amulet had been left in Charlotte's prophesized hands. The breakfast tea leaves had promised success, and Charlotte herself was determined to get the job done. She had her briefcase of documents, her mental script of conversations, and her exit plan all in order. No pirate shenanigans would stop her today.

As she walked, imagining the peaceful Hertfordshire meadow in which she would soon be sitting while admiring her amulet (albeit on a straight-backed chair, with a parasol overhead to protect her from the fresh air) she rubbed at her sleeve, breastbone, hip. She'd applied talcum this morning, and a few drops of lilac perfume taken from her mother's dressing table. Cecilia Bassingthwaite had smelled of talcum and lilac. Presumably, however, Cecilia Bassingthwaite had grown used to the rash caused by them.

And presumably she did not mind the aggravation of one gentle curl tumbling down her bare neck, whereas on Charlotte it was quite possibly going to cause insanity.

Furthermore, if Cecilia Bassingthwaite had some strategy for tolerating a lace-trimmed bodice, Cecilia Bassingthwaite ought to be morally bound to inform other women of it before they decided to wear a delicate, lacy, damned scratchy, white dress on the morning of an important robbery.

Thus dreaming and itching, Charlotte entered the museum.

The Beryl Black display had reopened despite a risk of fire (and theft, damaged books, broken statues, emotional trauma) and Charlotte hadn't been the only one with the idea to arrive early. At least a dozen witches mingled uncomfortably with a dozen pirates in a scene that looked like something on an African savannah, only with lace and polite smiles instead of fur and fanged teeth.

Charlotte paused to evaluate matters. She saw her cousin Eugenia Cuttle-Plim risk life and limb to pluck a stray thread from the sleeve of pirate maven Mrs. Rotunder. Another pirate was straightening Mrs. Chuke's golden bee brooch in an act equivalent to the unsheathing of claws. Guns, swords, and hatpins flashed in the electric light. One wrong move and twenty-four lionesses were ready to spring into action—and considering the only antelopes were a few museum staff trembling at the edges of the crowd, chaos was sure to ensue.

Charlotte smiled to herself in a manner that caused Bloodhound Bess, noticing it, to shudder and hurry away to the far side of the gallery.

Spying the exhibition's curator, Charlotte began to make her way toward him. She passed two witches debating the correct etiquette for stealing rubies from a baroness—before or after dinner?—and a wizened, white-haired pirate stealing pearls from them both.

She passed Cecilia Bassingthwaite, wearing a plain dress that looked extremely comfortable, and whispering to her husband, who was stroking her back as he listened to every word.

She accidentally murmured the incantation and sent a bust of Erato flying across the room, where it landed in a cradle once belonging to Beryl Black—which either foreshadowed a lovely future for Miss Bassingthwaite and her husband, or was just sheer chance.

And for one awful, heart-stopping moment she thought she saw Lady Armitage, the maddest and most dangerous of all pirates. But it was only a taxidermied cassowary bird that had been included in the exhibition because Beryl once wrestled one to death with her bare hands (or possibly shot it from a distance with a Winchester rifle, depending on whether you liked your stories interesting or true).

The curator was at the far end of the room, fussing with another of Beryl's wedding dresses, which had replaced the destroyed one. Charlotte found herself wondering if he had an abdomen rippled with muscle and seared with tattoos beneath his brown tweed suit, but the way he gulped as she arrived before him was so unappealing, she felt no desire to undress him and find out. Which only proved the general wisdom that what counts in a man is the quality of his character, not the swelling of strength beneath his sleeves, nor the warm color of skin that promises to taste like salt on a woman's tongue as she—

"Hello!" Her sudden, brisk greeting caused the curator to nearly leap out of his probably-not-tattooed skin. "Don't be alarmed," she told him. "I am not a pirate; I am an archaeologist."

He peered at her with eyes red-veined from constant wariness. "What, another one? I've spoken to three archaeologists and a historian in the past two days."

"Junior colleagues of mine," Charlotte said, dismissing them with a flap of the hand.

"Really? Both Mr. Jones and Mr. Brown claimed to be head of the Archaeological Society. Mr. Jones-Joneson was older than my grandfather. And Mr. Umblack had a document to show he ran the archaeological department at Oxford University (although I was suspicious, as there appeared to be a shopping list jotted on the back of it). Mr. Umblack also smelled of floral perfume and had a substantial bosom, but I am not one to judge. All wanted to inspect the amulet and all, regardless of their credentials, were refused permission."

Charlotte paused a moment to consider this. Then she smiled. "Did you think I said 'archaeologist'? Oh dear, excuse me, I said 'architect.' Yes. My name is Anne Smith. You will of course have heard of me; I was recently awarded Architect of the Year by the, um, Architection Society."

She held out her hand and the man shook it weakly. Charlotte strove not to grimace or to wipe her hand against her skirt. "I have no interest in any amulet," she said. "I've come to interview you about the design of this exhibition for a special paper to be presented at our next convention. What is your name, please, so I can quote you in my speech?"

A frown began to wither his expression. "You're actually an architect?"

"Yes."

"A female architect."

"Yes."

"Oh." Clearly instinct urged him to argue against the possibility of this, but his brain was swayed by Charlotte's unassailable confidence. "How do you do, miss?"

"Doctor," she corrected.

"A doctor of architecture?"

"Just so. Years of education, most edifying. Allow me to show you my credentials. There might be a small misspelling involved—it seems architect and archaeologist are often confused, ha ha, but pay it no mind."

"Ha ha," the curator said tentatively, quite overwhelmed. Charlotte gauged he would be easy to manipulate and allowed herself a small moment of happiness, for everything was going exactly to plan. Well, almost exactly. It should be simple enough to fake a mastery of architection, and in just a few minutes she'd be walking out of the museum with Beryl's amulet in her possession and her place of superiority in the magical community assured. Take that, Miss Beloved Cecilia Elegant Bassingthwaite.

Propping the briefcase against her hip, she reached for its latch.

"Hello, my darling," said a deep male voice. A hand covered her own. And just like that, everything went very wrong indeed.

Charlotte lifted up her eyes in amazement at Alex O'Riley, but was not too much oppressed to make any reply. "How dare you, sir!"

He smiled pleasantly in return. "And you too are dear, my sweet."

"Ah, now it makes sense," said the curator, sighing in relief as his world realigned itself properly. "Doctor Smith, I presume?" He nodded to Alex. "Which makes the little lady Mrs. Doctor."

"Little—!" Charlotte tried to take a calming breath, but it was not easy with clenched teeth. "I am *Miss* Doctor Smith," she said. And she pulled her hand out from beneath Alex's, causing a friction that sparked across her skin. He caught hold of the briefcase handle instead.

"Let go," she demanded.

"Never," he replied.

They struggled for possession of the briefcase as the curator watched nervously. This was not how he expected doctors or architects to behave (although he had to admit it did resemble his own married life).

"I'm confused," he said. "Just who here is Doctor Smith?"

"I am," Alex said firmly. "Do I look like I'd lie to you?"

The curator considered. The masculinity alone suggested doctor-ship, but the lack of a tie, not to mention the collection of terrifying weapons, cast some doubt on the matter. He gulped, his Adam's apple bobbing as if it feared someone might bite it.

"Doctor John Smith, at your service," Alex insisted. "This lady is my wife."

He had spoken normally, but a sudden gasp went through the gallery as if he had shouted. Charlotte looked around to see everyone staring.

"Knife!" she told them. "He said 'knife,' not 'wife'!"

The pirates and witches glanced at each other, united in this moment under the thrill of a possible scandal. "But dear," said a puff-haired little grandmother with a dragon tattoo up her arm, "how can you be his knife? Surely a blade is a gentlemanly metaphor?"

Several people snickered. Worse, Cecilia Bassingthwaite cringed sympathetically. Charlotte felt her stomach clench with shame. Only the fact her mother and Miss Plim were not present kept her from spontaneously combusting.

And then Alex winked at her, as if the situation were amusing, not horrifying, not appallingly messy, and not sure to feed gossip all over London for weeks. Suddenly, and for the second time since knowing him, Charlotte lost her temper and did something foolish.

"Miss Gloughenbury," she called out in a charmingly pleasant voice. "Didn't you tell me the other day that Mrs. Rotunder puts cream before jam on her scones?"

Another gasp shook the company. Charlotte's marital status was promptly forgotten as half of the ladies turned toward Miss Glough-enbury in shock at a witch having knowledge of a pirate's culinary habit, and the other half toward Mrs. Rotunder for the sin of that habit. Someone drew their sword.

"Clever," Alex murmured.

Charlotte ignored him. She was going to get her plan back on course if it killed—well, not her, but someone. Preferably an Irish someone with dark hair and an unscrupulous sense of humor. Turning to the curator, she lifted her chin imperiously.

"I require you to ignore this man, sir. He's lying, he is not my husband; he is a pirate."

"Aeronautical entrepreneur," Alex corrected.

There came the sound of metal clashing against metal as Mrs. Rotunder and her friends were called upon to defend her scone-spreading etiquette, but neither Charlotte nor Alex noticed, caught up as they were in a private war of their own.

"My love, you are getting overwrought," Alex said. "See, there is a flush on your face." He stroked the back of one finger across Charlotte's cheek, and in doing so turned his lie into reality. "You need to come home for a nice cup of tea."

She took a step away from him, struggling not to touch her face where it tingled. "I am not your love. I am a famous archae— I mean, architect."

"You really should do as your husband says, missus," the curator advised with a condescending smile.

"I will not!" Charlotte replied. "That is, I reiterate, he isn't my husband. He's a rogue, a thief, a buccaneer!"

"Aeronautical entrepreneur," the curator corrected.

Charlotte inhaled sharply in an effort to repress her temper, which was why the man was able to leave work that evening in full possession of his hair. "This is insane," she declared.

"It is indeed," Alex agreed, patting her shoulder in a way no actual husband would dare with his wife. "I did warn you what would happen if you forgot to take your pills, darling." He turned to the curator. "Mrs. Smith is quite unwell, I'm afraid. It's a tragic tale. She hammered in a nail to hang our wedding portrait last month and ever since has suffered an idée fixe about being an architect. I fear she wants to take your amulet to serve as our door knocker."

"Goodness me." The curator offered Charlotte a patronizingly sympathetic look that, if she was a pirate, she'd remove from his face through the energetic application of her knuckles. She was not a pirate, however; she was a witch. And witches were gentle, dignified people.

Suddenly the man's eyes crossed and he began tugging as discreetly as possible at his underwear through the cloth of his trousers.

"Come dearest, let's leave the poor man alone," Alex said, trying to pull her away. "We'll go get your medicine then tuck you up nice and cozy in bed. Wouldn't you like that?"

They were briefly distracted by a woman shoving past, long knife blurring as she made a literal point about the need for clotted cream beneath jam. Her conversational partner replied with a barbed walking stick. From somewhere beyond them came a mild explosion, and feathers drifted down through the air.

"Allow me to inform you precisely what I would like, Captain O'Riley," Charlotte replied, moving her feet apart and pressing them against the floor so he could not easily shift her. "By coincidence it also involves medicine—or should I say, poison!"

The curator, still attending to his twisting undergarment, gave an appalled gasp. "Good heavens! I see what you mean, Mr. Smith."

"It's all right," Alex said, sounding brave. "I've put up with worse. The other day I merely asked her to repeat a sentence and she threw a pumpkin at me."

"Egads."

"She's not easy, but she's worth it. Every time I look at her lovely face, my bicyc— I mean, my heart lifts."

He smiled with mock fondness at her. She stared coldly in response. Just then, a dagger flew between them and embedded itself, shuddering, in a map detailing Beryl Black's travels. The curator crouched down with a squeal, flinging his arms over his head.

Alex immediately took the opportunity to yank the briefcase from Charlotte's grip. He stepped back, his expression grimly triumphant.

"Consider this an annulment, sweetheart."

Charlotte glared. "You are the worst kind of—"

A flaming piece of wood clattered against her feet. Charlotte kicked it away. "Thank you!" an elderly pirate gentleman called out cheerfully, hopping over to retrieve what was in fact his left leg.

"—devil," Charlotte continued.

"But a devil once again in possession of his briefcase," Alex said. "Do beg the orphans for forgiveness on my behalf."

"No, I think I shall compensate them instead." Muttering rapidly, she held out her hand, and his ruby ring flew neatly into her palm. With a self-satisfied smile, she tucked it inside her bodice.

Alex's expression abruptly turned cold. "Give that back."

He looked genuinely frightening, and a frisson swept through Charlotte's body. Not fear, however—excitement. No one had ever stared at her in such a fashion before—undaunted by her reputation as the most powerful witch of her age, and prepared to absolutely dismantle every defense she possessed, should that be required. Even Miss Plim had become a little cautious of her lately. Alex O'Riley, however, clearly was not scared.

Delighted, she stared right back at him.

"I'll reach in after it," he warned.

"You'll try," she said complacently.

They ducked as a book flew overhead—and then, as Miss Gloughenbury whacked it with her stuffed poodle, flew back again. Charlotte straightened first; Alex did so more slowly, his eyes smoldering beneath their heavy black lashes. It might have been alarming had her inner Elizabeth Bennet not giggled at the sight.

"Mrs. Smith," the curator cried out from his huddle on the floor. "You really must let your husband take you to safety. These pirates are dangerous!"

"I'm not scared of pirates," Charlotte scoffed.

"You should be," the curator and pirate said in unison.

She sighed. It was a complex sound, containing more consonants than are regularly heard in exhaled air, and Alex's eyes widened.

"Don't be stupid," he said, but it was too late. He left the ground and traveled at a considerable speed across the chamber, meeting his rest abruptly against a display case.

"How did you do that?" the curator asked with horrified astonishment.

"I'm stronger than I look," Charlotte replied. "It comes from years of architecting." She strode away, making a determined path through sword-wielding, broom-smacking women, muttering incantations as she went. Bodies jolted out of the way and weapons swerved against their natural momentum to avoid touching her. The perfect serenity she usually felt was as shaken as the laughter in a pirate's mocking blue eyes, and suddenly all she wanted was that amulet in her hand, in a locked room, with a nice a cup of tea and a ginger biscuit to soothe her nerves.

Museum guards were blowing whistles to summon reinforcements; pirates were hollering; swords were clashing with a vibrant ring of noise. The whole world seemed to throb. Charlotte glanced back to see that Alex had got to his feet and begun stalking her. Everyone else remained oblivious to her actions, but although the pirate had only recently met her, he seemed to understand what she was about to do, perhaps because he'd witnessed just how foolhardy she could be when she ran out of patience.

Right now, her well of patience resembled a ditch in the African desert at noon on a midsummer's day. Twisting a word on her tongue, she sent a woman's peony-covered hat careening into Alex's face. But another glance saw him fling the hat off to reveal a hot, dark smile.

"*Concido, concido lente,*" Charlotte chanted, increasing her stride toward the plinth that held the glass-encased amulet. As her words flicked magic across the intervening space, the guard collapsed backward, smacking against the floor. The whistle between his lips shrieked once, then twittered into silence. A pirate in yellow satin leaped over him, swinging her purse from its strings as she chased a witch who preferred her scones Devonshire-style. Charlotte reached the plinth and laid a hand against the casing.

The amulet, lying back on a velvet cushion, sparkled as if to say, *Go on, take me.* For something of incalculable value it was rather tacky— a bulging disk of brownish glass framed in metal that looked more gold-colored than actually gold. It was set on a chain of heavy links that made Charlotte think inexplicably of men with hairy chests swaggering on a dance floor. She blinked the image away and focused.

"*Discutio.*"

The casing shattered.

Charlotte instinctively moved her hand back from the explosion of glass. A mere moment later she was reaching for the amulet—but a delicate, lace-gloved hand got there before her.

"Thank you most kindly," Cecilia Bassingthwaite said, snatching up the disk. With a brief, polite nod, she turned, stepped over the dazed guard, and began to hasten toward the doorway.

Shock clouded Charlotte's senses momentarily before being split by a lightning bolt of absolute fury. She threw words at the pirate. Cecilia stumbled, and the amulet floated out of her grasp. Catching it again, she hoisted her skirts and ran on. Charlotte took up the chase.

"The amulet!" someone shouted in belated realization.

Eugenia Cuttle-Plim barreled past several people to grab Cecilia's arm. The pirate spun about, her other arm rising in self-defense, but

Eugenia shouted a phrase of the incantation in her face. Cecilia reared back (less from the witchery than the fact Eugenia had eaten fried onions for breakfast) and Mrs. Chuke's maid neatly stole the amulet from her, then handed it to Mrs. Chuke. But before the woman could take even a step, Miss Habersham, a young witch dressed in layers of frantic white ruffles, pushed the maid aside, kicked Mrs. Chuke hard in the shin, and grabbed the amulet from her before darting away.

Charlotte strode through the crowd, incantating people out of her path. She'd stolen that amulet fair and square, and under any code (except the actual code of law, of course) it rightly belonged to her! As anger blazed in her throat, the unimpeachable rule about no overt public magic burned away—much like she herself would do if she was caught and prosecuted for witchcraft, but she did not stop to consider that. With one rapid phrase, she elevated herself several feet off the ground and leaped for Miss Habersham.

She landed a moment too late. Alex O'Riley had got there first. He picked up the beruffled witch and swung her around so her lower half collided with Charlotte's midriff. It was like being hit with a cream pie, only with knees inside. Charlotte staggered back, and Miss Habersham said a word that was not magical but certainly witchy. Alex laughed. Removing the amulet from her possession, he dropped her, and she bounced up off her bustle to crash again into Charlotte.

"Stop, thief!" Charlotte shouted with helpless fury, trying to divest herself of Miss Habersham so as to pursue the fiendish pirate. Alex did not pause, but he threw something over his shoulder at her. Miss Habersham ducked; Charlotte caught the item automatically, then scowled at its familiar leather surface.

"Devil," she muttered, tossing the briefcase aside. It crashed into a bust of Euterpe, causing a cacophony of disharmonic noises that ironically reached their crescendo as the marble bust met the floor. Charlotte extricated herself from Miss Habersham's ruffles, but it was too late; Alex dashed out through the doorway—

And fell flat on his face as a booted leg came out to trip him.

"Sorry, old chap," Ned Lightbourne said languidly, bending down to take the amulet from Alex's hand. Straightening, he turned to leave—

And got whacked in the face by a large pink purse.

"Take that, Master Luxe!"

"Constantinopla," Ned groaned, staggering back.

The pirate girl whirled to dramatic but purposeless effect, punched him in the gut, and snatched the amulet. "How's that for a dance move?" she said, and fled across the entrance hall with pirates and witches in hot pursuit.

Charlotte spun Miss Habersham away, shoved Miss Gloughenbury, and winced as someone yanked the hat from her head in an effort to slow her down. Farther across the hall, Cecilia Bassingthwaite leaped over the ticket counter and deftly kicked the amulet from Constantinopla's grasp. It sailed high into the air, flashing brightly, and the crowd staggered to a halt, all eyes lifting to watch its progress.

At that breathless moment, a young man wandered into the museum, hands in his pockets, hat tilted jovially to one side.

"What's up?" he said to the general assembly.

"Tom!" cried Constantinopla. "Catch it!"

Tom's eyes widened as he saw the amulet falling toward him. He reached out both hands almost mindlessly, and his entire body jolted with surprise as the treasure smacked into his palms. He stared at it.

"Run, Tom!" Constantinopla shouted. "Run!"

Tom spun about obediently and legged it back outside. As he raced down the museum steps and onto the forecourt, he glanced back at the crowd following him.

And thus it was he failed to see the tall, narrow house lowering itself before him. Nor did he notice its red door opening.

"Tom!" Constantinopla called out in a high, frantic voice. "It's Lady Armitage!"

But the warning came too late. Tom ran into the house and its door slammed shut.

Pirates and witches alike stood on the museum steps, staring in shock as the house most synonymous with true piratic horror rose from the forecourt and flew away, bearing with it Beryl's amulet (and Tom Eames).

✤ 6 ✤

HOT PURSUIT—THE BUTLER WOULDN'T DO IT—
AN UNWELCOME SIGHT—CHARLOTTE IS NOT A SPIDER—
HOT CIRCLING—THE WEAPONIZING OF TEA—
CHARLOTTE MAKES A MESS—WHEN ONE DOOR CLOSES—
ALEX SURRENDERS

The society of pirates entertained itself now and then with sending a few dozen women to air in houses fit to be employed in battle. Townhouses, mansions, a small castle or two—they made a brave sight when gathered (which is to say, a person had to be brave to stand still and behold them rather than run away screaming). Alex O'Riley's house, however, was generally agreed to be an eyesore. Never mind that it was also the fastest in the skies; a true pirate had consideration for appearances. He ought at least to whitewash the walls, fix the chimney, and submit to the superior opinion of the Wisteria Society on all matters since they really only had his best interests at heart.

But English people had been saying such things to the Irish for centuries, so Alex felt comfortable ignoring them. He liked his house. He liked its ruggedness and the way it always smelled of Donegal rain. He certainly liked how he could bash it into Mrs. Rotunder's house as they rose together off Great Russell Street and still its magic didn't falter—whereas Mrs. Rotunder's genteel townhouse tipped sharply to starboard and was rescued from complete collapse only by a telegram company office being in the way.

(It has to be said: she was saved by the bell.)

Alex harbored no guilt about this. Not only did it mean one less rival in the air, but on his own starboard side Bloodhound Bess was trying to do the same to him.

Everyone had rushed to their houses after seeing Lady Armitage abscond with both the amulet and a pirate lad—and not just because Tom's fiancée, Constantinopla, was screaming in the most aggravating way. An object of such power as Beryl's amulet having fallen into the clutches of Lady Armitage must be considered nothing less than a disaster. The woman had murdered several husbands and now therefore had nothing to do but to marry all the rest of the world—or ruin it, if she could. The Wisteria Society ladies did not generally agree on much, but they were unified in a belief that Armitage should not be allowed to get the upper hand, or else she'd be intolerable at parties. Besides, pirates were constitutionally incapable of letting something go.

Two elderly ladies had shoved past Alex, almost knocking him from his feet, as they raced toward their battlehouses. But as he got his house aloft, muttering the incantation's stanza for speed and turning the great oak steering wheel with an easy one-handed mastery, Alex knew he'd soon be ahead of the others. A pirate's house was their visible psyche, so the saying went. Alex liked his well enough, but in the end it was merely a way to get in the air. He'd push it as hard as he could—and if bits did happen to fall off, well, there was plenty of stone around to patch it.

Much the same as with his actual psyche.

Besides, he was determined to win that amulet, and not just because the look on Charlotte Pettifer's face when he got it would be priceless.

The witch had only herself to blame. Smashing pumpkins and throwing muses was all very entertaining, but of no real benefit when things took off, literally. Now, if she had been a pirate, she would have pulled the pins from her hair (he paused a moment to imagine it) and held one to his throat while demanding the key to his house. She wouldn't stand like the witches were doing on the museum forecourt, shaking their fists and parasols as pirates raised houses around them and sped away.

Alex didn't usually feel so competitive. Other than a friendship with Ned Lightbourne, his main involvement with the pirate community thus far had been in avoiding the pirate community. And only once before had he allowed a witch any space in his brain. But now, as he flew his battlehouse over the British Museum and toward Lady Armitage's rapidly dwindling house, he could not help but laugh, thinking about the Wicken League left hopelessly behind.

"Is something amusing, sir?"

Alex spun about, sword unsheathed and rising in a swift, automatic movement even before he completed the turn.

His butler paused in the cockpit doorway, waiting dispassionately for Alex's memory to pull itself together again. Dressed in a flawless black suit, his brown hair impeccable, he had a tray set upon one hand and a professionally unfocused look behind his spectacles. This was a man who would not recognize amusement even if it knocked on the door and demanded he say *Who's there?* before smacking him on the nose with a rubber chicken. He was a year younger than Alex but seemed ineffably older.

The tray held an onyx-handled pistol.

"I don't need a gun," Alex said. With a small apologetic shrug, he sheathed the sword and returned his attention to the view out the window. Cecilia and Ned's battlelibrary flew alongside. Alex eyed it thoughtfully. He ~~probably~~ obviously could not sideswipe his friends' premises, but he did mutter the phrase for speed once again, and the cottage trembled as it streaked through the light, outpacing the other cottage. At this rate, he would soon catch Armitage. "Prepare the grappling hook, Bixby," he ordered his butler.

"I am not sure a grappling hook would be appropriate in this situation, sir. It might damage the furniture."

Alex frowned, trying to work this out and failing. "What are you talking about?"

"I refer to the uninvited guest in your sitting room."

Alex turned, one hand still on the wheel, the other on his hip, to frown at the man. "Bixby, did you kidnap another Protestant so you could debate transubstantiation with them while I was out?"

"Not today, sir. And may I be so bold as to mention that you are about to collide with a manor?"

Alex spun back to the window and, with a rush of words and an urgent tug of a lever attached to the side of the wheel, banked the house over and away from Mrs. Dole's residence. The only furniture in the cockpit, a shabby armchair with several knives and brass knuckles cluttering its seat, shuddered across the floor. Alex frowned, for the stabilizing magic should prevent such things. Had he been so busy gloating about the witches that he'd recited the stanza incorrectly?

Annoyed with himself, he muttered the stanza again to be sure, then waved a hand to dismiss Bixby. "I don't have time for this. Lock him in the attic and I'll deal with him later."

"I already suggested that course of action to the lady, and she regretfully declined. She sat down on the sofa, and each time I approached to relocate her, she rose up again—several feet into the air, if you please—taking the sofa with her."

This news was narrated with the maximum disapproval possible in the minimum amount of tone. Alex closed his eyes wearily.

"Let me guess. Hair the color of wild honey, lovely eyes, holds herself as if she's a rifle aimed at its target and about to fire?"

"It is not in the compass of my employment to comment on the quality of ladies' eyes," Bixby replied. "But she does indeed have red-blonde hair."

Alex sighed. "Take the helm, Bixby. I'll deal with our stowaway."

"Are you not engaged in hot pursuit, sir?"

"Yes, in more direction than one, it seems."

"I beg your pardon, sir?"

"Never mind. Just follow that house at top speed."

"Top speed." The butler made it sound as if Alex had asked him to handwash his grandmother's undergarments.

"If you catch that house, there's a new duster in it for you."

"Hurrah," Bixby proclaimed dryly.

Alex snatched the gun and holstered it in his waistband, then tipped his head toward the steering wheel. Bixby did not sigh, but his entire posture, and the manner in which he tucked the tray beneath his arm, elocuted long-suffering disapprobation. He marched over to the wheel, sonorously intoning the pilot phrase as he went, and for one moment the cottage seemed to come to attention like a footman who knows who's really boss in a household.

Alex left him to it. Heading down the hallway, past crates of sugar waiting to be smuggled into Ireland, he tried to calm the tumult of thoughts suddenly overwhelming his mind. How had Charlotte Pettifer got into the house? And how could he get her out again, considering they were in hot pursuit, hundreds of feet off the ground? He could throw her out the door, but no doubt she'd just fly back up on that little metallic broom of hers and pester him by rapping at the windows.

With luck, she'd fainted at the mess in his sitting room. Then again, the way his own luck was going, she'd probably give him one long, slow-blinking look with her smoky green eyes and he'd be the one fainting instead.

Ha, he didn't mean that seriously, of course. He wasn't scared of some witch woman who barely came up to his chin.

Even if she was standing in the middle of the sitting room with a pistol in one delicate gloved hand pointed directly at him.

No, not scared, Alex thought as he looked at her. *Nor in any way stirred.*

Her hat was missing and her hair had escaped its bindings. It poured over her shoulders and down her back in an abundance of fine, soft waves that looked like they were getting their first experience of freedom in years and were making the most of it. Alex wrestled with a sudden strange compulsion to gather that hair in his hands and—

"Stop right there, if you please," she said archly, making his thoughts crash against each other: *gun, hair, such an elegant neck, yes but* gun, *neck again, do you think she'd shoot you if you tried to lick . . .*

"I said stop," she reiterated, holding the pistol a little higher, and Alex realized he'd continued walking toward her. He stopped, but his smile kept on going, budging up against her comfort zone. She took a step back.

"I have a gun," she said unnecessarily.

"And you're not afraid to use it?" he guessed.

"No, I am afraid to use it. But that won't prevent me, should you come any closer."

"I believe you." He held up both hands to show he was no threat. "To what do I owe the pleasure of this visit?"

"You know perfectly well. I intend to retrieve my stolen amulet."

He raised an eyebrow. "*Your* amulet? I've heard of reincarnation, but I always thought if Black Beryl came back to life it would be as a tarantula, not a London girl who doesn't even know how to release the safety on a gun before pointing it at someone."

She stared coldly at his smile, but her face was beginning to heat. Alex could not decide if that was due to anger or embarrassment, and he suddenly worried—for he might be a rogue, and making her walk the plank was still an option, but he never wanted to actually hurt her. His mother would have raised him better than that, had she lived beyond his first five years. Instinctively he took half a step forward, an apology forming in his mouth.

Miss Pettifer released the safety and shook back her hair, and he felt himself begin to heat too. Their eyes met.

Ah, said his brain, erasing the apology. *So it was* that *kind of heat*.

The air seemed to sizzle. Alex could not stand still, but did not want to risk rushing her. He made a careful sidestep.

She did the same in the opposite direction.

"I am the true spiritual heir of Beryl Black, prophesized by generations of witches," she said. "Therefore, the amulet is rightfully mine."

"Generations, hey?"

Her jaw twitched. "Well, two generations. But the principle remains."

"Fair enough. But I'm afraid you won't find any amulet in this house, darling."

He stepped; she stepped—circling each other.

"I doubt I could find an elephant in this house," she retorted, "considering the mess."

Alex smiled. The room was cluttered with boxes, treasures, piles of tarpaulin, all the usual detritus of a busy pirate. As he took another step he had to kick aside an old holster; as she did, she veered around a crate of gold cups. Only a sofa and low wooden table offered the suggestion of this being a home, although both struggled to serve their purpose, being as they were covered in books, dishes, laundry. And only the painted marble statue of the Virgin Mary, stranded with his mother's rosary and bolted to a little shelf halfway up one wall, was clean and polished.

"Why do you even have a butler if you don't let him tidy your house?" Charlotte asked, wrinkling her nose as she stepped on a dirty plate. "And scrub it . . . disinfect it . . . just burn it to the ground."

Irritation flared in his heart, but he replied with perfect nonchalance. "I see you've been talking with Bixby. He is my butler because he has a black belt in karate, can kill a man seven ways using a bowler hat, and makes the best lamb stew this side of the Irish Sea. If he wants to waste his energy with cleaning, he has to keep it to his own rooms. This is a working battlehouse, not a Mayfair mansion. We had goats in here last week, and a government minister as a hostage the week before that, if you want to know how really mucky it can get."

"I shall be sure to decontaminate myself later. But for now I require you to take me in pursuit of Lady Armitage, so that I may recover my amulet from her."

"It's true I just so happen to be going in that direction. Unfortunately, however, witches are not welcome in my house." At those words, a spike of old, poisonous hatred fired his instincts, and only by curling his fingers into a fist could he prevent himself from touching the scars left by a certain witch who'd got into his house, his family's heart, some twenty years ago. "But don't worry," he said, shoving the memory away with practiced brutality. "I have just the place for you to wait until we land and I can evict you. Nice and tidy, although lacking a view, I'm afraid."

"You speak of a closet," she said with remarkable perspicacity.

"I speak of a closet," he confirmed.

Their eyes, still focused on each other, blazed. If the air between them became much hotter, Alex feared his house—or at least his something—would go up in flames.

"Captain O'Riley, you seem to be under the impression you have authority in this situation," the witch said. "My gun, however, trumps your opinion."

"But you will only have your gun for the next few seconds," he told her calmly.

"I'll shoot if you come near me."

"Will you?" He didn't give her time to lie. "I'm not moving. Smithson will be taking it off you."

"Smithson?"

"Behind you."

Her eyes narrowed, and he could easily guess what she was thinking. Almost certainly no one stood behind her, and turning to look would leave her vulnerable to him. But "almost certainly" left room for doubt, and doubt was a dangerous thing when dealing with pirates. Alex shrugged one shoulder carelessly, smirking at something, or someone, just over her shoulder.

She turned.

She pointed her gun at nothing.

He had it out of her hand, and her hand twisted up behind her back, before she could even register that she'd made the wrong choice. Pulling her against his body, he wrapped one leg around hers so she could not deploy those interesting shoes as weapons.

But as her warmth sank into him, the fresh clean smell of her hair softening his mental awareness, the press of her bustle hardening his physical awareness, Alex forgot the most dangerous part of her.

He barely heard the whispering before a crate of tea slammed into him.

Charlotte jolted as the crate hit the pirate's shoulder. He staggered, grunting with pain. Immediately she yanked herself away, but he caught her again.

"Don't bother. There's nowhere to—"

"*Aereo rapido!*"

Maps flew up like wild geese, harsh and excited, to slap his face. He released her in order to bat them away, and Charlotte ran toward the hall that led to the wheelroom. If she got in there and barricaded the door, she could use her feminine wiles (i.e., witchcraft, weaponized shoes, multifaceted besom) on the butler to secure his help.

Suddenly her plan, and her body, lurched to a stop. Alex had snatched the bow of her ridiculous dress and, as Charlotte cursed Cecilia Bassingthwaite and her bad fashion example, he tugged her back against him.

"How dare—" she began, but his hand clamped over her mouth.

Charlotte was gobsmacked (literally) by the man's rudeness. This all could have been resolved in a civil manner if he'd just offered her a cup of tea and a comfortable seat while she hijacked his house. That he hadn't only proved what a scoundrel he was, and she would be sure to chasten him via lecturing or a moralistic burglarizing when she got the chance.

For now, however, she had no idea what to do. His grip was so strong, she could not even struggle; her heels clattered against the dusty wooden floor as he began dragging her backward across the room. Never before in her life had she done more than shake a gentleman's hand. To have his arms around her, his palm pressed against her lips, was—was—

Unacceptable! Atrocious! Rousing! No, wait, revolting!

Jane Austen's heroines, begged for assistance, offered bewildered silence. Unless he tried to propose marriage, they were at a loss as to how she might defeat him.

"Sorry about this," he said cheerfully. "Don't call me heartless, though. After I've retrieved the amulet I might let you look at it before I drop you back home."

"Mphm!" (For the record, she was calling him something a great deal worse than heartless.)

"Fear not, I'll set the house down before I drop you from it." She tried to bite his hand. "Probably," he amended.

She tasted sweat and her own bitter, unspoken magic. She cursed the gentleness of feminine literature that had left her so unequally educated in violence . . .

And then Amy March rose unexpectedly from the dregs of her imagination, manuscript in one hand and sharp smile on her face.

Alex cursed as the woman went suddenly limp in his arms. Had he hurt her? He'd not intended to, only wanted to ensure she was restrained from tearing his house apart with that damned witchy voice of hers.

"Miss Pettifer?" he inquired. She did not reply—of course, he'd covered her mouth. Perhaps she'd fainted because of that. Her eyes were closed, her fine-boned face pallid, and if he was not holding her she'd tumble to the ground. Worried, he hoisted her, intending to lift her into his arms and carry her to the sofa. But as his grip loosened she suddenly pulled free.

He scowled. "You—"

Whether this was to be a statement of relief or a curse must remain unestablished, for he got nothing further said before she raised her skirt, swiveled, and delivered a brisk, angled kick to his leg.

In that moment, Alex discovered she was wearing knee-high boots, and that those boots were studded. He would have been seriously thrilled had he not been staggering in pain.

She should have run then. But she overthought it, and snatched up a broken crossbow from the jumbled stack against the wall, preparing to smack him with it. Alex lurched forward, grabbing her hand and squeezing until she dropped the crossbow. It landed on one of her feet, causing a small explosion of sparks.

"Ow!" she cried, more in fury than pain. But Alex was merciless. As she tilted off-balance, he pulled her against him and hauled her up, over his shoulder.

"Put me down!" she demanded, kicking helplessly inside the layers of her skirts as he carried her across the room. "Put me down at once, or I will—"

He put her down. But his arm was still around her, holding her body close, so close, so soft and luscious, like a dream. *No*, he told himself—*a bloody nightmare*. She scowled up at him through a tumble of hair, sparks of witchfire in her eyes.

Alex grinned. "I'm afraid our guest room is a little small," he said, and reached out to open the closet door.

"Reciprico," Charlotte snapped, and the door slammed shut.

Captain O'Riley snapped a few words of his own, none of which required translation to the Latin to give them force. Charlotte gasped. Pressed against the length of his body, she not only heard those words but felt them vibrating through her bones, heating her blood further.

They looked at each other, gazes clashing like swords. He lifted his hand toward her mouth, she muttered quickly, and it was a race both of them lost—for he silenced her mid-word, but she got enough of that word out to make some difference. An empty wicker birdcage, already dreaming of wings, lifted in the air and began rushing toward them.

Alex turned, hunching over her so the cage cracked against his back. It was an act almost Darcy-like, protecting Charlotte from the consequences of her own irate choices, and she might have been impressed, even a little sorry for what she'd done, had she not known that everything was his fault. He straightened, moaning slightly, and she kicked him in the shin.

Abruptly he pushed her back against the wall. The impact ignited nerves and tossed magic words through her brain. She murmured them against the barricade of his hand, and although they were muffled, the front door flung open. Wind roared into the cottage. Charlotte felt her magic roar in response. She went on incantating against the pirate's skin, and small items began to fly about; her hair stirred.

Now *this* was witchcraft, she thought in exhilaration. Never mind stealing briefcases. This was stealing the sky.

She saw herself reflected like a flame in Alex's eyes. She inhaled his hot, angry breath and wanted more.

They glared at each other.

The house began to sway as witchery clashed with the flight incantation. The sofa was rising, windows swinging open. Charlotte wondered why she'd never before noticed the filament of gold in the pirate's left eye.

Alex lifted his hand from her mouth, taking all her words away with it. He brushed the hair from her face. A sword spiraled past; a bottle smashed against the wall beside them. The pirate was breathing as if he'd run a mile, but Charlotte felt her own hectic breath beginning to ease. A sultry, heavy stillness settled through her, even as the world turned wild.

Alex lowered his head. Charlotte lifted hers.

Their lips touched.

The ground beneath them shook.

❧ 7 ❧

GROUNDED—BAD LANGUAGE—DANGEROUS QUESTIONS—
JUST A SMALL PRICK—BIXBY OPTIMIZES THE SEARCH—
A PROPOSAL OF MARRIAGE—FUNNY BUSINESS—
THE SCENT OF A WOMAN

Kisses are foolish things. The pleasure of rational thought is not enhanced by them, and the inconvenience is often considerable. Therefore Charlotte was pleased—exceedingly pleased!—couldn't have been happier!—when the hard landing of the house caused Alex to stumble away from her before their kiss could properly commence.

"What the hell?" He looked around, blinking at the tumult in the room, the swinging windows and gaping front door. From the shock on his face, Charlotte realized he had somehow failed to notice until now what had been happening.

"Fluff!" he swore. (In fact it was a word vastly more potent than "fluff," but Charlotte's brain decided she'd had just about enough for one day, and took pity on her.) Without even glancing again at Charlotte, he stormed across the room, kicking strewn books and tools aside as he went, and disappeared into the hall leading to the cockpit.

Charlotte took a deep, unsteady breath. Her throat seemed full of ashes; her eyes ached as if light-burned. Never before had magic left her feeling this way. The intensity frightened her enough that she responded in true witchy fashion by sweeping it up, along with the realization she'd almost kissed a man; boxing them both neatly; and putting them alphabetized on a mental shelf. This left her brain calm and tidy again. Staid questions entered instead, wiping their feet first and speaking in level tones: *Where did Captain O'Riley put my gun? . . . What should I do now? . . .* and *Is there time to brush my hair first?*

Clearly, finding her gun amongst the disorder of the pirate's sitting room would be impossible, and she'd likely risk bacterial infection by trying. Instead, she smoothed her skirts and tidied her hair as best she could, until she felt calm settle through her once more. Then she picked a careful path over to the front door and peered out.

They had set down in someone's garden. This much was a relief.

Less relieving was the fact it was a rooftop garden.

And the edge of the roof was mere inches away.

Charlotte swallowed a word that might have doomed them. Just then, a townhouse and a cottage flew past. Toots emerged from the townhouse as if someone blew on a horn.

Charlotte huffed with an inexplicable feeling of offense. But there was nothing to do except watch as the other houses incinerated a quarter-mile from the advantage Alex's cottage had held. Shutting the door, she picked another careful path through the sitting room, toward the cockpit this time.

Alex and his butler were arguing therein.

"You shouldn't have landed here," Alex was saying, one hand on his sword pommel as he scowled at the butler. Bixby's expression of bored disapproval impressed Charlotte so much, she made a mental note of how she might replicate it.

"It was either land on this roof or land on *our* roof," the butler replied calmly.

"You're overreacting. So we were a little unstable—"

Bixby merely turned his head to look at the armchair, which was now propped upside down against a wall. Alex's mouth flattened with annoyance.

Then he caught sight of Charlotte, and the annoyance spread through his countenance into his eyes, his breathing; even his hair looked annoyed from having a hand tugged through it.

"You're still here."

"Yes," Charlotte replied with as much dignity as possible, considering a few moments ago she had almost surrendered that dignity beneath his lips. "I might be able to climb down from the roof of a four-story townhouse if I tried, but I still do not have the amulet in my possession and therefore am going nowhere. Speaking of which, why are we not in hot pursuit?"

"We?" Alex replied. "*We,* madam, are two men who were quietly attending to our disreputable business until hijacked. *We* do not include a meddling witch whose magic almost made us crash." (Charlotte scoffed, mainly because it was true.) "*We*—"

"We," Bixby interjected, throwing a reproving glance at his employer, "were just discussing the recommencement of hot pursuit. Miss Pettifer, would you care for a cup of tea while you wait?"

"Wait?!" Alex and Charlotte spoke in unified dismay.

"I'm a pirate; I don't wait," Alex said.

"My amulet is getting away," Charlotte added.

"I beg to suggest it has already gone," Bixby told her. "Seven houses and what appeared to be a ticket booth have flown ahead of us. Not even this house can go fast enough to outpace them all now."

"Shit." Alex shoved at his hair again as he turned to glare out the window.

Bixby's mouth pursed. "There is a lady present, sir."

"I am aware," Alex retorted. "She's the reason we're in this shitty situation."

Charlotte bristled. "I wouldn't be if you had done the gentlemanly thing and allowed me complete authority over your battlehouse."

"Madam, I advise you not to request *gentlemanly* behavior from a piratic rake unless you're prepared to accept all of the consequences."

"Sir, if you are truly a rake, then I am a milkmaid."

He turned to her with eyes that glittered dangerously. "I just kissed you," he pointed out, and his voice sounded like a kiss itself.

"You most certainly did not! A brief and temporary conjunction of lips does not equate to a—" She paused, because almost kissing a pirate was one thing, but speaking about it represented a whole new level of impropriety. "If you think that it does, sir, I can only pity your future wife."

He took a lithe step toward her. She stood her ground, cocking her mouth into a smile.

"Pardon me," the butler interposed before a fireball suddenly appeared on the rooftop of a London townhouse. Charlotte and Alex snapped their attention to him, but he did not even blink. "I doubt we would have caught Lady Armitage in any case," he said. "She had too much of a lead on us."

"Then it is not a matter of speed but intelligence," Charlotte answered.

Now both men stared at her, their eyes dark, their hard jawlines taut. She felt a sudden, uncharacteristic leap of anxiety, appreciating finally that, in her haste to pursue the amulet, she had entered without a chaperone into the private company of a notorious scoundrel and his assassin-butler. Not even flying a bicycle in public touched upon the scandal this represented. She'd be ruined if anyone learned of it, and worse—Aunt Judith would sigh in Disappointment.

The proper feminine behavior at this point would be to say no more, leave the room, and lock herself in the closet. Charlotte did not need to reference a Jane Austen novel to know that. Clearly, there was only one choice she could make.

Taking a deep breath, she shook back her hair, lifted her chin, and marched forward to the house's enormous, spoked wheel.

The men watched her, incredulous. Between the wheel and the window stood a tilted surface strewn with maps. Although these offered nothing comprehensible to her, Charlotte nevertheless tapped one officiously.

"I may be a mere London girl," she said, "but even I know one can plot a tractory—"

"Trajectory," Alex corrected.

"—to determine the probable course of one's prey."

"And this is something you learned in embroidery class, is it?"

She did not deign to look at him. "It is something every philanthropist is taught. Planning. Prediction. The subtleties of the art."

"Philanthropist," Alex echoed.

"Independent manager of wealth redistribution," she clarified.

"Ah. Thief."

"Do you want to listen or not?"

He shrugged. "Not. But don't huff—"

"Huff?!" Charlotte, alas, huffed.

"I will admit your idea makes sense. Armitage has to land sooner or later, and we may be able to get there before her—or at least before the other pirates—if we can find a shorter route. The question is, where?"

"If you will give me just a moment, sir," Bixby said. Turning to a series of alphabetized drawers set in the steering cabinet, he opened the uppermost and took from it a file thick with papers, which he proceeded to read.

"You should go home," Alex told Charlotte. "Seriously, I know you want that amulet, and I give you credit for your determination, but this is a dangerous business, not appropriate for a lady. Please understand, I'm only thinking of your safety when I—"

The thin but extremely sharp rapier at his throat prevented further speech.

"Perhaps you should think again," Charlotte suggested calmly, twitching her besom so the rapier point scratched his skin.

He grinned. His eyes became heavy with an expression Charlotte did not recognize but her body certainly seemed to. She could almost feel his pulse beating through the rapier into her own veins. Suddenly, holding a weapon to him seemed lewd, and she pulled it back, leaving a tiny red mark on his throat.

Without blinking, he reached up and touched a fingertip to the mark, then to his lips. His eyes smiled wickedly as he licked the finger. Charlotte sensed a blush erupting over her entire body. She snapped the besom shut and returned it so forcefully to a pocket that the fabric strained against its seams.

"How revealing," Bixby murmured.

Charlotte and Alex turned to glare at him. But he did not seem to notice what was happening between them. "Lady Armitage's dossier suggests she has a proclivity for the seaside. I venture to suggest, since she is heading east, she will be aiming for the coast."

"You have a dossier on Lady Armitage?" Charlotte asked with surprise.

"Madam, all professional butlers are tapped into an interconnected array of informational networks."

Confused, Charlotte glanced at Alex.

"They gossip," he translated.

Bixby bristled at this. "We participate in the sharing of resources and dub-dub-dub—" He paused, straightening his spectacles. "Excuse me. Dubbed copies of possible factoids."

Again, Charlotte looked to Alex.

"Rumors," he said.

If Bixby bristled any more, he risked exploding into sharp pieces. "I myself take the liberty of creating files, such as this one about Lady Armitage. A quick search for certain keywords enables me to suggest where the lady is heading."

"Tilbury," Alex guessed. "The Wisteria Society used to meet at the docks in the old days."

"And that is no doubt why everyone is flying in that direction, even though Lady Armitage is now out of visual range," Bixby said. "But I believe she is going to Clacton-on-Sea. Records show she has a friendship with the vicar there."

"Why should that be significant?" Charlotte asked.

Alex snapped his fingers, then pointed one at Bixby. "Because the amulet isn't the only thing she took—and perhaps not the most important to her. Right?"

"Indeed," Bixby said. "When dealing with Isabella Armitage, one must always consider the possibility she is wanting to marry."

"Poor Tom," Alex murmured.

"Tom? The boy who stole my amulet?" Charlotte tried to find sympathy for him within herself, but failed. "Marriage to Lady Armitage is the least punishment he deserves."

"Don't let Constantinopla hear you say that," Alex advised.

"Who?"

"Constantinopla Brown, generally known as Oply. Tom's fiancée, feisty young pirate, and as she would have it, close personal friend of Her Majesty, Queen Victoria."

"Oh." Charlotte recollected the girl in the museum queue. "I am not afraid of a sixteen-year-old."

"You should be," Alex and Bixby chorused.

"She has refined spoiled brattishness to an art form," Alex added. "What she wants, she gets, and woe betide anyone standing in her way."

"So you're saying she's piratic?"

"No, she—"

"Wait, I think I understand. She's a young female. Therefore her behavior, while typical for pirates, is, in her, mere brattishness."

Alex opened his mouth to reply, but upon seeing Charlotte lift one eyebrow in anticipation, closed it again wordlessly.

Charlotte tried not to smirk. "In any case, Oply is not here. We still are, however—sitting on this rooftop when we ought to be pursuing Lady Armitage. The question is, do we aim for Tilbury or Clacton-on-Sea?"

"Clacton," Alex said without hesitation. "Bixby is no twitter. His analytical ability is one of the reasons I employ him."

"Thank you, sir," Bixby chided.

Alex gave him a wry smile. "Set a course for Clacton. And, Miss Pettifer—"

"I'm coming too."

He sighed, and rolled his eyes, then turned his smile on her. Charlotte saw it coming, but felt unconcerned. After all, she was a Plim, and nothing daunted a—

The smile struck her with the full force of its crooked charm.

Sparks flew through her body as every nerve fell into utter disarray. She'd forgotten she was also a Pettifer. Suddenly she thought of her mother urging her to have a "conversation" with this man, and her nerves sizzled again. Furious with herself, she glared at Alex.

His smile widened.

"All right," he said. "I suppose I won't make you walk the plank. Yet."

In the British Museum's Grenville Library, silence crouched like an anxious curator who had been through too many fire alarms that week. It flashed here and there as light caught on shards of glass from the shattered display case. It wavered at its edges as museum patrons talked in the foyer beyond. If the silence had fingernails, it would be biting them about now.

The actual curator did not feel much better. Some fool in administration had thought calling the police about the stolen amulet would be a good idea, and now the curator had to stand smiling in the worried silence while Detective Inspector Creeve examined the crime scene.

"I fear we are wasting important police resources," he said finally, the words bursting out in near desperation for noise. "This is really not anything for you to be concerned with."

DI Creeve glanced up from beneath a pale, sparse eyebrow. His hair was so light and thin it seemed like cobwebs. His mouth was spectral. The look he gave the curator did not only pierce but twisted on its way through.

The curator laughed shakily. "Well, yes, I know there was a theft. And destruction of museum property. And Eustace did get his nose broken when that old lady hit him with her crutch. But for the publicity officer to have called the amulet 'gold' may be considered a liberal interpretation of the . . . well, to put it exactly . . . truth."

DI Creeve just went on wordlessly staring. *Those eyes*, thought the curator while his breath cowered and his instincts ran screaming for an emergency exit. It wasn't just that they were the color of bone. It was the way they assessed a man as if they saw . . . indeed, bone. And secrets, old, terrible secrets a man barely even knew he had. Shuffling back, he knocked into a bust of Thalia, which resulted in a moment of chaotic fumbling that would have been amusing to relate had not the policeman watched it impassively, casting a chill over the scene.

"Black's amulet was, of course, an important historical artifact," the curator said once he had the statue and his wits straight again. "We are upset at its loss. But what can you do when pirates want to take something?"

"It was not pirates," DI Creeve said.

"But they were everywhere! With their swords and guns and oh my God their hats, not to mention the smiles . . ." The curator shuddered.

"This is the work of someone even more nefarious." Creeve spoke the word as if it were a rich chocolate with raspberry at its heart, and he licked his thin white lips afterward.

"I assure you, Detective, that we have entertained no lawyers here."

Creeve did not respond to this hilarious joke. He just stood, staring. The curator had never seen skin splayed so awkwardly across facial bones before, nor been so doubtful of the life force behind it. One does not like to believe in ghosts when one is a historian, but this man menaced his imagination with the possibility. Many seconds later, there was a knock at the door, and the curator wrenched his eyes toward it. "That will be the cleaners."

"Let them in," Creeve said. "I have finished my inspection and know who committed this crime."

"You do? Goodness, how remarkably clever." *Please go away now and arrest them and never come back.* "Who was it?"

"Can you not smell her?" Creeve asked, and began to sniff the air.

"Um." The curator attempted a sniff, although it was a pathetic affair, tempered by embarrassment. He could smell old wood, older books, and blood from the pirates' melee. But he did not think Creeve would be interested in his olfactory report. The policeman was nosing the dusty light as if hungered by it.

"Bitterness," Creeve said, licking the word out of the air. "Heat.

From anger or perhaps passion; red heat, burning away all good sense. And—hm, lilac. A *witch* was here."

Laughter shot from the curator's throat. Creeve went still, and the curator hastily turned the laugh into a cough. "A witch," he sputtered. "Goodness, how dreadful!"

"More dreadful than you can imagine." Creeve moved his stare to a briefcase lying amongst the shattered ruins of a marble bust, and for a moment teeth appeared between his lips, small, sharp, and hungry. "A witch born of sin, raised in wickedness. An abomination."

"Oh dear," the curator murmured, tugging at his shirt collar, which suddenly seemed too tight.

"They are *everywhere*," Creeve hissed. "Fingering the secrets of our society, plucking, stealing, stirring things up. But this one in particular—" He sniffed the air again. "This one is their heart. Their promise for the future. Could they have been more stupid—and more helpful—marking it out with a prophecy so it's easier to hunt down? Fear not, however. I have been *watching*. Soon I will bring it in. And then I will destroy it."

"But we still want it for our exhib—" The curator blanched as Creeve looked back at him. "Oh, of course. You don't mean the amulet, but the—the witch."

Creeve's mouth sagged with disdain. "I see you don't understand the seriousness of this. Never mind. I plan to light a bonfire which will illuminate you. Which. Witch. Ha ha."

"Ha ha," said the curator.

Creeve sniffed at him. Then walking over the shattered glass, grinding it into smaller pieces beneath his boot heel, he departed the room.

"Upon my word," the curator muttered shakily, and had to spend the rest of the morning sitting down with several nice cups of tea.

❈ 8 ❈

LIFE IN THE FAST LANE—BARELY SPEAKING—
THE PURSUERS ARE HOT—A CUNNING PLAN—
CHARLOTTE IS CHANGED—INTO THE LIGHT—
SLOW BURN—CHARLOTTE'S HEART DOES NOT STAY COOL—
TWO HOUSES, BOTH ALIKE IN UNDIGNIFIED BEHAVIOR—DISASTER!

As the pirate's house flew toward Clacton-on-Sea, Alex and Charlotte had no conversation together. No intercourse (alas, in all definitions of the word) but what the commonest civility required.

"Would you like a seat?" he asked.

"Yes, please," she replied.

The armchair was restored to its normal position and Charlotte perched upon it, trying to balance between rest and making as little contact as possible with the stained surface. An uncomfortable silence passed, during which Alex steered the house and Charlotte amused herself with worry about what her mother would say when she did not arrive home by evening. She was at the point of imagining Mrs. Pettifer in most satisfying hysterics when Alex removed his coat and folded up the sleeves of his shirt.

Charlotte found herself captivated by the sight, as she'd never before seen a man's naked forearms and was surprised to discover them more interesting than thoughts of her mother. Dark hair shadowed the tanned skin; sleek muscles shifted with easy masculine power as he moved the wheel. Charlotte remembered that arm around her waist and imagined it there once again, but unclothed now as it gripped her firmly, hauling her toward what was not a closet but a bed . . .

"Ahem! Ahem!" She cleared her throat with a vigor necessitated by—by—the effects of altitude, or—yes!—all the dust in the room. So terribly dusty!

"Would you like some tea?" Alex asked.

"Yes, please," she replied.

Bixby was summoned, tea and biscuits were provided, and they flew on in a silence that burned all the way through uncomfortable into excruciating.

"Would you like me to kiss you when we get the chance?" Alex asked.

"Try and I'll slap you," she replied.

"Yes, please," he said, and grinned sidelong at her.

She looked away, nibbling a biscuit contemptuously.

The silence began to steam. Charlotte, fanning herself with the tea saucer, realized Alex was watching her reflection in the window. "Stop looking at me like that," she said.

"Like what?" He turned, looked at her directly, his gaze so deep, so intense, it made her feel naked.

"Like you want to eat me."

His lithe, sultry smile leaped. Her blood leaped in response.

At that opportune moment, Bixby reappeared, tea towel and grenade in hand. "I beg your pardon, sir. There is a house following us."

"Who is it?" Alex asked, still holding Charlotte in that unblinking gaze.

"Muriel Fairweather, judging from the yellow walls and pink curtains."

"No doubt she's taking a chance that following us will lead her to Armitage. Ugh, they don't call that woman Fox Terrier for nothing." He turned finally, glancing out the window, allowing Charlotte to breathe again.

"Actually, they call her Furious Fairweather," Bixby said. "Also Foulweather, Frightfeather for some unknown reason, and Muriel the Mad. She has no canine nicknames."

Alex frowned slightly. "Are you sure?"

Bixby's silence was an eloquent response.

"Well, in any case, I'll bring her to heel." He began unfurling his sleeves, and Charlotte put half a biscuit into her mouth to quell her disappointment. "I'll just jump over and toss a smoke grenade down her chimney, then we can get on with hot pursuit."

"Here you are, sir," Bixby said, and handed over the grenade as if this was something they did often. "But may I suggest a safer method of delivery?"

"Safer?" Alex laughed. "Are we pirates or w—" He stopped, glancing at Charlotte. "Er . . ."

"No, do go on," she said, regarding him with calm interest. "I am keen to know what you intended to say. 'Witches' or 'women'?"

To her delight, he flushed. "Never mind," he said grumpily. "Bixby, take the wheel. I'm going upstairs. The last time we tried to lob a grenade from the house, we missed, and nearly blew up a flock of sheep grazing below."

"Sir," Bixby argued, "I know you are a vegetarian, but that does not mean you should throw yourself off the roof." (Aficionados of the paleo diet may disagree.)

"Thank you, Daniel." Ignoring the butler's expression of offended dignity, he began pulling on his coat. "I'll be fine. Besides, we have no choice. It's not like there's a bicycle sitting around so Miss Pettifer can pedal over with the bomb."

Charlotte came at once to her feet. She drew breath—

"No," said the men in unison.

"But you have not heard me yet," she replied reasonably. "I will not allow Miss Fairweather to interfere with the plans to recover my amulet. In the absence of a bicycle, I can incantate across to the lady's premises."

"No," Alex reiterated. He put his hand on his sword pommel, as if that might in any way influence her. She looked at the hand, then up at his face, and blinked with absolute unconcern. In fact, so unconcerned was she, it practically served as a declaration of war. Alex took a deep breath to calm himself.

"No. One misstep or gust of wind and you'd fall. Eight hundred feet. To a ground that I can assure you is even more unyielding than a witch's opinion."

"I am not afraid of a little empty air."

"You really should be."

"Perhaps Miss Pettifer could levitate you instead, sir," Bixby suggested. "She would not need to emerge from the hatch any farther than shoulder height, and with most of her situated on the ladder inside the attic, she would be quite safe."

"So we are agreed," Charlotte declared.

"No, we are not," Alex said.

"I shall require a change of garments if I am to climb a ladder."

"No."

"Shirt."

"No."

"Trousers."

"N—" He stopped, a speculative look darkening his eyes. "Well, perhaps it is a good idea, I suppose. So long as you stay on the ladder. Bixby, do we still have those clothes belonging to the young Viscount of Sheffield?"

"I believe so, sir."

"Fetch them for Miss Pettifer. Shirt. Coat, if there is one. *Trousers.*"

"I have my own coat," Charlotte said. "I removed it when I entered your premises."

Alex stared at her unfocusedly.

"Come along, miss," Bixby said, gently placing his hand at her elbow. "Best not to mention removing clothes to the captain just now. Let us see what is available to outfit you more appropriately for shenanigans."

Ten minutes later, Charlotte re-entered the cockpit. Alex glanced around and nearly choked on his own breath. She wore a white shirt that had been tucked into tight-fitting black trousers, and while her long coat protected him somewhat from the provoking sight of her hips, there was no reprieve from her thighs or her knee-high studded boots. He hastily turned away, wincing at the discomposure her revealed form caused in him. No doubt she would have smiled with triumphant irony had she been aware.

"So," he said, then had to pause to clear his throat. "Are you ready to come—I mean—oh God."

"You wish to pray before the endeavor?" Charlotte inquired.

He laughed, rubbing his eye and temple, and smiled sardonically out the window. "No, but my priest had better set aside a whole afternoon soon to hear my confession."

"You're Catholic?" She sounded surprised. "A Catholic pirate."

"I'm Irish. Being both Catholic and a pirate are almost obligatory."

Adjusting his own trousers, he turned, and focused determinedly on her face. This did not help much. She had tied her hair back at the nape of her neck, but one strand curved over her cheek, stirring him almost as much as the revelation of her legs. How could a woman look so artless and yet so sensual all at once? And how was a man expected to properly breathe in the same room as her?

She's a witch, he reminded himself.

A witch with gorgeous lips, so lush beneath his . . .

Witch. Enemy. Briefcase thief.

And the way she can kick a man with those fierce boots . . .

He clenched his jaw. This woman was no different from Deirdre Riordan—bees at her wrist, ruthless magic in her heart. And like Deirdre, she would hurt him, no question. Hell, she already had. He was going to have bruises on his leg where she'd kicked him, and that was nothing compared to the discomfort he currently endured in his crotch.

"Oh yes," she said, her voice like velvet against his gritty thoughts. "This is yours."

She brought something from her coat pocket, held it out. Alex extended a hand automatically and she dropped his ruby ring into it.

He stared at the ring, feeling utterly blindsided. Kindness was the last thing he had expected from this woman—or anyone, ever. Something painful leaped in his heart. The ring was still warm from having lain between her breasts; slipping it on his thumb, he took a rather shaky breath.

"Thank you," he said, surprising himself with the words. "This is particularly precious to me."

She shrugged. "It wouldn't buy much for the orphans," she said, but he thought he heard an apology beneath the words. Suddenly he needed the restraint of every moral fiber he possessed to stop himself from taking the wicked little witch in his arms and kissing her, feud be damned.

But he saw the shadow in her eyes, and realized she probably felt vulnerable in the masculine clothes. And since he wasn't the complete cad he was reputed to be, he gentled his smile. "Ready to go?"

Charlotte looked down at herself. "Hm, let's see. I have a besom full of weapons in my pocket; I found my gun, so that's tucked into my studded, poisonous boots; I'm thoroughly trained in combat magic; and I moisturized this morning." She withdrew her sunglasses from a coat pocket and put them on. "I'm ready."

Alex swallowed dryly. "Er, good. Bixby!"

The butler appeared at once in the doorway. "Yes, sir?"

"We're going up. You have the helm."

"Very good, sir."

"Hmm. Get us alongside Fairweather's house and keep us there until I give the all clear." Turning to Charlotte, he grinned. "Tally ho!"

She tipped the sunglasses up to frown at him. "Is that some kind of insult? I demand an—"

Alex rolled his eyes and, stepping closer, clapped his hand over her mouth. She glared at him above his fingers, her own eyes a hot, flashing storm. Looking at them, he rather thought that was why he had done it. "It means *Let's go.*"

"Mphm," she said. He laughed, releasing her. She jammed the sunglasses back down and marched furiously from the cockpit—then stopped, foot tapping against the floor, waiting for him to catch up and show her which way to go.

Behind them, Bixby almost certainly did not snicker, although it sounded a great deal as if he did.

Charlotte followed the pirate up through dusty attic darkness into the wild light. Alex pushed open the hatch and hauled himself off the ladder to the roof; she emerged more carefully. With her feet several rungs into shadows and her face lifted to the sun, she thought how metaphorical a moment it was—and then she stopped thinking at all. The sky, so vast, filled her with its fierce, cool emptiness. The way Alex walked the ridgeline as if he were walking a parlor floor captivated her pulse.

"Stay there," he called over his shoulder.

The wind whipped his words like a red flag. "I will," she said, but knew it for a lie. Riding a bicycle up over buildings had been too uncertain a venture to enjoy at the time, but ever since, she'd felt heavy, slow, as if her body was meant for flying and she'd just never realized before. She steadied her hands on the rooftop and, climbing the last few ladder rungs, sat on the edge of the hatch.

Her spirit flung out its arms and laughed. Her actual body, rigid with the posture drilled into her from earliest childhood, sat quietly and used its proper good sense to clutch the roof tiles. But Charlotte knew in her heart she was ruined. Just like that, between an attic and a rooftop: utterly ruined for genteel life. All her dreams of rural peace collapsed. To sit in the shade on a fine day and look upon verdure was not the most perfect refreshment after all. To breathe the wild blue wind was so much better!

No wonder pirates always seemed so satisfied—which Charlotte was learning meant something quite different from self-satisfied, the witch's ground state of being. Everything in her longed to rise up and run after Captain O'Riley, who stood with his booted feet set apart on the ridgeline as he watched Miss Fairweather's house grow nearer. He was so steady he might have been anchored there by magic. Charlotte found herself moving, drawn unthinking toward him, and scolded herself back into submission. Even when sitting on a pirate's roof—or perhaps *especially* when—a lady must maintain her proper deportment.

Gently the cottage veered until it was easing alongside Miss Fairweather's garish townhouse. Alex swayed a little at the shift of angle. With his long black coat and black-sheathed sword, sunlight flashing on the silver dangling from his ear and the various knives strapped about his person, he looked casually dangerous. He did not say "Ahoy!" but he smiled it, a smile of crookedness and contentment. Clearly, staying alive was less interesting to him than all-out living. Charlotte realized he wasn't going to wait for her to safely incantate him between rooftops. The moment the houses aligned, he was jumping.

And if he fell—

She shook her head at the thought. He *must not* fall. If only because she'd never convince his butler to fly on in pursuit of Lady Armitage.

Besides, she was a seventh-generation witch and the Prophesized One who would next lead the Wicken League. She could easily keep him safe.

He would not fall. *Breathe, Charlotte.*

His coat billowed around him as he took the grenade from his pocket and tossed it up, caught it, restless. He glanced at her and winked.

Her heart winked back.

She began muttering. Magic awoke, sparking against words, sending trails of heat along her nerves. Charlotte frowned.

Something felt wrong.

Suddenly, Alex leaped. All the thoughts in her head seemed to go with him; blank, she incantated by habit alone. He landed with ease and began running up the roof toward its ridgeline as if he could outrace gravity. Would her magic reach across the distance to him? Worried, Charlotte removed her sunglasses to see more surely. She incantated in a louder voice. Wind shook through the sound, shook her awareness, making her realize she'd somehow got to her feet and was standing on the cottage roof, anchored only by magic. Her heart leaped like a pirate.

She swayed, hands reaching out as if she could grasp hold of the wind to steady herself. Magic whipped inside her in a way it never had before, rowdy, messy . . .

Exhilarating.

She laughed.

The sound shocked her. A witch ought not laugh when reciting the incantation. Magic was not fun. It shouldn't delight, nor disturb, nor tug at instincts deep and secret inside her until she felt like dancing. Charlotte told herself sternly to get back onto the ladder where she could be safe and focus her thoughts on protecting Captain O'Riley. That was the sensible thing to do. And no one was more sensible than a witch.

She nodded in agreement with herself.

And began to walk toward the chimney at the far end of the roof.

On the other house, Alex had reached its chimney and was dropping in the grenade. Charlotte watched him from the corner of her eye. Smoke erupted from the chimney and he turned to run back. In that moment, he saw her.

He stopped, his body teetering on the narrow ridge. "What the hell do you think you're doing?" he yelled.

Charlotte put a finger against her lips to shush him as she continued to mutter the incantation. The ladies of the Wicken League would be aghast if they saw her. But those ladies were not present. And Elizabeth Bennet had nothing to say, since not even exploring the rooms of Pemberley equated to such a daring perambulation. Charlotte was alone and utterly bewildered by herself. She needed encouragement from a literary character who understood that walking the ridgeline was her only reasonable option. But if such a heroine could exist, she had not been written yet. Left to her own narrative devices, Charlotte inhaled sunlit wind and exhaled enchantment as she swayed on through the ancient, sea-washed, unburied dreaming of the incantation's magic.

"Goddamn idiot!"

From the corner of her eye, she saw Alex running to leap back onto his own house. No doubt he intended to chastise her, but she did not care. After all, she was a grown woman, capable, intelligent, and mature. He was not the boss of her.

She'd just reached the chimney when he caught up to her. She turned, a little unsteady, and he grasped her arms, pushing her back against the brick column as if that might save her from plummeting into the depths of a wayward enchantment. She stared up at him, half-drunk on magic and wanting to fly.

Good heavens but he was gorgeous. Those black-lashed eyes reflecting the vast, bare sky . . . that mouth more alluring than anything she'd envisioned on Mr. Darcy . . .

Suddenly Charlotte found herself wishing they'd let her read *Madame Bovary*.

Alex drew a breath as if to chastise her. She smiled, daring him.

And then he kissed her.

And she discovered there was a magic beyond words.

She had supposed he would take her in the way of a rogue, capturing her body and plundering her mouth and doing other things described with equally piratic metaphors until she was robbed of all good sense. But he was astonishingly gentle. His mouth lay soft on hers, tentative, wishing. His stubble was like a hundred tiny kisses against her skin. Every nerve in her body began to sing.

An aria. From a grand opera. With magnificent costumes, an entire orchestra, and flowers tossed onto the stage.

And yet, she wanted more—wanted something forceful, so she could be sure of what was happening, and how she must react. He would not give it to her. He brushed her lips with such a light touch that she almost sobbed with yearning. Lifting on her toes, she pressed against him, hands clutching in his windswept hair, trying to pull him into passion. This was not anything close to ladylike behavior, and Jane Austen would have ripped it out of her notebook and thrown it away, but Charlotte could not seem to help herself. The wind was to blame—or magic—or the pirate's aggravating nature.

He responded with a smile, and flicked her lips with his quick, devilish tongue. The fiend! This was outrageous! He was kissing her, and yet—not quite. He was coaxing a flame in her and then blowing it out, over and again, until the singing along her nerves reached such a pitch it would have shattered glass, had any been in the vicinity.

He shifted back an inch, leaving her bereft, and an old, aching loneliness rushed into the space between them. Charlotte could not bear it. She moved toward him, and he allowed their lips to touch gently, desperately briefly, before shifting back again. His smile tipped like a hook. She wanted it to pierce her, wanted kisses and sighs and his bare hands on her skin, but no book had equipped her with the necessary conversation to request such things. And Alex just stared back in provoking silence, as if he knew perfectly well how she felt and was enjoying it.

Charlotte realized then it was a game, like the briefcase had been. She considered reaching for the besom in her pocket so as to hold him at rapier point until he damned well ravished her. But if he wanted to play, she could play. She could be flirtatious. Books went that far, at least: Mr. Tilney had flirted with Catherine Morland in *Northanger Abbey*, and she recollected the way of it perfectly well. She gave one smirk and began to turn her head as if she had lost all interest in this irrational kissing venture—

Suddenly, Alex surrendered. Catching her face in his hands, he kissed her with a passion that utterly engulfed her senses. For one exciting moment she thought she might combust. Smoke swirled around them—granted, from the Fairweather chimney, but it was still conveniently metaphorical. Charlotte's knees trembled, and she grasped at the pirate's coat, arms, anything she could, to keep herself from tumbling. He pushed her back against the chimney again, his body pressing to hers, trapping her between a rock and a hard place. In that moment she discovered what an inadequate education statues had been. That which she felt through Alex's trousers wasn't so much a storm in a teacup as a teapot—a samovar, even—and the thunder was in her blood.

The whole world thundered.

And then shuddered.

They pulled apart, their eyes glazed with passion, realizing a moment too late that something was wrong. The Fairweather house had collided with Alex's cottage. It jerked away, then back again, brick smashing against stone with a screeching crash.

"Hell!" Alex swore, wrapping his arms around Charlotte in futile protection. The cottage rocked violently, tipped to port, and before either could think of what to do they were thrown off the roof.

❊ 9 ❊

EVERYTHING TURNS TO CUSTARD—A HORDE OF BARBARIANS—
WITCHES EXPLAIN THAT WITCHES DO NOT EXIST—
CECILIA CREATES AN EXPLOSION—
THE DIFFERENCE BETWEEN PIRATES AND WITCHES

If there is anything disagreeable going on, mothers are always sure to get into it—even when at several miles' distance. Mrs. Pettifer, sitting to afternoon tea with Miss Plim, jolted suddenly in her chair. The tea she had been about to sip shook in its cup, and she set it down in the saucer with a slight clink that immediately alerted Miss Plim to trouble.

"What is it, Delphine?" she demanded, peering over the rim of her spectacles. "You look as if you've seen a ghost."

"It's Lottie," Mrs. Pettifer gasped. "Oh my dear girl." She pressed a hand against her pearl-swathed bosom, in which her heart was suffering tremors of anxiety (or too much tea).

"What about Charlotte?" Miss Plim asked impatiently.

"I fear— Oh, Judith, I fear she went forth this morning without a parasol, and that she will come home most dreadfully suntanned!"

"Nonsense," Miss Plim declared. She proceeded with the custard slice from which Mrs. Pettifer had distracted her. "Charlotte is far too sensible to tan. Never in all my life have I known a girl more cautious and circumspect. She will stay out of the weather, you mark my words."

"Perhaps you are right." Mrs. Pettifer sighed, then murmured a short phrase. A shawl floated across from the sofa to her outstretched hand; Mrs. Pettifer wrapped it around herself comfortingly. "Lottie is down-to-earth," she said, trying to convince herself. "And she is an adult, I must remember. She can be trusted not to be flighty, and to keep in the shade. Although I must confess, I thought she would be home by now." She sighed again, to Miss Plim's aggravation. "No doubt she has taken up with one of her jolly friends and lost track of the time."

Miss Plim almost choked on custard slice. She did not know what was more amusing—the idea that Charlotte had friends, or that Mrs. Pettifer actually believed it. Unfortunately, the opportunity to mock her sister was lost as at that moment Woollery appeared.

"A Miss Bassingthwaite is at the door, madam," he announced.

"Good heavens!" Mrs. Pettifer ejaculated in astonishment. Miss Plim actually choked on custard slice. "A flying bicyclist come to visit! The shame!"

"And Captain Lightbourne," Woollery continued.

"Not the Dreaded Lightbourne of Leeds? I've heard he threw his own house off a cliff because he didn't like the wallpaper anymore! Pirates, Judith, at our very door! Quick, hide the silver!"

Alas, Miss Plim, busily engaged with smacking herself on the chest and trying to breathe, left the silver to its doom.

But Woollery had not finished. "Also, Mrs. Rotunder."

"No!" Mrs. Pettifer gasped. "Revolting Rotunder! Are we goners, Judith?"

The only reply she got was a wordless, wheezing cough.

"And Miss Constantinopla Brown, madam."

Mrs. Pettifer frowned. "Who?"

A fragment of patisserie shot across the room and splatted against Woollery's face. He blinked. "Shall I say you are not at home, madam?" he asked as half-digested custard dripped from his cheek.

"Gracious, no," Mrs. Pettifer said, more alarmed than ever. "That would be rude. Let the barbarians in."

The butler turned to perform this task.

"Wait! Woollery!" Mrs. Pettifer recalled him urgently. He turned back, inexpressive. "Bring more tea for our guests. And cake."

"Madam," he intoned, and departed. Mrs. Pettifer looked pale-faced at her sister.

"What a disaster. Four visitors and not enough tea to offer them! Thank heavens I remembered in time!"

"Hmhgh," Miss Plim replied, reaching for a glass of water. Her life had flashed before her eyes while she was dying from custard, and although it had been entirely satisfactory, she realized there was still much to do to improve the lives of others around her. But before she could embark upon helping Mrs. Pettifer by means of a lengthy corrective lecture, the visitors entered.

Mrs. Pettifer rose graciously to welcome them (and check her sixteenth-century golden goose statuette was safely out of their reach). Mrs. Rotunder, a distinguished matron in purple (and red, green, lavender) swooped into the room in a manner that would have made even a grand duchess feel gauche. Behind her came Constantinopla Brown, bedecked in lace and ribbons. She in turn was followed by a pretty, red-haired woman, then a man in such a ghastly waistcoat Mrs. Pettifer's polite smile sagged somewhat.

"Such an unusual pleasure to be visited by members of the piratic community," she lied. "Will you sit down?" After all, the chairs could easily be reupholstered. And if the pirates were seated, they could not be stealing.

(In fact, Cecilia Bassingthwaite pocketed a gold pen she found on a side table and Mrs. Rotunder surreptitiously tore the braiding off the cushion set at her back, repurposing it later as a hat trim.)

The pirates arranged themselves on the sofas and Mrs. Pettifer angled her chair to face them. Miss Plim, however, would not come out from behind the tiered cake plate. "Sister, dear," Mrs. Pettifer said through her smile, "won't you say hello to our company?"

"I most certainly will not," replied Miss Plim, for whom social graces were something that happened to other people. "Never in my life could I have imagined pirates in the house of an alleged witch."

"Witches do not exist, dear," Mrs. Pettifer said, the smile tightening.

"Hence 'alleged,' dear," Miss Plim snapped, and set about mauling a new custard slice with a fork.

The pirates glanced nervously at each other. They knew trouble when they saw it. Miss Bassingthwaite sat forward a little, attempting to ease the tension. "I do not entirely understand the feud between the Wicken League and the Wisteria Society," she said. "Surely pirates and—er, alleged witches are much the same?"

She might as well have tossed a bomb into the room. With one sentence she managed to offend both parties. Eyebrows lifted, mouths pinched, bosoms heaved. Captain Lightbourne, wincing, pressed a thumb knuckle against his forehead.

"Cecilia," Mrs. Rotunder murmured through clenched teeth, "you are too young to understand."

"I'm younger than her," Constantinopla interjected, "and I understand. And Tom . . . oh Tom, my beloved, what has become of you? . . . He would understand too." She produced a great shuddering sigh.

"Tom Eames is a pirate," Captain Lightbourne explained to Mrs. Pettifer, and gave her such a winning smile, she blushed. "We have come to discuss with you his kidnapping."

"Witches are nothing like pirates," Miss Plim said from behind the cakes. "They are Beryl Black's true descendants and use the incantation as it was intended."

"Be that as it may—" Captain Lightbourne began.

"Black Beryl's first use of the incantation was to fly a hut back to England," Mrs. Rotunder said. "Therefore pirates have the correct usage of magic."

"If we could just focus on—" Captain Lightbourne attempted.

"Witches," Miss Plim said, rising from her chair, "are subtle."

"Pirates have imagination," Mrs. Rotunder countered, hat feathers shivering.

"Witches are not thieves," Miss Plim said.

"You steal things all the time!" Constantinopla argued, gasping with indignation.

"We redistribute wealth," Miss Plim explained.

Mrs. Rotunder huffed a laugh. "Redistribute into your own purses."

"That is for the good of society, dear," Mrs. Pettifer explained, smiling sweetly. "After all, no one is happy unless a witch is happy. Alleged witch. Goodness, where is the tea?"

"Witches swindle," Mrs. Rotunder said, digging her heels in metaphorically and, alas for the Pettifers' expensive Oriental rug, literally also.

Miss Plim directed her fork like a dagger toward the pirate lady. "We creatively encourage behavior. Pirates wreck lives."

"Witches interfere."

"Pirates—"

"Witches—"

They spoke over each other in an excess of indignation, although they actually said the same thing: "—are the lowest of all scoundrels!"

The air seemed to ring with undrawn swords, unthrown vases. Captain Lightbourne spoke quickly before someone said or did something that brought war to London, or at least to the Pettifer drawing room.

"It is true the two communities are not exactly simpatico—"

Everyone stared at him in bewilderment.

"Sympathetic," he clarified.

"Ah yes, Captain Lightbourne is half Italian," Mrs. Rotunder said in the same way one explains that a person has fungal infections.

"Mr. Pettifer is half French," Mrs. Pettifer said, and the sigh she gave made everyone shift uncomfortably in their seats.

Cecilia cleared her throat. "Ned is trying to say that, although our communities do not all agree on . . . well, anything, we nevertheless have something in common now."

"And what is that, pray tell?" Miss Plim asked, clearly offended by the very idea.

"As you know, Beryl's amulet has been stolen—"

Cutlery crashed as Mrs. Pettifer and Miss Plim both grasped the table in horror. "Stolen?" they chorused.

Cecilia, growing pale, stated the obvious: "You don't know."

"We were attempting to feed orphans all day, but could not find the little blighters," Miss Plim explained. "We have not been to the museum."

"The amulet was stolen by Lady Armitage," Cecilia said.

"No!" Constantinopla cried, flapping a handkerchief dramatically. "Lady Armitage stole Tom, who was holding the amulet."

"What? Why?" Mrs. Pettifer reeled from shock to confusion.

Miss Plim ground what remained of her custard slice into a gritty puddle. "It would be bad enough *any* pirate running off with our amulet," she said, "but Armitage embodies pure evil. Such power in her hands could prove catastrophic. She is the Wisteria Society's responsibility— you must stop her!"

The visitors looked grim. "That is true," Ned agreed. "However, not only has Beryl's amulet (along with Tom) been stolen. The difficulty we all share is that a male pirate has flown off with an alleged witch."

The sisters gasped.

"No witch would keep company with a pirate," Miss Plim averred.

"Surely none would be so incautious, so careless of her reputation, and more than that, so dismissive of her family's reputation," Mrs. Pettifer agreed. "Your information must be wrong, Captain. I appreciate you don't understand our society, since you are of the piratic inclination yourself. But I know of no witch, alleged or otherwise, who would do such a thing!"

"It was your daughter."

Mrs. Pettifer would have swooned, but Miss Plim hastily muttered words from the incantation to keep her upright.

"I beg your pardon, Mrs. Pettifer, bringing you such tidings," Ned continued. "But several witnesses confirm Miss Pettifer entered the premises of Alexander O'Riley, an Irish pirate of ill-repute, and remained on board as it flew away."

"At least he is of ill-repute," Mrs. Pettifer said weakly as she grasped for a cup of tea. Ned, frowning a little in confusion, glanced at Cecilia, who shrugged. But before he could speak further, Miss Plim cleared her throat with what was an attitude of either authority or obnoxiousness, depending on who heard it.

"Clearly Charlotte has kidnapped Captain O'Riley and forced him to pursue the amulet."

"Not at all," Mrs. Rotunder said tightly. "Clearly Captain O'Riley has kidnapped Miss Pettifer."

"She is too powerful to succumb to kidnapping."

"He is too rude to be kidnapped."

Cecilia frowned delicately. "Every indication points to Miss Petti-fer having entered the house willingly, and we all know if Captain O'Riley did not want her there he'd have expelled her."

The two older ladies exchanged a look that would have been a skir-mish had they possessed fewer manners (and less cumbersome cloth-ing). Eventually, both blinked. "Someone kidnapped someone!" they insisted, their voices merging in reluctant alliance.

"But—" Cecilia began.

"An unmarried woman has absconded with a bachelor," Mrs. Ro-tunder explained in the slow, carefully enunciated manner that seems desirous of promoting comprehension but suggests its listener is inca-pable of such a thing. "This has occurred in public view. Under ordi-nary circumstances, a marriage would be required. But clearly a pirate cannot marry a witch! Kidnapping is a far more palatable scenario."

"I concur," Miss Plim said. "The idea of Charlotte marrying any— er, *that* man is not to be entertained!"

"Well . . ." Mrs. Pettifer said, having been fortified by tea. "It actu-ally *might* be entertaining." She caught Miss Plim's scowl in much the same way a person catches a primed grenade, and hastily added, "But of course it is entirely wrong. Abysmal. Insupportable. Even if the cap-tain is a very handsome gentleman."

"Hmm," Ned murmured, in lieu of mentioning all the other things Alex O'Riley was.

"I have only met Miss Pettifer briefly," Cecilia said. "But it seems to me she and Captain O'Riley would be well suited."

Her observation cast a chill over the gathered company. Even Woollery arriving with tea and cake reinforcements did not dispel the mood. Ned threw Cecilia an exceedingly married look.

"Imagine if they wed," Mrs. Rotunder said. "All the opportunities it would offer for goodwill between our two societies!"

Everyone shuddered.

"Charlotte must be retrieved," Miss Plim declared, smacking her hand against the tea table, "before the perfectly lovely feud we have enjoyed these past two hundred years is ruined."

"Captain O'Riley must be censured," Mrs. Rotunder added. "And also made to paint his windowsills, but that is perhaps less urgent."

"Furthermore, the amulet must be recovered from that ghastly Lady Armitage before she can make a mess with it," Mrs. Pettifer said.

"And Tom must be rescued!" Constantinopla cried—although by this time everyone had become occupied with teacups and slices of ginger cake, so her addition went unnoticed.

Mrs. Rotunder sat forward in her seat, teacup held like a sacred object before her. "I understand that you, Miss Plim, are not the leader of a nonexistent league of alleged witches. In this non-capacity I assume you do not have the authority to speak for those others who are not in the hypothetical league?"

"No," Miss Plim agreed.

Mrs. Rotunder nodded. "Excellent. As a member of the Wisteria Society, I am taking it upon myself, with no jurisdiction whatsoever, to approach you and suggest our two societies call a temporary truce, and combine forces in order to hunt down"—she paused at a startled look from Mrs. Pettifer—"er, I mean ascertain the location of the two flyaways, and restore them to their proper spheres."

"And rescue Tom!" Constantinopla added vehemently.

"Of course, dear," Mrs. Rotunder said, smiling at her. She turned back to the adults. "And retrieve the amulet."

"A temporary truce in the interest of preserving the feud seems like a sensible idea," Miss Plim said. "I would authorize it if I was in a position of power over a group of witches."

"I think I'm getting a headache," Ned murmured to Cecilia.

"Sh," she whispered, trying not to smile, and they shared a glance that Miss Plim, happening to notice, felt go through her like sunshine. She grimaced with disgust.

"And so we are agreed," Mrs. Rotunder declared. "This is not a romance; it is a cautionary tale." She chuckled in the tone of an interfering old woman, which is even more chilling than that of a pirate. "Parting those two shall be sweet, even if it causes them sorrow. I shall let the Society know our plan, and be in touch with you again regarding details. If we manage this truce carefully, it should lead to a swift return of hostilities."

She quaffed tea then stood, a ravaged cushion dropping down behind her. Fortunately (or unfortunately, depending on whose perspective you favor), Mrs. Pettifer was too distressed about Charlotte to notice. The pirate maven snapped her fingers at the others. "Tally ho!"

The younger pirates rose to go. But after nods and murmured farewells, suddenly Mrs. Pettifer stepped forward and caught Cecilia's arm.

"Please," she said, her voice almost quavering. "My Lottie is a fragile girl, tender of heart and sensitive of spirit. Will she be safe with this Captain O'Riley?"

"I'm sure she will," Cecilia said, discreetly putting away the dagger she had instinctively drawn. Out of kindness, she refrained from mentioning that perhaps Captain O'Riley was the one who should be cautious. Charlotte Pettifer had seemed fierce enough to overawe a pirate, no matter how big and scary he might be.

"You needn't worry," Ned added with a smile that eased Mrs. Pettifer's heart, despite his waistcoat. "I've known Alex O'Riley for years. He's a blighter and a rogue, with no respect for any rule and no consideration of manners . . . indeed, he once robbed the Princess Royal while wearing nothing but a bathrobe . . . and when someone accused him of burning down three police stations in Ireland he threatened to shoot them because in fact it was four . . . then there's his habit of—"

"Ahem," Cecilia interrupted quietly, having noticed the increasing pallor of Mrs. Pettifer's face.

"Er, yes, well." Ned grimaced an apology. "That's all to say he is ultimately a good man. Rest assured, madam. I am absolutely certain no harm will befall Miss Pettifer."

❊ 10 ❊

A FALLEN WOMAN—IN MORE WAYS THAN ONE—
A REMEDY FOR PNEUMONIA—ALEX IS SWEPT OFF HIS FEET—
THEY AGREE TO DISAGREE—SAVAGE SLIPPERS—
A FISHY STRANGER—THEY DO NOT RACE FOR IT

Falling off a roof hundreds of feet above the ground is certainly the finest balm for the pangs of disputatious lust. As Charlotte plummeted toward the ground, still locked in Alex's arms, she recollected Miss Plim's warning that kissing a man was bad for one's health. Terror flashed through her entire body. But her mind, well trained for messes like spilled tea, conservative governments, and tumbling toward one's death, reacted calmly. She was speaking the incantation before she even realized it.

At once, their descent slowed. Adding the *momentum automatica*, Charlotte was able to settle her pulse (and appreciate just how convenient trousers were in an updraft).

"You might have spoken quicker," Alex said. "I'm dizzy now."

"I can always let you go," she replied. "Smashing into the ground would undoubtedly cure your vertigo."

"No, that's fine, thanks. Besides, better late than never, I suppose."

"You're welcome."

"We're still going a little fast, though."

"Any slower and a blackbird will nest in your hair."

"And be careful of gusts."

"I know what I'm doing." She winced as a speck of rain fell on her eyelid. "Women of sense, whatever you may choose to say, do not want men thinking them silly."

"The last word I would use for you, Miss Pettifer, is 'silly.'"

"Besides, this is all your fault. If you hadn't tried to seduce me, we would have been prepared for the collision."

"Tried?" he repeated, scoffing. "Madam, considering how passionately you were kissing me back, I think I succeeded quite well in seducing you."

She gasped. "Rude man! If we weren't airborne, I would kick you in the—er, I cannot mention where, but you may be sure it would hurt."

His eyes blazed hungrily. His face, freckling with raindrops, seemed to sparkle. "If we weren't airborne, the things I'd be doing to you would be very rude indeed."

"Upon my word, you are the worst kind of scoundrel!"

"Being called a scoundrel by a termagant is a rather comfortable compliment."

"Termagant?!"

"Better than 'silly,' yes? Watch out for the lake."

"We're nowhere near the lake."

"It's right beneath us."

"Nonsense."

"Veer starboard!"

"What?"

"Right! No, other right. That way!"

Splash.

In vain Charlotte struggled, but it would not do. Her efforts to swim out of the lake were repressed by the weight of her coat. She came toward Alex in an agitated manner, kicking legs that, booted as they were, did more to drag her down than keep her swimming. "You must allow me to help you," he insisted ardently, and at last secured her agreement—and her person, which he pulled ashore.

As he brought her to safety, Alex felt a rush of pleasure. Not often did a pirate get the chance to be heroic. That he had saved this stubborn, irritating woman from drowning made him happier than he'd have guessed it would. Granted, she had just saved him from falling to his death, so they were infuriatingly equal. But he was not the most notorious buccaneer in all of Eire, half of England, and two southwestern provinces of France for nothing, and he felt sure he'd get the better of her soon. He'd rescue her *even more,* or arouse her further, or steal the bloody amulet first just so he could triumphantly give it to her.

Maybe then she'd be dislodged from his traitorous heart. How she'd even got in there was a complete mystery. One day he was cursing her for stealing his briefcase and the next he wanted her under him in bed. Or on top of him. Or rolling around with him. Really, any position would do.

But more than that, he wanted her to insult him, argue with him, provoke him fearlessly as no other woman had ever dared. Even Cecilia, who wasn't scared of him, didn't go out of her way to cause tension between them. But Charlotte Pettifer seemed to find tension as thrilling as he did. She utterly disrespected his reputation, and he liked her for it.

A week ago, he'd have thought such a thing impossible. A week ago, a witch was to him the sort of woman who'd steal a husband, smirk at a wife's funeral, and thrash a child with such regularity that even years later he kept at least one weapon to hand in case it might be needed for defense. He'd always supposed he'd drown a witch if he had her in his hands within proximity of a lake. To not only have saved this one, but even now, crouching beside her on the rain-washed shore, to be wanting his mouth on hers again, his fingers pressing into the lush softness of her skin—it bewildered him. And Alex did not like bewilderment. He liked smug certainty and hitting things with his sword.

He glanced at Charlotte. Even on her knees in the mud and drizzling rain, coughing up lake water, she looked entirely proper, as if there was only one right way to recover from near-drowning and she had mastered it. God, but he wanted to make her messy in the most licentious manner.

With a sigh, he got to his feet and held out a hand to her. She looked at it darkly. "You do realize my amulet is getting even farther away while we waste time with shenanigans?" she said.

"You do realize my house has made an emergency landing I don't know where?" he answered.

Her expression sobered. She reached for his hand. "I hope Bixby will be all right."

"I'm sure he's fine." Alex hauled her to her feet. She stumbled against him, and as their eyes met, it was as if they fell all over again. He caught her with an arm around her back and was kissing her hard, even before she could force him to.

The rain, a mere sprinkle until now, tapping shyly on the lake, burst forth suddenly like a diva in a feather boa bursting through stage curtains, as if inspired by their passion. It poured from their hair and eyelashes and slicked their kiss. A shadowed wind gasped cold between them, but they were burning inside. They were a dangerous storm that promised mutual electrocution if they did not stop. Finally, Charlotte pulled away, pressing the back of her wrist against her mouth.

"What atrocious behavior!" she said, although it wasn't clear exactly to whose behavior she referred.

"It was medicinal," Alex replied. "Your lips were turning blue. I thought it wise to warm you rapidly."

She almost huffed, but he watched her stop herself in time, settling dignity over her face and standing taller for all the world, as if she were in a reception room, dressed in silk and pearls, rather than on the dirty, rain-beaten shore of a lake, wearing a man's shirt that had turned so transparent the delicate lace of her camisole could be seen, and beneath that—

He hauled his gaze upward and found her glaring at him.

"I have never met a more aggravating man," she said. "If I didn't need to abduct you in order to recover my amulet, I would gladly never see you again."

Alex laughed in astonishment. "Abduct me? Madam, I assure you, I am not abducted. I would leave at this very moment if you weren't a fragile female lost God knows where in a downpour, vulnerable to—"

She yanked his arm suddenly, tucked her leg around his, and flung him to the ground.

It would have been a great triumph for her—except he grabbed her coat as he tumbled, and she went down too, smacking against him. He rolled them over so he was lying atop her, heavy against her softness. Instantly his body reacted. He could see she felt it, but that she did not understand exactly what it meant. Strange that such a competent woman could be so innocent. The thought aroused him even more, and he decided for safety's sake to get off her. But suddenly, without warning, she lifted her head and kissed him.

He inhaled sharply, nerves flashing.

It was only a brief, soft kiss, making him think of a kitten lashing out with claws so tiny they barely tickled. Alex had never before experienced such an intoxicating mix of lust and sweetness.

"You are a tyrant, Charlotte Pettifer," he said against her mouth.

"You are a fiend."

He kissed her back, although neither soft nor sweet. Their tongues tangled. Their ankles tangled. She twisted hers, and in the scuffle managed to tip him off her. With a leap, she was on her feet again and drawing forth the vicious little multipurpose device.

Alex lay on the ground and grinned up at her. "Do it," he said. "Go on, do it."

She flicked the device and there was a sharp click as an implement sprung out.

Alex considered the teaspoon a moment, then laughed. Flushing, Charlotte snapped it shut and brought forth the rapier.

He licked his lips. Getting up slowly, he held her gaze. She swallowed—for he really was very big and scary. He drew his sword from its scabbard.

Her eyes widened.

"I suggest you give up and let me take you to safety," he said, raising the sword.

She followed it up with her gaze, then looked back at him. He realized then it wasn't fear in her eyes, but exhilaration.

"Aereo," she said. The incantated word levitated her several feet off the ground. "I suggest you give up and let me steal your house."

"That's not going to happen, sweetheart."

She kicked toward his head.

He ducked, and moving behind her, thumped the pommel of his sword against her booted ankle.

Sparks shot out from the back of her heel. Alex laughed, delighted. (And also winced as a spark burned into his breastbone.) Charlotte somersaulted midair then spun about, rapier sweeping toward him. But he met it with his sword, and as metal cried out, the rapier fell from her hand.

"Ow," she said, shaking her hand and glaring at him in indignation. He tossed his sword aside, grasped her shirt, and pulled her down toward him. She was still floating as their mouths met. They kissed with such force, Charlotte's magic flared, and in the next moment Alex was rising off the ground along with her. He clutched her head; she dug fingernails into his back. Their coats billowed as the rain around them sizzled from magical energy.

"Just surrender," Alex growled between kisses.

"You first." Tipping her head back, she offered her throat. He dragged his tongue up it, pressed lips against her pulse—tasting soap, rain, the heat of aroused blood. He very nearly spoke then to yield all his heart and will to her, but old, barbed instincts stopped him in the nick of time. He could almost hear a voice, still sharp despite being two decades past, calling him a bloody fool. He flinched as if a fist boxed his ear.

At his sudden movement, the magic unbalanced, and they dropped to the ground. Charlotte immediately turned away but he caught her, pulling her back against him, trapping her within the compass of his arm. Although he couldn't see the expression on her face, he could imagine its fury, and he grinned.

"I dare you," he said in her ear, hot and tempting. "Step on me with those vicious boots of yours."

She tried to tug herself free. "Brigand!"

"Virago."

"Excuse me."

They turned their heads in surprise.

"I beg your pardon," said a gentleman standing placidly in the rain. He wore enormous galoshes, and on his head a cap bristled with hooks. A fishing rod lay propped against one shoulder. As Alex and Charlotte stared at him, he smiled beneath his thin, crooked mustache. "I say, have you by any chance spotted a pike gudgeon?"

Charlotte blinked dumbly. Alex narrowed his eyes. "Is that some kind of weapon?" he asked.

The man laughed. "Good heavens no, my dear chap. Fish." He waved at the lake as if this explained all.

Charlotte and Alex turned their heads toward the lake, then back to the man. "Can't say I have," Alex said. "You, darling?"

"No," Charlotte replied. "And if you call me darling again, I'll bite you."

He grinned. "Promise?"

"Well, bother," the newcomer continued in a blithe tone, despite the rain and the two strangers paused mid-struggle before him. "I'm sure it's in there. Only one in the whole district, you see, imported especially for our little contest, and it'd be a dratted shame if Peddick got it before me. And will you look at this! Someone's left a sword just lying around. Not safe, that. A person could stub their toe on it."

Alex shifted slightly, adjusting his hold on Charlotte. "Can I ask, sir—"

"Hooper." He offered a hand to shake and then—noticing the knives strapped to Alex's thigh, and the long dagger extending out of his boot, not to mention the sword scabbard—made a little wave instead. "Arthur Hooper, three times Dagenham district champion angler (bait form) and butler to Sir Rufus over at Rothbury House, at your service. Well, at Sir Rufus's service, but you know what I mean."

"Mr. Smith," Alex replied. "And this is my sister, Miss Smith."

The man's eyebrows raised with astonishment. "I'm guessing you are northerners, for I've never seen anyone around here kiss their sister quite so vigorously. It almost looked like you were jumping off the ground, ha ha."

"Did I say sister?" Alex shook his head. "I meant wife. She's my wife. Mrs. Smith. On account of me being Mr.—"

"Shut up," Charlotte said. "Mr. Hooper, would you kindly direct us toward some shelter, please?"

"Shelter?"

"From the rain."

He blinked up at the gray deluge. "Oh, you mean this mizzle? You could go to the Angler's Retreat. Local pub. Just on the other side of the lake there." He pointed with his fishing rod.

"Thank you."

"Right you are," he said, smiling and rocking on his heels as if intending to stay and watch whatever remained of their show. They stared at him with expressions like drawn swords, and an awkward laugh fell from his mouth. "Well then. No pike gudgeon. Right ho, I'll be just on my . . . um . . . tah-rah, then."

"Tah-rah," Alex said.

"Good-bye," Charlotte added.

The man scurried away.

"I'll give you three seconds to let me go," Charlotte said, "before I demonstrate my technique for killing a man using one elbow and the anchoring phrase of the incantation."

Alex sighed. "Are you always like this?"

"You bring out the worst in me."

"I meant—"

She pulled away. He thought she might run, but instead she placed her hands on her hips and glared at the scenery as if it were making an effort to personally annoy her. "We should try to locate your house."

Alex considered the distant trees. "It's too far. Bixby knows how to land in a hurry. He'll be fine. We'll wait in the Angler's Retreat and make a search when the rain clears."

"That's a long walk."

"Hardly."

"You've crippled me, hitting my leg with your sword's pommel as you did."

His heart swooped with dismay. Taking a step toward her, he glanced at the leg in question, its shape explicit within the soaked trousers, then blinked hurriedly and looked at her face instead. "I'm sorry, does it very much hurt?"

"I am in agonizing pain," she lied calmly.

Hearing her tone, he rolled his eyes. "I'm walking," he said, bending to pick up his sword. "You can come or not, as you choose. If not, I wish you all the best in your efforts to steal the amulet. Good afternoon, madam."

She gave him a vicious look and muttered beneath her breath. The little besom flew up from the grass into her hand. With a snap, a long thin metal broom shot out. Its bristles flared like a bare-bones umbrella.

"Don't tell me you're going to sit on that and fly," Alex said incredulously.

"Certainly not! Don't be ridiculous!" She shook back her wet hair. "I am going to hold on to it and fly."

"That's daft."

"It's quicker than walking."

"Aren't you afraid of falling off in the middle of the lake?"

"I am not afraid of anything, Captain."

"You really ought to rethink that attitude."

"Perhaps I shall, once inside, warm and dry, and drinking tea with a splash of sherry."

"Sherry?" He laughed. "That's a drink for grandmothers in fluffy slippers and hairnets."

She gave him a cutting smile. "Sir, if I wore fluffy slippers, they would have poisoned darts hidden amongst their fluff."

His blood turned suddenly hot. He swayed a little toward her, and she swayed a little toward him, and thunder shook a warning that had them moving prudently back again.

"I believe you," he said. "But for God's sake, drink a proper whiskey."

"It's ungentlemanly for you to tell me what to do. Actually, no, I take that back. It's entirely gentlemanly. You, sir, represent all that is wrong with our patriarchal society!"

"And you, madam, are the most enticing creature I have ever known. I want to lick every inch of you."

She stared at him, open-mouthed. "Upon my word! Only two minutes ago you were asking, 'Are you always like this?' Such inconsistency is what gives pirates a bad name."

"And here I was thinking it was the pillaging, terrorizing, and rampant hooliganism. I beg your pardon, Miss Pettifer, but as I tried to tell you at the time, what I actually meant was, 'Are you always this strong, fierce, gorgeous, brave?' A question entirely consistent with my more recent statement."

"Oh." She looked away, frowning. "Well. Hmph."

He grinned. "Daft woman."

"Poor communicator."

"Fair enough. I'll get explicit, shall I? Are you afraid of premarital sex?"

Her eyes narrowed as she considered this. At last she spoke, her tone cool. "I reiterate, I'm afraid of nothing."

His grin deepened. He felt its pleasure all the way down in a part of his anatomy that really could not sustain much more pleasure right now. "Race you to the inn?"

"Certainly not!" she replied, indignant. "A lady never races. I shall merely make haste and await your presence."

And with that, she gave her broomstick a flick, muttered a word, and flew off through the storm.

Then flew back again, picked up her sunglasses, which had fallen from her coat pocket earlier, and with a haughty expression flew off once more.

Alex looked heavenward for patience, but only got an eyeful of rain. It was enough to make him believe God was a witch. He began to walk.

And then, thinking of Charlotte Pettifer all warmed up with whiskey, he began to run.

❊ 11 ❊

ONLY ONE BEDROOM—INCORRECT UNDRESSING—MANHANDLED—
CHARLOTTE WISHES FOR SOME BEDTIME READING—
ALEX IS UNHYGIENIC—JANE WHO?—
THIRD TIME, LUCKY—MUTUAL DEFEAT

G ive a girl an education and introduce her properly to the world, and ten to one but she will find herself alone in an inn bedroom with a gentleman rogue. Charlotte (who really should have been allowed to see the interesting pages of biology textbooks after all, and therefore had her curiosity safely assuaged) stood beside the bed with her arms crossed sternly over the simple dress the innkeeper's wife had given her, and glared at Alex.

And he, looking dangerous in borrowed trousers and shirt that strained against his muscles, shrugged in insouciant reply.

That they had landed less than a quarter mile from a public house was coincidental only if you forget this was England, where many thousands of pubs thrive around the country. That it had just one bedroom still available will not be surprising to connoisseurs of romance. The sole astonishment was it contained two beds.

Alex and Charlotte had quickly fixed that.

And now, the beds having been pushed together, the hot whiskey toddies having been drunk, they stood waiting to see who would make the first move.

"I don't know why you insisted on getting dressed, since I'm only going to undress you again," Alex said.

"I don't know why you are so confident of that," Charlotte replied. She swayed a little, for there had been just enough whiskey in the toddy to loosen her muscles along with several of her dearest inhibitions. Somewhere at the back of her mind, Jane Austen's heroines were shouting, waving volumes of *Mansfield Park*, and trying to remind her of the fate awaiting unchaste women. But they were drowned out by the echoing memory of Alex calling her *strong, fierce, gorgeous, brave*.

Her heart sighed. Something about the man—his laughing eyes, perhaps, or wicked mouth, or dear lord his boots—caused her entire being to thrum. She felt as if she had been sleepwalking through life and had woken finally on that day in St. James's when one conversation with him had literally flung her skyward. But there was no call to let him know this. "It goes to show your male arrogance," she said, "that you assume you can simply undress me on your own authority."

"Fair enough," Alex said languidly. "So shall I just leave?"

"By all means, if you are a lily-livered, trembling—"

She stopped, blinking in surprise, as he stepped forward and began tugging at the buttons on her bodice. "No," she said, smacking at his hands. "Not like that. You have to push them more care—"

He caught her chin, lifted it, and kissed her until words dissolved and her knowledge of correct button removal procedures was utterly lost from memory.

The bodice managed to get open despite his rough method, and after some struggle with sleeves, during which both parties lambasted each other (and kissed each other with increasingly urgent frustration), the entire dress fell in a heap to her feet. All that remained was a plain cotton chemise the innkeeper's wife had also provided.

Charlotte stared down at the dress, rather dazed, and unsure what to do next. She'd just allowed a man to disrobe her. Jane Austen would be weeping into her inkwell.

Alex had the situation in hand, however. Literally. Taking hold of her by the waist, he simply lifted her up, kicked the dress aside, and set her down again.

"Oh," she breathed. "Goodness gracious." Her stomach filled with a dozen fans flapping urgently in an effort to cool her.

Alex smiled, biting his lower lip in an expression of endearing wickedness. Reaching for the chemise straps, he began to slide them off. Charlotte grasped his wrists, and although she had nowhere near enough strength to actually stop him, nevertheless he stopped.

"I am not convinced that is wise," she said.

He smiled. "What, are you hiding a rifle and three attack dogs under there?"

"Of course not. You may check if you want."

His eyebrow raised at the invitation. Using one finger to gently draw back the chemise's neckline, he peered beneath.

Charlotte held her breath.

He did not touch her, but his gaze seemed to stroke every nerve ending. After a long, wordless moment, he looked into her eyes again. He had seen her—and now apparently wanted to see *her*. Charlotte lowered her own gaze, for he could have her body, but no one was trusted with her heart.

And her body, hearing that thought, tossed aside the fans and installed a steam turbine instead. Certain parts ached for the pirate to not just look, but to touch with his strong, calloused fingers. But her mind, already aghast at the turn of events, and composing a lecture it suspected the body would completely ignore, was determined. She might well be *strong, fierce, gorgeous, brave,* but adding *naked* to that list surely crossed the line of Proper Femininity. Charlotte had spent her entire life trying to balance on that line, pulled one way by the dictates of society, and the other by her own sensitivities and intelligence. She could usually approximate nice behavior by watching people and reading books. But the etiquette of trysting in a country inn with a pirate was not something easily guessed at.

If only Jane Austen, Elizabeth Gaskell, or even Charles Dickens, had written on the subject of copulation so she knew what to do, and in what correct sequence. Were there particular words one ought to say? An action one always must take?

No doubt Captain O'Riley had an encyclopedic knowledge of the subject, but Charlotte could hardly quiz him without revealing her own ignorance. And never must she do that. A witch was nothing if not superior in all understanding.

"So," Alex said musingly. "I can look but I can't take the thing off?"

"You can do anything you want," she said, and he made a noise in the back of his throat. "But according to how I was raised, a woman does not disrobe under any circumstance."

"What, not even in the bath?"

"Absolutely not!" She was shocked at the very thought.

"God, and I thought my upbringing was awful." He looked at her for a long, steady while, assessing her courage for what lay ahead. She waited, heart pounding, for him to call a halt to the whole endeavor. But at last he shrugged.

"Your choice, darling. It stays on."

Relief washed through her. "You, however, may disrobe as you wish," she added. "Or retain whatever items of clothing you choose. I suppose you'll take off the trousers so as to freely access your—um—gentleman's small tumescent limb."

His eyes flashed. "I beg your pardon?"

"Is that not used in this activity?"

"Yes," he said in a rather strained voice. (*Oh dear*, Charlotte thought—

perhaps he'd got pneumonia in the rain after all.) "Let me give you two pieces of advice, Miss Pettifer. First, never use the word 'small' in relation to a man's—er, that."

She sighed testily. "I meant small compared to an arm or a leg."

"Never. Ever."

Apparently, this was a firm rule. "Very well," she relented.

"And second—just lie down on the goddamn bed, will you?"

She glanced over her shoulder at the furniture in question. "Do you think it's clean?"

His expression tightened, and she got the sense he was only just holding on. "Unless you want me to take you against the wall, you'll just have to risk it."

Charlotte gasped—but after a moment's hesitation, decided on no, and pulled back the eiderdown.

Alex watched as Charlotte lay on the bed. There followed an endless minute in which her chemise twisted around her hips and she had to raise them to rearrange it, and then do the same with her hair, and then shuffle over to avoid what must have been a loose spring in the mattress. Alex waited with an exasperation that bordered on intense, pulsing arousal. The woman was going to annoy him into an orgasm before he even placed a hand on her.

Finally she lay still, almost rigid, her gaze fixed on the ceiling. He hesitated, not wanting to go ahead if she was as anxious as she seemed—

"Tsk," she said, clicking her tongue impatiently, and he yanked off his shirt and trousers, first taking out the item of protection he always carried with him (not necessarily because he was an incorrigible rake—after all, the item had many handy uses, such as tying up bank workers and holding stolen coins).

(He was, however, *also* an incorrigible rake.)

As he fitted the item, Charlotte did not shift her gaze from the ceiling. Looking at her, Alex frowned. If she wasn't anxious, why did she lie there as if the world was a great scratchy weight on her body?

The question flipped itself into its own answer. And with it, Alex felt something loosen around his heart. He lay down on his side next to her and pulled the eiderdown over them.

"Come here," he whispered, tipping her to face him. She swallowed a breath, her eyes huge and dark but, thank God, not frightened. The same could not be said so surely for him. Bloody hell, he'd done this often enough—there was no need to be nervous.

Then she blinked her long, thick lashes over her stormy eyes, and his heart trembled.

"You've taken more of the blanket on your side," she grumbled, laying a hand against his tattooed chest. Her touch, soft as rose petals, was so gentle Alex thought he might break apart beneath it.

"You're a she-devil," he answered, brushing damp strands of hair from her face.

They stared at each other for a long, intense moment. *Breathe,* Alex reminded himself. *Do what now?* his lungs replied.

"This is merely to clear the air between us, you understand," Charlotte said.

Alex grinned. "Darling, I assure you there will be no *merely* about it," he countered, and Charlotte rolled her eyes. "However, you are essentially right. We are just releasing the tension."

"It is not a commitment."

"Agreed."

"Furthermore—"

He kissed her. And all her words turned to chaff, leaving her with a more honest silence.

The kiss turned slow, explorative. The stroking hands over bare skin set them both shivering despite the cloistered heat. Charlotte's bracelet tinkling against him reminded Alex she was a witch to whom he should not even be speaking—but he did not care. In this moment, in this bed, she was Charlotte Pettifer, nothing more, and if he could not get inside her soon, he would likely perish from wanting.

But he tried to be patient, because piracy only went so far, and he'd never take from a woman if it would hurt her. Charlotte's body was as tight as her attitudes, and no matter how she muttered that they needed to get on with things so they could resume the chase for her amulet, Alex was determined to be gentle. Using first one finger and then two, he offered a preview of what he planned to do to her.

At first, her astonishment was extreme. "Are you sure?" she said, squirming against his hand. "This doesn't seem very proper to me."

"It's entirely improper, darling," he agreed, moving the fingers slowly, delighting at her adorably censorious frown. But her body was beginning to ease as he drew her with long, stroking movements toward a state of warm, wet disarray.

"I don't under— Oh!" She went abruptly taut again.

He paused. "What?"

"Do that. Again. With your thumb."

He rubbed again. "That?"

For the first time since he'd known her, the sounds emerging from her throat were not complaints. In broken syllables and shuddering gasps, she related how he was finally doing something perfectly, and he smiled with the particular triumph of knowing he had pleased her. Continuing as instructed, he watched pleasure swell in her eyes, felt it clench around his fingers as she climaxed. The sensation in her body seemed to spark through his own, and he had to take a deep breath to calm himself.

"Goodness me," she said at last. "That was—remarkable."

"I'm glad." He kissed her, as if he might taste the rare compliment on her lips.

"How do I reciprocate?" she asked, businesslike.

At the question, an unfamiliar emotion tangled up inside him, but he could not identify it and did not dare try. Far safer to just get on with being a rakish pirate and let the murky depths of his psyche deal with themselves. He smiled down at her. Damn, she was beautiful, all flushed and softened by pleasure. He had a sudden fierce urge to protect her from himself, even knowing that turning away now would be physical torment. But she scowled at him, wanting an answer, and the protective urge was overwhelmed by more desperate urges that her own impatience seemed to encourage.

"You are giving me all I want just by being here," he said. And surprised himself with the truth of it.

Alex did not like surprising himself. He wasn't particularly fond of truth either, for that matter. He did, however, like kissing Miss Pettifer, so he went back to doing that.

Charlotte had a talent for certainty, and one thing she was very sure about was that she didn't approve of what they were doing. She liked it—in fact she would happily continue doing it for the rest of the evening if required, and furthermore take it up the next morning should the opportunity arise—but *approval* was a different matter entirely.

Captain O'Riley had touched her in a way that was certainly unhygienic. And goodness only knows what kind of nervous damage she had acquired when that strange, powerful sensation of bliss overtook her. There was also still the fact of the amulet being unsecured.

Then Alex stroked a hand over her breast, causing all thought of the amulet to explode in a golden blaze. And now the blasted man was kissing her again. Worse, his gentleness completely ruined the happy image she had of him as a cur. She had been expecting a brief, furious event, such as their arguments had been. But instead he gave her this tenderness, this inexplicable consideration.

Thankfully, she had at last cobbled together somewhat of a script for response. Mr. Darcy also had proved himself a considerate fellow beneath his aloof exterior, and Elizabeth Bennet had reacted with sincerity and love. Charlotte thought this rather extreme, but she could at least kiss the pirate's jaw, enjoying the texture of stubble against her tingling lips, following the hard curve up to his earlobe. That she bit gently, his earring clattering against her chin.

"Hhnngh," he said, which was possibly an Irish word; it seemed to express approval.

"You're welcome," she whispered into his ear.

He shivered. "Wicked witch," he said, and Charlotte remembered yes, that's what she was. Casting aside her nice script, she drew a fingernail along the tattoo of barbed knots that swooped across his chest then down, over his heart, around his navel, into the dark hair at the base of his, er, fifth and definitely not small limb. His breath hitched, and Charlotte smirked with satisfaction. She had a fair idea now of what he intended to do with that particular part of his anatomy, and she stroked a cautious finger along the blushed, velvety skin . . .

Within seconds, he had her flipped onto her back, legs pushed open, knees up, breath gone. He lay over her, and his eyes blazed with a feral heat.

Charlotte grinned. "I dare you."

"Are you sure?"

"I wouldn't be here if I wasn't."

"Very well then." His hand moved down to where it had been so effective before, and she gasped as sensation rampaged through her. She tried to think of a response but suddenly something else was there, pressing hard, and her body tensed, sensing a moment from which there would be no going back. Her heart thundered in trepidation.

Then the world literally caved in.

Alex blinked with confusion as they dropped a depth of two feet to an abrupt, although rather soft, landing. Moments later he realized the beds had slid apart and they'd fallen through the gap to the carpet below. A tangled sheet lay beneath them. The eiderdown stretched across the gap above like a tent.

"Are you hurt?" he asked Charlotte—but she was already laughing. It sounded wild and delighted, like a woman surprised by life and surprising herself that she didn't mind it.

All of a sudden, Alex found his heart fill with sincere affection. This woman drove him absolutely mad, both mentally and sexually, and yet he really did like her despite it. Perhaps even because of it. There was something so invigorating about her, and at the same time so reassuring—certainly different from the women who approached him with caution or used him for a thrill. Charlotte was neither afraid of him nor seeking mere titillation. She made him feel safe enough to be himself—not the dread pirate, the impious rake. Just Alex, wanting her.

God, wanting her so much he could not wait another moment. He'd only known her a few days, but his body swore it had suffered an eternity of desire for this woman. With a warm smile, he looked into her beautiful, lavish eyes.

"Hurry up," she demanded.

His smile blazed into a grin. Well then, damn it if he had any choice left but to prove in one long, unrelenting movement exactly how a man used that most interesting part of him.

Her thoughts shattered. She grasped mentally at wise pages, good quotes, but it was of no use. She could barely recall the name of any author, let alone something they might have written. Alex dominated her, body and mind. She could feel nothing but him, think of nothing but him. Overwhelmed, she clutched the tumbled sheet in a kind of despair. It was too much; it was unbearable.

Then he moved back, and she grabbed his hips, pulling her toward him again.

"Don't stop," she grumbled.

He laughed. "No fear of that." He began a gentle pace, inching deeper, all the while keeping his thumb occupied in a way that made Charlotte breathe jaggedly. He kissed her throat, as if trying to ease her airway. "Are you doing all right, darling?"

"Fine," she gasped.

"Does it hurt?"

"No."

"Are you—"

"Is conversation usually standard at this time?"

He laughed again. "I beg your pardon, Charlotte."

It was the first time he'd said her name, and she spun into bliss at the sound of it wrapped warm and sensuous around his accent. Oh dear, this was proof—her nerves were completely in disorder. And her toes might break from curling so hard. Not that she minded, considering how splendid it felt.

"My God," Alex breathed. The smile had gone from his face; he frowned as if deep in sacred contemplation. Charlotte had not realized he was such a devout man. Mind you, she felt rather prayerful herself at that moment. "You're so sensitive," he whispered.

Her stomach swooped.

She'd heard those words over and again throughout her childhood, words that felt like a rap on the knuckles or a prod against the heart. *You're so sensitive, Charlotte. You feel too much, you are too much. It's messy. A witch must be more restrained.* She'd built a hundred layers of calm and coolness over the years in response. She'd worked hard to become something other than her altogether wrong self. Now she shrank.

Alex sensed it, and paused, brushing the hair away from her face, lifting her chin so she had to look at him. His bright, fierce gaze pierced the shame. "So responsive," he said, and the words sounded like a smile. "Like a bird in the singing winds."

Charlotte frowned, not quite understanding. But he kissed her again, murmuring against her skin, and she finally comprehended that he was actually voicing approval. The realization jolted through her, shattering a thousand blocks and barbs around her soul, filling her with the pieces like hot, glimmering stars. The emotional release felt as incredible as the physical one she had just experienced. Clinging to him, she was grateful and frustrated all in one beautiful, messy tumult. He gave her such pleasure with his body, his words, even just the expression in his eyes—

Blast it, the man was besting her! She wanted to make him feel the same way—*more* the same way, more ecstatic, more electrified than her. But she didn't know how to achieve it.

"You seem to be rather good at this," she said, trying a compliment.

He smiled, a sweet, charmed smile, suggesting she had got it right. "Thank you, darling," he said. "But let's see if I can do it well enough that you're too breathless to tell me so."

He lowered himself farther upon her, and all the sensations shifted, sparking anew. Charlotte gasped in astonishment. Alex's smile became an altogether wicked grin. She tried to speak, to query this new development, but instinct elbowed reason out of the way, rolled up its sleeves, and took charge. Wrapping her legs around the pirate, she lifted her hips to better meet him. The murmur in his throat encouraged her, so she moved again, and again, and his rhythm quickened, and his breath too. She was pleasing him. This was excellent! There was only one problem.

It was pleasing her all the more also.

Electricity began building again within her body. Every muscle clenched in anticipation. She could not breathe, just as he had planned—could not think—she moaned indecorously as the pirate filled her so deep, every proper word dissolved and tumbled right out of her. She clung to him even as he wrecked her; she inhaled his hot, ragged breath as her only hope for survival. It felt as devastating and exhilarating as being tossed from a roof high above the ground.

Abruptly the fire erupted, fiercer than before. Her very soul seemed to go up in flames. At the same moment, Alex's entire body clenched. Charlotte pulled him close, just as she had when they'd fallen through the rain. They began to shiver as they came down together into softness, heaviness, peace. His mouth kissed across her face, searching desperately for her mouth. She turned it toward him, and they met in a long, deep, mutual kiss.

And closing her eyes, Charlotte felt for the first time in her life the experience of sharing a perfect moment with someone else.

✳ 12 ✳

SLEEPLESS IN DAGENHAM—BREAKFAST IS DELIVERED—NEWS—
HOUSEWORK INTERRUPTED—THE ONLY WAY LEFT IS UP—
DÉJÀ VU—ALEX REGRETS HIS CHOICES—
CHARLOTTE KNOWS WHERE SHE STANDS—
THIEVES DO NOT STOP—HANGING BY A THREAD

Charlotte had to declare after all there was no enjoyment like love-making! How much sooner one tired of anything than of sex. When she had a husband of her own, she should be miserable if he did not have an excellent skill in the bedroom. Captain O'Riley had quite altered her expectations on that account.

They repeated variations of the activity several times throughout the evening and night, since after all there had been a great deal of tension between them that needed clearing. They were only being efficient, dealing with it all at once. Granted, Charlotte now felt so tension-free she was unsure she could actually walk, but mobility seemed a small sacrifice to make for such pleasure.

Somewhere in the midst of this, Alex had organized dinner to be brought to the room, and they'd eaten while still tucked up on the floor between the beds, wrapped in sheets and with an eiderdown beneath them for added comfort. The food had been bland, and they'd argued pleasantly over that while twining their feet and ankles together and agreeing at least that the wine was nice. For a while they'd slept, only for Charlotte to wake to find Alex already roused, his tongue drawing her out of vague dreams, his hands disturbing her peace in the most criminally delightful manner.

The man possessed remarkable stamina, which was fine with Charlotte as she seemed to have a remarkable tolerance for it. She even discarded the chemise (in other words, folded it neatly and set it aside) since allowing him to see what his hands had already comprehensively explored was only rational, despite how her body trembled at the choice. But he did not look. He drew the sheet around them, holding her close until she eased within his arms, nakedness forgotten. It proved he was altogether too clever at this whole business, and had Charlotte not been reaping the benefits of it, she would have found a way to bring him down a size or two. Instead, she insulted him as often as she could, and he retaliated by making her cry out with some new and fascinating delight.

Finally, the morning upon them, they agreed it was necessary to rise and go on to Clacton-on-Sea. Charlotte consulted leaves from the evening's leftover tea and prophesized a good day for flying. The amulet really needed be removed from Lady Armitage's insane clutches (and Tom Eames rescued, time permitting).

This agreement was promptly followed by a disagreement about how to locate Alex's missing house, which they enjoyed while dressing in their now-dried clothes. They became so heated in their opinions, they were on the verge of throwing each other to the floor and undoing all their good work with buttons and tuckings-in, when a knock sounded on the door.

Alex drew his gun instantly. He waved for Charlotte to get out of sight, rolled his eyes with exasperation when she ignored him, and then carefully opened the door.

"Good morning, sir," Bixby said, standing in the corridor in a suit and bowler hat, a silver tray of folded newspapers set on his hand. "Miss," he added, nodding past Alex's shoulder to Charlotte.

She blushed and hurriedly pulled on her coat as if that could hide all her sins. While it had occurred to her that people might learn of what she'd done, which would be bad, she had not appreciated until this moment that they might *imagine* what she'd done, which was exceedingly worse. And although Bixby's expression was inscrutable, this offered little comfort. Charlotte was only too aware of the interesting thoughts that could take place behind a blank countenance.

Alex, on the other hand, seemed entirely nonchalant about what his butler might be thinking. He holstered his gun and opened the door wider. "Newspapers, really?" he said tetchily. "Why didn't you bring breakfast?"

Bixby laid the tray on a sideboard then returned to the corridor. Seconds later he returned, pushing a food-laden trolley ahead of him into the room.

"Hmph," Alex said.

"Thank you," Charlotte added, smiling at the butler. He nodded brusquely, as if she had said something offensive but he was too well-trained to comment.

They ate breakfast at a small table beside the window while Bixby stood nearby to attention, his eyes politely unfocused. Charlotte dared not offer him food. She did glance at him occasionally, however, still fretting about what he might be thinking. (Considering the state of the beds, it was actually not too hard to imagine what he was thinking about: sheet thread counts and the best laundry detergents.) He had explained that he'd landed safely after the collision with Miss Fairweather's house, and having seen Charlotte and Alex descending gently under the power of the incantation, had felt unworried enough to spend the evening washing dishes and sweeping floors—or in other, more accurate words, drinking brandy and reading a George Eliot novel. Dawn had routed him to Rothbury House, where he made inquiries with the butler, Hooper, and exchanged packets of information according to secret household service protocol. Hooper informed him as to the whereabouts of a gentleman and oddly dressed lady.

"I swear," Alex said over a cup of hot black coffee, "you butlers rule the world behind our backs."

Charlotte laughed a little at this. Bixby stared ahead expressionlessly.

After a small meal comprising only toast and eggs, baked beans, buttered muffins, fried tomatoes, and kippers, Alex took up the newspapers while Charlotte set about making the beds. She had got as far as gathering the sheets from the floor when Alex's sudden curse word stopped her.

"What's wrong?"

When Alex did not reply, so intent was he on reading the frontpage article, Bixby supplied an explanation.

"I suspect the captain has just learned that Miss Charlotte Pettifer of Mayfair has been kidnapped by the dread pirate Rotten O'Riley."

Charlotte stared at the butler. "Kidnapped? I? Outrageous!" She folded a sheet in half and flapped it so briskly it made a loud cracking sound. Out of the corner of her eye, she saw Alex flinch. "Next they will be describing me as—"

"'An innocent damsel of unimpeachable reputation,'" Alex read aloud from the newspaper.

"Confound it!" Charlotte exclaimed. "How am I supposed to blackmail or swindle anyone from here on? They will just laugh at me!"

"Nice picture of you, though," Alex said.

"Huh." Charlotte folded the sheet again—at least if you understand *fold* as meaning *bashed together in a fervent motion that created its own tiny cyclone*—and the whole thing slid into disarray. Bixby, stepping over, quietly took one edge and moved back, separating the corners at his end. Charlotte copied him.

"I wonder how they got the information," Alex mused, drinking coffee as he read.

"It was probably my cousin Eugenia," Charlotte said, stepping toward Bixby so their sheet edges met. He took the whole thing, made a few quick maneuvers, and handed her back an immaculate rectangle of linen along with a brief, rare smile that seemed to communicate reassurance, kindness, and an admonishment to hereafter leave sheet folding to the professionals. The smile disappeared as soon as Charlotte gave her own in return.

"You think your cousin would betray you to such a degree?" Alex was remarkably astonished for a man who had spent his life amongst pirates.

"Oh yes," Charlotte said as she set down the sheet. Snatching a pillow, she started yanking the cover from it. "Eugenia has always hated me for having been prophesized as Beryl Black's true heir before she could be. Besides, she pours the milk into the bowl before the cereal. And calls me Char. There's no end to her villainy." She plumped the pillow so hard Bixby winced.

"Maybe you should try to calm down," Alex suggested.

"I am calm." The pillow exploded in a cloud of goose feathers.

Alex and Bixby exchanged a wordless glance. Bixby was just stepping forward to take what remained of the pillow from her grasp when a knock came upon the door. Before Charlotte even saw them move, both pirate and butler had guns in hands. Without a word, Bixby hurried over to stand by the door while Alex pressed against the wall so as to peer carefully out the window. They glanced at each other again; Alex made some hand gestures.

"Who is it?" he called out.

"Only the housekeeper," answered a high-pitched voice. "I have fresh towels for you."

Alex cursed under his breath. Holstering the gun, he pulled on his coat, slung his sword belt over one shoulder, then took Charlotte by the arm and tugged her toward the window.

"I hope you were right about being able to climb down a building."

Charlotte frowned. "It's just the housekeeper bringing towels."

"Immediately after breakfast, in an English pub?" Alex snorted with bleak humor.

"But—" Charlotte protested.

"There are policemen on the other side of that door," Alex whispered fiercely. "The innkeeper must have seen the newspaper and tipped them off."

"Then we must tidy the room before we leave," Charlotte said, trying to pull out of his grip. "Imagine what they will think!"

"I'd rather imagine it than have them tell me while taking me to prison." He threw an intense look at Bixby, who nodded in response. Apparently they had been in this situation often enough to need no words. Alex stepped onto a chair as if it were a stair, and then onto the breakfast table, his boots smashing plates and tea cups. Charlotte would have gasped in horror were she not distracted by being hauled bodily up to join him. She carefully nudged a teapot aside as Alex unlatched the window and flung it open.

He took her hand and looked her coolly in the eye, and her stomach flipped with what felt awkwardly like lust and trepidation. "Bixby will divert them," he said, "then bring the house round. But we have to go now."

Together, they looked out the window. Twenty feet below lay a paved courtyard that glinted like bared teeth in the morning light.

Alex shrugged casually. "We can jump that."

Charlotte stared at him in incredulous horror.

"Coo-ee," came the voice through the door. Its falsetto rang out

INDIA HOLTON

cheerfully, but the knock that followed was hard and brisk, and even Charlotte recognized it as the sound of a man whose sense of authority was exceeded only by his impatience. Her heart leaped.

"I have an idea. Hold my hand."

Without questioning, Alex did as she asked, and she gripped him tightly. *"Aereo,"* she said.

Her blood swooped as the incantation lifted them gently into the cool, fresh sunlight. She allowed them to rise, holding on tight to Alex's hand and trying not to look down, until she felt certain within herself. Then she said, *"Descendeo."*

They started to plunge toward the ground. *"Lente!"* she called out hastily. *"Descendeo lente."*

Their bodies jolted as the rate of descent abruptly slowed. Alex grinned at her.

"I've got to say, you really know how to get a man up."

"It's fairly simple witchcraft," Charlotte replied pedantically, and he laughed.

"If you ever change, Charlotte Pettifer, I will hunt you down and kill you."

She frowned through windswept strands of hair. "I cannot decide if that is a threat or a compliment."

"It's a joke, darling."

"Ah." Her tone seemed to express that she considered joking equivalent to a cup of green tea—distasteful and to be politely ignored if at all possible. "Are you ready?"

He bounced his eyebrows in reply.

They somersaulted, and their booted feet hit the pavement in unison. Still holding hands, they leaped a low border of box shrubs and ran across the lawn toward an elm grove. From the inn came a shrill whistle as a policeman, leaning out the open window, sighted them. Most impudently, they failed to stop or to return to the inn so as to be arrested.

"Will Bixby be all right?" Charlotte asked. The unenchanted words sounded odd, shallow, her voice crackling.

"Sure," Alex said. "Who blames the butler for anything?"

Skipping over a fallen branch, they entered the grove. Their pace slowed, and Alex tugged Charlotte's hand, pulling her toward him and kissing her. She clutched at his shoulders in an attempt to maintain her balance, and they stumbled back until she was pressed against a tree. It quivered slightly as if offended.

"There should be a law against men like you," she gasped between kisses.

"There is," he said, biting her earlobe. "Someone should lock you in a room and only let you out on Sundays."

"You just described my childhood." She thrust fingers into his hair, tilting his head back so she could kiss his throat. "Who can I hire to have you beaten to a pulp?"

"And you just described mine," he said. "I thought we released this tension?"

"These are mere reverberations, Captain," she explained. "We will stop now."

"Absolutely. Stopping at once." And he pressed his lips against hers with a kiss so deep she thought she'd drown in it, there amongst the trees.

But a whistle squawked again in the distance, making little bursts of noise as if someone was blowing it while jogging, and they pulled back, looking at each other with rather blurred eyes.

"If they're chasing us now," Alex said, "Bixby should be free to go get the house."

They ran on through the grove, motivated by calls of "Stop, thief!"

"You know, I resent being called a thief when I haven't yet been able to steal anything," Alex grumbled.

Past the trees, they came to a field, and as they ran across it they looked over their shoulders to see the stone cottage rising beyond the inn's rooftop. But the policemen were coming faster, whistles shrieking. Alex evaluated the situation with calm, professional speed, then pointed to a tumbledown wall. They ran to it and, ducking behind, sat with their backs against the mossy stone, catching their breath. Alex smiled at Charlotte.

"Are you having fun?"

She frowned. "As a matter of fact, I am."

He laughed. But as he continued to regard her, his eyes darkened. His smile faded. Finally he shook his head. "Damn, you're beautiful. And what—nineteen?"

"Twenty-one," she said warily.

He shook his head again. "I haven't been thinking straight. What happened last night—it was wrong—I'm sorry."

She flushed, taken aback by this unexpected statement. "I beg your pardon. If you found it so unpleasant, sir, you might have said at the time."

"No." He reached out to touch her face, but she leaned away. "No, I mean it was—extremely nice. My God, it was incredible. But you're an unmarried woman, and I've corrupted you. When your future husband realizes you're not a virgin, what will you tell him?"

"To angle slightly to the left, and rub with his thumb."

He laughed, despite himself.

"Cecilia Bassingthwaite is younger than I am," she said in a dangerous tone.

"Cecilia's a pirate," he replied, and avoided being maimed only because her escape from several policemen in hot pursuit was dependent on his able-bodied presence.

"I'm a witch," she retorted.

He frowned. "Don't remind me."

"I'm also an adult woman who is capable of making her own deci-sions about what she wants to do in the company of a man. Your house just flew past."

Glancing up, he saw the house move away over the field. "Shit." He stretched up to look over the wall.

"How many?" Charlotte asked.

He sat down again. "Four. I'm flattered."

"They're coming for me, not you."

"Braggart."

The house began to circle back. Alex stood, pulling Charlotte up with him. In one swift, casual movement, he drew his gun, turned, and shot. A startled noise leaped from Charlotte's throat even as a police-man's helmet leaped from the head of its occupant. The policeman flung himself to the ground, yelping as he cowered.

"Please tell me you didn't miss your target," Charlotte said rather shakily.

"I didn't miss my target," Alex replied, tugging her into a run. "I may be a scoundrel, but I'm not a murderer."

They hurried across the field. Alex's cottage swooped near and a rope ladder dropped from one window. He caught it.

"Take hold and don't let go," he ordered Charlotte.

"I can incantate—"

"In front of the police? Take the bloody ladder."

She grasped hold of the swaying rope and clambered up onto its second rung. Immediately Alex moved behind her, standing on the lowest rung with his body protectively against hers as he clutched the rope above her hands. The house lifted, causing the ladder to swing wildly.

"Keep holding on," Alex said in Charlotte's ear.

"Stop right there!" shouted a policeman and blew his whistle furiously.

Charlotte sighed. Men simply couldn't help themselves, telling a woman what to do. As if she was stupid enough to either let go or stop and be caught! Really, Miss Plim was right: if males weren't necessary for procreation and opening tightly lidded jars, womankind could get along quite nicely without them.

Mind you, considering what Alex had done with his tongue last night, perhaps it was worth admitting his value for that alone.

As the ladder swerved from side to side, Charlotte clung to it so tightly her hands burned. But she was unafraid, knowing the pirate would not let her fall. And if he did, she always had her own magic to catch her. They swooped over a cluster of pine trees and flew east toward the sea, leaving behind four breathless policemen, an unpaid innkeeper, and a highly shocked chambermaid.

✣ 13 ✣

MISS PLIM KNOWS BEST—WITCHCRAFT IN THEIR LIPS—
GREAT MEDDLERS THINK ALIKE—HOW NOT TO BE SEDUCED—
MRS. ROTUNDER KNOWS BETTER—THE TIGER IS ROUSED—
SOMETHING'S IN THE AIR

There was nothing Judith Plim would do for those who were really her friends. She had no notion of loving people; it was not her nature. Vague stirrings of affection every now and again kept her from outright villainy (presuming one did not count robbery, tax evasion, and a penchant for Marmite-and-banana sandwiches as villainy). But actual love—the powerful, coiled instinct that so often springs without warning, putting out an eye so people don't see all the things that should keep them from committing to their beloved—was in Miss Plim's case a mere boiled noodle.

And yet, when she received word from the police that Charlotte had willingly evaded them with Captain O'Riley, the noodle stirred. She had contacted as many of the Wicken League as were in London, summoning them to a coven gathering at Pettifer House—her own house being far too clean and tidy to have that gaggle of overdressed miscreants traipsing through it.

"My dear friends," she addressed them once everyone was seated around the dining table. "Thank you for coming at this troubled hour."

The witches murmured words that sounded pleasant but, if recorded, slowed down, and separated from the mass of sound, would be clearly heard equating Miss Plim to the devil and suggesting some unmentionable (and surely uncomfortable) places she could store her spectacles.

Tea and tiny pink cakes had already been served, for food is a great weapon when dealing with women whose power resides in their throats. A witch with a mouthful is a witch disarmed, and Miss Plim knew no enemy worse than the coven she led. However, in a deft counterattack, each cake had been altered in some small way by its recipient: the icing scraped off, the glazed cherry removed and placed neatly to the side, where it effected a silent, subtle insult to the hostess throughout the meeting.

Such militant passive-aggressiveness was practically de rigueur for witches. Although the Wicken League had been formed as a mutual support agency, witch uplifting witch (often with the consequence of heads bashed against ceilings and ankles broken upon descent, until they got the hang of the magic), its ongoing unofficial mission was to provide an exercise ground for hostility. Unlike pirates, who clashed openly and literally—swords, battlehouses, cannonballs—witches employed a discreet and dignified violence in their friendships. Invitations arriving late. A slow, precise blink of the eyes upon noticing someone's new hairstyle. Cucumber slices removed from sandwiches with a grimace that shifted immediately into a polite smile. This culture served to keep everyone in their place, so that few witches had the self-confidence to take their magical powers, not to mention their knowledge of who performed criminal acts of witchcraft, and go dangerously rogue.

Until, that is, the League president's own heir ran off in the company of a pirate.

Or, as Miss Plim put it: "Our dear, brave Charlotte has nobly sacrificed her own safety and comfort by kidnapping a ferocious pirate in a valiant effort to regain Beryl's blessed amulet for our League."

"I read that she was the one to be kidnapped," Miss Habersham said. Miss Plim nodded tolerantly, for it had cost her an expensive favor to get that information in the newspaper so as to protect Charlotte's public reputation and make her more visible for recovery efforts. But before she could explain this, Miss Habersham continued: "Not a good example of supposed Plim superiority, if you ask me."

Miss Plim scowled. She drew breath to argue—

"I heard she was working in cahoots with Lady Armitage," Mrs. Vickers added, looking around the table while nodding vigorously, as if this would make everyone else automatically agree.

"I heard the amulet theft was just a diversion, and actually she eloped with the pirate," Eugenia Cuttle-Plim said. She gave a nasty little flick of her head that would have had Charlotte grasping Alex's arm and saying, "See what I mean?" had she been there to witness it.

"Descendeo," Miss Plim muttered through tight lips, and Eugenia's head-flick ended in her hat falling over her face.

"Lottie would never elope," Mrs. Pettifer countered staunchly. "She dreams of having a large wedding, with a beautiful gown and magnificent white cake."

Miss Plim rolled her eyes. Delphine had always been deluded about Charlotte. Many times Miss Plim had tried to explain that the girl was not a romantic, would never marry, in fact had no interest in men whatsoever. But Delphine could not bear to listen, her identity too fused with what she supposed Charlotte's to be.

"Charlotte is entirely immune to the supposed charms of Captain

O'Riley," Miss Plim insisted. "I myself saw them together the other day and can assure you there is nothing between them but disregard and disdain. Charlotte almost certainly took an opportunity to commandeer his house so as to join in the pursuit of Lady Armitage. It shows excellent leadership skills, unsurprising in a Plim."

She tapped the table in front of Miss Edwardina Fox, who was keeping the minutes of the meeting. "Excellent leadership skills," she repeated, and watched as Miss Fox wrote the words in the special shorthand she had devised when first she was voted secretary (and had since mostly forgotten, as a consequence of which "excellent leadership skills" was noted down as "excellent vegetable socks").

Satisfied that her perspective had been recorded for perpetuity, Miss Plim returned to scowling at the group. "While we must give the public impression of her being a victim, so as to forestall any talk of marriage, privately we must acknowledge Charlotte as the finest example of witchery. It only goes to prove that she is indeed—"

"The Prophesized One and True Heir of Beryl Black," the group intoned with a weariness born from twenty-one years of reminders.

"Just so. Besides, I don't notice any of you rushing off to find our precious amulet."

The room filled with mutters. Sicknesses were evoked, twisted ankles displayed, times declared to be difficult, husbands castigated as tyrants, and several other excuses presented as to why the ladies present were not in current hot pursuit of Beryl's amulet. Some swore they had begun—but then a stray cloud or random blue symbol had prophesized trouble if they continued. Others had been on their way out the door *this very morning* to start the pursuit when Miss Plim's summons came.

She looked down her nose at them all. "Charlotte is doing important work for the League. She must be supported at this time! I'm calling for volunteers."

See above for the response to this.

Miss Plim sighed and shook her head. "Ladies, ladies, are we witches or are we worms?"

"Witches," murmured the group sulkily.

"Excellent. The first thing we must do is prevent the newspapers from publishing any further articles on the subject. They have served their purpose admirably thus far, but we don't want to allow them free rein. Journalists are always sneaking around uncovering facts, solving crimes, and generally being intrepid in the most insufferable of ways. I need volunteers to—"

"Write letters to the editors, describing Charlotte's sweet and gentle disposition?" someone suggested.

"Provide an alibi for her?" someone else suggested.

Miss Plim frowned. "Incantate a series of natural disasters at the newspaper offices—fallen tree, exploded printing press, typhoon in the paper storage cupboard—so they cannot publish at all."

This received an excited response. If there was something witches loved better than tidying, it was making a mess for other people to deal with. Several ladies raised their hands and were sent forth to do their worst.

"And now another group to locate Lady Armitage and retrieve from her our amulet."

Ten hands were promptly sat upon or made busy stirring tea. But with cajoling (berating), encouraging (threatening), and cheer (just bloody well making people do it), Miss Plim put together a team and sent them on their way.

That left four in the room, a perfect number for the final task: tracking Charlotte and ~~dragging her home~~ rescuing her.

"I say," Eugenia piped up, "just exactly why did Char choose to hijack Captain O'Riley's decrepit cottage, considering all the possibilities parked outside the museum?"

That left three in the room.

Miss Plim glared at her sister and Mrs. Chuke. "Ladies, we must find Charlotte before my—before her reputation is completely ruined."

"It should be easy," Mrs. Pettifer said. "Lottie is such a kind, biddable girl."

Miss Plim and Mrs. Chuke exchanged a glance.

"Of course she is, darling," Mrs. Chuke said. "I might just have Dearlove bring along a gun and some handcuffs anyway. In case the pirate makes trouble," she added hastily, upon seeing the horrified look on Mrs. Pettifer's face. "Not that he will," she added further, when the horrified look worsened. "But how shall we find them?"

"We already have," Miss Plim said. "Delphine's butler was contacted by a butler in Dagenham. He had information that Charlotte and Captain O'Riley spent the night in a public establishment there."

"In a pub with a pirate?" Mrs. Chuke said, her eyes growing wide. "Oh dear."

It was to be a sentiment murmured several more times that morning. The witches consulted the auguries, traveled by carriage to Dagenham, and located the Angler's Retreat with efficient speed. They proved, alas, not to be in the nick of time, for Charlotte was well gone. Nor were they close to the nick of time, for any clues left behind had been either taken by the police or cleaned away by the chambermaid. In fact, they were so far from the nick of time that, when they arrived at the inn's bedroom, they found Mrs. Rotunder, Ned, and Cecilia already there.

Three besoms flicked open to become daggers.

Three swords were drawn from pirates' belts.

"What are you doing here?" everyone demanded in unison.

"Looking for the renegades," everyone answered at once.

"My butler told us they were here," Mrs. Rotunder explained. "But we arrived too late; they had already flown the coop. The bad news is that they had policemen hunting them. The worse news is that the innkeeper said the room was rented by a *married* couple."

Her emphasis was not so much an innuendo as an out-and-out slur. But Miss Plim only shrugged.

"That is a standard ploy, claiming to be married in order to secure the last room in an inn. It means nothing. Besides, look—two beds!"

Mrs. Rotunder smirked. "Oh well, two beds, you're quite right—that completely saves your girl's reputation. Everyone knows two beds are the best deterrent there is to seduction."

"Exactly," Miss Plim said with a nod.

"I'm not sure, Judith," Mrs. Chuke said worriedly. "A pirate can be unscrupulous."

"But a witch can be deadly," Miss Plim reminded her. "And remember, Charlotte has been raised by strong women who would never let a man dominate them."

"That's true," Mrs. Pettifer said with a dreamy sigh. "I once mixed gunpowder in Claude Monet's paints and swore I'd light a match if he did not paint me like one of his French girls."

Everyone stared at her.

"Wasn't that just before he ran off to join the army?" Mrs. Chuke asked.

"That's not the impression I got," Mrs. Pettifer replied with a sniff. "My point is, no doubt Lottie also threatened to blow Captain O'Riley up."

There was a slight pause at an interesting juncture of that sentence, causing everyone to glance at each other.

"Mrs. Pettifer," Cecilia said cautiously, "am I right in thinking you actually *want* Charlotte's reputation ruined?"

Mrs. Pettifer flushed. "Heavens no, dear! Egads, the very thought! My antisocial, bookish daughter being forced to marry a man who is handsome, owns his own home, and is presumably rich?" She cast an inquiring look to Ned, who shrugged then nodded.

"Rich," she repeated, rolling the word around her mouth as if it were a bonbon. "And I think I already mentioned handsome. Lottie could do worse."

"No, she couldn't!" Miss Plim fumed, her topknot of hair reverberating with the force of the words. "He's a pirate! She's a witch! Imagine if they had a big, joyful wedding! Or worse, children whom everyone adores! If this goes on, Delphine, we're risking an end to two centuries of successful hostilities!"

Her face had become so red, she looked almost healthy. But Mrs. Pettifer remained unconvinced. "A wedding would be an opportunity for exciting trouble," she argued. "Brawling. Poisoning each other. Screaming."

"Dancing. Sharing food. Laughing," Miss Plim retorted.

An unhappy murmur went through the company.

"Captain O'Riley won't marry Miss Pettifer," Ned said somberly. "His father dallied with a witch, and it caused his mother such distress she died from a broken heart. Well, and a broken neck after throwing herself down the stairs. The father then married the witch and . . ." He shrugged uncomfortably. "It's a bleak story, too bleak for ladies' ears— even if the ladies are witches and pirates. Let's just say O'Riley hates the Wicken League perhaps even more than the Wisteria Society does, and certainly for better reason."

Mrs. Pettifer frowned anxiously at this news, but Miss Plim was gleeful. "Thank you, sir, this has eased my mind." She bestowed upon Ned the tight, brief twitch of lips that she liked to consider a smile. He stared back at her coldly. "Charlotte will come home with her own heart broken and should behave more cautiously from here on. I consider that a win."

Mrs. Pettifer made a small sound of dismay. Cecilia and Ned

looked grim. Even Mrs. Chuke seemed rather aghast. But Miss Plim continued blithely. "It should not be hard to trace them farther. Someone must have witnessed which direction they headed after leaving."

"East," said a quiet voice. Everyone turned with surprise to see Miss Dearlove standing by the open doorway, where she had gone unnoticed the entire time. She lowered her eyes shyly. "I beg your pardon. The innkeeper just now informed me he saw a battlehouse flying that way."

"Battlehouse." Mrs. Rotunder spat a laugh. "You mean shack."

"Authentic historic cottage," Cecilia corrected, unable to help herself.

Mrs. Rotunder gave her such a contemptuous look, Ned half-raised his sword. The older woman stepped back, hat feathers quivering.

"Well I never!" she huffed. "Young people these days quite astonish me. Running off together, standing up for each other! Mr. Rotunder would never consider defending my honor in such a gallant way!" She paused, realizing her outrage was perhaps misdirected, then the feathers shook once more. "I for one am in agreement with Miss Plim. The hooligans must be stopped and brought to justice—er, I mean, returned to the bosom of their communities. We simply cannot tolerate this kind of romance! Who will join me in heading eastward to find them?"

"I will!" Miss Plim declared in a ringing voice. "Delphine, go home and wait in case further information comes there. Mrs. Chuke—"

"I'm coming too, darling! My breakfast muffin this morning was in an unusual shape, which seemed to predict travel for me." She snapped her fingers. "Dearlove, fetch my purse and poisons from the carriage."

Mrs. Pettifer stared in amazement at her sister. "You'll fly in a pirate's house?"

"For the sake of the Wicken League," Miss Plim replied, lifting her chin heroine-fashion.

"And for the sake of Charlotte," Mrs. Pettifer added.

"Of course." Miss Plim dismissed the concern with a wave of her hand.

Cecilia turned to Mrs. Rotunder. "You'll allow witches in your house?" she asked incredulously.

"It might be fun," Mrs. Rotunder replied with a shrug. "Besides," she added in a whispered aside, "have you seen their jewelry? If I don't make a profit out of this trip, I'll relinquish my black flag in shame."

And so the ladies trooped out of the inn room, dresses flouncing and hat feathers swooping, leaving Ned and Cecilia alone. The young pirate couple looked at each other in dazed silence.

"You know we'll have to catch Alex and Miss Pettifer first," Cecilia said. "We cannot leave them to the machinations of that woman. She makes my aunt Darlington look like a small, fluffy kitten."

Ned frowned. "I hope you're not harboring any romantic ideas about the pair. You know Alex has sworn to never marry."

"And Miss Pettifer is destined to lead the Wicken League," Cecilia added, "therefore would never choose a pirate."

"It's a doomed relationship."

"No hope at all."

They glanced at the two beds set neatly apart, and the long dents in the carpet where they had been previously pushed together. Catching each other's eye again, they shared a smile.

"You'll have to wear a plain suit when you stand up as his best man," Cecilia said.

Ned sighed mournfully, then put his arm around her waist. "You won't be able to drink wine in a toast to them."

"Not unless they have a seven-month engagement," Cecilia agreed, touching a hand to her stomach. They switched off the light (and stole the complimentary mint chocolates) before leaving the room, nodding politely to a chambermaid waiting in the corridor outside.

As soon as they were gone, the chambermaid took off her cap and apron and hurried down the road to Rothbury House. She knocked at the servants' door.

"Hooper?" she whispered when it opened, glancing around to be sure no one else could hear. "I have some information for you."

Later that day on the outskirts of Bath, Cecilia's aunt, the dread pirate Miss Darlington, received a note from her housemaid. She began hyperventilating even before she'd finished reading it.

"Prepare the house at once!" she commanded, clutching her letter opener like a sword as she rose from the chair on which she had been lounging. "Battle stations! Close all windows and start incantating the unmooring phrase. And ready the medicine kit. There is not a moment to lose!"

"What's wrong?" asked her husband, setting aside the book of Byron's poetry he had been reading aloud.

"Cecilia is in mortal peril," Miss Darlington explained. "I have just received information—good God, I cannot believe she is walking about in her condition!"

"What condition?" asked her husband anxiously.

Miss Darlington collapsed back into the chair, unable to bear the weight of her newfound knowledge. "The interesting kind!"

"Oh dear," murmured her husband, trying not to smile.

"And I just know she's not wearing any protection."

"It's a little late for that, isn't it, dear?"

She pinned him with a scowl so sharp he flinched. "Hat," she snapped. "Scarf. Rubber-soled shoes. You know how delicate Cecilia is at the best of times. We must rush to her side!"

"Where is she just now?"

"Heading in the same direction as every other pirate: toward Isabella Armitage. We need to get there first. And I know just where Izzy will be." She stabbed her letter opener so hard through the note that the oak tabletop beneath it cracked. "Tally. Ho."

Miss Plim might not be kittenish, but if she had been able to take one look into the pirate maven's eyes at that moment, even she would have fainted in terror.

A knock came again at Hooper's door. "It's Mary," whispered the Angler's Retreat chambermaid. "I have more news for you."

Hooper brought out his secret notebook. "Go ahead."

"Another policeman has just been sniffing around the room where the pirates stayed. And when I say sniffing, I mean that literally."

"Are you sure he was a policeman?"

"He said his name was Detective Inspector Creeve. He gave me the shivers, to be honest. Not just the sniffing, but the way he stared at me. It was downright creepy."

"Hm," Hooper said, for he himself stared at the pretty chambermaid often enough and didn't want to think he might have been downright creepy too. (He had been.) "I doubt this is significant, Mary. Maybe the man sniffed because he had a cold."

"But—"

"I'm sure it's nothing." He cleared his throat. "I say, is there any chance you're free Friday night? I know a nice little restaurant in the village . . ."

The door shut in his face.

❊ 14 ❊

CHARLOTTE FINDS MUCH TO ENTERTAIN HER—
AN UNEXPECTED PROBLEM—FLYING LESSONS—FAMILY JEWELS—
THE DISAPPOINTMENT OF AN UNTROUBLED CHILDHOOD—
CLACTON-ON-SEA—ALEX IS IRRATIONAL—A LIVELY DISCUSSION—
THE GHOST OF MISCHIEF PAST

If Charlotte disapproved more of Captain O'Riley's house, she might be able to talk about it less. But she knew what she was. Alex and Bixby would hear nothing but truth from her. For three hours as they flew east toward Clacton-on-Sea, she blamed them, and lectured them, and they bore it as no other men in England would have borne it: so badly, they considered locking her in the closet, until they remembered what happened last time that was attempted.

She had much to occupy her. The dust. The spiderwebs. The sluggish rate of travel, second only to the sudden dangerous speed. The dust (again). Not enough tea. Bixby remedied the latter, along with a provision of fresh scones, after which there was the pleasure of discovering just what exactly gentlemen pirates considered adequate for a lavatory. Charlotte was able to entertain herself with expressions of horror about that one for quite some time. Eventually Bixby locked *himself* in the closet and Alex, forced to remain at the helm, decided to offer her a flying lesson.

Charlotte was ~~disappointed~~ surprised to discover this was not a metaphor for something more interesting. She eyed him suspiciously as he demonstrated the various pieces of navigational equipment. "Are you just trying to distract me from suggesting improvements to your home?"

"Not at all," Alex responded tonelessly.

"Because it is only my intention to be helpful."

"Of course."

"If you alphabetized your boxes of loot, you would feel so much—"

"Charlotte?" He smiled at her.

"Yes?"

"Shut up."

She gasped. "Well I nev—"

He caught her by the front of her shirt, pulled her close, and kissed her. And if he felt her triumphant little smirk against his lips, he was wise enough not to say so.

The kiss was pleasant in its own way (i.e., the way of coffee-flavored chocolate melting in one's mouth, its warmth spreading through one's body until remaining upright becomes increasingly, but deliciously, difficult). But it failed to convince Charlotte of there being any charm in the pirate's messiness.

She had to admit, however, that she rather liked the messiness of his charm. After a lifetime of carefully crafted narratives, having someone show her just how delightful unexpectedness could be—sudden kisses, sensuous smiles—proved enlivening. But also rather frightening. How could one prepare a correct response to the unexpected? Charlotte knew that over the past two days she had behaved so unlike Elizabeth Bennet or Anne Elliot as to be almost authentically herself, and that was far too risky to be considered a good thing.

She did not mind exposing her flaws to Alex O'Riley, for he was just a pirate, and as soon as she had her amulet she would undoubtedly never see him again. And oh dear, Bixby's scones must have gone down the wrong way, for suddenly she felt an odd heartburn.

The real trouble would come if she got into the bad habit of being herself when she returned to regular society. No one wanted to see a young woman dressed in trousers, or laughing with abandon, or *feeling* things.

The kiss ended finally, and with a mutual sigh they returned their focus to the flight lesson. Alex guided her to stand at the great spoked wheel, and then positioning himself behind her, he set his hands on hers.

"The wheel is a conduit for the magic," he explained. "There are no mechanics involved. So long as it can be attached in some secure manner to the house, and then moved to provide direction, it does not even strictly speaking have to be a wheel. But convention helps, because the pirate's state of mind is all-important, and it's less easy to believe yourself piloting a house by means of a stick or hairbrush or something."

"If state of mind is all-important—considering most pirates seem to be utterly mad, how do they keep their houses aloft?" Charlotte asked.

"Aren't you going to add 'present company excepted'?"

"No."

He grinned. "Fair enough. To be honest, it depends on the madness. Delusions of grandeur are actually helpful in our trade."

"What's this?" She put her hand on a lever protruding from the wheel shaft. Alex hastily pulled it away.

"Careful. That's my emergency vertical thrust accelerator."

Before she could make the kind of reply that would horrify even a penny-dreadful heroine, Alex began intoning the phrase to take them out of *momentum automatica*. The house creaked, shifting into his manual control. At once, Charlotte felt magic press her hands more firmly against the wheel. The sensation was uncomfortable, and not in the way her own magic recently had become, igniting nerves and stroking carnal instincts. Rather, it felt heavy, suffocating. This was indeed what she'd always imagined a bombastic pirate's magic to be, or perhaps a man's magic: forceful compared to the fine raveling of witchery.

"Your accent is stronger when you incantate," she noted.

"Oh?" The word was like a shield. With spikes on it. Bloodstained spikes. But before Charlotte could question why, he went on incantating, low and lilting. He slipped his fingers between hers, back and forth, until her breath was moving in time with it. Gently together they turned the wheel, and the house veered, moving into a pale haze of clouds.

"Can you feel the magic?" he asked between phrases.

"I hope you are talking about the incantation," she said. "Otherwise, that is a ridiculously lewd question."

He chuckled.

"Don't laugh. Magic is not fun."

"Really?" He shifted her hair aside, murmured *aereo* against her neck, then cooled the warmth of it with his tongue. The house began to climb, even as Charlotte felt her stomach sink.

"It's hard to breathe," she whispered.

Immediately he moved back. "Sorry. I suppose a house would be rather burdensome after a lifetime of lifting teacups and powder puffs." He incantated the *momentum automatica*, and magic eased into the wheel.

"Powder puffs?" Charlotte turned to present him with an affronted glare, but he only grinned down at her, undaunted. "I'll have you know, sir, that witches do important work. We effect real social and political change—"

"And steal lots of lovely jewels?"

"Well, yes, but it's not *fun*."

"Then you've been doing it all wrong, darling."

"*Tsk.*" She tried to move away, but he stepped closer, his thighs pressing hers to the wheel behind them. The house swooped, or perhaps it was her stomach. Alex slid a finger down the line of her shirt buttons. "Is the flight magic bothering you now?"

She considered this. The air around them had become almost cozy, as if they were swathed in eiderdowns. It throbbed slightly with self-perpetuating enchantment but no longer dragged on her senses, making her feel like she was turning into stone, wood, glass.

"I'm fine," she said. His hand was at her trouser buttons now. The throbbing of the air became stronger, and in the back of her mind Elizabeth Bennet was surprisingly, and rather enthusiastically, nodding. That Charlotte's behavior over the past two days had so corrupted a literary figment of her imagination would have troubled her were she not focusing instead on committing such behavior once again.

Besides, she was merely being practical. It had become apparent the tension between them needed releasing on a regular basis, for the sake of their health—no, wait, for the sake of obtaining the amulet! Charlotte could not focus on that goal if constantly arguing with a pirate. It was her League duty to have sex with him.

"Absolutely fine," she reiterated (although it must be said she could no longer recall what the question had been).

"Grand." Alex smiled. "Let's have a different kind of fun then."

Ah, excellent, things were going to get metaphorical after all.

Alex lay it down as a general rule that if he doubted whether he liked a woman, he certainly ought to keep his hand out of her underwear while she leaned forward with her brow pressed against his shoulder, whimpering every now and again. But he did like Charlotte Pettifer—would like her even if she wasn't doing interesting things with her own hand inside his underwear. And since he could not tell her so (of course not!

he was a pirate and a rake; he did not talk about *emotions*), he could at least make her feel very good.

That she made him feel just as good was a bonus.

"I've always wondered something," he said afterward, his fingers tangling with her bracelet as he tried lazily to distract her from tidying herself. "Why bees?"

Charlotte slapped his hand. He smiled and reached past her instead to take hold of a wheel spoke, casually navigating the house away from a flock of geese.

"Bees represent industry and community," she explained, continuing to button up her trousers. "Therefore they are well suited to witches, as we work for the sake of England."

He laughed. "You're joking."

"I most certainly am not." But she paused, biting her lip, for witches are not only industrious but unfailingly truthful. (Except when stealing, swindling, evading taxes, providing details to law enforcement officers, and assuring their mother-in-law that a knitted yellow tea cozy in the shape of a chicken was exactly what they'd always wanted for their birthday. All for the sake of England, of course.) "Also, bees feature on the Wicken League founder's ancestral coat of arms."

Alex frowned, recollecting Black Beryl's heraldic design. "No, it's ravens."

"Yes, er, I meant the deputy founder, Andromeda Plim. Beryl Black was, of course, our first leader and in no way whatsoever betrayed or murdered. Since we are making bold inquiries, Captain, why do you have a ring containing a portrait of Cecilia Bassingthwaite?"

Taken by surprise, Alex blushed. The realization she had found his ring's secret compartment and looked therein threw him back into old memories—nuns searching his laundry for sins, Deirdre finding the money he'd secretly saved to run away from home. But his brain had long been a minefield of buried misery, and he was used to its sudden explosions. That they became more frequent when he allowed himself emotional intimacy with another person was why he generally did not do so. Hands in underwear—fine. Hearts involved—not.

But damn if Charlotte Pettifer and her spiky, fearless, witchy gorgeousness didn't keep drawing out his heart.

He scowled at the sky as if he could fly away from her, even though she was in his house—standing between him and his wheel—smelling so enticingly of soap and softness that he wanted to lick her.

And now he was blushing again, like a callow boy.

Charlotte stared in wonder at the pirate. The sight of his reddened skin was made all the more endearing by how he tried to hide it, lifting a hand to push back his hair. The ring in question, circling his thumb, glinted as if it knew it was being discussed. Charlotte recollected the feel of its hard, smooth ruby between her breasts, pressing firmly into the soft flesh, and then she was blushing too.

"Are you in love with Cecilia?" she asked. The words did not feel like grit in her throat, nor did her pulse shudder as she awaited his reply. Any suggestion that she cared about whom Captain O'Riley fancied was utter nonsense.

"Well?" she prompted, having given him one and a half seconds to respond.

"No." Flicking his gaze to her, he allowed her to see the truth in his eyes. There was indeed no love in the dark blue depths, only an old, weary cynicism Charlotte recognized all too well. "The portrait isn't of Cecilia but her mother, Cilla, a famous pirate who was murdered many years ago. And before you ask, I didn't love her either. I never knew her. The ring used to belong to Ned Lightbourne. It was all he had of Cecilia for years before he finally met her. I grew tired of him mooning over it, muttering promises, dreaming of a girl he didn't even know. So I took it for safekeeping."

This sounded too much like an interesting romantic tale for Charlotte's liking. Of course Cecilia would have a murdered mother and pining adorer. No doubt her father too had been remarkable—a great poet, perhaps. Charlotte did not wish for her own mother to die horribly, but that Mrs. Pettifer suffered nothing more fascinating than lumbago, and that Mr. Pettifer was a—a—um, whatever it was he did when he left the house each morning—did not furnish her with a particularly exciting history.

She scowled at Alex as if Cecilia's wondrousness was his personal fault.

"How is stealing someone's ring and wearing it yourself 'safekeeping'?"

"Not the ring," Alex corrected. "Safekeeping his heart. But it's a long story and it has a boringly happy ending. Ned and Cecilia are married now. I offered to give the ring back to them, but they've had enough of ghosts. I wear it for—" He stopped, shrugging, as if the explanation did not matter as much as the shadows in his eyes suggested.

"For friendship," Charlotte guessed.

He shrugged again. "Pirates don't have friends. Not really."

Charlotte leaned back against the wheel and regarded him for a long, quiet moment. His expression as he returned her gaze was wry and unblinking. *Dangerous,* it reminded her. *Lawless.*

But what she saw was a mess. And being a witch, she wanted to fix it.

Alex O'Riley might be a proud, unpleasant sort of man, but this was everything since Charlotte really liked him. She leaned forward abruptly to kiss his cheek.

The cottage shook with surprise.

"Stop trying to crash my house, Charlotte," he muttered.

They shared a sardonic smile. And if it trembled a little at the edges with wishing, aching—well, they both looked away before they noticed.

By midafternoon they arrived at Clacton-on-Sea. With no other pirates in sight, they decided to land the cottage on a pier, and Alex immediately suggested a walk along the beach. Certainly, Lady Armitage must be found and the amulet retrieved (and Tom rescued), but there was no particular hurry. It was not as if the amulet had an expiry date (best not to think about Tom). A little fresh air and sunlight would invigorate them all for the search.

Charlotte and Bixby disagreed. "I should like beaches infinitely better," Charlotte replied, "if they were paved in a different manner. It would surely be much more rational if cobblestones instead of sand made the order of the day."

Bixby nodded in agreement, but Alex sighed and rolled his eyes. "More rational, my dear Miss Pettifer," he said, "but it would not be near so much like a beach."

However, the lady could not be convinced. Her boots' bomb compartments would get clogged with sand. Her hair would be tossed about abominably. She would risk *suntan*. Furthermore, she must find Beryl's amulet. Enough time had been wasted already on shenanigans! Even now Lady Armitage might be learning the amulet's magic. That she would use it for diabolical ends was beyond question. England's safety could well be at risk if Charlotte did not succeed! Worse—Miss Plim would be displeased. Did Alex want that on his conscience? Did he? Well?

"We should plan for a methodical search," she concluded.

"I recommend a grid pattern," Bixby said.

Alex exhaled a sigh. "You are both being too fastidious."

"Too fastidious?" Charlotte frowned, clearly struggling to connect those words. "This is a town of some size. The woman might be anywhere."

"Except the beach?" he added facetiously, just to watch her eyes flare. "Stop worrying so much, darling. A little stroll first—"

"You may *stroll* if you wish, but I intend to search. Bixby will accompany me."

Bixby raised a disapproving eyebrow at this proclamation. Alex, for his part, raised two.

"I beg your pardon, madam, but Bixby is in my employ, and—"

"And I am a young, innocent lady," Charlotte interjected, smiling and batting her lashes (and then needing to stop, wincing as she strained an eyelid). She did indeed look young and innocent, having changed back into her preposterously frilled white dress, and with her long, rich hair unbound. She looked like a pure English rose, delicate and easily bruised. Alex's heart softened as he gazed at her.

His brain, however, laughed sardonically.

Charlotte must have sensed it, for she tightened her smile until it resembled nothing so much as a thorn. Producing lace gloves from a pocket, she yanked them onto her hands with such violence Alex was surprised she didn't break a finger. He and Bixby exchanged a wary glance.

"Gentlemen," she said stridently, "I require escort. I am certain you agree no lady is safe walking alone through a strange town."

She lifted her skirts a little to check the gun tucked in her weaponized boots.

"I do agree," Alex said. "You are indeed not safe walking through this town. God only knows who you might hurt."

"Well!" Charlotte flung down her skirts with a huff. Then producing her little red besom from a pocket, she flicked out a tiny item that she fanned with brisk energy before her face.

Alex carefully maintained an unaffected expression as he watched her. The fact the fan was actually a shuriken, or small, star-shaped weapon, had apparently escaped her attention, and he felt no inclination to point this out, lest she throw it at him. From the corner of his eye he saw Bixby bite his lip in an effort to repress a laugh.

Bloody hell! It was bad enough the woman had got under his skin—that she'd driven Daniel Bixby to the verge of human reactions was the final straw!

"I shall accompany you through the town, madam," he said. "We shall find Lady Armitage, recover the amulet, and have you back home in London by tomorrow. Bixby can remain here and—and—sweep a floor or something."

"I beg your pardon," Bixby said reprovingly.

"Nonsense!" Charlotte replied.

"God damn it," Alex grumbled.

All at the same time.

The house shuddered. Its doors began to slam.

"Stop doing that!" Alex shouted at the confounded little witch.

She propped her fists against her hips. "Do you hear me saying the incantation?"

"You don't need to, woman! You are magic on legs!"

Silence clanged down. Bixby blushed. Charlotte stood with her mouth ajar. And Alex sighed, rubbing a thumbnail so hard against his brow it left a red mark.

Then the shouting began again.

Outside, a dozen or so people who had been perambulating along Clacton pier until a great ugly stone cottage landed on it, and who were at that very moment about to knock on the door and ask if the pirate might please move his premises just a little aside so they could get past, paused to glance nervously at each other.

"I would not risk it, if I were you," advised an elderly lady at the edge of the group. She looked rather like an electrified ghost in a stiff black dress, her gray hair standing erect beneath a black lace parasol and her face stretched over thin, sharp bones. Her smile, however, seemed to crackle with life. "I am a daughter of the Fairley clan, and as such I recognize trouble when I see it. That's an *Irish* pirate house, you mark my words."

The group gasped, mostly because her tone seemed to demand it. "And we all know what that means," she added significantly.

"Yes, yes, hmm, of course," muttered the crowd—which might be translated as, "Actually no, wouldn't have a clue, surely pirates are generically bad, whatever their nationality?"

Suddenly, from inside the house came an exclamation: "Fiend!" The building clattered against the wooden planks of the pier.

"I suggest you swim for it," said the elderly lady.

The group hesitated, for they all were dressed in rich and heavy clothing, not to mention shoes that, if stolen by a Wicken League member, would have fed several orphans for a month.

"Virago!"

The building leaped two feet before smacking down again.
Splash.

The elderly lady watched the dozen or so gentlewomen and men paddle desperately for the shore. She chuckled a little to herself. Then, with a contentedly wicked smile, she edged past the pirate's house and ambled away toward her own, stopping only to purchase an ice cream from a vendor on the beach as she went.

❈ 15 ❈

THEY ARE LOST—LOBSTER AND LAUNDRY—LIVE ENTERTAINMENT—
A SUDDEN EXIT—IF ONLY—TAKING THE LONG WAY HOME—
TWO HEARTS IN THE DARK—TURNING BACK—THEY ARE FOUND

The most incomprehensible thing in the world to a woman was a man who rejects her offer of directions. Charlotte might never have set foot in Clacton-on-Sea before, but as soon as she obtained a map of the town (not stealing it, since if the shopkeeper wanted money for his maps he obviously would not display them on a wall rack, but instead lock them in a cabinet behind the counter, guarded by himself, a pit bull terrier, and two alarm systems), she automatically became an expert through the simple expedient of reading. Alex, however, just seemed to go any which way he happened upon.

"I'm familiar with this town, and know a shortcut," he insisted, tugging on her hand as he attempted to lead her down entirely the wrong street.

"But it's not on the map," she replied, tugging back.

"*Map,*" he scoffed, as if the word itself was pure nonsense, let alone the concept.

Thus went the conversation, on a looping circuit, over the two days they spent searching the town for Lady Armitage. At night they barely spoke beyond instructions like *More, faster,* and *My God don't you dare stop or I will smack you with my shoe,* as they engaged in what Charlotte liked to think of as reasonable constitutional exercise, and Alex viewed more frankly—i.e., using other words beginning with *f.* But the days were full of argument.

For example: "You're eating your lobster all wrong," he said as they picnicked on the cottage roof at twilight, looking out over the sea. (Officially, they were searching—after all, who knew when Lady Armitage might take a skiff out for an evening's sail?)

"As a vegetarian," Charlotte retorted, "you have no right to comment. I do declare—"

She paused, suddenly breathless, as a cool, whispering breeze swept up from the shore, the sky's own incantation, making her shiver. Her derelict imagination stirred with dreams. Why had Jane Austen not advised her of how vast an expanse a woman's wonder might encompass? Could she even return to her scrupulous existence after watching wild stars dance out from beyond the edge of the world?

Of course, the question was redundant. It was her prophesized fate and her duty to remain in London and one day lead the Wicken League. But perhaps it didn't have to be as dreary as she'd always anticipated. "When I get my amulet back," she said, mostly to herself, "I will use it to help other people know life can be this beautiful."

Alex stiffened. She glanced at him, and found his eyes dark with wary amusement as they stared down at her.

"What?" she asked anxiously.

"You surprise me."

"Why, because you doubt I will beat you to the amulet?"

She'd meant it as a joke, but there was no humor in him. "No, because you don't talk like a witch would."

Charlotte laughed a little, frowned a little, considered running away to hide a little. "And how does a witch talk?"

"I don't know." He looked away, pushing a hand through his hair. For a minute it seemed that he'd rather jump off the roof than answer.

"Alex?" she prompted, rather unnerved by this sudden seriousness in a man she'd not thought capable of it.

He shrugged. "Not interested in beauty. Or in helping other people."

"Oh." It wasn't *her* he thought wrong; it was all witches. She relaxed teeth she did not know she had been clenching. "It's true: some of us care nothing for beauty or charity. My aunt does good works only to spite others. But some are caring and good—not *legally* good, that is, but they use the incantation whenever they can to aid others. My mother is one such."

Alex did not reply, his expression closing even further. Charlotte nudged him with her elbow. "I myself am not so good, however, that I'm going to let you win the amulet."

He laughed then, like she'd hoped he would. He removed his coat and wrapped it around her shoulders, tucking her close against him as if he feared she might fly away.

"Reprehensible lout," she murmured, leaning her head on his shoulder.

"Wicked little witch," he answered, and kissed her hair. She sighed, and the sun set like summer passion in their eyes.

And later, as they prepared for bed: "You are exasperating," Alex told her when she picked up his clothes from where he'd tossed them on the floor.

"You are disorderly," she replied, folding his shirt and placing it on a chair.

"Oh?" His eyes smoldered as he turned to look at her, and Charlotte swallowed dryly. She retreated behind the chair, but it was a useless defense; within two steps the nefarious pirate caught her. When he hoisted her over his shoulder, Charlotte did all she could to not laugh as she faked a struggle. He tossed her onto his ramshackle bed and demonstrated various unanticipated benefits of disorderly behavior—after which she was willing to concede it perhaps hadn't been the dreadful insult she'd supposed.

"But you should still employ a mop or flamethrower around this house occasionally," she said as they sat on the bed later, eating biscuits they'd stolen from Bixby's kitchen.

"Next you're going to want me to wear perfumed pomade in my hair," Alex grumbled; then, at the contemplative look in her eye, hastily kissed that thought out of her mind—and every other with it.

And the following morning: "Stop being so bloody well aggravating, woman," he said when she stole from him five pounds he'd stolen from a passing tourist, and gave it to a ragamuffin girl instead.

"Stop being uncivilized," she countered, handing him the gold bangle she'd stolen from that same tourist.

"I like being uncivilized," he replied, grinning. And he sold the bangle to buy her a pair of embroidered ankle boots and several darts to weaponize them.

"Besides," he added later, as they sat with Bixby in a tavern booth, quenching their thirst after a long day's futile searching. "I'm a pirate and smuggler. It's my job to be uncivilized." He had his feet on the table as he drank beer. Charlotte sat primly beside him, sipping tea. Bixby, on the other side of the booth, with his fingers propping up his chin and pressed against his mouth, was gazing at something across the room.

"I believe the Wisteria Society would disagree with you," Charlotte said.

Alex grinned at her sidelong. "Are you complimenting pirates, my darling?"

"Certainly not. They are uncivilized to an extreme degree. However, within that context, they have their own simplistic notion of manners. They would not put their feet up on a table."

"Only because their clothing won't allow it."

"Bixby is a pirate and he manages to sit with appropriate decorum."

"He's a butler, not a pirate. And his elbow is on the table."

"Your behavior is corrupting him."

Alex laughed. "Daniel, old chap, Miss Pettifer just called you corrupt."

"I did not," Charlotte retorted, but Bixby didn't notice in any case. He remained focused on the distance. Frowning slightly, Alex glanced over his shoulder to see what had transfixed the man. A young, brown-haired woman in a plain dress was walking quietly across the room toward the door.

"Pretty," he said, shrugging his mouth. "You should go and say hello."

"One does not just 'go and say hello' to a lady," Bixby murmured reproachfully.

Alex laughed again. "Of course one does! Granted, she doesn't look your type, since she's not a diagram in an etiquette manual, but you might get lucky. Go, say hello. I dare you."

"Oh well then, if I have been *dared*, I should of course immediately act in a manner contrary to all my education and character," Bixby replied, deadpan.

"Yes," Alex said. They gave each other looks that would have involved tongues sticking out were they twenty years younger.

"I was not even looking at her," Bixby said.

"Sure." Alex hid a disbelieving smirk by drinking more beer.

Charlotte leaned forward with a frown, judging this *pretty* woman for herself. "Good heavens!" she remarked. "That is Miss Dearlove."

"Who?" Alex asked.

"Mrs. Chuke's maid." She looked anxiously about the room. "Mrs. Chuke is here?"

"Mrs. Chuke being a witch, I presume." Alex slipped his feet down from the table as if expecting trouble at any moment. "Well, the jig had to be up sometime, I suppose. It's been fun, darling, and if you need a lift home—"

"I beg your pardon?" Charlotte stared at him, bewildered.

He shrugged, not quite meeting her eye. "I assume you will join with this Mrs. Chuke to continue chasing the amulet."

Charlotte felt suddenly as blank as the space at the end of a chapter in which the heroine has been left in exciting circumstances, but one's visitors are due any moment now, so reading on is impossible. Both men looked at her, and she swallowed dryly.

"Why would I join with Mrs. Chuke?"

"Well, she is a witch; you are a witch," Alex reasoned. "You are in league with each other, literally."

"Yes, but—" She frowned, unable to explain why her heart was pounding. After all, while the past few days had been, as Alex put it, "fun," her goal remained to retrieve the amulet for the Wicken League. It did make sense to reunite now with her own people. "But—"

"But Miss Pettifer must remain in temporary alliance with you," Bixby supplied in the calm, reasonable voice Charlotte herself could not manage, "because a flying house may still be needed in the pursuit of Lady Armitage."

"Exactly!" Charlotte smacked her hand against the table for emphasis, causing her teacup to rattle and pain to shoot up her arm. Alex raised an eyebrow; Bixby almost smiled. Fiends, the both of them! (Her foolish heart tried to budge an *r* into that word, but she ignored it.) "However, I would not call this an alliance. We must never forget, gentlemen, that I have kidnapped you."

"Oh, absolutely," Alex said cheerfully. "Pretzel?"

Charlotte ignored the basket of snacks he handed her. "Furthermore, although this kidnapping has been done in the name of the League, Mrs. Chuke would not approve, since I am a reputable lady and you are—"

"Rogues?" Alex suggested.

"Knaves?" Bixby offered.

"Deplorable pirates," Charlotte said. "Therefore, I must hide from her—and from any and all other witches we might encounter. For the sake of the amulet, you understand."

"I understand," Alex replied in a tone that suggested he understood only too well. Looking her in the eye finally, he tipped his smile between wickedness and sweetness. *My God*, Charlotte thought, *how many women have drowned in that charm? And why do I envy them?* Flustered, and annoyed at being flustered, she leaned forward again to scrutinize the pub's inhabitants.

"I cannot, in fact, see Mrs. Chuke anywhere."

"No," Bixby agreed, "but I count three pirates."

Alex's beer mug met the table's surface with a *thunk*. "Details," he ordered brusquely.

Bixby did not move more than his eyes as he indicated each pirate in turn. "Mrs. Etterly is sitting three tables behind us, sharpening swizzle sticks with her dagger. And the Rotunders are playing cards over there. Mr. Rotunder just discarded his entire hand. Literally. He's screwing on a hook instead."

Alex straightened. "Time to leave."

"I don't think they've seen us," Bixby said.

"No, but it sounds like they've seen each other. You create a distraction and I'll—"

Smash!

Alex's instructions were rendered unnecessary by the arrival of an independent distraction: to wit, a beer mug thrown at Mrs. Etterly's table. The glass shattered and beer splashed widely, causing an outraged "Well I never!" from Mrs. Etterly.

Bixby's eyes widened in an excess of astonishment.

"Is there a fourth you didn't count?" Alex asked.

"No. The mug was thrown by Miss Dearlove."

"Huh. In any case, we're leaving. You go out the front, and I'll take—"

"I see you! Scoundrel!" There came a shudder of furniture as Mrs. Etterly rose abruptly from her chair, the bustle of her dress shoving it back to smack against the floor.

"I smelled you ten minutes ago!" Mrs. Rotunder leaped from her own chair, cards flying.

Mrs. Etterly gasped. "I am wearing an eau de toilette the Duchess of Uzes gave to me in thanks for not shooting her or burning down her house."

"Eau de toilette? Smells more like water you took from the toilet."

"Well I—"

Smash!

Another beer mug exploded on the floor between them. The pirates looked at it in momentary bewilderment, since clearly neither had thrown it, then cast such petty considerations aside and drew their swords.

"En garde!" Mrs. Etterly shouted.

"Prepare to die!" Mrs. Rotunder shouted in reply.

"Never!"

"Um, dearest," Mr. Rotunder said, tugging on his wife so he might whisper to her. She listened, then straightened again, her expression poised between fury and dignity.

"Prepare to be wounded!" she shouted in amendment. "But not so badly that you cannot sing at my soiree next week! The prince will be there, and you know how he admires your voice!"

"Never!" Mrs. Etterly repeated. "By which I mean never in this context! I of course look forward to the soiree!" And she leaped forward, sword raised. A table crashed over, blades met with a loud metallic ringing, and several patrons screamed.

"Blighters!" roared the innkeeper, waving a cricket bat as he entered the fray.

"Up," Alex said, climbing on to the bench seat and hauling Charlotte with him.

"Be careful not to spill the tea!" she urged as a chair went flying past to shatter against the bar.

With some difficulty, due to the inconvenient volume of Charlotte's clothing, not to mention beer mats whizzing past with a stinging speed, they clambered across the table, over the side of the booth, and dropped to the ground unnoticed by anyone (except three waitresses, the bartender, and an old lady who had just been trying to enjoy her fish and chips in peace). As Bixby headed for the front door, Alex led Charlotte out the back into a dark alleyway. He shut the door moments before a plate shattered against it.

"You have destroyed my skirt, sir, with these shenanigans," Charlotte said, brushing at a slight mark on the fabric. "I declare, you appear to have a genius for mess. If only you weren't such a scoundrel!"

"If only you weren't so enchanting," Alex countered.

This made no sense at all, since she had not done magic, and Charlotte was on the brink of telling him so when he grabbed her, pushed her against the alleyway wall, and kissed her until she forgot every word he said or she ought to say in response.

Kissing was one thing she never disputed. Her body had an irrepressible attraction to the man and, despite the several lectures it received daily from her brain, refused to care about either ill-mannered feuds or well-mannered behavior. Alex seemed to be caught in the same dilemma. They could barely cross a street without afterward dragging each other into a passionate embrace.

Indeed, by the time they traversed the two hundred yards from the pub to Alex's cottage on the pier, disheveled, breathless, and significantly unbuttoned, Bixby had brewed a pot of tea and retired with Thomas More's *Utopia*.

Later that night, lying beside Alex in his bed, watching him sleep in the gauzy moonlight and trying to pretend there were no spiderwebs on the ceiling overhead, Charlotte attempted to reason through what was happening to her and just where along the way she had left a large portion of her good sense. Captain O'Riley was not a suitable obsession. He seemed just as dangerous asleep as he did awake. His long, dark eyelashes, curving against his cheeks, were akin to a sword at her throat; his dreaming smile was a lure that would draw her out of all propriety.

If only he wasn't as tempting as he was perilous. If only he lived in a boardinghouse, and worked in an office, and didn't look at her as if he wanted to lick the bittersweet words right out of her mouth. As she surveyed him covetously, Charlotte wondered whether concern for the amulet had inspired her to hijack his house, or whether she had still been flying a bicycle somewhere inside herself, lawless, longing for freedom, and in love even then with the pirate's sky-colored eyes.

Well, not *in love*. In like. Intrigued. She might share his bed, but there was still no call to involve emotions. The fact her pulse rushed when he smiled at her meant nothing beyond physiology. The odd loneliness that made her ache when he left the room for even a short while was inconsequential. She'd been lonely all her life, after all.

No, Charlotte concluded; their relationship was nothing more than temporary fun, and when it was over she would go back to her proper life, taking with her some interesting memories (and the amulet).

She sighed. *I am most certainly not in love,* she told herself, reaching out through the darkness to touch the pirate's face.

And Alex, lying quiet with his eyes safely closed, indulged in the comfort of Charlotte's presence after years of not sharing this bed with any woman out of fear they'd also want to share his heart. (Rugs being different, and beds in other buildings, and a convenient tabletop in more than one case.) He felt the drift of her fingers and tried not to smile. She bewitched him even without incanting. It wasn't that she stirred his nether regions at a mere glance—although she certainly did that too. It was how her rosy loveliness and her thorn-sharp wit stirred his heart, making it shove painfully against the stone wall he'd built around it more than twenty years ago. That heart wanted to share with her, yearned to share, trembled so fast with its desperation to share that Alex began to feel dizzy, even lying in bed.

He could not allow it. But he could not lie still either while his blood shook and Charlotte stroked her soft, clean fingers against his skin. So he tipped her back and pushed her legs apart, and she arched to welcome him in. They moved together fiercely, wordlessly, holding on to sheets and headboards and each other for dear life.

Not love. Not needing. Just exercise in the dark.

But afterward she wept, and he tried to brush the tears from her beautiful, moonlit cheek. "Did I hurt you?" he asked anxiously.

"No," she said. "I'm—I'm feeling, that's all."

"Are you cold? Hungry? Do you want a cup of tea? What is it?"

She caught his hand, holding it against the calm steadiness of her heartbeat. "It's nothing. Only feeling. Is that not acceptable?"

She sounded so defensive, he kissed her damp face. "Of course it is," he assured her, although he still did not entirely understand. But tucking her closer, he just let her be.

She held on to him like a pirate holds on to the wheel through a storm. As if she needed him. As if he represented safety. He felt her smile shift across his bare skin, and he sucked in a breath as sensation trembled through him. It was nothing, he told himself—sex always left his body sensitive for a while. This woman was just another lover, another way of getting through the dark. He was not going to go *feeling* simply because she did.

However, there was no harm in smiling too, like a soft, boyish fool, in the darkness where no one could see it.

"The map says there is no shortcut," Charlotte reiterated as the three of them trudged through town, following the afternoon's light toward sea-tanged shadows. This was their third day now in Clacton-on-Sea, and Charlotte was so wearied by searching that she had fallen into an uncharacteristic irritability. "I doubt Lady Armitage is even here. Bixby's information must have been faulty."

Bixby did not reply to this; his silence, however, was scandalized.

"Impossible," Alex argued. "Don't give up, sweetheart. Remember the jewelry store yesterday that was robbed of all its gold rings? And the burned-down church? Not to mention the man who saw an unusual red-doored townhouse on Anchor Road? Parking in that street would appeal to Armitage's sense of humor."

"But you are walking in the wrong direction for Anchor Road."

"No, it's just down here a bit. Trust me." He tugged on her hand without effect.

"Ha. If you will look at the map—"

She turned to gesture at said map, which Bixby was carrying to assist them, and went abruptly still. Alex turned to see what had troubled her.

Bixby was gone.

"That's odd," Alex murmured.

"He obviously disdained your shortcut and has taken the correct route," Charlotte said smugly.

Alex rolled his eyes. "He obviously got sick of your harping on." He began walking back along the narrow street in search of the missing butler. Charlotte, by dint of her hand still being held in his, necessarily followed him.

"I have not been harping on," she harped. "I have been attempting to educate you."

"The last woman who tried educating me used to apply a birch rod when I gave the wrong answer," Alex replied cheerfully. "Or when she simply didn't like my looks. Are you going to beat me, Lottie?"

He flashed a seductive smile at her, but she stared back open-mouthed. "My God. I am so sorry."

Surprise flittered across his expression for the briefest moment before he laughed. "Don't be. Sister Andrew—and the other nuns—and Deirdre—and Dadai—were all good training for the life of a pirate. Hell, my father still tries to give me a refresher course every time I go back to Ireland. He may be retired now and living the life of Riley, ha, but let's just say he hasn't forgotten how to be piratic."

"Well, I am not a pirate, and I don't want to hurt you," Charlotte averred—although in fact a moment ago it had been her plan to score a verbal hit. But as she hastily assessed her motivation, she found only a desire for game playing. In fact, what made exchanging barbs with Alex so enjoyable was the thought no one got truly harmed by it. Never mind Darcy; he had somehow managed to become her Mr. Knightley, a witty sparring partner, and while she did not expect a happy ever after like Emma Woodhouse, at least she was having a good time staying up late, turning pages, even dog-earing a few like a real scoundrel.

Now the vision of Alex as a whipped little boy shook her so deeply, she stumbled as he pulled her along. They turned a corner they had not taken earlier, but Charlotte was too distracted to notice.

"Don't reassure me in that way," Alex said, his voice lilting more than usual. "What would I do without the thrill of your deadly footwear, or the ravishing bite of your teeth? Now just down here and around this corner—damn." He stopped suddenly, causing Charlotte to collide with him. He steadied her automatically, but his focus was on the high stone wall that stood ahead of them.

Charlotte could not help herself. "It seems like your shortcut has been cut short."

"Very funny." Pushing a hand through his hair, he looked around, scowling. "I would have sworn this led to Rosemary Road. And where the hell is Bixby?"

"Having a rather pointed conversation with my maid."

They turned to see Mrs. Chuke in front of them, smiling like a thundercloud looking down on a parade.

✳ 16 ✳

PRIDE AND PREJUDICE—THE BUTLER HAS IT DONE TO HIM—
OUT OF THE FIRE—SUDDEN ACROBATS—INTO THE FRYING PAN—
CHARLOTTE GOES WITH ALEX BECAUSE SHE WANTS TO LIVE—
MAD HATTING—GETTING IN THE SWING—CHARLOTTE IS A VILLAIN

Mrs. Chuke's character was despised in general society for its sincerity and frankness, and in such a moment as this, she certainly would not depart from it. "Charlotte, darling! How dreadful you look! Your face is all rosy, and what is that sparkle in your eye? Thank goodness I found you before you go completely to rack and ruin! I shall save you, dear girl, from this wicked pirate who kidnapped you!" She eyed Alex darkly.

"I didn't—" Alex began, but Charlotte spoke over him with a confidence plagiarized from Elizabeth Bennet.

"You have been widely mistaken in my character, madam, if you think I can be kidnapped by a pirate."

Mrs. Chuke gasped. "Surely you are not admitting to being in his company on a *voluntary* basis?"

"Why not? He is a scoundrel; I am a scoundrel; so far we are equal."

"But pirates and witches, who-do-not-exist-but-if-they-did, are mortal enemies! Think of the League, Charlotte darling! Think of your mother, who even now is ordering caterers for the wedding!" ("Um," Alex said, blanching, but the ladies ignored him.) "Your reputation will be a disgrace; your name will be constantly mentioned by all of us. Good heavens, Charlotte, *you have allied with a pirate!*"

Charlotte frowned, although in fact she felt thrilled at this opportunity to face a nemesis in the same way Lizzie did with Lady Catherine de Bourgh. Admittedly, Mrs. Chuke was inferior in style and temper to Lady Catherine, and a dusty urban street was nowhere near as romantic as a copse, but it seemed bookworms could not be choosers when it came to real life. "If I had allied with him," she said, "I should be the first person to confess it. And I do not. Captain O'Riley continues to be my worst enemy."

"It's true," Alex interjected with a pleasant smile.

"And whatever my connections may be, if the Captain objects to them, that must be everything to you."

"I do object to them," Alex said, nodding cheerfully.

Glancing at him, Charlotte felt a fluttering in her stomach. She knew she shouldn't have eaten fish for lunch! On the other hand, could it be . . . friendship? At least what she supposed friendship was from reading about it in books. She expected one day she would marry, for such is the general fate of womankind, but having a *friend* was a dream she had never dared entertain. That Alex might be this made her want to laugh in delight.

But delighted laughter was the sphere of girls like Lydia Bennet, and tended to escalate into scandalous behavior, such as running off with scoundrels . . . er . . .

Blushing, she lifted her chin, tightened her lips, and glared at the captain, Mrs. Chuke, and a nearby seagull.

"Well!" Mrs. Chuke was nonplussed. This was not the response she had expected from Judith Plim's niece. She muttered a word, and old brown leaves littering the street began to rise, swirling around her ankles. She'd been a witch longer than Charlotte had been alive, and Chosen One or not, the girl would be made, either by wisdom or outright witchcraft, to remember her place. "You are clearly discomposed, my dear. This situation must not continue!"

Charlotte opened her mouth to reply, but she was indeed discomposed, and could not immediately recollect how the scene in *Pride and Prejudice* had continued. So she closed her mouth and pulled out her besom instead.

Mrs. Chuke paled. "You would not dare."

Charlotte shrugged. From the corner of her eye she saw Alex lower his face to hide a smirk. *He* knew she would dare. She felt another surge of delight.

"Just put down the broom and come home quietly," Mrs. Chuke said. "I read the runes this morning, and they predicted you traveling back to London with me." But her own hand was sliding down toward a secret pocket wherein no doubt she kept her besom.

It was time for the Andromeda Choice. The last resort, the worst possible weapon, designed specifically to disarm a fellow witch. Charlotte had always felt it would come to this one day, but her heart did lurch a little. A witch might attack another witch (indeed, it would be strange if she didn't), but using the Andromeda Choice was like flying a bicycle over a crowded street. Only the wildest person would do it.

Click.

A cloud of dust burst from the besom. Mrs. Chuke shrieked in horror. Raising her own besom, she activated its broom with an immediate instinct to tidy. As she swept madly at the air, Charlotte and Alex turned to flee.

The wall blocked their way.

And in front of the wall stood Mrs. Rotunder, arms crossed, jolly black hat feathers swooping in the sea breeze.

Two streets away, Bixby was staring down the barrel of a gun.

It was a very pretty gun, with an engraving of tiny flowers on its silver body and pearls set in the handle. Its owner, Miss Dearlove, clutched it with all the delicacy such a weapon deserved. She herself was also very pretty, but that seemed rather beside the point at this moment.

"Keep walking into the dark and narrow alleyway, if you please," she said. Her quiet voice offered no threat—so long as one ignored the words it was actually saying and the loaded gun behind them. It had lured Bixby away from Alex and Charlotte, requesting assistance in finding a dropped shilling; and then humbly begged his pardon as it explained he must do as he was told or else be shot. Bixby had obliged because he feared the woman would start crying if he did not. But allowing himself to be guided into a convenient place for murder went beyond his notions of chivalry.

"Forgive me, miss," he said, since abduction at gunpoint should not prevent one from using good manners. "I'm afraid I cannot do that. May I suggest instead you hand over the gun, and I will allow you to depart unharmed."

Miss Dearlove did not so much blink as wince her eyes briefly shut then open. She bit her lower lip. It made her appear so vulnerable that Bixby would have felt his heart melt if such a thing were biologically possible. Although he remembered her throwing beer mugs at pirates last night in the tavern, he could barely reconcile that image with the timid creature before him now. The simple brown dress, the calm face, and the quiet voice that spoke only when necessary, made him think of book-lined shelves and the Dewey Decimal System of an outstanding library. A man's instincts (and other things) roused automatically for a woman like this. It was all Bixby could do to prevent himself from offering to buy her a cup of tea and escorting her safely home.

Indeed, notwithstanding the fact she was proposing to murder him, he rather thought her entire attitude reminded him of a doe—i.e., gentle and shy—and he could not endorse such a one being involved in dangerous shenanigans like these. Somebody might get hurt, and it would not be him.

Smiling kindly, his eyes soft, he reached out to remove the gun from the girl's anxious, fine-boned grip.

Fifteen minutes later he woke on the dirty ground of the alleyway, bound hand and foot, and groaning through a lace handkerchief stuffed in his mouth. His wallet was gone, as were his gold cufflinks.

Had someone been on-site with an encyclopedia of nature, Bixby would not have needed them to explain that the true description of a doe was "powerful and unpredictable." Spitting out the handkerchief, he turned onto his back and laughed.

Mrs. Rotunder had no such sense of humor. Indeed, after spending several days in the company of witches, she could barely remember what humor looked like. Crossing her arms with the self-awarded authority of older women everywhere, she frowned at Charlotte and Alex. "Now, my dears, you know this can't go on. Not the least because it's far too clichéd. We are in England, not Verona! Have some literary subtlety and separate, for everyone's sake."

Irritation flashed through Charlotte's nerves, sparking a low mutter that caused Mrs. Rotunder's sable feathers to shake. Alex glanced at her sidelong, excitement in his eyes. She half-expected him to kiss her right there and then. "Madam," she said, her voice strong with righteousness, "I can assure you the captain and I are not together."

Mrs. Rotunder's response was to direct a trenchant stare at their joined hands.

"This is because I am keeping him under my control," Charlotte explained.

Alex shrugged and nodded complacently.

"So *you* kidnapped *him?*" Mrs. Rotunder gave a brusque laugh.

"And why not?" Mrs. Chuke interjected, striding forward before Charlotte herself could reply. Dust covered her face, but so great was her anger, she did not even notice. "Charlotte would be a witch if witches existed. That makes her just as dangerous as him!"

Mrs. Rotunder *tsked*. "No one is as dangerous as a pirate."

"Ha! Having traveled in your house, drinking that tepid stuff you pretend is tea, and sleeping on a mattress so soft I was in danger of becoming relaxed for the first time in six—in fifty years, I know perfectly well that piratic danger is false advertising."

"Oh?" said Mrs. Rotunder chillingly. There came the long, slow hiss of steel being drawn from a scabbard.

"You call that a weapon?" Mrs. Chuke pulled out a fly swatter. Made of black metal. With spikes all over its surface.

Charlotte and Alex sidestepped as Mrs. Rotunder whirled her sword in a complicated maneuver.

"Shall we go?" Charlotte whispered.

They winced as Mrs. Chuke whacked the sword with one hard blow from her swatter.

"Probably wise," Alex agreed.

"*Aereo,*" Charlotte said. At once, they elevated over the witch and pirate, who were too involved with each other to notice their precipitous departure. They crossed the wall and came down to the street on the other side.

"Rosemary Road!" Alex said delightedly. "I told you this was a good shortcut."

"Braggart," Charlotte replied.

A small throng of American tourists turned away from a shop window to stare at them open-mouthed. "I say, how did you do that?" one asked with alarm.

"There was a ladder on the other side of the wall," Charlotte said. "We climbed up, jumped down."

The tourists exchanged dubious glances.

"She's only joking," Alex said. "We're acrobats with a traveling circus. Trained to leap over high obstacles in a single bound."

The tourists began to murmur excitedly, and several inquired about tickets to the show. Suddenly a woman in a pink turban pointed at Charlotte.

"I recognize you! Your photograph was in the newspaper. Wait—didn't this man kidnap you?"

Charlotte smiled tolerantly. "No, not at all."

"That photograph was of her twin sister," Alex said. "Three minutes younger and not as pretty."

"Ahh." The crowd nodded.

Charlotte stared at him, surprised. "You'd call me pretty?" *Strong, fierce, gorgeous, brave . . . pretty.*

He grinned. "That is the least I would call you, my darling."

The tourists cooed.

"You said Miss Dearlove was pretty," she persisted. "Perhaps this is an adjective you apply to all women."

He laid a hand against her cheek, looking down at her with his particular tender-smile-despite-all-the-sharp-weapons expression, which Charlotte suspected was probably what had earned him his reputation for deadliness in the first place. Several of the tourists sighed dreamily. Charlotte would have done so herself were it not for years of rigorous Plimmish training.

"Oh, Lottie," he said. "You are—"

"Stop!" roared a voice from behind the wall. "Kidnapper!"

Charlotte glanced over her shoulder. "Was that my one or yours?"

"Wicked kidnapper!" came a different voice.

Alex shrugged. "It doesn't seem to matter which."

"She is the wicked one," retorted the first voice angrily.

"Nonsense. He is a pirate; it's in his job description to be wicked. Clearly he is the worst!"

"No one is more wicked than a witch!"

There came another sharp clash of metal. The tourists leaped with startlement. Charlotte and Alex took the opportunity to hasten along the street—

And stopped abruptly.

Miss Plim strode around a corner, sunlight flashing on her spectacles.

Till this moment, Charlotte never knew herself. But now, watching Miss Plim aim toward her like an inevitability, she felt bird wings flap madly against her bones and wind roar through her mind, and she realized that a lifetime of considering herself self-contained had been a lie. *Imprisoned* was the better word. In fact, she had a vast longing in her—a whole sky's worth of longing for life and love, rooftops and running wild—and here was Miss Plim now to bring her back to earth.

The woman moved with a cool, measured stride. The hem of her black dress swept methodically back and forth against the street; her topknot of hair knuckled the clear, bright sky. And her hand, emerging slowly from a pocket, unfurled with blade, shuriken, eyebrow tweezers.

No weapon was more deadly, however, than the look on her face. *You are wrong,* it said. *The way you have been behaving proves just how wrong you are deep inside. Charlotte Pettifer, you are A Disappointment.*

Don't listen! screamed Charlotte's brain. *Run away!*

No, quick, curtsy! Apologize! Promise to be better! argued her body.

Caught between the two impulses, Charlotte was unable to make a choice that would not in some way be incorrect. She could not move, could not breathe.

Besides, it was too late. Aunt Judith's presence meant everything was over. The escapade; the kissing in alleyways; the midnight snacks in a lamplit kitchen, hoping Bixby did not catch them. Just as soon as she reached Charlotte, Miss Plim would transform her from an independent woman making admittedly wild choices into once again a proper witch. It would only take a shake of the head, a click of the tongue. In fact, Charlotte could feel it happening already. Jane Austen began chanting: *Be wise and reasonable.*

But alas! Alas! She must confess to herself that she did not want to be wise yet.

Luckily, she was in the company of an entirely unwise pirate. "Quick," Alex said, tugging on her. "This way!"

He half-dragged her off the street and through the nearest shop door. As the doorbell tinkled merrily, Charlotte came back to herself—and into near-collision with a peacock.

Stumbling back, she ascertained this was not an ironic statement from the universe but in fact a hat the shopkeeper was transporting across the shop. "I say!" the merchant declared, but Charlotte and Alex skidded past and made for what they could only hope was a rear exit behind a curtained door.

They found themselves instead in a silk floral jungle inhabited by flocks of stuffed birds.

The doorbell tinkled again. "Good afternoon, sir," came a woman's voice, the aural equivalent of a bayonet being jabbed into a wagon that is hiding escapees amongst its load.

Charlotte's breath caught raggedly in her throat. Alex grasped a decorative shepherd's crook that was propped up nearby and began whacking at wings and flowers, papier-mâché beaks and long lace vines, clearing a path through the mad hat jungle. Discovering a rear door, he immediately applied his bootheel to it and the door slammed open at once, not having actually been locked. They rushed out even as Miss Plim stalked into the workroom.

"She'll never stop," Charlotte cried.

"Trust me," Alex said with a piratic smile. "I'll keep you unsafe."

They ran down the street, took a corner, and Alex led them to a random door that he opened in the conventional manner of turning its handle. It revealed a large hall crowded with yet another flock of birds—which is to say, people dressed in vivid colors and plumes, fluttering around, their voices warbling through the air. Two long lines of dancers swooped together, then apart, while a group of fiddlers played.

They had stumbled upon an afternoon ball, Charlotte realized, and she felt a certain narrative satisfaction. As Alex shut the door and shoved chairs against it, she watched the dancers, evaluating the quality of their muslins. Then Alex tugged on her hand so she spun toward him; grasping her other hand, pulling her close, he grinned.

"Madam," he said. "May I have this dance?"

Elizabeth Bennet would have said yes from sheer surprise. Fanny Price would have said no and hidden her face. But Charlotte did not consult either. Instead, she frowned at the pirate, called him a fiend, and let him dance her in long strides across the floor. His smile was a hook, holding her up out of fear. Her hips moved in a manner she had not known them capable of. The two lines of dancers moved apart, with hands connected and arms raised to make a steepled lane. Witch and pirate danced through like shadows in the lamplight, portending night, leaving everyone blinking and enchanted.

As they reached the end of the lane, the lines of dancers moved together again, and Charlotte and Alex copied them—hands still clutching, gazes locked. The world seemed to suspend in a haze of noise and color. Miss Plim was gone; Lizzie Bennet was gone; all that remained were Alex's smiling eyes and the disordered beat of her heart.

She did not want to breathe lest she break the spell. Here was some magic greater than witchery. She, Charlotte Pettifer, was participating in a romantic ballroom moment such as Jane Austen herself might have composed—albeit without a dreadful aunt in pursuit. Nor a hero who was utterly devilish, with an earring and a hefty sword, not to mention a pair of boots that on their own would be censored from any decent novel. And alas, she doubted the heroine would be quite as worldly as she herself had become this past week.

In fact, she rather suspected she would be the villain in a Jane Austen novel.

But Charlotte was surprised to find she did not care. Rising on her toes, she kissed that devilish pirate, and thrilled at the smile she startled onto his mouth.

It was an imperfect moment, but she would remember it for the rest of her life.

And then the music surged, and they moved apart with the rest of the dancers. Alex held up Charlotte's hand, and laughing, she spun beneath it. If she was being wrong, at least it was enjoyable.

Crash!

Chairs scattered as the hall door smashed open under an assault of Latin poetry. The music faltered and the dancers staggered to a confused halt. Charlotte looked up to see Miss Plim inject herself into the crowd. The woman was not running; she did not even appear to be flushed or breathless with the effort of the chase.

"It's time to come home, Charlotte," she called out in a pitiless monotone. And then she began chanting.

"Abi. Abi."

Bodies flung away from her. Hats spun across the room.

Charlotte stared in horror. "Come on," Alex said, grasping her hard and pulling her. They ran for the nearest door. Unfortunately, "nearest" was a relative term, involving a crush of dancers, waiters with trays of lemonade glasses, a row of chairs, and a pirate.

Ned Lightbourne leaped seemingly out of nowhere onto one of the chairs, sword drawn. The crowd screamed and attempted to scatter, but as bustles tangled with lace trimmings and gloves snagged in ornate brooches, they quickly became something resembling an exploded wedding cake. Alex and Charlotte stood trapped amongst them, frowning up at Ned.

"Don't make me fight you, old chap," Alex warned.

Ned rolled his eyes. "You know the last time we fought I beat you so thoroughly you were limping for a week."

"You mean the time you beat me at backgammon. I was limping because you danced around in celebration and knocked me off my chair, twisting my ankle."

"Nonsense." Ned paused, glancing at the crowd quaking in fear as they watched him. "Never mind. O'Riley, you have to stop. This isn't as simple as an enchanted amulet that, in the wrong hands, could destroy the world. By running off with Miss Pettifer, you've annoyed a lot of old ladies. Both groups are tracking you across England, determined to prevent you from spoiling their feud."

Alex shrugged.

"Good grief, man, how can you shrug? We're talking about the Wisteria Society!"

The crowd gasped.

Alex looked around at them, hands spread so they could see the several weapons strapped to his hard, muscular form. "Do I look like the sort of person to be scared of lady pirates in ridiculous hats?"

"You should be," a waiter said. The crowd murmured agreement.

"Oh for heaven's sake," Charlotte said testily. "Captain O'Riley and I remain perfect enemies."

To which Ned replied by looking wordlessly at their joined hands.

"It's so I can weaponize her if necessary," Alex explained.

"Exactly," Charlotte agreed. Glancing anxiously over her shoulder, she gasped as she watched Miss Plim elbowing her way deeper through the crowd. Any moment now, she would be upon them. Alex might not like to fight his friend, but Charlotte liked even less the idea of returning meekly home before she'd had her fill of happiness (and, er, recovered the amulet). She reached for the besom in her coat pocket.

Too late.

"I'm sorry to do this," Ned muttered, and lifted his sword.

☙ 17 ☙

AN INTERVENTION—MISS PLIM ARRIVES—CHARLOTTE IS BRAVE—
AN AFTERNOON SNACK—A PEDESTRIAN CONVERSATION—
THEY COMMIT TO A FITNESS REGIME

Generally speaking, Charlotte disliked the frank, the open-hearted, the eager character beyond all others. She preferred those who kept their thoughts to themselves, so saving her the inconvenience of listening to them. However, in the circumstance of someone wielding a sword, a little candor could be a good thing. Ned Lightbourne offered no explanation as he raised his weapon, and Charlotte was able to remain calm only because she had been so well educated that not even imminent mortal peril could make her cry out.

Unexpectedly, the sword left Ned's hand and flew over their heads, arcing gently as dancers screamed and cowered. Watching it, Charlotte caught sight of Alex's face, of the perfect tranquility there, and realized he had not worried for even a moment about what Ned might do. It astonished Charlotte and, were she not standing beneath a sharp, flying blade, and—worse!—with her furious aunt bearing rapidly toward her, she might have felt a moment's fierce longing for that degree of friendship and trust.

The sword came down precisely as it was aimed: into the upraised, lace-gloved hand of Cecilia Bassingthwaite.

Typical, Charlotte thought dourly. (One of course did not wish Cecilia any harm . . . but if she'd failed to catch the sword, or dropped it on her foot perhaps, scratching her gorgeous shoes, then one would be more inclined to believe in the benevolence of the universe.)

Cecilia spun the sword dispassionately, turned on her heel, and applied the pommel with a professional degree of force against Miss Plim's head.

Charlotte gasped in horror—and the merest breath of delight.

Miss Plim went down in a heap of black crinoline. Her topknot thwacked as it hit the floor.

"That should give you ten minutes or so," Ned said. He jumped from the chair and slapped Alex's shoulder in a friendly manner.

"Thanks," Alex muttered.

"I shouldn't have done it, since it only encourages your bad behavior." Ned frowned first at Alex and then Charlotte, who would have stared back imperiously if she wasn't aware of Cecilia coming up behind her, cool and elegant, not a hair out of place. As a result, she only managed to look queenly, which is not as noble as it sounds. Ned reached between her and Alex to take his sword back from Cecilia, and the smile he gave his wife was so unconsciously tender, so melting with love and regard, that Charlotte's look degraded to common envy, and out of the corner of her eye she saw Alex grimace.

"You really need to separate," Ned continued as he sheathed his sword. "Alex, go quiet for a while. Smuggle some sugar, rob a few minor lending institutes. Miss Pettifer, go home. I know it's enjoyable stirring up trouble, but you'll find a more lasting contentment in your own spheres."

"What nonsense!"

All three turned to stare at Cecilia. She stared back unperturbed.

"Don't listen to him. He just doesn't like the idea of wearing a white waistcoat to your wedding—he thinks doing so at ours was enough for a lifetime. The man is a fool."

"But a debonair fool," Ned argued.

"Wedding?" Alex said weakly.

"Besides," Ned added. "I would wear a pink dress to their wedding if they asked me. That is entirely beside the point."

"Excuse me, what wedding?" Charlotte said.

"The point is," Cecilia contended, "they have an amulet to retrieve."

Ned raised an eyebrow. "*We* have an amulet to retrieve."

Alex glanced at Charlotte. "Wedding?" he whispered. She shook her head with bemusement. The crowd, now silent in fascination at the scene unfolding before them, smirked and nudged each other.

"Yes, dear," Cecilia continued. "This is why we must keep an eye on them, which we can do more easily if they are running around together, attracting policemen, outraged pirates, and wit— Er, women who are in no way involved in witchcraft. Better this than them working independently in secret."

"Well, they won't be running anywhere if they don't start before the aunt recovers."

At this reminder, Charlotte jolted to attention. "Thank you for your assistance, Captain Lightbourne, Miss Bassingthwaite," she said, "but we must be leaving. Were Captain O'Riley and I not committed enemies, with absolutely no plans for a wedding, we would invite you to afternoon tea in our—er, that is, Captain O'Riley's house. But I'm afraid we must dash."

"Of course," Cecilia said. "I am the last person who would inflict a woman's aunt upon her. It was lovely to meet you again, Miss Pettifer. I hope you will come to me when you are planning your baby shower. My housemaid has developed a mania for knitting booties, and we now have more than we will hopefully ever use."

"Baby shower?!" Alex echoed in a strangled voice.

A few voices in the crowd chuckled. Alex's glare repressed them back into prudent silence.

"Thank you, Miss Bassingthwaite," Charlotte said stiffly. "I would one day enjoy a discussion on footwear." She ignored the small noise Alex made, for she felt like she was crossing a chasm on an uncertain rope bridge, and needed no distractions lest she plummet into mortal embarrassment. "I am keen to know where you bought those charming shoes you are wearing."

Cecilia smiled warmly, and the rope bridge became a little steadier. "I would be happy to tell you. Perhaps we might defy the feud and take luncheon together one day soon. We could admire Black Beryl's amulet displayed above my hearth."

Charlotte's own smile in reply was tepid, but only because it had originated from a lifetime of being out in the cold. "I would be pleased to bring Beryl Black's amulet on my visit, and set it temporarily above your hearth so we may admire it together."

They looked at each other with a steady silence that, for any two other women, would have been a chuckle. Charlotte realized she'd crossed the bridge, and had a moment's pride in herself before panicking and running back along it to safe ground again. "Come along, Captain O'Riley. We must be leaving. Although we are not *together*"—she gave Ned a fierce look, and he raised his hands to surrender the point—"we had better return to the house before Aunt Judith rouses."

She gave Cecilia a sharp little nod then strode away, Alex following in somewhat of a daze, his hand still in hers. "How did we get from a wedding to a baby shower in one conversation?" he could be heard asking as they made their way through the crowd to a door someone hastily opened for them.

Ned smiled sidelong at his wife.

"You shouldn't really have teased them like that," she chided.

"I wasn't teasing them," he said in a noble tone. "I was testing them."

"Ned Lightbourne, fairy godfather?"

"Well, I am rather dressed for it."

Cecilia laughed. And as Miss Plim raised herself groaning from the floor, they nonchalantly walked past her and out the way Alex and Charlotte had come in, pocketing wallets and a particularly fetching emerald ring as they went.

Outside the hall, Charlotte and Alex disengaged their hands self-consciously. Charlotte put on her sunglasses; Alex shoved at his hair as he frowned up and down the street.

"All right," he said, "I give up. I don't know where we are. In fact, I'm completely lost."

Charlotte swallowed back an instinctive "I told you so," for she too possessed no idea of their location. This, however, did not prevent her from striding purposefully southward. "Follow me," she announced in the tone of a woman who knew exactly where she was heading. With a shrug, Alex obeyed.

They reached the end of the street, incantated over a fence, hurried through a garden, and then walked another street eating grapes they had obtained from a vine in that garden. Miss Plim would struggle now to find them, and Charlotte began to relax. Her posture stiffened. Her boot heels smacked more decidedly against the cobblestones.

"Despite recent circumstances, I would like you to consider yourself still under abduction, Captain," she said. "My elders are not entitled to enforce a prejudiced injunction on my plans; I remain independent of opinion and therefore of action."

Alex frowned as he worked this through. "Ah. They can't tell you what to do," he translated finally. "I agree. But sweetheart, sooner or later you're going to have to face the truth that we're choosing to stay together." He shifted a grape between his teeth and grinned at her. "I could have tossed you out my door any time I wanted, and you could have walked away as soon as we reached Clacton. We are not exactly being sensible."

She narrowed her eyes at him. "Do you want me to leave?"

His expression leaped as if in alarm. "No. No, I'm not saying that. But you're risking your reputation if you stay."

Charlotte lifted her chin so high with affronted dignity, she pulled a muscle in her neck. "I have a perfectly fearful reputation. There is no reason people shouldn't believe that I kidnapped you."

He smiled wryly. "I meant your reputation as an unmarried woman."

"Oh. Well. I will not deny it would be politically sensible to relinquish your company. But you have not yet brought me all the way."

"Your reaction last night suggests otherwise."

She cast him a brief, disdainful look. "I shall ignore that. Only an uncouth person employs lewd innuendo. It shows a kink in the imagination, and I urge you to take a more somber, penetrating perspective, Captain. It's not hard."

"It is now," he muttered, but thankfully she did not hear him.

"I meant all the way to Lady Armitage's house, which will be the climax of our efforts. Once I have my amulet, you can withdraw."

Alex laughed. "Oh dear, I do love you," he said—

And silence clamped down between them.

"Um," he added, pushing a hand through his hair. "Metaphorically speaking, of course."

"Of course," Charlotte agreed hastily. She realized she had stopped walking, possibly because her heart seemed to have stopped beating; she began to stride once more along the street. "Do not look so concerned on my behalf, Captain. It is a common enough statement. For example, I myself love that house there with the wooden shutters. I love tea. I love you, and your smile, and the way you sigh in your sleep. See, common. Unconcerning. We are still enemies."

"Mortal enemies," he agreed, smiling rather self-consciously.

"Enemies born to utterly despise each other. Mind you, this doesn't mean we can't take a little nocturnal exercise together now and again, in the interest of our health."

"I am also partial to exercise in the morning," Alex said, "to start my day right."

Charlotte nodded. "It is important to keep fit. Especially in our line of work."

"Don't let the Wisteria Society or Wicken League hear you say that. Our work is completely different, remember."

Somehow their hands had become entangled again. They swung them as they walked. "Everything about us is different," Charlotte said. "To begin with, pirates are wrong and witches are right."

He laughed. "I disagree with you so heartily, I want to take you home and exercise your brains out this very moment. But if they found us, they've probably also found my house. I doubt it's safe for us to return just now."

"Bother. How will we give chase if Lady Armitage suddenly leaves town?"

Alex shrugged. "I can fly anything. But to be honest, I suspect Armitage is long gone."

"Excuse me," came a mild voice behind them.

They shifted aside automatically to make space on the footpath. "I fear you may be right," Charlotte agreed. "Look, that street sign says we are on Anchor Road, and yet I see no red door ahead of us anywhere."

"Excuse me," came the voice again.

They shifted in the opposite direction. "Bixby will have to get down another load of information," Alex said, "and reroute us to a likely new port."

"Excuse! Me!"

At the irritated shout, they turned, eyebrows raised in surprise that anyone would yell at a pirate who was more weapons than man.

And found a woman standing in the doorway of a townhouse five feet behind them on the pavement—and five feet *above* the pavement. She smiled down at them, revealing large teeth that glinted menacingly in the sunlight.

Her hair was a rigid gray fan.

Her door was blood red.

"I hear you have been looking for me," she said.

"Lady Armitage!" Charlotte dragged off her sunglasses as if doing so would improve the vision before her. Alas, she was still staring at a bony woman encased in a dress so black, it went beyond mere darkness into an eclipse of all possible light, hope, and happiness. This was a dress that might have been marketed as *Couture de la Tragédie* were it worn by a younger woman, but despite her erect stance Lady Armitage exuded age to the worrying degree of close-to-death. (Or possibly close *with* death, which is considerably more worrying when associated with a pirate.)

"At your service," replied the lady. "Although whose service, exactly? I recognize this boy." She pointed a long, loose-skinned finger at Alex. "You once played with my grenade collection while your father tried to sell me a bag of turnip seeds. He thought I was stupid enough to buy them—but where would I plant seeds in a battlehouse, I ask you? I remember your pretty eyes, so blue—and black and purple. My, how you've grown."

Alex took a small step back as her lecherous gaze stroked him from head to foot and halfway back up again. Charlotte shifted protectively closer to him, and Lady Armitage's attention snapped her way. Charlotte flinched so slightly it might have been a mere blink. No wicked old pirate woman scared her!

Not completely, anyway.

"Who are you?" the lady demanded.

"Charlotte Pettifer," she replied. "I have come for my amulet."

"Pettifer, Pettifer. Goodness me, not by any chance niece to Judith Plim, who leads the Wicken League of witches?"

Charlotte stared silently in reply. Lady Armitage had a smile like a hangman's noose.

"Well, well, a pirate and a witch standing together at my door. I must have lived forever because now I've seen everything."

"We are not together," Charlotte replied with exasperation. "Why does everyone keep saying this?"

"We are merely in proximity to each other," Alex agreed. "As enemies. Mortal enemies."

Lady Armitage leered at their joined hands. "That's a very interesting degree of proximity. But why are two nice children like you bothering me? Have you not heard I am an evil genius, scourge of the skies, voted World's Most Notorious Pirate in 1882?"

Alex and Charlotte glanced at each other. Charlotte shrugged. "Actually, no."

"I heard you use snake oil for your arthritis and have a habit of parking on other people's roofs," Alex added.

"Well I never!" The smug grin snapped shut. The door followed its example and before Charlotte could knock on it in a peremptory manner, or Alex hit it with his sword, the house lurched and flew away.

✻ 18 ✻

CHARLOTTE IS NOT TOO PROUD—
THE NARRATIVE BECOMES A BODICE-RIPPER—LEAP OF FAITH—
A TRAITOR IS REVEALED—ALEX AND CHARLOTTE DISAGREE—
DODO BONES AND DOOMED TREASURES—THE POINT OF NO RETURN

A lady's anger is very rapid; it jumps from annoyance to vexation, from pique to incandescent rage, in a moment.

"Damn!" Charlotte swore, her internal Elizabeth Bennet combusting in one irate syllable.

Alex released her hand, and Charlotte supposed he was disgusted by such an unfeminine outburst. Her heart cracked and fell heavily into her stomach. But it became apparent he had merely been freeing himself to pull a long-barreled pistol from a thigh holster and aim it toward Lady Armitage's house. Charlotte did not even have time to question the sense in shooting a house before he did so.

A thin dark streak sped through the air. The gun had fired what looked like a string that was now attached to the house by a small, deeply embedded hook. Alex caught Charlotte about the waist and pulled her close.

"Hold on to me," he said. "And perhaps give us a boost of magic in case the grapnel doesn't stick and we plunge to our certain and horrible death."

"Um," was all Charlotte had the opportunity to say before they began to lift off the ground, towed by the ascending house. Astonishment silenced her. Until a few days ago, the greatest height she had visited was the belfry of St. Stephen's clock tower, where she inspected Big Ben (and stole a gold pocket watch from the tour guide as a souvenir). Now, it seemed, she spent half her life in the air. And while she liked to think of herself as an open-minded, adapting kind of person (which goes to show just how self-delusional even the most intelligent woman can be), suddenly finding herself swinging on a length of string beneath a house was rather unnerving.

Seeking in her mind for the calm good sense of Elinor Dashwood or the capability of Anne Elliot, she was surprised to find instead images of her mother.

Until now, Delphine Pettifer, née Plim, had been a whimsical creature in soft focus at the edge of Charlotte's life, warm, cheerful, and doting for twenty minutes before supper or at bedtime. Charlotte had never thought of her as anything more than Mother. Now here were memories of Delphine surreptitiously reading a French novel. Slipping pepper into Miss Plim's tea. Using Miss Gloughenbury's taxidermied poodle in an impromptu game of toss-and-catch with the parlor maid when Miss Gloughenbury was not looking.

Charlotte realized for the first time in her life that Plim did not only mean Aunt Judith, and tightly pinched lips, and going through life with a broomstick stuck up one's opinions. It also meant writing a wicked, handsome pirate's name on one's dinner invitation list.

"*Aereo!*" she said with her mother's verve, and they flew up toward the red door.

But Armitage House tipped abruptly, as if someone had hiccupped in the middle of incantating. It veered toward a rose-vined bungalow, carrying Charlotte and Alex in a long swoop to collide with the bungalow's roof. Alex turned with both arms around Charlotte to protect her from the brunt of impact, an act of chivalry she suspected not even Mr. Darcy could equal. They scrambled to catch hold of the roof tiles with hands and boot heels. Armitage House veered again, and Alex tossed his gun aside before they were pulled in another wild course straight into a chimney or the hard-paved road.

"That house is as mad as its owner," he said. Touching Charlotte's face, he seemed to draw her heart back up from the pit of her stomach, into her throat instead. "Are you all right?"

Charlotte nodded, her voice tumbling over Latin words as she created a bolster of air around them. They were able to haul themselves to their feet, halfway up the roof (or halfway down, which they did not want to think about). Charlotte began tugging urgently at the tiny pearl buttons of her bodice.

"What are you doing?" Alex asked, watching her in bewilderment.

"I can't move properly in this blasted thing," she explained, grimacing as the buttons refused to cooperate.

"Wait." He brought out a large, serrated knife and set about efficiently relieving her of her dress by means of tearing it apart right down the front.

Charlotte raised an eyebrow, impressed. "You've done this before."

"Maybe," he said through a small smile. Charlotte pulled out of her sleeves and the dress fell away, tumbling down the roof like an errant cloud. Charlotte was left barely clad in a thigh-length chemise, a corset covered by a silk camisole, white lace drawers that reached below her knees, stockings that encased the rest of her legs, and ankle boots. Her hair swept in blushing, breeze-stirred waves against the shocking nakedness of her arms. She felt light, liberated—and ready to apply those boots to the posterior of anyone standing between her and her amulet.

Alex was looking at her with eyes more vivid than the afternoon sky. Charlotte knew her own eyes held the same intense energy. He holstered his knife. She began to incantate. They ran along the slope of the roof.

And leaped to the neighboring roof, the incantation propelling them smoothly over the intervening space. Armitage House was swaying as it tried to gain height under the influence of an apparently inept pilot. Racing toward it, boots smacking against the roof tiles and making the cottage's occupants look up from their afternoon tea in confused horror, they leaped again.

Soaring past chimneys and over the road, they landed with a thud on the roof of Armitage House. Laughing, Charlotte shook back her hair. She had never felt more alive. If someone handed her a first edition of *Pride and Prejudice* in this moment, she would throw it away just to watch it fly.

They skidded down the slope of tiles, vaulted the gutters, and came down on a small, wrought-iron-framed balcony. Alex unsheathed his sword. Charlotte smoothed her hair, then opened the balcony doors. They stepped into Lady Armitage's gilded, pink-walled sitting room.

"Ah," said the old lady from where she reclined on a sofa. "There you are."

She cast a smile at them, smug, disdainful: a reprobate needing only one fluffy white cat in order to reach arch-villain status.

"Stand up, madam," Alex ordered, brandishing his sword.

Lady Armitage elevated her eyebrows but, alas, no other part of her body. "Why don't you sit down, boy? Both of you, yes? We can have a cut-throat. No, wait, I mean chin-wag. Ha ha."

On the other side of the room, Tom Eames called out in a voice deprived of its vowels by the cloth tied about his mouth. In a fine suit, his hair slicked with pomade, a red rose in his lapel, and quantities of rope attaching him to the chair, he had been all dressed up and then given no place to go. Nearby, a vicar was also obliged to Lady Armitage's unyielding hospitality. (The two men were, if you will, bridled.) A footman standing by the door had the stark expression of someone who knows that, if he does not obey orders, he'll be married next.

Alex glanced at the men, assessing the risk of the situation in one professional glance, but Charlotte's attention was entirely devoted to the glass-and-gold pendant Lady Armitage wore against her breast.

"I have come for my amulet," she announced in a businesslike tone. "However, I do not wish to intrude, as I know this is not a proper hour for making calls. If you'll just hand it over, please, we shall leave straightaway."

"And," Alex prompted quietly out of the corner of his mouth.

"Oh, yes. And kindly do not steal it again."

"I meant Tom," Alex murmured.

Charlotte blinked a few times. "Tom?"

"Fellow over there all suited up for a wedding, albeit not to his actual fiancée?"

"Of course. Tom. I beg your pardon, Lady Armitage, but in addition to my amulet I require you to hand over Tom Eels."

"Eames," Alex corrected. Charlotte shrugged.

Lady Armitage laughed merrily, a sound like rattling bones. "My, what a forthright girl. I like that. Won't you stay and have some tea? We'll discuss amulets and"—she flashed Alex a matrimonial glance—"other matters."

Charlotte set her jaw. "No, thank you."

"I insist, dear."

"And I insist on leaving."

"Ah, but my insistence comes with bullets."

She directed a significant look past them, her smile uncoiling once more. Charlotte and Alex turned—

And sighed.

Miss Dearlove stood by the balcony doors with a pistol in each hand, aimed directly at their hearts. Or, more precisely, given their height difference, at Charlotte's heart and Alex's stomach, although this seems a nitpicking detail under the circumstance of being held at gunpoint by a cold-eyed traitor.

"You!" Charlotte said.

"Who?" Alex asked.

"Mrs. Chuke's maid," Charlotte explained. "The *pretty* girl."

Miss Dearlove gazed at them expressionlessly.

"In fact, she is my maid," Lady Armitage put in from the sofa. "Excellent servant, pours a perfect cup of tea. Perfect aim, too, so I suggest you don't make any sudden moves. It has been most tiresome having her away spying on the Wicken League—although since it ultimately resulted in my acquisition of Black Beryl's amulet, I ought not complain." She caressed said amulet lovingly, and Tom squirmed in his bonds. "Such an elegant piece of work, and so rich with magical potential. I have been trying different words from the incantation to unlock it. Thus far all I've managed is to explode one little church." She waved cheerfully across at the vicar, who glared back in a most unholy manner indeed. "I can *feel* the power within the glass. At first I was thinking it might help me destroy the Wisteria Society, but why aim so low? After all, we in England are blessed by the most delightfully flammable cities."

She paused to chuckle at the thought, her eyes brightening as if with a lit fuse. Then she shook her head. "But enough exposition of my wicked plans. It is most rude of me to keep you hanging around at gunpoint like this. Dearlove, kindly ring for tea and some poisoned bisc—"

Suddenly the house reeled to port. Lady Armitage toppled off her sofa, hitting the floor with a twang of interesting undergarments. Miss Dearlove staggered. Immediately, Alex spun about, his foot rising to kick the guns from the maid's grip. She tripped backward, hissing in pain. Alex completed the turn, double-punched the footman who had rushed forward, and strode over to capture Lady Armitage before the woman could retaliate. Hauling her up at swordpoint, he winced as she spat curses (and a fragment of boiled lolly) at him.

At the same time, Charlotte incantated the guns from the floor into her own possession. "Nobody move," she said in a tone that might have been more compelling had she remembered to put her fingers on the gun triggers.

"You!" Alex snapped to the footman. "Go and tell whatever idiot is trying to pilot this house to bring it down at once. Carefully."

"Or else?" the footman inquired, scowling as he clutched his reddened jaw.

"Or else you're the first one I kill on my way up to the cockpit to take the wheel for myself."

The footman came to attention, ankles clapping together smartly. "Right you are, sir," he said, and dashed from the room.

"This is insufferable!" Lady Armitage declared. "How dare you come in here and interrupt my evil plotting to behave in such a—a— piratic manner!"

Alex laughed, but Charlotte was less amused. "Excuse me," she said, the words bristling with offense. "I am in no way piratic. I am merely hijacking your house, holding you and your servant at gunpoint, and preparing to steal that jewel around your neck. Captain O'Riley, please take the amulet from Lady Armitage and hand it to me."

"Don't try anything foolish," Alex advised the lady as he attempted to lift the amulet on its chain over her stiff hair.

"I say, is that musk cologne you are wearing?" she murmured in a caressing tone.

Alex replied in kind by yanking on her chain. It snapped. "Thank you, madam," he said, smiling as he dangled the amulet before her face.

"You're going to regret this," she warned him gleefully.

Alex shrugged. "Do I look like the sort of person who has regrets?" (A statement he immediately repented as Lady Armitage stroked his body yet again with her gaze.)

"Captain," Charlotte said impatiently, taking a step forward. "If you just pass the amulet to me, we can depart forthwith."

"Mmph," Tom interjected, but nobody noticed him. Alex was regarding the amulet with a slight frown, and Charlotte was regarding Alex with a sterner one.

"Captain," she repeated.

He looked across at her, and a lovely, tender smile touched his lips, but his eyes were oddly dimmed, as if he saw something through her and far away. "You know, we probably should have paused for a real conversation at some point over the past few days."

Charlotte frowned. "What do you mean?"

He tipped his head to one side, taking the smile with it into an emotion more aslant of tenderness. "We have to destroy this amulet, Lottie."

"Destroy?!" she and Lady Armitage echoed in matching tones of horror.

"I understand you have beautiful ideas for its use, and I admire you for that. But no woman should possess such power."

"No *woman?*" Charlotte felt her eyes—and her heart—narrowing.

"Ignore him, dear," Lady Armitage advised. "Every man is a chauvinist at heart. Or at another part of their body they treat as their heart. Better just to shoot him. Go on; no one will blame you."

Charlotte did not even hear the old pirate's words. It seemed as if

218

the entire world had shrunk down to Alex standing opposite her, holding Beryl's amulet. "We cannot destroy it!"

"Why not?" he asked.

"Because . . ." She gestured rather aimlessly with the guns. "*Because*. It is mine. Even if I had not stolen it, thus making it my property—which I did—but even if I had not—although in fact I did—then it would still belong to me by reason of my being the Prophesized True Heir of Beryl Black."

"You know that's just an invention to keep your family in power."

"Ooh," Lady Armitage said. She grinned, looking from Charlotte to Alex as if watching an exciting theater production.

"Of course it was invented," Charlotte replied with a dignity so stiff, Miss Plim could have used it to prop up her topknot. "That doesn't devalue its effectiveness. A prophecy is something a witch intends to make true."

"Fair enough," Alex said, and Lady Armitage's hair vibrated as she turned back to him. "But that only supports my argument. And for all that I trust you, darling, I do not trust your aunt. There can be no risk of her getting hold of such power. We have to destroy it. You know that's the right thing to do."

Charlotte did not care to know what she knew. "You're a pirate," she retorted. "What do *you* know about the right thing?"

He shrugged. "I certainly know enough about the wrong thing. I know what a witch is capable of when she has no limits on her behavior. No empathy. No one who will rouse themselves to stop her. I *know*, sweetheart, and I won't let anyone else experience that if I can help it."

Silence hung between them. Alex's face was stony, but Charlotte saw bruised memory in his eyes, and felt decidedly unwitchy tears rising to her own. Lady Armitage looked like she would murder someone for a bag of popcorn—literally. On the other side of the room, Miss

Dearlove was creeping sidelong toward the bound men and, beyond them, the sitting room door.

"Tell me what's in your heart, Lottie," Alex said in a soft voice that might as well have been full of daggers and spikes, considering its impact. Charlotte flinched with unexpected pain. No one had ever asked her that question. They had regulated her life, her dreams, even the words she spoke—and she'd striven to be exactly what they required. She'd tried so hard, even when it had confused her, even when she had to plagiarize novels to furnish the proper response—because, after all, what else was there? Beneath the prophecy and the rules and the old Latin magic, did she even really exist?

Damn the pirate for believing that she did.

She took a deep breath to answer him, and the world flickered with shadows at the edges of her vision. Raising the guns, she shouted.

"No!"

Alex jolted, but it was too late. Miss Dearlove had tossed a dagger to Lady Armitage, and the old pirate, catching it expertly, had grabbed him, yanking him back against the groaning structure of her gown and pressing the blade to his throat before he could even blink.

"Let this be a lesson to you, boy," she said, her breath hot against his ear, as she snatched the amulet away from him. "I always say that nothing is to be done in robbery without steady and regular attention. If I had known your mother, I should have advised her most strenuously to engage a burglary tutor for you."

"You criminal!" Charlotte exclaimed, the pistols trembling dangerously in her grip. "You are mangling Lady Catherine de Bourgh's words most dreadfully!" Alex gave her an incredulous look; blushing, she added, "And you are wicked indeed to hold Captain O'Riley at knifepoint! Let him go or I will shoot you!"

Lady Armitage smirked. "And risk hitting him? I don't think so. For people who are 'not together,' you two certainly have a fine repertoire of passionate looks. Besides, there are no bullets in those guns."

Charlotte regarded the weapons with frustration, then tossed them aside. Alex saw the magic flare in her eyes and he grasped hold of Lady Armitage's hand with both of his, clenching it so tightly he heard the bones grind together a moment before she yelped and dropped the knife.

"*Aereo!*" Charlotte snapped, leaping into the air. Magic propelled her higher, and as she cartwheeled forward, angling her elegant and explosive boot toward Lady Armitage's head, Alex ducked, escaping the pirate's clutches effortlessly. He heard a loud twang, and turned to see Charlotte being flung backward as she bounced off the solid fan of Lady Armitage's hair.

Alex caught his breath, but she spun with practiced ease and came down on a sideboard. Its display of dodo bones went flying in a bittersweet moment that had Lady Armitage squealing, and Alex took advantage of her distraction to snatch back the amulet. Lady Armitage immediately lunged for him. He stepped away, holding the amulet high out of reach, but the woman kept coming, heedless fury blazing in her small dark eyes. Every instinct in him suggested drawing a dagger or sword and ridding the world of her wickedness once and for all. But in front of every instinct stood a nun in a black habit, smacking a ruler against her hand and frowning. *Do we hurt frail, elderly ladies?* each demanded in a strident Irish accent. *No,* he answered obediently— and winced as they whacked him anyway with their rulers for the inconvenience of having had to ask the question. So he retreated until his back met the sofa, and then realizing himself trapped between a rogue and a hard place, he drew a breath—

And without further thought threw the amulet to Charlotte.

She was so astonished by his trust in her, she missed the catch. As the amulet fell to the floor, their eyes met, and the wry humor in his countered the wonder in hers. Before either of them could blink, Miss Dearlove had appeared between them, calm and quiet as if strolling in a rose garden. She gave one efficient sidelong kick, and the amulet scooted across the floor to disappear beneath the sofa.

"Ha!" shouted Lady Armitage and punched Alex hard.

Then winced as her bones shuddered against his abdominal muscles.

He pushed her away and turned to shove at the sofa even as he heard Charlotte's voice crackling through the room.

"*Proximare!*"

She pointed to the sofa, presumably aiming her magic at the amulet beneath. But the sofa, already in motion, responded instead. It lurched violently into the air, rocking back and forth as its sedentary nature vied with the magic, and then shot toward Charlotte. Instinct had Alex running for her even though he knew he could not outpace speeding furniture.

Charlotte jumped from the sideboard just as the sofa smashed into the wall above, and Alex grabbed her, throwing them both aside. The sofa tumbled to earth with a bone-shaking thud.

Clinging to each other, they inhaled shakily, and Alex rolled so they could more easily get to their—

"Stop right there."

Looking up, he saw a gun barrel, and behind it the sharp red smile of Lady Armitage. His arms tightened around Charlotte.

"It has been a long and tiring week," the pirate complained, "between organizing my trousseau, blowing up the church, and kidnapping the vicar. I appreciate the entertainment you have provided here, but that's enough now. Time to bring an end."

"There are no bullets in that gun," Charlotte reminded her.

Lady Armitage's smile quirked. She pulled the trigger.

Alex hunched over Charlotte protectively as the floor next to them exploded in a screaming shower of sparks and wood chips.

"I am a pirate," Lady Armitage said coolly. "You didn't think I was telling the truth, did you? Dearlove, kindly go and dust the torture chamber. I do believe I shall give myself a hen's party before my wedding tomorrow." She chuckled as she kicked Alex with her booted toe. "Although these two will be the ones squawking."

❈ 19 ❈

Miss Plim was the unhappiest creature in the world. Perhaps other people have said so before, but not one with such justice. She was unhappier than even Miss Darlington; that lady only grumbled, Miss Plim grouched. Everyone could tell what she suffered! But no one cared, for those who complain are never pitied. It would be enough to bring Miss Plim to despair, did she not already live there permanently, with a drafty house, a perpetually withered garden, and a holiday home at the edge of melancholia when she felt like a change of view.

Charlotte's behavior had left her so unhappy indeed, she did not even kneel on Mrs. Rotunder's drawing room carpet to pick out unsightly fluff, as had become her habit since traveling with the pirate. The memory of Charlotte running away from her, hand in hand with a pirate, lurked at the edge of her consciousness, clutching its portfolio of images and chewing on its lower lip, too nervous to venture into Miss Plim's immediate awareness. The last time it tried, it got beaten back by fury and dissociation. It still had the scars: Charlotte had reverted to a young girl and the pirate's face was a snarling shadow flashing with teeth. The memory was taking no further risks, and nudged onto the field instead a gaggle of shivery, high-pitched little complaints about Mrs. Rotunder's weak tea.

Miss Plim set her cup back on its saucer with an expressive *clink*. But no one else in the drawing room noticed. Mrs. Rotunder was busy chastising Mr. Rotunder for taking his arm off in company (it was a wooden arm, fashioned from a leg of a mahogany bedside table, and yes, sadly, Mr. Rotunder did tend to joke about his arm that was a leg). Mrs. Chuke paced with as much agitation as is possible in a heavily bustled dress, fretting about her absent maid, Miss Dearlove. Had the girl been mugged? Murdered? Stolen away to be the bride of a half-mad baron in the Scottish highlands? Or indeed, all three?

Miss Plim lost patience. A sigh exploded from her mouth, followed by a *tsk tsk* that rolled away from it like a burning wheel.

But no one noticed that either, for just then Mrs. Rotunder's butler appeared at the door.

"Visitors, madam," he announced. "Miss Fairweather, Miss Fairweather, Mr. Bassingthwaite; Miss Brown, Miss Brown, Mrs. Eames." He paused, swallowing nervously. "And Miss Jones."

The pirates trooped in like a sentence full of adjectives, adverbs, and exclamation marks, punctuated finally by the tiny black full stop of Verisimilitude Jones, who was generally called, or more precisely, screamed, "Millie the Monster." Even Miss Plim felt rather overwhelmed by it all. She stood, forced another quarter inch of height out of her already straining spine, and glared superciliously at the newcomers.

But since pirates are composed entirely of superciliousness and sweetened tea, no one paid her any notice.

Miss Brown senior stepped forward to greet Mrs. Rotunder. "Gertrude, I love what you've done with your hair! It suits you so much better now!"

"Anne," Mrs. Rotunder replied, smiling. "That dress! You always inspire me with your fashion choices—I wish I too didn't care about what other people thought of me."

Before Miss Brown could counterattack with another brutal compliment, Mr. Frederick Bassingthwaite imposed himself upon the conversation. "Ladies, how magnificent that we are unified here today on this momentous occasion of togetherness, pirate and witch, our hearts singing with the sublime harmonies of true and courageous—"

Miss Plim coughed a word. Frederick's lips began to veer left and come in for a landing.

His wife, Miss Fairweather junior, frowned. She was a grim, bespectacled woman who clearly would have made an excellent witch had she not been born on the wrong side of the incantation.

"Did you just use witchcraft on my husband?" she demanded.

Miss Plim had nothing to hide (other than the silver teaspoon, vintage earrings, and guest soap she had thus far stolen from Mrs. Rotunder). "I did."

Miss Fairweather bowed slightly.

"Ladies, we have come to join the campaign against Isabella Armitage," Miss Brown explained. "She must be prevented from using the amulet in some terrible and dangerous manner before we ourselves have had the opportunity to do so."

"Should be simple enough," Mrs. Rotunder said with a shrug.

"And we must rescue Tom!" Constantinopla Brown added.

"Well, I don't know, dear," Mrs. Rotunder murmured. "After all, the risks involved, and the difficulties of getting . . ."

"We understand there have been some shenanigans involving Captain O'Riley and Miss Pettifer," Miss Brown continued, regaining control of the conversation. "But we must prioritize our efforts. We do not believe they are in any current danger."

"I agree," Miss Plim said coolly. "If there is any danger, it will be *from* my dear niece Charlotte, not to her." Besides, rebellious girls who run from their wise and loving aunties deserve to be left unrescued on their path straight to hell.

"And," Miss Brown continued, "they might be anywhere, whereas we have information stating Lady Armitage is parked on Anchor Road, a mere half mile hence. We must hurry to ambush her. Gertrude, your new grasshopper cannon from America will provide a valuable addition."

"The Whopper Hopper," Mrs. Rotunder said proudly. "I shall fire it up at once."

Excitement filled the room. But Miss Plim cleared her throat in a manner resembling fingernails down a chalkboard, and everyone turned to stare at her.

"Rushing in is foolish," she said. "We must plan our assault carefully."

"Sure," Millie the Monster said, grinning. "Here's the plan: fly over and shoot 'er up."

She hauled forward the enormous rocket launcher she had strapped on her back. It was almost as big as she was, but she propped it against her hip with ease.

Miss Plim eyed the launcher with distaste. She could imagine the mess it would create—someone would be sweeping up dust for weeks afterward. "Perhaps a little more nuance might serve us well," she suggested.

"Nuance?" The pirates looked at each other in confusion. "Nuance?"

"I think she said 'no aunts.'" Millie growled, turning her weapon in Miss Plim's direction. "We can agree with that, can't we?"

Miss Plim raised a smile, which looked as deadly as the rocket launcher.

"Ladies," Mrs. Rotunder said hastily. Having spent the past few days with witches, she understood something now of how their minds worked. (Hence the weak tea, which she had suffered herself just for the enjoyment of seeing their faces as they tried to drink it.) "We are fortunate to have with us Miss Plim, the greatest witch of her generation." Catching Miss Plim's sharp glance, she politely amended, "And several generations before that. We also have Mrs. Chuke, authoress of various pamphlets on Correct Etiquette for the Burgled and Importuned."

"Darlings," Mrs. Chuke murmured bashfully, and would have brought said pamphlets from a pocket of her dress, but Mrs. Rotunder plowed on.

"I suggest we make the most of these ladies' exceptional talents."

"Hm," Miss Plim responded, lifting her chin with regal acceptance of her due.

"Hmmm," the pirates responded more ponderously, mouths twitching as they tried not to glance at each other.

And so it was that the two witches were sent to the front line of Anchor Street, where they were given the vital role of keeping pedestrians at bay while the Wisteria Society did the tedious work of storming Armitage House.

"This is a bad idea," Miss Plim said with a mixture of disapproval and glee as she watched the four pirate battlehouses gather for attack. "You mark my words, Mrs. Chuke. Or rather, my word. Nuance, Mrs. Chuke. *Nuance*."

"Sure," Mrs. Chuke agreed (despite not actually knowing what *nuance* meant) and pulled out a bag of bonbons while she awaited the show.

The battlehouses lowered themselves toward the street, magic crackling in the air as butlers chanted the navigational incantation. Their black flags whipped in the sea breeze. Their flowering window boxes suggested the colors of blood and gore—poppies and azaleas being currently in season. Four windows swung open to expose enormous gun barrels and rocket launchers.

The elegant, red-doored townhouse set halfway along the street did not respond. Whatever Lady Armitage was doing inside it, she failed to realize she was about to be blown into a thousand pieces.

Mrs. Chuke popped a bonbon into her mouth. "I wonder where Charlotte is?" she mused.

Miss Plim shrugged. Hard-eyed, her jaw clenched with a brutal silence, she waited impatiently for the explosions, as if they would satisfy the well of emotion plugged up tight within her body.

For Mrs. Ogden, resident of 23 Anchor Road, Tuesdays meant a supper of bangers and mash while reading the latest *Women's Penny Paper*, perhaps with a bit of pudding afterward if she'd had a hard day and needed a treat.

Mrs. Ogden usually had a hard day. Life in Clacton-on-Sea was difficult indeed. For instance, yesterday she had gone to the store for dandelion wine, but they were all out of stock. And just this morning she'd nearly been knocked down by a pretty strawberry-blonde-haired girl waving a map and saying, "North, I tell you! North!" as she strode ahead of a man, clearly her husband, whose expression was far more irritated than you wanted to see on someone carrying so many weapons.

Mrs. Ogden sighed, spooning herself another heap of pudding. It never used to be like this. Back in the days Mr. Ogden was still alive, it used to be a whole lot more boring. He did not condone pudding, for one thing. Bad for the bowels, he'd said. Mr. Ogden had been big on bowels, almost as much as he had been on bathing daily in seawater, which is why it was such a dark and terrible tragedy that he'd accidentally swallowed some unknown sea creature while swimming and died after a week of severe dysentery. "This is for you, Walter," Mrs. Ogden would say in memorial every time she brought a sticky date pud out of the oven and poured custard over it.

Mr. Ogden had not liked sitting at the window looking out either, since it led to hemorrhoids; but in widowhood—to be precise, seventy-five minutes into widowhood—Mrs. Ogden had taken to tucking herself up on the cushioned window seat, bowl of pud or glass of wine in hand, and watching the various doings along Anchor Road. She could rely comfortably on being presented with some dreadful sight: young women and men perambulating together unchaperoned; hatless babies being taken out in cold breezes; Mrs. Witters next door chatting to the milkman even though she was married, the hoyden.

But this evening, as she settled down to watch the day fade into twilight, Mrs. Ogden was met with a sight more dreadful than any she had before experienced. She almost choked on pudding as she stared out at it, her lace curtains twitching.

Four pirate houses hovered in the street outside.

Pirates! In Clacton-on-Sea! Egads, how ~~exciting~~ ghastly!

The windows flashed in the lowering sunlight. The chimneys puffed little white clouds that floated away like sheep—er, flying sheep that slowly disintegrated. (In all fairness, living with Mr. Ogden would weaken anyone's imagination.) The scene might have been quite picturesque were it not for the whopping great guns protruding from some of those windows.

Suddenly, Mrs. Ogden's house shook with an enormous booming sound. The pudding spoon clattered against her teeth; her heart clattered against her ribs.

"Well I never!" Mrs. Ogden grumbled as a shiver of dust fell into her pudding. Just what did those pirates think they were doing? Anchor Road was a peaceful place (except when Mrs. Witters giggled loudly at the milkman). People couldn't come around shooting cannons willy-nilly. Lucky for them Mr. Ogden was no longer alive, or they'd be getting the sharp edge of his—

Boom!

The house shuddered again. Mrs. Ogden nearly fell off the window seat. More dust was falling, and an unpleasant odor of smoke began to fill the room. Mrs. Ogden got unsteadily to her feet. A moment later, the window exploded as a small rocket howled through it, passing her at such proximity her puffy white hair sizzled, and then embedded itself in the far wall. Three clay ducks that had been flying perpetually toward the ceiling finally achieved their goal, albeit only briefly and in pieces.

"Oh I say!" Mrs. Ogden clasped her bosom with astonishment.

"Surrender!"

The demand roared out, accompanied by copious door-thumping. Mrs. Ogden reached automatically for her rolling pin.

"We know you're in there!"

Mrs. Ogden's eyes narrowed. She recalled Mr. Ogden saying those same words on their honeymoon as she hid in the outhouse, eating leftover wedding cake. She'd been squidgy back then, but marriage and widowhood had fired her spirit (and had a remarkable effect on her feces). Tugging on her cardigan to straighten it, she marched to the front door, yanked it open, and swung out wildly with the rolling pin.

"A Brit never surrenders!"

Several women in magnificent hats leaped back. They stared at Mrs. Ogden in horror.

"You're not Isabella Armitage," said one. The ostrich plume in her turban swooped as she surveyed Mrs. Ogden's brown cardy and woolen skirt.

"I most certainly am not," Mrs. Ogden replied, then noticed the wreckage of timber and roof tiles in her front garden. She looked up at the gaping hole that had been her spare bedroom's wall. "What have you done to my house?!"

"It was an innocent mistake," the plumed lady said. "Why on earth would a civilian paint their door red?"

Mrs. Ogden's cardigan buttons strained against the swelling of her bosom. "I chose that color for the sake of my poor dead husband!" Mr. Ogden had always despised red.

"Oh. Er. Well." The pirates shuffled awkwardly, rubbing the backs of their necks and casting embarrassed glances at each other. "Terribly sorry. Awful shame. I say, you haven't happened to see another house around here with a red door? It has white shutters same as your house has—er, had."

"No." Miss Ogden's eyes had begun narrowing again. She placed one fist against her hip; the other still gripped the rolling pin with all the determination of a Boudicca, or Queen Elizabeth, or the person who'd dobbed in the milkman for fraternizing with his married customers. "So what are you going to do about compensating me?"

The pirates murmured amongst themselves. The plumed one turned back with a dazzling smile. "Would three diamond necklaces suffice?"

"No," said Mrs. Ogden.

"Oh." Further consultation took place. "How about three diamond necklaces and an emerald ring?"

"No. I know what I want."

She smiled then, her cheeks rosy and her eyes bright, looking for all the world like someone's dear old granny. The pirates as a group went suddenly pale, remembering their own grannies and recognizing just how big a mistake they had made.

Half an hour later, the pirates and their witch guests departed. Mrs. Ogden stood cheerfully beside the remnants of her picket fence, holding a piece of paper containing scrawled Latin poetry, and deciding which of the houses along Anchor Road she was going to steal.

She chuckled. Mr. Ogden would certainly not have approved.

Miss Plim, on the other hand, was silent as she sipped tea and watched Mrs. Rotunder navigate south across the town in search of Armitage House. She did not mention *nuance,* or even smirk once. But Mrs. Rotunder knew, and thus learned the power of witchcraft even without words.

On the shore road below, Daniel Bixby glanced up as the Rotunder house cast its shadow over him. He had escaped the bonds Miss Dearlove had left him in, despite their surprisingly strong knots, and was now leaning against a wall with his hands in his trouser pockets, watching several women poke around Alex's house on the pier. At first he thought they were pirates, for they appeared to have been involved in some kind of catastrophic haberdashery incident, but after several minutes passed without them drawing guns on each other, he realized they were, in fact, witches. One woman holding a small white dog was applying a tool to the door's lock with a determination that should soon have entertaining results, considering the booby trap Bixby had installed only last week.

"Fine weather we're having," someone said.

Bixby turned to see a bony, pale-haired man standing next to him. "Hm," he replied, squinting up through his spectacles at the gray sky, which promised rain.

The man sniffed, and Bixby restrained an instinct to pass him a handkerchief. "I'm looking for a girl."

A small silence passed, in which someone with an easier sense of humor would have said, *Aren't we all,* but Bixby simply regarded the fellow until he blinked those strange, uncomfortable eyes.

"Twenty-one, strawberry blonde hair, name of Charlotte Pettifer. I wonder if you've seen her?"

"No," Bixby said.

"Are you sure?"

"Yes." He went on gazing with such dispassionate stillness that the man actually took a step back.

"Well, now." The man sniffed again. "I think you may be mistaken."

"I am never mistaken," Bixby replied.

The man scowled. It should have been frightening, but Bixby had worked for years with half-mad pirates, had even spent ten minutes in polite conversation with Miss Darlington, and a mere scowl from what was clearly a policeman did not trouble him. He turned to go—

And the man caught his arm.

The question of whose humerus bone would have been broken must remain unanswered, for at that moment the witch sprang the door's booby trap.

Boom!

The pier shook. The witch fell back with a second, smaller explosion of supportive undergarments. Her white poodle soared into the air, coming down with unexpected force on the head of the pale-eyed policeman.

There followed a third and inexplicable explosion of sawdust. Bixby coughed disapprovingly. When he could see again, he realized the dog was beyond saving, and obviously had been so for several years. The witches were in a flutter that proved them all alive. And so with a shrug he stepped over the policeman's unconscious body and went off in search of some dinner.

EVERY LADY NEEDS A SHE SHED—ALEX IS ENTERTAINED—
CHANGE OF TACTICS—ALEX WISHES FOR AN EXPLOSION—
MUTUAL DISAGREEMENT—WATER-COLORED MEMORIES—SILENCE

L ady Armitage was excessively fond of dungeons. There was always so much discomfort, so much elegiac charm, about them. She had built herself one in the cellar of her battlehouse, where she might drive husbands down at any time, and collect a few gruesome memories, and be happy. She advised everyone who was going to maraud, plunder, marry, or generally commit piracy, to build a dungeon.

Alex himself also had a dungeon in his cottage, since the house had belonged to another pirate before him. He stored his beer and potatoes there.

Sitting now on the stained wooden floor of Lady Armitage's oubliette, staring into the shadows, he thought he had never been more content. His back ached as he leaned against the wall, he was literally in sore need of a cushion, and he very much wished he had not thought about beer and potatoes, considering his last meal was hours before. But none of this signified in comparison to the pleasure of Charlotte's company.

She appeared to have forgotten he existed, other than the times when, in the course of her pacing, she stepped over his outstretched legs. Each time she did so, her expression was careless, but her boots gave an eloquent clack against the floor, and Alex had to struggle not to laugh. He knew if he did, she would ignore him even more vehemently.

The dungeon's bolted door, high tiny window, wall shackles, and spikes occupied all her attention. She worked upon them with an effort that went undeterred by its complete and utter failure. At one point she even levitated parallel to the ceiling, searching for a possible trapdoor. But incantation, boots, fingernails, outraged witch glare all proved inadequate. Alex watched her grow more pale, more furious, as time wore on. He thought she had never looked more beautiful.

But then, he was starting to realize she could be covered in effluent and he'd still think her beautiful. She could be deeply asleep and yet fascinate his senses. In fact, more than once this week he had accidentally woken her by stroking the smooth little half-moon of her thumbnail or tasting the pulse at her wrist. There always followed a moment in which their eyes met undefended, as bare as their bodies in the night-shrouded bed, and he could see in hers the same loneliness and longing he felt himself. Seconds later they would be hiding them again behind passion—mouths burning together, legs tangling, bodies having a conversation their hearts were not brave enough to undertake. But Alex found himself scarcely able to sleep for the sake of that tiny moment. He looked for it through the day also, yearning, frightened, more vulnerable than he'd been in years.

Even now, while she applied herself yet again to the door's handle as if she might have missed something all seventeen previous times, he watched her in case she glanced back. He followed every movement of her lips as she muttered magic. He guessed what she would do next, and grinned with a boyish thrill when she did so. He was fascinated by her, spiky little witch that she was, and being locked in a dungeon with her now did not feel grievesome in the least.

He himself saw no need for wasting energy on escape attempts. This was not his first stint in a dungeon, even if not counting the time he got drunk on beer in his own and accidentally locked himself in. He felt confident Lady Armitage would eventually turn up to gloat, threaten torture, or propose marriage, and so they might as well wait as comfortably as they could. Charlotte did not seem to appreciate this. He could have sworn he heard her mutter *work ethic* once or twice amongst her magical Latin. It endeared her to him all the more.

At last, as visibility decreased with the fading of daylight through the window, she came to sit on the floor beside him. The manner in which she did so, stiff-backed and precise, communicated clearly that this was no surrender to the situation, but rather a change to more subtle, long-term tactics. She gave Alex one sidelong glance then looked away, adamantly disapproving of his piratic insouciance.

He shifted slightly closer.

She sniffed, raising her chin and glaring at a spiderweb in one high corner. Alex could almost see brooms in her eyes.

He put his arm around her shoulders.

She huffed—

And leaned rigidly against him.

Smiling to himself, Alex closed his eyes, breathing in her now-familiar scent of good plain soap. Even after a day of running, leaping, and generally scraping herself against the rough edges of life, she smelled like he imagined perfection would smell if someone managed to bottle it. He was hard-pressed not to take off his coat and lay her down on it so as to while away the cloistered hours kissing every single inch of her luscious skin. But he was not quite that much a scoundrel; besides, he suspected Charlotte would consider it improper behavior for a dungeon.

"Everything will be all right," he promised. These were the same words he'd used when they were first locked into the room, and she appeared to like them as little now as she did then.

"That is impossible to determine," she said, her voice sounding remarkably similar to how her heels had on the floor. "What if Lady Armitage is even now discovering how to use the amulet to its full capability? Think of what she might destroy while we sit here *resting!*"

"Refusing to purposelessly exhaust myself is not the same as resting. Try to preserve your energy too, darling. You'll need it when Armitage returns for us—as she certainly will before she attempts any destruction. She's the sort who likes an audience."

Charlotte muttered under her breath, and Alex tried not to smile, recognizing in her vexation a reluctant agreement. She squirmed, apparently trying to get herself more uncomfortable. Her shoulder pressed at a difficult angle against his rib cage, but he dared not stir even a little to relieve the annoyance, lest she decide to move entirely away from him.

"Where do you think we are?" she asked.

Alex looked around the room. "This is called a 'dungeon,' I believe. You can tell from the great big lock and the torture device on the wall."

She clicked her tongue with exasperation. "I meant, the house itself."

"Still in Clacton, I'd say. Armitage might try to escape under the cover of darkness, but that's risky, even for one so deranged as her."

"Certainly she has qualities which I had not before supposed to exist in such a degree in any human creature."

Alex opened his mouth to reply, then closed it, frowning with puzzlement. "I feel like I've heard those words before."

"I doubt it," she muttered. "I've seen the kinds of books you have in your house."

He did not understand what that had to do with anything, but he was at least wise enough not to inquire. Instead, he kissed the top of her head, then bent to kiss her brow. It was as if each kiss eased the great aching knot that bound his heart. He would have continued on, but she hummed contentedly and relaxed against him, and he sat back with a sigh.

Slowly Charlotte's breath slowed, her Plimmish stiffness melting into a warm, quiet lassitude. Alex frowned as the knot shifted up into his throat. She'd slept in his arms over the past week; he ought to be used to it, not feeling like any moment he might cry.

He held her tighter, for no reason except to flaunt the muscles in his arms. He laid his big strong hand with its ruby thumb-ring against her dainty one. The juxtaposition of rough, tanned skin against a smoothness that had been protected by gloves and crèmes thrilled him.

How odd. He'd spent years developing his potency, stocking it with weapons and outfitting it with leather and boots, bashing it against the world so he could steal whatever was left afterward—only to feel more powerful in this moment than ever before, although all he did was quietly hold a woman in her gentleness.

A woman—a witch.

Memory twisted suddenly in the pit of his stomach. Instinctively he clenched his hand to reach for a weapon, despite the fact they had been taken from him by Lady Armitage's footmen. He might have punched the wall instead, but then Charlotte was speaking, and the hushed blur of her voice distracted him.

"You were right."

Alex blinked. "I was what?"

She tilted her face up to give him a sleepily factitious look. "You heard me, sir. You merely want me to say it again. Very well, since you do deserve the acknowledgment: you were right. The amulet must be hidden away—or broken apart—or, I don't know, thrown into the sea. I confess, I am not sure I'd trust even myself with it."

He went on blinking, his vision switching between Charlotte's beautiful, luminous eyes and the darkness inside him. "You'd give up such enormous power?"

"Yes." Wariness tightened her expression. "You seem to find that unbelievable."

He tried to answer, but his pulse had begun thudding with such force, it broke his breath into soundless pieces. *You were right.* The words were turning him all soft inside, and he began to panic. Softness meant his defenses were failing. Already he could hear whispers rising from the dark. He wanted his sword. He wanted to bloody well stop feeling at all. But Charlotte was touching his face now, muttering something about how he could trust her, and a barrage of hope, lust, fear, grief threatened to completely overwhelm him. Damned if the witch wasn't doing housekeeping in his heart.

He could not bear it. So he picked his favorite of those feelings and, capturing her jaw a little too roughly in his fingers, began kissing her out of her sleepiness into a tumult of emotion right along with him. She murmured against his lips but did not pull away, and he took that as permission. He tasted the warmth of her—*felt the crack of a birch switch against his back*—tilted her chin so he could kiss the silky white throat beneath it—*crawled into a corner*—clenched a fist in her bright, honey-colored hair—*turned his face to the wall, although that was no sanctuary from birch or bootheels or the spitting Latin that fired books across the room at him until he said one word enough times for it to count* . . .

"Sorry," he whispered again now, the sound trembling against Charlotte's pulse.

She answered him, but her words echoed with the clatter of tiny golden bee charms as a fist slammed against his ear. "Sorry," he said again, following a path of tiny freckles down, down, toward shadow and secrets . . . He breathed in for one last desperate moment before memory drew him under.

He cringed as the closet door slammed shut on him. The whole world turned to shadow. *Sorry,* he cried, and the darkness crawled into his lungs, filling them with the sensation of clinging, corrupting damp. He imagined rotting away in that darkness, amongst his father's old coats. When Deirdre unlocked the door for him two days later and demanded a proper apology for whatever it was he'd done, he was unable to answer, all his words decomposed.

"You don't get out until you say sorry," Deirdre warned, smiling in the way that always made him think of hooks and bones. She held the door half-open, ready to slam it shut at a whim's notice. Her voice, dry and crackly from years of incantating instead of walking across a room to pick up whatever she wanted, dropped hard little promises at his feet. "Say sorry and you can come out. Say sorry and you can have dinner. There's bacon, Alex. We all know how much you love bacon. Say sorry and there's hot chocolate."

He tried, but only managed a crippled sound. "S-s-s-"

Deirdre laughed and started to shut the door again. *At least I'll die in peace,* he thought.

But his father, furious and determined to make a man of him somehow, pulled him out—dragged him through the kitchen where he could smell the bacon and thought only with surprise that Deirdre had been telling the truth—and tossed him out of the house ten feet above Lough Caragh . . .

His body flashed cold as if it were hitting the water again. He felt himself being sucked terrifyingly deep into the old dark. With an instinct of hope and longing, he reached up toward light—and as he moved, the shift of his legs against hard wooden planks beneath him brought time crashing back into place.

Floor, not lake bed, he told himself. *Walls, window. Now, not then. Breathe . . .*

"Breathe, Alex." Charlotte's voice came out of the dark, taut but certain, like a lifeline. "Tell me what's wrong."

He supposed her sensitivity had sensed tension in the air; either that or he'd been screaming without realizing it. Which, judging from past experience, was always possible. "Nothing's wrong," he said. He could swim for himself. He always had. He didn't need anyone now.

And then he felt a warmth against his heart. She was touching him again.

Oh God.

"Alex," she said, uncharacteristically gentle. "Your pulse is racing."

He gave her a swaggering smile. "It's because you're so close, sweetheart, and I want to—"

He stopped, choking on the words as if they were lake water. She *was* so close. She was right inside his soul, prodding bossily at all the things he kept hidden there, making him forget how to be sardonic, or seductive, or any of the measures that had protected him from himself these past twenty years. This was why he'd worked hard to create a reputation that would attract only the kind of women who wanted to ring his doorbell then run away before they were caught. But of course witches made it their business to get in.

"What do you need?" Charlotte whispered, still prodding.

He answered her in the same way he drew his sword whenever someone disturbed him—immediate, unthinking, with sharp edges and a brutal warning. "For all the bloody witches in the world to have their power stripped away."

But Charlotte only stroked the wall across his heart, undaunted. "All of them, you say?"

"One of them," he relented. "One Lancaster witch who found herself in Donegal some two-and-twenty years ago with a fancy for a man, never mind that he was already taken, and a determination to get herself a home even if it had to be made from bones pasted together with blood."

"That doesn't sound very weatherproof."

He laughed. Good God—she made him laugh, even in the midst of talking about Deirdre. It was some kind of magic. *She* was magic.

Her hand pressed with a firm serenity against his pulse as if she could settle it just from her will alone. "This witch hurt you."

"Aye, well, who didn't, darling? Once one person starts, seems it's hard for everyone to stop."

"And is she still alive, resident in Donegal?"

The calm, conversational tone of her voice sent a thrill along his nerves. "Will you fly on over there, Lottie, and wreak vengeance for me?"

She shrugged. "I may. If I have nothing more pressing in my calendar next week."

"My terrifying girl. But fear not, the witch died from consumption some years ago. The father's totally banjaxed from whiskey half the time, can hardly stir himself, let alone his house. And the nuns—"

He stopped, memories extinguishing any humor in him.

Charlotte went back to stroking, soothing. "I'm so sorry."

He shrugged. He shoved a hand through his hair, glaring at the torture device on the far wall even though he could see nothing but darkness. Why couldn't Armitage have put them in it, rather than leaving them to talk about feelings? Clearly the ferocious old pirate understood well how to best employ her dungeon on a man.

"It's all grand, my darling," he said, as if that might have some hope of stopping the conversation.

"Don't be preposterous!" Charlotte said. "It is not grand; it is appalling and utterly intolerable that anyone caused you harm. Well, it shall not happen again so long as I am in your company. Lady Armitage may have confiscated my besom, but I still have my voice."

He grinned. "You'll keep me safe, will you?"

Her eyes narrowed in the way he loved, all fury and adorable deadliness. "Are you laughing at me, sir?"

He did laugh then, but he also raised a hand in assurance. "By God, Charlotte Pettifer, I would not ever."

"Excellent. Because I am serious. And I am a powerful witch, Alex. I prophesize that no one will hurt you again. Not even you yourself."

He drew her closer. "Ah, you're awful good to me, Lottie."

"I am not," she protested, all stiffness in her voice but growing soft again, warm and lush like the aftermath of magic, in his arms. "*Good* is for civilians."

"True, that."

"You told me once you knew a woman with a bee bracelet. Was that her?"

"Aye."

She reached for the bracelet on her own wrist, and Alex frowned as he watched her try to tug it past the heel of her hand. The bee charms clattered as if in protest. "What are you doing, my darling?" he asked.

"I would not want to wear anything that reminded you of her."

She yanked harder, wincing as metal dug into her skin. Alex's heart leaped. He laid his hand over hers. "No, it's fine. Thank you. But you're so far from being like Deirdre as to be holy water on my memory." Lifting her hand, he kissed the knuckles.

"Oh." She blinked as if he'd whispered some spell over her and now all she could see were sparkles in the deepening dark. But it took her only a moment to sweep them away and restore her equanimity. "Well, good. I'm glad that is all sorted."

She patted him, woman-like, clearly believing her job done. He had been ruffled—discomposed—and reorganized—in thorough witch fashion.

But even as he began to relax, she proved to have one more intervention up her sleeve.

"You know, when your accent comes through, you sound like a poet standing on a wild shore. I remember when I first met you I thought you must be strewing poetry like bombs all through London, making a ruin of women's hearts. I suspected you of being very untidy indeed."

"And now?" he asked warily.

She shrugged her mouth. "Now I know exactly how untidy you are. It is . . ."

He held his breath . . .

". . . compelling."

He laughed again, and marveled at the way the dark, endless suck of lake water in his mind ebbed away.

"What do you want, Alex?" she asked.

He imagined inside her brain a tiny Charlotte standing in her knickers and chemise, holding a clipboard and waiting to add his response to her checklist of How to Manage Alexander O'Riley. An answer rushed at once from his warmed-up heart, but he dared not speak it. All his weapons were gone, but even if he had them he'd not feel safe enough to tell her the truth. *You, witch. I want you.*

And he certainly would not admit to her how she'd infiltrated his defenses from the very start—at least not by using words that were half-buried like land mines inside of him. *Love, beautiful, naked.* He loved the darts in her beautiful, deadly shoes. He loved the way her hair felt, slipping over his naked skin. And he loved how her own defenses came apart like a windblown rose when he smiled at her, for all she tried to hide it from them both. He'd spent the past few days smiling more than he ever had in his life, just to watch its effect on her, the darkening of her eyes and the way her properness cracked until she was muttering insults that not only rang his doorbell but his fire alarm as well. He loved it.

He loved her. And not just in the metaphorical sense. The thought of her leaving him, returning to London and the witches' League, hurt like hell.

Damn.

He was most definitely not telling her that.

But it was true. The aggravating little witch had crashed him with her magic, and there was nothing he could do about it. He'd fought smugglers and talked back to Irish Catholic nuns, but there was no defeating this soft-skinned, sensitive grenade of a woman.

"Alex?" she prompted.

"What do I want?" he echoed lightly. "Dinner, my darling. I want dinner, and a bottle of wine."

She sighed. "You are incorrigible."

"At last, something we can agree upon." He smiled, and lifted her gently onto his lap so she would be more comfortable than on the cold, hard floor. She nestled close, laying her cheek against his shoulder. It felt like a whole-body kiss.

I love you, he thought silently, trying not to tremble.

"Fiend," she muttered.

"Witch," he replied, stroking her hair as her breathing grew lighter, lighter, until at last she slept.

And he sat there staring into the darkness, thinking, *Damn, damn.*

❊ 21 ❊

There is no charm equal to the tenderness of a soft mattress. Charlotte certainly felt that as she woke in the morning light after sleeping on the dungeon's icy wooden floor. Her bones ached and her skin, unprotected by layers of muslin, silk, and wool, was ready to start a petition for a return to conservative clothing.

But none of that mattered as she opened her eyes and saw Alex's face. He was still asleep, his arm curved around her protectively, and thus Charlotte had the luxury of a few private moments to indulge in staring at him.

She had always considered him handsome, even from the start of their acquaintance, when she shared the same first impressions of his character that Elizabeth Bennet had of Mr. Darcy's. But now she saw courage in his sanguine attitude, wit in his wayward smile, and in the flickering of his ravishing eyelashes a vulnerability she would fight always to protect. He was a fiend, but also truly a friend, and their conversation last night had proved that. She wished she could demand justice from anyone who had so much as scratched the little boy he had been. Certainly she would punish anyone who tried it now—and would do so even after he left her for his next adventure, as she knew was inevitable. Even after he welcomed the next woman into his bed. He was worth it for his own sake, not just for how he made her feel.

But oh, how he made her feel . . .

There was no denying now that she really liked him, the rogue.

There was, however, denying that she actually loved him. She was not quite brave enough to admit such a thing yet.

Besides, she had known him only a week. How could she fall in love with someone in a week?

Ah, whispered her heart, *but it's been a lifetime of aloneness, waiting for him, and now here he is.*

Nonsense! her brain declared, arms folded tightly and chin tilted, even while her heart waved a volume of Jane Austen's *Persuasion* at it in supporting argument. Besides, Alex almost certainly did not feel the same way about her. He'd said *love* yesterday, but that was clearly a joke. He went to bed with her, but she could mark that down to a desire for entertainment. And while it was true that last night he'd held her with tenderness, Charlotte felt sure with a little effort she could contrive an excuse for this also. Her education had provided her not only with superior wit and a complete understanding of English law (and how to break it) but also what amounted to a bachelor of arts in cynicism. She could explain away just about any kindness. No doubt existed in her mind that Captain O'Riley planned to snatch the amulet and fly off with a farewell kiss and a jovial cry of *tally ho!*

But looking at him now, feeling his quiet breath against her face and realizing that at some point in the night he'd put his coat like a blanket over her, she resolved for that plan to fail. He belonged to her!

Elizabeth Bennet would no doubt be shocked by such indelicacy. But then, Elizabeth Bennet really should have boxed Mr. Darcy's ear halfway through chapter three. Just as Emma Woodhouse should have shut the door in Mr. Knightley's condescending face and Fanny should have slapped some sense into Edmund then gone off to London to get herself a decent education. Having now experienced various degrees of communion with a man, Charlotte was of the opinion that Jane Austen's heroines were ninnies.

Maybe from here on she ought to read Mary Wollstonecraft instead.

Of one thing she was certain. She would get her amulet *and* her man. No one would be able to persuade her otherwise.

Suddenly, Alex's eyes opened. He smiled even before they were focused. Charlotte's pulse began to dance, and when she tried to scold it into decorum, it laughed at her and skipped happily on, singing *love, love.* For goodness' sake, it's just *like,* she reminded herself, to no avail. She felt a softening within, and hastily frowned.

"Good morning," she said in a somber tone.

"Good morning, my darling," Alex replied, his Irish accent rolling like music out of sleep's peace.

Charlotte blushed scarlet, powerless to stop the disintegration of her frown and the resultant smile. Mary Wollstonecraft would have turned over in her grave (depending on who was on it at the time, and what they were doing). Elizabeth Bennet and her authorial sisters smirked as their character choices were vindicated. Who was the ninny now?

Alex did not seem to notice her response. He clambered to his feet, taking his coat from her and putting it on. Charlotte sat up more slowly.

"It's simply rude for you to have so much vigor after sleeping the night on a floor," she said, rubbing her aching back.

"It's less vigor than impatience," he said, grasping her hand and pulling her up. She staggered against him, and he gave her a quick one-armed embrace. "I want breakfast. And my regular morning exercise."

His grin made her blush flare again. The accent was gone, taking with it the vulnerability in his eyes, but apparently his ardor remained.

"You might find yourself thwarted in both by the fact we are imprisoned," Charlotte said. "And take it from me, there is no way out."

He laughed. "There's never any point in saying 'Take it from me' to a pirate."

Charlotte stepped back, hands on her hips. "You saw me working last night. You know I found no means of escape."

"I do know," he said, striding across to the door and grasping its handle. "But you didn't try—"

The door swung open.

"—shouting," he finished numbly.

They exchanged a shocked stare. Then Alex laid a finger to his lips and, drawing the door open wider, peered out.

"Huh."

Charlotte came up beside him. "Why is there a rose lying on the threshold?"

"I don't know," Alex said. "Perhaps Lady Armitage is playing some kind of game."

"So what do we do now?"

"We play." Taking her hand, he led her out of the dungeon, closing the door behind him. "Which way, magic girl?"

"Left," she said, indicating where pink rose petals made a trail along the narrow corridor.

"Like sheep to the slaughter. Very well. Tally ho!"

"Really, that is such a daft phrase," Charlotte muttered. "You would never hear a witch say something so ridiculous. We are far too sensible."

"No, you are far too boring," Alex corrected.

Charlotte refrained from arguing, partly due to the need for stealth, and partly because she agreed with him. They followed strewn petals up a flight of uncarpeted stairs, around a corner, and halfway down another stretch of corridor. Whoever had created the trail must have run out of petals, for this could not be the actual destination. Several doors stood shut; the house was silent.

Charlotte judged from the faint light glimmering through a window that dawn had broken only recently. In Pettifer House, no one stirred until at least nine (except the cook, dishwashers, chambermaids, scullery maids, footmen, and butler). It appeared this was also the case in Lady Armitage's household. Now if they could only locate the amulet before anyone woke, they could be out of there without further trouble, and home before the end of the day.

The realization lurched in her stomach. Convincing the League that she was going to marry a pirate would be the most difficult magic she'd ever attempted. Cleaning Alex's house would come a close second. Perhaps best to simply crash it "accidentally" and seek new premises. She did not need a Pemberley per se, but there ought at least to be a decent bathroom and the certainty of no opossum living in the kitchen's chimney.

"Which way now?" Alex whispered, drawing her out of visions of Georgian columns and marble floors.

"Down the aisle," she replied. He looked at her oddly. "The corridor," she amended, managing not to blush. "Down the corridor and up those stairs."

She assumed Lady Armitage would keep her bedroom on an upper floor like a proper (albeit mad and murderous) lady. So they went up, wincing at every slight noise their boots made on the treads. Then they walked another corridor until they met a closed door, with no further passage available. Charlotte was about to suggest they turn around when a slight clattering came from within the room. Alex reached instinctively for his sword, then mouthed a curse as he remembered it had been taken from him. Despite this, he opened the door before

Charlotte could supply him with one of a dozen excellent reasons not to do so.

Lady Armitage's cockpit lay before them. Either that or a lounge in a brothel, but since the latter generally did not include large, spoked wheels, Charlotte felt confident in her initial assessment. (She might have been surprised had she actually visited such a place.) The room contained several pastel-colored fainting couches, statues of unclothed gentlemen who were more happily endowed than those in museums, the aforementioned wheel, and lying on the floor beneath that wheel, Miss Dearlove.

The traitorous maid sat up hurriedly as they entered. In her hand was a screwdriver.

"What are you doing?" Charlotte demanded.

"What does it look like?" Miss Dearlove replied in a quiet, even tone.

"Like you are carving your name on the wheel shaft in an act of petty vandalism common to household servants."

Miss Dearlove and Alex stared at her incredulously.

"She's sabotaging the wheel," Alex said.

"I'm sabotaging the wheel," Miss Dearlove agreed. She got to her feet, folding the screwdriver back into a besom. "Why are you up here? I left you a trail of rose petals leading to the sitting room, where Lady Armitage is preparing to hold a marriage ceremony."

"Why did you help us?" Charlotte asked.

Miss Dearlove regarded her coolly, and Charlotte had a sudden, inexplicable desire to run out and pay taxes. She had never before given much attention to the bland little maid, not even when Miss Dearlove had been aiming a gun at her. She realized now the woman's inconspicuousness had been a clever disguise.

"Lady Armitage will no doubt include the amulet in her bridal ensemble," Miss Dearlove replied. "I suggest if you want it, you hurry downstairs."

"You sabotaged the wheel yesterday too, didn't you?" Alex said. "Loosened its connections so the incantation pathway was disrupted and the house couldn't be properly steered?"

Miss Dearlove ignored this question also. "Vicar Dickersley has agreed to perform the ceremony. Lady Armitage offered him a substantial compensation: his life. Tom Eames is in imminent danger. You really should make haste."

"Just who are you, Miss Dearlove?" Charlotte demanded.

The woman sighed. "You people have the most confusing priorities. But why am I surprised? Pirates are mad; witches are lunatic. These past few weeks have made me want to join the circus for a rest. I recommend you two get married, so as to keep the insanity contained as much as possible. Now if you'll excuse me, I have somewhere else to be."

They stared in dumbstruck astonishment as she took up a plain, wide-brimmed hat from a table and, pushing ajar a window, stepped up onto the windowsill.

"You're a witch!" Charlotte realized—for someone would exit from an upper-story window only if they possessed the facility to incantate (or had grandiose delusions of invulnerability, which is why so many pirates were injured doing it).

"I am not," Miss Dearlove said, and stepped out.

With a gasp, Charlotte rushed to the window, only to see Miss Dearlove dangling beneath the hat, one hand holding its white ribbons, as she sank at a genteel pace to the ground.

Armitage House was parked beside a Bible bookstore, where the Wisteria Society would never look for it. Once Miss Dearlove set foot on the pavement, she folded the hat remarkably small, tucked it into a pocket, and marched away down the street with the steely manner of a librarian who has just seen someone dog-ear a book's page.

"Who is she?" Charlotte wondered aloud. "And where can I get a hat like that?"

"Why do you need one?" Alex asked. He leaned past her to take a pearl-handled penknife from a desk, tucking it into his boot. "You can levitate with a word."

"But it seems to be operating on a hitherto unknown magic."

"Don't you have enough magic yourself to be going along with?"

"Do you have enough money?"

"Good point." He found a chisel amongst the navigational array and tucked it into his other boot. "We should probably go get that damned amulet." With a sudden pleased sound, he grabbed a long-barreled pistol that happened to be lying atop some unfinished knitting. After checking that it was loaded, he turned with a grin to Charlotte.

"Don't say it," she warned.

"Tal—"

"Don't."

"*Tell* me that you will come downstairs with me, sweetheart."

She gave him a disgusted look and marched from the room, and with a self-satisfied smile he followed her, picking up a letter opener on the way.

It is a convention of adventures that the heroes will arrive in perfect time to save a wretched victim from their doom. Charlotte and Alex considered themselves the heroes in this instance—and certainly Tom Eames was about as wretched as it is possible to be without entering a darker genre of narrative. Therefore it was to general astonishment all round when they burst through the doorway to Lady Armitage's candlelit sitting room just as Vicar Dickersley pronounced these words:

"Man and wife."

Charlotte and Alex staggered to a halt. Lady Armitage, looking up from gazing with adoration at her new ball and chain (and the young man attached to it), smiled cheerfully and waved at them. Dressed in mauve, and with lilies overflowing her grasp, she looked as happy as any woman observed in the middle of her favorite hobby.

Tom had a more furious response, but since he was gagged it came out as mere annoyance.

"I see you found Kitty," Lady Armitage said through her smile.

"Kitty?" Charlotte asked, bemused.

Lady Armitage twirled a finger at the gun Alex was aiming toward her.

"You name your gun?" At that moment, Charlotte realized Miss Dearlove had been right: pirates *were* mad. "Well, hand over my amulet or else Kitty will be shooting you."

"And Tom," Alex added. "Er, that is, Kitty won't be shooting Tom; what I meant—"

"Now see here!" This from the vicar—Lady Armitage showing no concern at the choice of being robbed or shot. "You cannot interrupt a sacred moment like this!" He lifted a hand to gesticulate, and the chain binding him to a table leg rattled obtrusively. Candles set upon the table trembled, and a vase of lilies threatened to topple. But the vicar did not notice. "Have some respect for true love!"

Alex stared at him in amazement. Charlotte, however, only had eyes for the amulet. "Give it to me, madam," she said, striding forward and presenting her hand, palm up, for delivery.

"Never!" Lady Armitage avowed.

Charlotte's patience, driven to its limit, and smelling coffee somewhere in the room, abruptly snapped. *"Proximare!"* she incanted. The amulet rose on its chain, straining toward her.

"Be careful," Alex said, but it was too late. Magic stretched through her body, pressing against bones and muscles. She felt her feet rise off the floor. The amulet flew violently to her.

Unfortunately, Lady Armitage came with it.

The two women crashed. Lilies scattered everywhere. Candles toppled from a nearby table, and the table went too, cloth, tea service, and all. Charlotte fell backward, the pirate atop her, and as they smacked against the floor she immediately rolled over to exchange their positions. But she had not factored in Lady Armitage's hooped petticoat. Once it started rolling, it did not stop. The women flipped over each other several times before being halted by a wall. Immediately, Charlotte began pulling at the amulet, and Lady Armitage began pulling at Charlotte's hair, and the only thing that prevented it from being a catfight was that Alex could not see a clear enough shot to fire Kitty.

Behind them, a candle flame got about its business with quiet dignity, burning a hole through the fallen tablecloth to the carpet beneath. Several new flames leaped up, spreading across the floor. Vicar Dickersley, who had collapsed to his knees as the table fell, began whimpering as he tried to clamber up and away. He liked to consider himself a religious man (always a bonus in his job), but really, martyrdom by fire would be the final straw today.

"Free Tom!" Charlotte shouted to Alex. Granted, it sounded more like *fee om,* since Lady Armitage was smacking a hand against her mouth, but Alex understood. He quickly evaluated the situation and decided she did not need his help. Holstering Kitty, he hurried over to the captive groom and used Lady Armitage's pen knife to slice through the wrist ties. At once, Tom pulled the gag from his mouth and gasped a desperate breath.

"She put the key to our chains in her bodice!"

Alex glanced at Lady Armitage. Charlotte was sitting atop her, tugging furiously at the amulet while Lady Armitage attempted to break her wrists. Charlotte's hair had come free of its bindings and tumbled everywhere; Lady Armitage's had shattered a fallen teacup. As Alex watched, the pirate snatched a porcelain shard and began using it to saw at a long strand of Charlotte's hair. He cringed, for even as a male he recognized the battle was about to explode. There was certainly no acquiring a key under those circumstances.

Suddenly, the candle's fire, having got all its notes together, and with a deep, excited breath, stepped forth onto the stage—or, more precisely, a velvet sofa that was covered in shawls and cushions. With an ironically chilling rush of sound, the whole thing went up in flames.

Vicar Dickersley swooned. Tom grasped the chain attaching him to a table, tugging on it as if that could in any way help. Charlotte and Lady Armitage had resorted to slapping each other's hands wildly. Two footmen rushed into the room—and as Alex pulled the chisel from his boot and threw it at them, rushed right back out again. They slammed the door hard behind them. A tall standing candelabra shook at the reverberations, then toppled against some drapes, which promptly caught alight.

Alex looked around at the chaos and grinned. "Now," he said to himself with satisfaction, "it's starting to get fun."

✳ 22 ✳

ASSAULT WITH A DEADLY TEACUP—LADY ARMITAGE WINS—
BLOOD, SMOKE, AND TEARS—TAKING FLIGHT—
TOM HAS AN AWAKENING—ALEX DOES THE FORBIDDEN THING—
CHARLOTTE IS NO HEROINE—THE MOMENT OF CHOICE

Charlotte knew her own happiness. She wanted nothing but the amulet—or, to give it a more fascinating name, total dominance over the fate of England. Granted, she intended to be good in the most outrageous fashion by destroying said amulet, but that did not detract from the central fact: as Prophesized Heir of Beryl Black, the choice was hers to make. It would be the pinnacle of her duty. And if she represented it as a magnificent victory over the Wisteria Society, it might just appease witchy tempers that were bound to erupt when the Wicken League discovered that not only had she been in cahoots with a pirate but she hoped to go on cahooting with him in the future.

Absolutely, she needed that amulet.

Unfortunately, Lady Armitage disagreed.

They wrestled and slapped each other until the lady pirate managed to stab a teacup shard into Charlotte's arm. Pain rushed through her like a cold wave, smashing everything in its way.

At first she could not understand what had happened; she saw the shard protruding from her arm but did not recognize it; she forgot entirely about amulets and maniac pirates. A moment later, Lady Armitage yanked the shard away and the pain rushed back out, dragging any last fragments of sense with it. Charlotte collapsed onto the floor. Her vision went white, then red, then stayed red. She realized dimly that she was looking at flames.

Lady Armitage hauled herself up, muttering something about annoying girls who did not respect their elders. "You're worse than Cecilia!" she yelled at Charlotte. "At least she did not stain my favorite dress with her blood!"

Charlotte laughed. At last, she had bettered Miss Bassingthwaite! She sat up rather dizzily, wincing at the pain. Her wound did not seem too terrible, but she frowned upon seeing the astonishing amount of blood. Bixby was going to be most displeased when he came to do the laundry.

An unhappy butler posed the least of her problems, however. The sitting room was worryingly alight. Alex had smashed the tables to which Tom and Vicar Dickersley had been chained, and both pirates were dragging the vicar toward the door. Lady Armitage pushed past them, intent on escape. Charlotte tried to incantate a braking phrase to stop the old pirate, but smoke swirled into her mouth, making her cough. Lady Armitage pulled open the door and ran out.

"Alex," Charlotte called out roughly. "She's getting away!"

Alex looked up. Upon seeing her blood-stained form, his eyes blackened with emotion. Charlotte would have found it wonderfully flattering were they in more pleasant circumstances. As it was, she might swoon, but not from romance.

Alex dropped his side of the vicar and, with three great strides, was across the room and crouching before her, grasping her arms urgently. "Are you all right? Where are you hurt? Charlotte?"

She grimaced. "I'd be better if you weren't squeezing exactly where she stabbed me. I'm fine. Let me go; I need to chase her. She still has the amulet!"

For a moment she thought he would argue. She watched emotions wrestle with his countenance until at last something dark and fierce triumphed. Looking at it, Charlotte did not know whether to be awed or frightened. He brought her to her feet and started pulling her toward the door.

"I'll go after Armitage," he said. "You get out. Take Tom and the vicar to safety. Promise me, Lottie."

It was a sensible plan. He had more chance of overcoming Lady Armitage than she did. As a witch, she approved it.

As a woman, she clutched his coat, trying not to cry. "Promise me you will stay safe too."

He grinned with his usual flippant wickedness. "Of course. I know what I'm doing. This is a regular day's work for me, darling. Now out!"

He gave her a little shove, and for once she obeyed without further debate. Rushing over to the vicar, she took up the shoulder Alex had dropped, and disregarding her pain, began helping Tom to haul the man out of the room. The effort was made difficult by the weighty chains, not to mention the sight of Alex dashing up the stairs in pursuit of Lady Armitage, smoke swirling behind him. Charlotte forced herself to just focus on breathing.

A footman ran past, his arms full of silverware. As he barreled down the stairs toward the ground floor, Charlotte realized there was no hope of getting the unconscious vicar down those stairs in time. "We'll have to go out the window!" she shouted to Tom over the crackling of the fire.

The young pirate glanced at the window then back at her, his eyes wide. "It's too high!"

"Not for a witch."

"You don't mean to use magic? But you're a woman; we'll be too heavy for you."

In lieu of answering that, Charlotte threw a dark, sorcerous word at the window. Glass exploded outward, along with a portion of the wall. As Tom stared agog, she gave him a smile as polite as a witch's besom with every device extruded.

"Out you go, young man."

"I think you should—"

Alas, his manly opinion was lost to posterity as he suddenly jolted up from the floor and, along with the vicar, swept on out the window. Charlotte waited, counting in her mind, as Tom's scream informed her of how long the descent took. She gazed up the stairs to where Alex had gone. Everything in her yearned to follow him. But smoke was filling the corridor, and she knew she would be foolish to remain inside. Running to help Alex would be like Tom telling her how to do magic.

And yet, leaving him was agony.

She should have persuaded him to come with her. Never mind the amulet—nothing mattered, nothing, if Alex was not safe.

But such thoughts were neither sensible nor dutiful, and although Elizabeth Bennet might sympathize with her, Charlotte knew most heroines would not. They would tell her to run away and let the man save the day.

And so she climbed onto the windowsill, muttering magic reluctantly. Smoke billowed around her. Heat stroked her back. The house was shuddering as it began to rise, and Charlotte clutched the window frame lest she fall before she could fly. The world had become a blur—she was capable of tears after all, it seemed, for they filled her eyes, blinding her with grief and terror.

I do love him, she thought.

Damn.

She could not leave, regardless of good sense. If love made a pyre for her this morning, then so be it. Turning back carefully on the window-sill, she prepared to run upstairs—to save Alex, and herself along with it.

But magic was not sentimental. It had no heart or heroism. With a witchy calm that felt altogether callous, it tossed her out to the wind.

Alex staggered, colliding with a wall. The house was rising—and at the same time he could have sworn something was falling, dragging his heart down with it. *Let it be Charlotte*, he prayed. Let her be leaping to safety.

And then he continued on along the corridor, because he'd been a pirate all his life and he knew the fate of the world (not to mention the fire consuming Armitage House) was not going to take a break, drink a cup of tea, read a magazine, while he managed his emotions.

Lady Armitage had locked herself in the cockpit. He could hear her voice declaiming the incantation and he winced, for she sounded like an opera singer with laryngitis. She was also mispronouncing the in-cantation in a manner that would be funny had she not just said *accendo* instead of *accedo*, thereby causing the fire to further inflame. Alex began to kick the cockpit door with his boot heel.

"I am not taking callers at the moment, thank you!" Lady Armit-age called out.

"But I think you'll really appreciate what I have to tell you about life insurance!" he called back.

The door proved more durable than he expected. Smoke thickened the air. Suddenly the house rocked, almost tipping him off-balance, and Lady Armitage's chanting devolved into a mad cackle. Damn. She was going to crash the bloody building—amulet, him, and all.

He kicked more urgently at the door. It swung open suddenly, causing him to stagger through, falling to his knees. In his surprise he dropped the gun Kitty, and it scattered away across the tilting floor.

Lady Armitage, holding the door ajar, looked down at him with the kind of smile that really ought to be put in a straitjacket. "You needn't kneel to me, sir," she said. "A mere bow would suffice."

Alex clenched his teeth so as to prevent a reply that probably would have doomed them both. Out the cockpit window he could see the town's rooftops bobbing like boats on a smoke-colored sea. Keeping Lady Armitage as stable as possible was his best chance of keeping the house stable until he could take charge of its steering.

He pushed himself upright, inhaling heated air, groping for calm inside himself. His makeshift weapons would be inadequate against a wily old villain like Isabella Armitage, but he did still have one powerful force in his array.

He was smiling even before he turned to face the old pirate.

"Madam," he drawled charmingly.

She punched him in the mouth.

"It's a disaster!" Tom wailed, clutching at his hair. "An absolute disaster!"

Charlotte frowned. "Pull yourself together, boy. I'm sure Constantinopla will forgive you."

Tom laughed with such a violent hysteria that Charlotte turned away from the swaying, smoke-belching house to stare at him. "No, no, she most definitely won't," he chattered, clutching at his hair. "I married another woman, three weeks before our own wedding!"

"For heaven's sake." It was all Charlotte could do to not slap him. Cecilia Bassingthwaite had been right, a statement she never thought she would make, but it was irrefutably true—men could not be relied upon for rational behavior. "I am certain the marriage was not even legal. Did you say 'I do'?"

"Yes!" he wailed.

"Oh." Charlotte bit her lip. "Well. You shall simply have to not tell Constantinopla."

Tom gaped at her. "Not tell?"

"That's right Keep it a secret. No one is going to believe Lady Armitage, and I'm sure the vicar can be convinced it was a delusion caused by too much smoke inhalation."

They looked down at the man who lay sprawled unconscious on the footpath.

"Won't I get in trouble?" Tom asked anxiously.

Charlotte shrugged. "I would count it as the merest of sins, under the circumstances."

"I didn't mean with God. I meant with"—his voice lowered—"Oply."

"Not if she never finds out."

He drew in a breath to argue—then comprehension began to dawn. Charlotte watched as his expression of dazed misery slipped into a new wonderment. She would have feared what this portended for Constantinopla but at that moment her attention was diverted by a sudden gasp from the crowd of residents who had gathered in their dressing gowns and slippers to watch the dramatic scene. She turned back toward the house just as something exploded in its sitting room. Flames burst from a window. Charlotte's heart felt as if at any moment it would burst too.

"No," she said. "This is not acceptable."

She was no heroine, bravely facing whatever life sent her way. She was a witch, capable of inverting the laws of physics to get things done.

She began striding along the road, half-undressed and splashed with blood, her deadly boots clicking against the road like a *tsking* tongue, her eyes as fiery as the hovering battlehouse overhead. All her life she had tried to restrain herself, to be like a woman in a paper world: a Plim with a teacup and impeccable posture; a nice, proper lady. But now she felt only a bone-deep relief to be Charlotte Pettifer, wicked witch. She did not even care that, as she walked, people scampered away from her, recognizing power when they saw it.

Life had become messy, and Charlotte was going to clean it.

Alex waited to drop dead. He was sure it would happen, for striking a woman was a crime punishable by immediate divine retribution. Never in his life had he even contemplated doing such a thing. He may have sparred with Charlotte, but that was almost like dancing, and he certainly intended her no harm. But when Lady Armitage punched him, instinct responded faster than thought, and he smacked a fist into her midriff so hard, the old woman stumbled backward.

The blow actually hurt him more than it hurt her, as she was wearing a steel-boned corset. But Alex waited on a thunderbolt from the heavens . . . for about two seconds, before receiving Lady Armitage's less-than-holy fingernails clawing at his face instead. Grabbing her wrists in self-defense, he tried to restrain the woman without actually harming her, whereupon she kicked his shin and then kneed him in the groin.

Or rather, she would have kneed him in the groin had not her crinoline petticoat prevented her knee coming within twenty inches of its goal. Instead, Alex found himself gently bumped. This miscalculation set Lady Armitage off-balance, and he took the opportunity to firmly (but carefully) push her back against a wall.

"Why, sir," she said, batting her eyelashes. The ones on the right eye fell off, leaving just a few white wisps. "You only had to ask."

Disgusted, Alex yanked the amulet from her neck and turned away, chanting the pilot stanza as he strode toward the wheel. The house began to tremble like a bashful girl at the sound of his voice.

"Thief!" Lady Armitage cried, throwing herself upon his back.

Her bony arms around his neck tried to throttle him, but Alex was undisturbed. He continued on toward the wheel, incantating loudly over the growing rumble of the fire downstairs. Lady Armitage groped at his mouth, attempting to gag him, and he tasted dust and old perfume before managing to pull her hand away.

The wheel was attached to a plinth in front of a grand floor-to-ceiling window. Alex had just reached it, his fingers touching the wood and his body tingling with ancient magic, when Lady Armitage shrieked in his ear. As he winced away from the noise, she thrust out a leg, hooking it around one of the wheel spokes. The wheel jerked, and the magic stumbled wildly in Alex's throat.

"Stop it!" he yelled. "You'll crash your goddamn house!"

"I'll crash you," she replied, and hooked her other leg around the wheel. The house tipped back and forth like a child's toy. Alex had no choice but to relinquish his plan. If the mad old pirate wanted to go down with her battlehouse, he had little interest in debating the matter with her. He had a green-eyed witch to get back to, and soon thereafter Ned Lightbourne, to seek advice on how to woo Charlotte in the best, most romantic way possible. She may not like him now, but pirates always got what they wanted. He'd steal for her, recite sonnets for her, until she surrendered.

Forcing Lady Armitage off with some difficulty, he pushed the old pirate onto one of her fainting couches and turned to leave.

"Thank you!" she called out, laughing.

Turning back, Alex saw her splayed on the couch, red shoes propped up, amulet dangling from her fingers. He cursed aloud. Somehow she had snatched the blasted thing from his hand without him realizing. While part of him could not help but feel a certain professional admiration for her skill, another part wanted to strangle her with the goddamn gold chain.

"Give. That. Back," he demanded through a clenched jaw.

She rose from the couch, letting the amulet sway. "Come and get it, boy."

Alex strode toward her, but she moved unexpectedly, darting aside, and pulled a lever on the wheel's plinth. The great cockpit window folded open.

Armitage House lurched as its magic destabilized even further. Alex staggered, reaching for the nearest object to steady himself—a naked marble gentleman. It rocked beneath his hands, thus proving Charlotte, Cecilia, Miss Plim, and probably most women of England correct as to the unreliability of men. Alex was immediately pushed into a tripping gait toward the open window.

He grasped at the window frame. His hands caught it firmly, and he almost breathed in relief.

But the rest of his body kept moving, following the tilt of the house, tipping him out fifty feet above Clacton.

Charlotte was still some distance away when Alex tumbled through the window. For a moment her body seemed to fracture internally from the force of her horror. But then she saw he had hold of the window frame, and she pulled herself together in ruthless Plim fashion. This was no time to be emotional.

Around her, the bystanders were gasping, pointing, and passing a bag of biscuits amongst themselves. Charlotte knew she could not levitate to Alex's rescue in front of so many witnesses, but a subtle use of the incantation might still be possible. *Don't let go,* she urged him silently. Aloud, she began to whisper in Latin.

She could see at her periphery a man pushing his way through the crowd, but she ignored him. Only one man concerned her now, only one fear. As a consequence, the fellow was upon her before she realized, grabbing her arm.

"What are you doing, sir?" she demanded, glaring at his pale eyes and bony face. "Unhand me at once!"

He did not oblige. Indeed, his grip became firmer. He had a bandage on his forehead and an expression of revulsion on his thin, pallid face; looking at him, Charlotte felt she ought to know him, as if his presence had dwelled in her life since she was born, just awaiting this hour to become manifest. "Charlotte Pettifer," he said, sniffing moistly. "You are under arrest for witchcraft."

Horror shocked her again. And yet also a strange, weary relief. *I knew it would happen one day,* her mind said, even while her heart began flapping itself in panic. *At least the dread is over.* But although her vision washed with light and she did not know when the next breath might come, she straightened to the full extent of Plimmish righteousness and gave him a cool, contemptuous look.

"Don't be ridiculous, my good man. Witches do not exist."

"Are you quite sure about that?" he asked, a smirk slithering across his lips. And then, with slow deliberation, he looked up.

Following his gaze with her own, Charlotte choked on a cry. Lady Armitage was standing at the open window, bashing Alex's hands with a telescope. One lost its grip, causing him to swing perilously, and the crowd gasped with excitement. Any moment now, he was going to plunge to his death.

Oh God.

This is no time for emotion! her brain reminded her sternly.

Arrrgh! her body replied.

The man leaned forward, snuffling at her hair. "You smell of smoke," he said, and licked the words from his lips. "How appropriate."

His fingers around her arm were as sharp as sticks on a bonfire. His voice was flames. Charlotte wanted to scream now as she knew she would scream when they set a torch to the pyre. What should she do?

She could not think—she knew only that she stood in smoke on a seaside road, inescapably caught between life and love, and nothing in any novel had prepared her for a moment like this.

"I am not a witch," she said out of old, witchy instinct.

The man hissed a laugh. "Let's see, shall we? I give it less than a minute before the pirate drops fifty, sixty feet onto this extremely hard road. Then we shall find out, Miss Pettifer, just exactly who you are."

"I am—" Charlotte began, but her words turned to fire and her heart to ash.

Alex fell.

❋ 23 ❋

CHARLOTTE MAKES HER CHOICE—A SENSELESS QUOTE—
A VOICE RIPPLES THROUGH THE SMOKE—WOMAN'S LIBERATION—
AN INVITATION—THE CAVALRY ARRIVES—THE BUTLER DOES IT—
MISS PLIM EXPLODES—A DISASTER OF TITANIC PROPORTIONS

*D*escendeo lente!" Charlotte shouted.

The man grasping her arm laughed with vicious triumph. But she did not hear him. *"Descendeo lente, proximare,"* she continued, her voice ringing clear and loud above the crackling fire and murmuring crowd. She raised her free hand as if to draw energy from the sunlight to intensify her magic. The words flared. Her hair began to stir around her as the air shimmered and swayed.

And Alex floated through the smoke to land gently on the road.

Immediately he tipped to his knees, coughing. But Charlotte could see through the crowd swarming toward him that he was safe—provided, of course, Armitage House or its burning timbers did not crash down upon him, nor the excited crowd trample him. She felt a pain she could not at first comprehend, until realizing it was her un-conditioned facial muscles striving to manage the vast smile demanded of them.

"Thank you for giving me all the evidence I need," the pale-haired policeman said, his words licking close to her face. But again, she did not hear him, for the crowd was cheering. A group of American tourists explained to everyone nearby that these were circus performers, and immediately a chant began, accompanied by the rhythmic clapping of hands, requesting an encore performance.

The policeman slapped handcuffs onto Charlotte's wrists. "The only performance you will be giving, *witch,* is your funeral speech on the bonfire."

Charlotte jolted as fear once more slammed through her body. "Let go of me," she demanded, tugging against the man's grip, but he had remarkable strength for such a desiccated fellow and clearly no intention of allowing her escape. He continued along the street, dragging her with him. Charlotte saw ahead a horse-drawn police wagon, two uniformed officers standing at its open door. Her heart skittered in panic. Her thoughts flailed as if they too had been cuffed. There seemed no escape. Even if she used her weaponized ankle boots against the man, his colleagues would be upon her instantly.

Striving to recollect any element of the incantation that would save her, she could summon nothing more than the complaint of Marianne Dashwood: "Had I talked only of the weather . . . this reproach would have been spared." Which, while true, was about as helpful as one might expect quoting a novel during one's arrest would be. The irony of being arrested for witchcraft yet unable to command even one word of witchery would have made her laugh, were she not terrified.

Looking desperately over her shoulder, she saw nothing but bystanders dancing and hugging each other as a fiery Armitage House struggled higher over the rooftops. (Nothing quite like the imminent demise of a pirate to encourage community spirit.) Alex was out of her sight—which meant that she was out of his. He'd be unaware of her peril, and therefore unlikely to provide a rescue in the nick of time. She was going to disappear into that police van and out of the world.

She tried to take a breath deep enough that she might shout for him, but even had she managed it, the crowd began roaring as another pirate battlehouse appeared on the horizon to double their entertainment. He would never hear her over that noise. Charlotte had no hope, just as Miss Plim always warned. That had been a daily lesson, between embroidery and how to run a blind heist. *Get caught doing magic and you're alone. No one will come to save you. No one will even remember your name.*

But as the tight-lipped specter of ruthless Plimmishness that had haunted generations of witches threatened to break her with its sharply tapping finger, a bolder figure appeared through the smoke. Trousers—upraised sword—magnificent feathered hat; Charlotte gasped as it took shape.

"Get away from her, you son of a bitch!"

The policeman barely had time to sniff contemptuously before the pirate spun dramatically on a gorgeous pink bootheel and kicked him in the gut. As he pitched forward, a cry of pain bursting from him, the pirate then applied her knee to his forehead with an efficiency Lady Armitage would have killed for. (Literally.) The man went down like a sack of wet handkerchiefs. His fellow officers rushed over, truncheons waving.

Charlotte and the pirate exchanged a brief, amused glance. Charlotte saw then that she had been rescued by a young woman, suntanned, swaggering, and her heart swaggered in response. Fear fell away—or, rather, was kicked away by the spiked boots of her Wicken pride. No witch was going to look scared in front of a pirate girl! She turned toward the policemen and began incantating. The pirate lifted her sword.

And the policemen, taking professional stock of the situation, ran away as fast as they could.

"*Subsisto et concido!*" Charlotte shouted after them. They fell to the ground, and whether due to unconsciousness or good sense, stayed down. The pirate, appearing disappointed at this efficient end to the trouble, brandished her sword uselessly for a moment, then shrugged and gave a complex whistle. Hearing it, the police horses trotted off, taking the wagon with them.

"Thank you," Charlotte said, attempting to offer the pirate a handshake before recollecting the iron cuffs.

The pirate grinned. "You're welcome. I owed you."

"You did?" Charlotte frowned a moment before finally recognizing her. "Upon my word! You are Constantinopla Brown."

"At your service," the girl said, bowing extravagantly. "Well, you know, not actually at your service, since pirates serve no one, not even Her Majesty the Queen (a personal friend of mine), and I regret to inform you that I've already robbed you of your earrings, but nevertheless, colloquially speaking, at your service and pleased to meet you."

While Charlotte was blinking in an effort to process this speech, Constantinopla reached down and acquired a set of keys from the unconscious policeman. She sorted through them with practiced ease and used one to release Charlotte's handcuffs. "I am ever so grateful that you rescued my Tom from the clutches of Lady Armitage," she said as she worked. "He might have been wed to the old hag had you not intervened."

"Oh yes," Charlotte said. "It was a close shave. But we arrived in the nick of time and Tom absolutely, definitively, did not marry anyone, least of all Lady Armitage, of that you can be sure."

Constantinopla's face lit with a smile. "So it seems I owe you again, Miss Pettifer. I say, will you come to my wedding? I know we shouldn't associate, but I'd be honored by your attendance, since you are responsible for it happening at all."

Charlotte hesitated. "I'm not sure that would be wise."

"Oh."

"And therefore I am happy to accept the invitation."

Constantinopla grinned so widely, Charlotte feared she would crack something. Then she pocketed the handcuffs, and when Charlotte noticed, she blushed. "I thought I might take them on my honeymoon."

And now Charlotte blushed.

"After all," Constantinopla continued, gazing adoringly at Tom, who was now hobbling toward her, "one never knows when one might want to do a little independent looting, and these handcuffs will prevent my husband's intervention. Even a married woman should maintain her self-sustenance, you know."

"How modern of you," Charlotte murmured. This idea (albeit in a more metaphorical sense that shall not be related here) interested her so greatly, she left Constantinopla with a nod and smile, and approached the other two policemen in the hope of finding handcuffs on their persons. Besides, the young pirates were joyfully expressing their pleasure at being reunited, and she could not help but disapprove. Laughing and embracing in full view of several dozen people was appalling behavior, even for pirates, and she had a good mind to turn back and scold them.

"Lottie!"

Alex emerged from the crowd, his face soot-covered but his eyes such a clear blue Charlotte felt she could have flown away in them. Forgetting the policemen, she ran to him, engulfing him in an embrace even before he stopped walking. He laughed, and she wrapped her legs around his hips, overcome with such joy she felt the air crackle with it. Alex's arms encircled her in return, providing a strength she knew she could trust.

He was her big scary pirate, and she was safe with him.

"Are you all right?" she asked, touching his face, brushing back his hair.

"I'm grand, my darling," he said, grinning as if he'd just come from the pub rather than toppling some considerable distance out of a burning house. "Are you?"

"I am now."

"Thanks for rescuing me."

She opened her mouth to say it was nothing. Risking her own life, exposing witchcraft, betraying the League—nothing. But that was not true, and she found herself saying instead, "You are everything."

Heat bloomed between them, and the air crackled louder. The world seemed to drift away like smoke from a house fire. Alex blinked, his eyes growing heavy. Charlotte smiled. They drew together in a soft, gentle kiss.

It felt like they had never kissed before, never touched. A tender new promise blossomed between them, and Charlotte knew she would gladly battle the League, or even abandon it altogether, to keep the pirate in her life. She sighed against his wicked mouth.

A moment later, she realized the crackling sound was in fact from the flames that continued to ravage Armitage House above the crowded street, and the warmth she felt may have been romantically metaphorical, but it was also literal due to the burning shards of floorboards and furniture raining down. Slipping from Alex's arms, she stared up at the aerial drama. A tall and elegant townhouse had begun to circle Armitage House with a somber, rather supercilious dignity that reminded Charlotte eerily of her aunt. Its gable window cycled open to reveal a large cannon.

"Is it going to shoot her out of the sky?" she asked with astonishment. "People on the ground will be hurt!"

"That's Darlington House," Alex said. "Miss Darlington and Lady Armitage have been rivals for longer than I've been alive. I expect to see—"

Suddenly the cannon fired. Water sprayed from it onto the Armitage House flames, creating enormous billows of smoke. The crowd cheered, and Charlotte cocked an eyebrow at Alex.

"Yes," he said, nodding authoritatively, "that's exactly what I was about to say."

Charlotte had no chance to scoff, for the battlehouses began moving toward the shore as Armitage House tried to evade Darlington House's rescue efforts. The crowd hastened to follow, and Charlotte and Alex went with them automatically.

"I wasn't able to get the amulet," Alex said as they hurried along.

"Good," Charlotte said.

"Excuse me?" His eyebrows did not seem to know whether to lift or huddle in confused surprise.

She shrugged with an audacious nonchalance she had learned from him. "Now we will simply be forced to continue together in our pursuit of it."

Alex grinned, and Charlotte felt a shimmer beneath her heart that she knew was reflected in the long, hungry gaze she gave him. His footsteps slowed, and he reached out to touch her face—

"Oh hell," he said, his expression turning grim.

"What's wrong?" Charlotte looked around for the trouble he had noticed, and her own expression leaped over grim and landed straight in appalled.

Miss Plim marched along the street, aimed directly toward her like a poisoned arrow.

"Oh hell," Charlotte agreed.

It was as if Aunt Judith had not stopped pursuing them since being briefly stalled in the ballroom yesterday afternoon. She strode methodically, without weariness or mercy. Her topknot of hair had been knocked aslant, but her elbows were still in working order, jabbing left and right at the people rushing past. And her face was so stormy she could have put out the Armitage House fire just by glaring at it.

"Hell," Charlotte repeated, the word fluttering madly in her throat. "Pardon me."

They turned to see Bixby standing inscrutable beside them. In one hand he presented a silver tray holding two pistols.

"How do you always manage to find me?" Alex asked as he took one of the pistols and passed it to Charlotte.

"One does try to perform one's job adequately," Bixby replied.

"Or maybe you're trying to catch me off guard, so I'll scream in fright and you can scold me for being noisy."

"Certainly not, sir," Bixby said in a tone so deadpan it sounded like it had been bashed to death by laughter.

Alex gave him a dark look. "I'm tempted to make you walk the plank," he said, taking the other gun and checking its bullet chamber. "But you'd no doubt critique the wood and refuse to walk until I'd hammered all the bolts in properly. Is the house safe?"

"One moment, sir," the butler replied. He lifted his tray without looking and whacked it against the head of a young man who had been attempting to pick his pocket. The boy crumpled to the ground.

Alex glanced down. "Isn't that Dominic Etterly?"

"Jonah, the younger son," Bixby corrected him.

"Good heavens, Joe Etterly, old enough for piracy. I feel ancient. Do me a favor, Bixby, and steal that fobwatch he has attached to his waistcoat."

"Yes, sir. Also, the house is quite safe, although we will need to repaint the front door. And if I may be so bold as to mention: irascible aunt at two o'clock."

Alex turned, raising his gun automatically.

Charlotte stared at him in horror. "Surely you don't intend to shoot my aunt?" she demanded.

"I—"

"Because that is my privilege." She tried to cock her own gun, then frowned and tried again. Alex winced and, taking the weapon, released the safety and cocked the hammer for her before handing it back.

Charlotte might have gone on to shoot Miss Plim, or she might not have; before the decision could be made, the aunt herself arrived. At this point, shooting her would be a decidedly intimate matter—and make an awful mess. Charlotte found herself hiding the gun behind her back like a naughty child caught with forbidden cake.

"Charlotte Pettifer," Miss Plim declaimed, crossing her arms and managing to look down her nose at Charlotte despite the latter being half a head taller. "I am appalled to find you in such a state—standing on the street in your unmentionables, covered in blood and soot, and worst of all, with your hair unbound! You have been behaving shamefully, not only dragging the good name of your family through the mud, but also the wicked name of witches everywhere. Pirates have begun to consider us approachable! I have received two invitations to tea this morning alone! Such an intolerable state of affairs must cease at once. I require you to return home and make a public denouncement of this—this—" She flapped a hand toward Alex as if naming him would defile her tongue.

Charlotte shook back her hair in a gesture of defiance not quite as powerful as aiming a gun at her aunt's face, but good enough that it made Miss Plim scowl furiously. "The man to whom you are referring, Aunt Judith, is my friend."

Miss Plim spat out a laugh. "Friend? What nonsense! I would say you've been afflicted with piratic foolishness, Charlotte Judith Pettifer, but sadly there has always been a deep flaw in you, a propensity to delinquency, no matter how hard I have tried to improve you. It makes me sick when I—"

She stopped, her mouth wrinkling up into a knot.

"You'll notice," Alex said languidly to Charlotte, although not moving his attention from the gun he had pressed against Miss Plim's temple, "I have the safety off, so will be free to shoot when I do this."

He cocked the gun.

Miss Plim flinched.

"I'm afraid I did not get the memorandum about being friendly to witches," he said. "Hell, I'm not even friendly to the one I intend to marry. So I'm telling you right now, madam: one more nasty word to Lottie and I'll ensure you never speak again."

His expression was so cold, so ruthless, even Charlotte shuddered. Miss Plim huffed in outrage, her nostrils flaring, but no actual words emitted from her pursed mouth. Charlotte could not believe it.

"Sir," Bixby murmured.

"Yes, I know," Alex said testily. "Don't be rude to a lady."

"Actually, sir, I detect no lady other than Miss Pettifer. I was trying to explain that the houses are advancing beyond our view."

Alex pulled his gun back, releasing the hammer. "I suggest you leave quietly," he told Miss Plim. "Before I change my mind."

She threw him a look so vicious it would have scythed through the confidence of most people. Alex just laughed. "You don't scare me. I was educated by nuns. They would sort out a woman like you in the space of one Hail Mary and half a Paternoster, then have you spend the rest of your days doing laundry. Go. Now. Fast."

To Charlotte's utter amazement, Miss Plim actually obeyed. "I'll see you at home," she said with a final scathing glance to Charlotte, then turned so briskly on one heel that Charlotte half expected her to spin right around. Shoving her way through the crowd, she vanished.

Charlotte stared after her, stunned. Never before had anyone chastised Miss Plim in such a manner. Certainly never before had anyone defended Charlotte from her haranguing, as if Charlotte might be vulnerable, soft, with a heart that deserved protecting.

Hastily she affected an arch amusement before Alex could realize how touched she felt. "Goodness me, it was worth jumping out of a burning house, getting arrested, and betraying my entire heritage, just to see that moment happen. But may I raise one small question, Captain?"

"No," he said. And the way he looked at her, so steadily, so deeply, made her realize he saw right through her affectation. She swallowed heavily—and yet, she was not scared of him.

"No?" she echoed, her heart swaying.

"Not until I'm ready to say it again in a proper manner."

The swaying became a waltz. "Oh, I see. With a ring?"

"And down on one knee. Yes."

"Yes," she said breathlessly.

His solemnity broke into a smile unlike any Charlotte had seen from him before. Its beauty and warm sincerity shone on her heart, which gasped and hugged itself.

"I'm glad you finally agree with me about something," Alex said, cupping a hand to her face. The dangerously beautiful eyes were gentle as they looked down at her. "Hold on to that answer."

She tried to huff, but it came out as a dreamy sigh instead. "I will."

"That one too."

They gazed at each other, grinning rather foolishly.

"*Tsk.*"

Turning, they found Bixby shaking his head with exasperation. "I beg your pardon," he said without the least hint of apology in his voice, "but is this a romance or is it an adventure? For I will remind you, we are missing the ongoing action."

Charlotte and Alex exchanged a smiling glance. "I think what this is defies definition," Charlotte said.

"Which is only right," Alex added. "We, Charlotte, are the makers of manners."

"Ooh," she said, her smile brightening, "Shakespeare! I didn't know you read—"

His eyebrows shot up in amusement.

"—such things," she added. "I didn't know you read *such things*."

He shrugged. "There's a lot you don't know about me, darling."

"Good, for I am not too old to learn."

She took his hand, and they hurried after the crowd toward the shore.

❋ 24 ❋

THEY UNHAPPY TWO—UNEXPECTED EMPATHY—
A SOLUTION POPS UP—PORK PIES—NED ADVISES ALEX—
CLACTON'S ANGELS—CREEVE GETS JUSTICE—
NO BECHDEL TEST FOR MEN—CHARLOTTE TAKES AIM—
THE ULTIMATE SOLUTION

Gentlewomen in England still a-bed would no doubt think themselves accurs'd they were not on the shore promenade of Clacton-on-Sea, and hold their womanhoods cheap whilst any spoke that watched the pirate battlehouses fight each other that morning. By the time Armitage House and Darlington House reached clear skies above the harbor in which to skirmish properly, more than half the town had gathered, flags were being flown, the constabulary had given up trying to get order, and several young fellows in red-and-white-striped jackets were going through the crowd selling pork pies and cheese-on-a-stick.

The fire in Armitage House having been extinguished by Miss Darlington's water cannon, and Lady Armitage keeping her battlehouse aloft by what must have been sheer force of will (or being too insane to realize that she was now flying nothing more than an upper story and half a staircase), the two danced around each other, exchanging shouts.

"Shouldn't they be exchanging shots instead?" asked one woman.

Her question was voiced rhetorically but Alex happened to be nearby, so he answered.

"Miss Darlington and Lady Armitage have been trying to kill each other for decades. It would be strange if they started *actually doing so* now."

The woman turned to acknowledge his reply and, seeing he was a pirate, nearly expired on the spot. Scurrying aside, she accidentally stepped on the foot of a blond fellow whose smile was as gleaming as a sword. (The woman felt confident in applying this metaphor due to the literal sword he was holding.) With a shriek, she fled through the crowd.

"Still charming the ladies, I see," Alex drawled as Ned came to stand beside him.

"Still making a mess, I see," Ned replied, eyeing Alex's soot-stained hair and clothes.

"Why are you waving your sword around like that? You could put out someone's eye."

"There are four pirates and at least two witches in this crowd. I skirmished with Olivia Etterly just now and promised to meet Mr. Rotunder with pistols at dawn."

"Will you?"

Behind them, a woman laughed. "I doubt Ned even knows what dawn looks like."

Alex turned to grin at Cecilia, who gave him a cool look then nodded to Charlotte. "Miss Pettifer, how do you do?"

Alex watched Charlotte's eyelashes swoop down then up again, the only sign on her otherwise calm visage that she was rapidly assessing how to behave in this unexpected moment. His heart did a little flip of worry for her, then a little flip back again with adoration. God, but he loved that she didn't automatically know how to be normal. He longed to fly her away into a wild sky where she'd have the freedom to be as strange and sensual and indescribably wonderful as she wanted to be.

"I am well, thank you, Miss Bassingthwaite," she said after a pause so tiny only Alex noticed it. She nodded with impeccable elegance. "And you?"

Cecilia sighed, fanning herself with a white-gloved hand. "To be frank, Miss Pettifer, I am overwhelmed. All this clamor and crowding exhausts my senses."

Charlotte's eyes grew wide in amazement, but she recovered quickly and gave Cecilia a polite smile, as if she herself was not on the point of doing something terrible, such as scowling, or perhaps even exhaling loudly in exasperation, due to her own overwhelm. Alex bit his lip to stop himself from grinning.

"Shall we take a short walk?" Cecilia suggested. "I would appreciate your company as I try to find a quieter location from which to view my aunt's derring-do."

"Aren't we supposed to be getting to our house and chasing after the amulet?" Alex asked.

Charlotte hesitated. He could sense the conflict in her between duty and a new friendship. Instantly, he knew which one he valued more. Friendship meant nothing to him—nothing!—but he wanted with all his heart for her to have it for herself. And if the two women did become chums, then he would have an ~~excuse~~ obligation to spend more time with Ned. Perhaps he and Charlotte, Ned and Cecilia, could even go so far as to have long conversations, travel together, and meet at dining establishments. He would do it for Charlotte's sake. He would risk anything, even the perils of emotional intimacy, for her.

"Go," he said. "We have no need to hurry."

Charlotte looked at him doubtfully, and for a moment the whole world seemed to become still, awaiting her reply.

Then she smiled.

"It would be my pleasure," she said to Cecilia, who smiled in return.

But before she departed she took one more glance at Alex, as if to check again that he was still alive. It reached right into him and squeezed his heart. How long had it been since anyone had cared he was living?

In fact, had he only realized, it was the previous week, when Bixby saw him walk in the door after spending the night in a gambling house, bankrupting opium dealers; then six months before that, when he stood beside Ned at the altar, watching Cecilia glide toward them in a white and gold dress; and three months before that, when he flew an old woman's house to a warmer climate so she suffered less from arthritis; and indeed the whole of 1884, when he smuggled enough flour and sugar into Ireland to keep three villages fed all year.

Ignorant of this, Alex gave Charlotte a look so full of love and gratitude that she frowned. Luckily, she turned away with Cecilia before she saw him sigh like a dreamy boy.

Ned, however, saw only too well. "You're in love," he chuckled, prodding Alex with his sword.

Without even blinking, Alex had his gun aimed directly between Ned's eyes. This caused the other pirate to laugh even more. "Never mind, old chap," he said, slapping Alex's arm—a risky move, considering it was the arm with a loaded weapon at the end of it. "I have a book of poetry you can borrow."

Charlotte and Cecilia strolled arm in arm through the crowd, a process made easier by the fact that most people recognized Cecilia as a pirate (the piquant little red hat was a clue, not to mention the two guns strapped to her waist) and hurried out of their way.

"Goodness, but it is close," Cecilia said, bringing forth a handkerchief and waving it delicately in front of her face. Charlotte noticed that it was the one Captain Lightbourne had implored her to pass on, several days or a lifetime ago, in the British Museum. The glimpse of Asiatic lilies made her heart sigh. She too loved lilies, but Cecilia had even this.

Although I've always loved lilies of the valley best, she reminded herself—and then flushed in horror as she realized she had spoken aloud. Panic began swelling into her throat.

But Cecilia only smiled. "To each her own, Miss Pettifer," she said.

And just like that, Charlotte could breathe. A single sentence from the pirate and years of reproachful Plimmish education unraveled, making her feel at last acceptable in all her shy, brittle sensitivity. The irony was so Jane-Austen-like, she almost laughed.

"I am glad you were able to save Captain O'Riley," Cecilia continued blithely, as if validating a woman's true heart was such everyday work for her she did not even need to pause afterward. "Beneath his weapons and roguishness . . . and bad manners . . . and simply awful language . . . not to mention that catastrophe he calls a battlehouse . . . and then there are the dubious politics and the tendency to drink a little too much when he is in a bad mood, which seems to be often . . . er, yes, beneath that, he is a good man."

"I will agree that he has a few worthy qualities," Charlotte said.

"And he's remarkably handsome," Cecilia added.

"He is tolerable to look at, I suppose," Charlotte agreed.

"Also rich."

Charlotte paused, thinking back to the first day she met him, the outrage and the secret wry appreciation she felt, as a fellow swindler, when his briefcase opened and shredded paper fell out. "Money isn't everything," she said.

"Good heavens!" Cecilia ejaculated. "I fear you have inhaled too much smoke from the fire, Miss Pettifer."

Charlotte did not answer, for she had noticed how Darlington House was casting out a grappling hook, as yet unsuccessfully, and a dreadful thought occurred to her. "Pardon me, Miss Bassingthwaite, I may be prejudiced in the matter of aunts, but what if your Aunt Darlington was to get the amulet from Lady Armitage?"

Cecilia smiled complacently. "Aunt Darlington is a noble character who will keep the best interests of England first and foremost in her thoughts," she replied in ringing tones.

"I'm pleased to hear it," Charlotte said.

"Or to be more precise, we are doomed."

At that lowering moment, a voice called out from the edge of the shore road. "Ladies! Ladies! Over here!"

Charlotte turned to see Constantinopla Brown standing before a garishly colored popcorn stall. The young pirate leaned one hand in a proprietary manner against its shuttered frontage, while with her other she waved cheerily.

Cecilia turned to Charlotte with a smile that was now less complacent and more wickedly piratic.

"I say, Miss Pettifer. Are you by any chance up for an adventure?"

"The secret to a successful relationship," Ned was saying as he and Alex ate pork pies they had stolen from a passing vendor, "is communication. Cecilia knows I will never (again) install a tennis net in the parlor without talking to her about it first, and I can be sure she won't go off harum-scarum without letting me know. This is why we are so blissfully happy. I urge you to take my advice, old chap, if you want the same happiness with Miss Pettifer."

"Uh-huh," Alex said, watching Cecilia spin a small, portable wheel inside a popcorn stall as it rose above the crowd. Constantinopla was pointing to the dueling battlehouses while calling out unnecessary navigational directions, and Charlotte stood between the two pirate ladies, counting the bullets in her gun.

"Of course, I'm blessed to have a wife like Cecilia," Ned continued. "So gentle, so demure."

"Hm," Alex said, grateful for the mouthful of pie that restrained him from further response as he witnessed Cecilia bashing a bag of popcorn against a decorative piece at the front of the stall that was obstructing her view. The piece broke off at the same moment the bag split open, sending popcorn down upon the crowd in an appropriately circus-like version of manna from heaven. Alex swallowed pie and said carefully, "By the way, do you have a spare wheel on you?"

"Sorry," Ned said. "Cecilia carries ours in her bustle. Pirate women really do have the best fashions, you know. Visionary, even. Mark my words, one day all women will have secret compartments and pockets in their skirts as a matter of course. But why do you want a wheel?"

"I don't. I was just wondering how your demure wife managed to get that popcorn stall aloft."

Ned glanced up at the colorful little stall flying toward the battlehouses, three women jammed inside. He rolled his eyes. "Another thing you will learn about successful relationships, O'Riley, is that you'll always be wrong. Besides, you can't keep a good woman down, and that goes literally for a buccaneering one. I see your Miss Pettifer is getting into the swing of things in a manner I'd not have expected from a Wicken League member."

Indeed, Charlotte was literally swinging herself up to crouch on the roof of the stall, lips moving as she whispered the incantation. She had a gun in one hand and a long pink ribbon tying back her hair, and Alex thought he would swoon at the very sight of her.

"Lottie is unique," he said.

"Do you think we should chase after them?" Ned asked without much enthusiasm.

"I think they left us behind for a reason. This is women's business."

"Sounds about right. Be a friend, steal me a coffee from that vendor."

Alex was just about to do so when an angry voice shook through the crowd. "Witch! Witch!"

A pale-haired man staggered toward the shoreline, pointing a long, thin finger at the rising popcorn stall. "Stop that witch!"

Alex frowned, having no idea who the man was but no interest in stopping to inquire. Drawing his gun, he stepped forward to save the situation. But he was too late.

A bag of roasted nuts plummeted from the stall onto the man's head. He collapsed at once in a tumble of elbows and spindly legs, and the crowd cheered with delight at this clownish addition to the show.

"That's my girl," Ned murmured with a smile.

"Actually, that was my girl," said a new voice. The pirates glanced around to see Tom arriving. In his arms was an iron ball, its chain still attached to his ankle. Ned smacked him cheerfully on the shoulder, making him wince.

Alex turned back to watch the popcorn stall close in on Armitage House, Charlotte riding its roof with perfectly calm balance. "Does anyone else get the feeling," he said, "that in fact we're their boys?"

Charlotte rose to stand upright on the corrugated iron roof. Wind rushed against her face and her heart. Magic rushed out. She did not look down, for she did not care who might be watching her or what they might be thinking. She kept her eye on the open window of Armitage House and the shadowed figure inside. It wasn't that she particularly worried about regaining the amulet. That was a job to be done, but it no longer possessed her heart. The chase was what she'd come to love. The chance to stand in the wild, being wild.

She had always thought pirates needed to be more like Wicken League ladies, decorous and sensible, with smaller hats. On the whole, she still did. But goodness, mixing piracy with witchcraft certainly was exhilarating.

How had other witches not known about this? Had they never experienced magic surging through them like hot, sensual passion? Or were they prim and proper because they had, and feared it?

"Well," Charlotte told herself, "I am not frightened of being afraid." At least, she hadn't been ever since a wicked pirate pushed and shoved and kissed her right off the plank, into the depths of herself.

For example, she could admit that falling from this popcorn stall scared her. Although she might easily *descendeo lente,* she would still drown, since swimming was unladylike; and besides, witches had always been too haunted by the cultural memory of witch-trial dunkings to tolerate anything more immersive than a bathtub. But the fear did not own her. She laughed in its face! (Or, more accurately, she frowned in its face and thought of how it might be improved upon—a shark, perhaps, or a sudden gust of wind.) Furthermore, she did not think she would actually fall, for she was determined to have her happy ending, and therefore reality could just do as it was told for the next little while.

In the interior below, Cecilia was expertly maneuvering so as to draw level with Armitage House's cockpit. Constantinopla was shouting insults at the old pirate—an enlivening, if ultimately useless, contribution. Lady Armitage, clutching her great wheel, laughed with disdain. Her face was smoke-smudged, her hair sagging, but a light in her eyes suggested she had enough spirit (or cocaine lollies) to stay in the fight.

Charlotte raised her arm slowly, pushing against the buffering force of magic, and pointed the gun at the mad pirate. "Give me back my amulet!"

"Do you mean this thing?" Lady Armitage held up the amulet,

swinging it back and forth tauntingly. With the chain wrapped about her fingers, there was no hope of Charlotte incantating it without bringing the whole woman along too, and that much magic would probably destabilize both airborne buildings. "Why don't you come and get it, little girl?"

"Just surrender, Aunty Army," Cecilia called out. "Then we can all go and have a cup of tea and some biscuits."

Charlotte rolled her eyes. Even the more reasonable pirates were essentially mad.

"Oh well, if there are biscuits." To Charlotte's astonishment, Lady Armitage moved away from the wheel. But her smile was crooked like an old moon and held just as many secrets. Charlotte took an instinctive step back.

"I'll jump over and hand it to you, shall I?" the pirate asked through that smile.

Charlotte thought she was merely teasing, for surely it would be impossible for an old woman in heavy clothing to make a jump of some twenty feet unless she used witchcraft—and Lady Armitage was no witch. For one thing, her dress sense was far too vulgar. But as the pirate stared at the gap between the houses, her eyes squinted, gauging the distance, and Charlotte realized she was serious. She intended to make that leap, regardless of its certain failure. Charlotte could not comprehend such madness!

Then again, no doubt Alex would make the same leap. Witches feared too much, but pirates did not fear anywhere near enough.

Sighting along the length of the gun, Charlotte began calculating. Not the head; she didn't want to actually kill the woman. But not the legs either, risking ricochet from the crinoline petticoat. Probably the shoulder would be safest. One good shot, then make the leap herself to recover the amulet—which would be *entirely safe* and *not at all mad*, as she'd be supported by witchcraft. (Never mind that Armitage

House would surely plummet if its pilot was shot, not to mention the lady pirates on hand who'd immediately snatch the amulet from her, and a dozen other considerations that pirates would have known to factor in. Although, to be fair, they'd make the leap even *with* that understanding, thus leaving no actual difference between a witch's arrogance and a pirate's insanity.)

Now if the stall, house, and pirate could just stop swaying in different directions for a moment . . .

"For goodness' sake, Isabella, this behavior is deplorable, even for you!"

Charlotte looked from the corner of her eye at the other battlehouse. Miss Darlington was frowning out through her open cockpit window, one lace-gloved hand on her wheel, the other holding a cup of tea. "Besides," the grand lady called out, "magical amulets are passé these days. Every hero and her sidekick has one. You must learn to take a modern perspective, Isabella. I hear Countess Strabe has a cursed sword that would suit you much better."

"Indeed?" Lady Armitage seemed piqued by this information. She took another step away from her wheel. Her skirt swept against it and something fell out of the shaft, clattering across the floor and out the window. Charlotte remembered Miss Dearlove sitting up from beneath the wheel, screwdriver in hand, a professional degree of mystery in her eyes. "*I'm sabotaging the wheel*," she had said in that dangerously calm, quiet voice of hers.

The wheel spun, untouched. The house began to tremble. Inside the popcorn stall, Cecilia gave a horrified gasp as she realized what was happening. "Aunty!" she called out—although which aunt she meant, Charlotte did not know.

Suddenly the house tilted. Charlotte saw startlement flash onto Lady Armitage's face. For one hideous moment, it looked like sanity. She clutched at the air, trying to keep her balance. Charlotte's heart began to race. Dropping the gun, she held out her hand in an instinctive offer of rescue. A dozen words of the incantation rushed up—

The house tilted again.

And just like that, Lady Armitage was tossed out the window. No grandiose death speech. No wail to wrench at the heart of even those who feared her. In gruesome silence, she fell a hundred feet into the sea.

And the amulet went with her.

✷ 25 ✷

The pirates' feelings would not be repressed. They allowed each other to tell how ardently they had hated and despised Lady Armitage. And yet, oh, for a house of fire, that would ascend the brightest heaven of Clacton! Armitage House had gone down soon after its mistress, and the fact it would never again menace England, parking in the middle of traffic intersections, luring in bachelors, was almost impossible to comprehend.

Together the pirates stood shoreside, staring out across Clacton Harbor. Or, rather, squinting, since the morning sun shone on their faces in a decidedly unfuneral manner. Lady Armitage would have been outraged. They made somewhat of a crowd, since several members of the Wisteria Society had arrived unnoticed during the aerial battle and now joined the stunned gathering. Servants had set out lace-clothed tables laden with tea, cakes, and little crustless sandwiches, as is done in times of community grief, albeit not usually in the middle of the street and guarded by gun-toting butlers.

The locals, on the other hand, had rapidly dispersed. Pirates dueling aloft in flaming battlehouses was one thing; pirates standing quietly on the footpath, murmuring amongst themselves and drinking tea, was altogether more terrifying. Doors had been locked and then barricaded with various pieces of furniture. Jewels had been hidden and children told to come away from that window at once. On the harbor, fishing boats headed rapidly out to sea, even those with holds full of fish. An eerie peace lay upon Clacton.

"This does not seem a fitting end for Aunty Army," Cecilia said with a sigh. She was swathed in scarves and shawls, which Miss Darlington had insisted upon and Cecilia had patiently allowed, despite now being at risk of fainting in the midsummer heat. After all, Miss Darlington had just suffered the loss of a nemesis who tried for decades to kill her; she needed whatever comfort could be provided.

"I don't know," Ned argued gently, slipping an arm around his wife and easing her close. "It seems to me only the sea is vast enough to contain Isabella Armitage."

Charlotte glanced surreptitiously at the pirate couple. She felt an odd stirring in her heart, and she tried to define what it might be. Not jealousy of their intimacy, for she had her own with Alex, who had dressed her in his coat and now stood behind her, arms about her shoulders, chin resting on her head, his strength and warmth encompassing her as he sheltered her from the prying eyes of lady pirates. Nor was it a desire to steal their jewelry. She suspected it might be that rarest of delights: comradeship.

The thought she might experience this with someone other than Alex, and to a milder extent Bixby, was utterly wondrous. And also disconcerting. It was one thing to like a pirate captain with seductive blue eyes who knew just how to soothe her heart and inflame other parts of her anatomy. Charlotte defied any witch to ignore her own womanhood to such a degree. But liking *several other* pirates, and for the very things that made them pirates—the fervor, the histrionics, and the ridiculous joie de vivre—this was something altogether different.

Just exactly what kind of witch was she?

The kind that was a little too similar to Beryl Black, she realized worriedly. And look what the Plims had done to her.

Even so, she could not stop herself from wanting to smile at Ned and Cecilia. So she turned away—and saw Constantinopla on the other side of her, holding hands with Tom. The pirate girl winked.

Overwhelmed, Charlotte nodded briskly in reply, then frowned out at the water, which had the decency to not smile back. Alex seemed to sense her emotion; he tucked her in even closer, kissing her temple.

Charlotte sighed, more happy than she'd ever thought she had the right to be.

She ought not allow his embrace in public. Every moment, she awaited opprobrium from the elder pirates surrounding them. It appeared, however, that riding the roof of an airborne popcorn stall had earned her some respect from the Wisteria Society—or perhaps *disrespect* was more accurate, for they treated her like a fellow pirate, even if (maybe because) she had been instrumental in the death of one of their own. Several ladies had shaken her hand, and others had actually gone so far as to not steal her bracelet of bee charms or the pearl buttons on her dress. Charlotte did not know whether to grimace or smile at the thought of how this would horrify the Wicken League, were they aware of it.

In fact, witches were present and watching Charlotte's behavior with disapproving eyes. The amulet retrieval team, having recovered from Bixby's booby trap, not to mention the night they'd been forced to spend in a cheap hotel room with only one bed (which is not so romantic when it has to serve five women who all had the garlic prawns for dinner), had been drawn to the shore road with the instinct for trouble all witches shared. But they remained cautiously back by the tea table, restraining themselves to tight smiles and criticism of the silverware. While witches were not worms, as has previously been established, neither were they about to confront Charlotte in the middle of a pirate crowd without the express permission of Miss Plim. Stretching racks and ducking stools had nothing on what Judith could do with a mildly inquiring smile.

Charlotte, for her part, did not notice their presence, not even when Miss Gloughenbury accidentally spilled the contents of a teapot, thereby nearly starting a war. But then, no one ever noticed anything except pirates when in the company of pirates.

"Now that Lady Armitage is gone, it's the closing of an era," Constantinopla said with a dramatic sigh.

"Excuse me?" Mrs. Rotunder set her teacup down in its saucer with an indignant *clink*. Everyone near her shuffled a few steps aside. "I am the same age as Isabella, and just as notorious. You may be assured that the era remains open."

Constantinopla gave no reply, but smirked and rolled her eyes at Tom. Everyone near her shuffled a few steps aside, including Tom.

Noting the smirk, Mrs. Rotunder bristled. "Now see here, young lady . . ."

Charlotte found herself being abruptly pulled away by Alex. Behind them came Ned and Cecilia, glancing over their shoulders and murmuring for Alex to hurry.

"What is the matter?" Charlotte asked testily, not liking being manhandled in this way (although other ways, involving sheets and pillows, were fine).

A clash of steel answered her.

"Upon my word!" she gasped as Constantinopla and Mrs. Rotunder began to parley. "Cannot pirates restrain themselves for even one hour?"

Alex, Ned, and Cecilia exchanged a glance. "No," they chorused.

After all, the collective noun for pirates was "a quarrel." The air rang as a dozen more swords came into play.

"But Lady Armitage has just died!"

"And now this is a fitting end for her," Cecilia said, ducking as a teacup flew past. "I, however, would rather like to leave before Aunt Darlington breaks my leg so I am forced into months of bed rest."

"Come on, my love," Ned said, taking her by the hand. "Let's go steal some liver cleansing tonic in Aunty Army's honor."

Cecilia smiled at him rather sadly, then turned to Charlotte. "Good day, Miss Pettifer. Please do call on me soon."

"I will, thank you," Charlotte replied automatically—and then realized not only did she mean it, but she was excited at the prospect of doing so. At the back of her mind, Elizabeth Bennet glanced up from a hammock where she was sipping lemonade and reading *Frankenstein*; she gave an encouraging nod and then vanished. Charlotte felt the swelling of emotion that she recognized now as friendship—true friendship for her own self.

She smiled at Cecilia as a purple-feathered hat cartwheeled past, throwing off sparks. "I hope you will come to my—er, that is, to any interesting events I may hold in the near future."

"I already have my shoes picked out," Cecilia replied. Noticing Miss Darlington looking about with a medicinal gleam in her eye, she began tugging at her husband's hand.

"Hurry, Ned, or she will start prodding me again to make sure the baby is sitting up straight. I just know it."

Ned slapped Alex's arm in farewell. Alex punched Ned's shoulder. Ned punched him back, and Alex reached for a knife. The ladies shared a dry look then drew the men apart. They headed in opposite directions along the road.

Alex gathered Charlotte against his side as they walked. "What happens now?" he asked, his tone light, careless.

"Breakfast," Charlotte said. A witch ran past, swinging her reticule at a pirate. "A bath. Then home to London, I suppose. Mother will be wondering where I got to."

"There will be an uproar when you return in a pirate's house."

Something exploded behind them. They stumbled a little at the force of it then kept walking. Charlotte smiled, although her heart trembled. "Yes. I'm expecting to make quite a mess indeed."

Later that day, in the dusky calm of Pettifer House's drawing room, Mrs. Pettifer looked up from her embroidery with a mild frown. "Dear, what light through yonder window is shining into my eyes in that aggravating fashion?"

Mr. Pettifer shifted the lace curtain and peered out. "It is the stagecoach, and Judith is the passenger."

They sighed in unison. "She looks sick and pale as always," Mr. Pettifer muttered. "I'm going upstairs. You deal with her."

"Oh no, sir," Mrs. Pettifer declaimed, thrusting down her embroidery and arising like a moon—bright, shadow-eyed, and capable of causing madness in otherwise reasonable gentlemen (and a certain amount of dancing around naked, although that was before she married). "I demand the equal right to be unsociable. Let's both go upstairs, and leave her in Woollery's capable hands."

"But what if she is bringing news of the girl?" he asked as they hastened upstairs like furtive children.

"Lottie is perfectly well," Mrs. Pettifer replied. "Not a scratch on her, I can feel it in my motherly bones."

Woollery watched them disappear into the bedroom, then opened the front door even before Miss Plim did not knock. "Madam," he said. "I am afraid Mrs. and Mr. Pettifer are not accepting visitors."

Miss Plim glared. She was not a visitor. She was a Plim! Furthermore, she cared nothing about Delphine and—um, whatever his name was—the husband. She had come for Charlotte. When Woollery moved to close the door, she snapped a phrase of Latin that shoved him aside, then marched without a backward look toward the drawing room.

Woollery met her at its door in a show of butlering skill that verged on magic. "Madam, I am afraid—"

"Of course you are, stupid man," she retorted. "I am going in to wait for Charlotte. I require tea. Snap to it!"

Woollery relented. Thus left alone, Miss Plim paced the drawing room with all the vigor of a woman who has just spent hours in a rattling stagecoach. She did not know if Charlotte would return tonight, but she intended to wait as long as required. Her fury knew no bounds. Indeed, it had been many years since she'd had such an exemplary outrage. Bad enough that Charlotte had spent several days *enjoying herself*, but worse that she'd done so in the company of a man. If only she'd been able to convince Delphine that cold black tea and unbuttered toast were essential to the girl's formation, they would not be seeing now this disastrous outbreak of individualism.

Miss Plim emitted a sigh tainted with incantation. Mrs. Pettifer's volumes of Byron toppled from their shelf, making a loud clatter against the floor and riling up her nerves in a most pleasant manner. She was tired of everything. Charlotte be damned, Miss Gloughenbury and the orphans be damned—it was time for a new prophecy.

Woollery brought tea. Miss Plim poured herself a cup and was on the verge of drinking it when the drawing room door opened once again and a man stepped in unannounced. Miss Plim stared at him, cup halfway to her mouth. His magnificently chiseled face and pearl-colored eyes arrested any rebuke she would have made. Although he wore dusty clothes and two large bandages patched his temples, she had never before seen such an Adonis. Her spectacles fogged, and within her chest cavity came a peculiar sensation, as if she had already swallowed tea and it was heating her.

The man stopped abruptly to stare at her. The air between them held its breath.

"Madam," he said finally, bestowing upon her a look so revolted, so soured with contempt, that Miss Plim almost gasped. Here was a kindred spirit indeed! "I am Detective Inspector Creeve. I have come to arrest Charlotte Pettifer on charges of witchcraft. I demand you surrender her to me at once."

Miss Plim would have shaken back her hair if it hadn't required a hammer to do so. "Witches do not exist, my good fellow. But you can certainly arrest Charlotte after I have finished lecturing her on her bad—although non-witchy—behavior. She is not here at present, but I await her return, and you may also. Will you have tea?"

He sniffed. His eyes glimmered as he looked her up and down. His tongue slipped out to lick what could be called his lips by only the most charitable observer.

Fortunately, Miss Plim was a renowned philanthropist.

"We have green tea," she said in the same way another woman would have mentioned wine. Served in a slipper. In her bedroom.

He blotted moisture from one nasal cavity. The pallid gaze that had wandered all over her body lingered at the brittle line of collarbone peeking out from above her gray wool bodice, and he looked as if he would like to sniff it.

"You are a fetid witch."

Miss Plim blushed. "And if I am not mistaken, sir, you are that revolting and heartless scourge of the earth, a witch hunter."

He took a few steps toward her, his hips jerking in an attempt at manly swaggering. "What is your name?"

"Judy," she said.

"Matthew," he told her.

He'd come so close, she could smell the saltiness of blood beneath his bandages. Her heart pulled itself up from its stiff-backed chair, rubbed its aching hip, and put itself to stirring. She needed no crystal ball to justify the future she began to see for herself.

"I am fetid, bad, reprehensible," she said huskily. "How are you going to punish me, Matthew?"

His dainty eyelashes fluttered and a yellowish hue began to infuse his expression—lust, or perhaps indigestion. He reached out, touched her face, then lifted his fingers to his nose. Miss Plim shivered at the romantic gesture.

"You belong on a flaming pyre, woman," he growled, stepping so close their shadows fused into one trembling, distorted shape.

"Oh yes," Miss Plim replied, her voice little more than a breath made steamy with feminine magic. "Burn me. Burn me alive."

When Charlotte arrived home not long after, hand in hand with a pirate, it was to find the drawing room empty. Woollery informed her parents of her presence, and Mrs. Pettifer rushed downstairs in a flurry of lace and laughter. Embraces were issued and welcomes made to Captain O'Riley, whose occupation was forgiven in light of his wealth and good looks, not to mention the fact Mrs. Pettifer had nearly completed the wedding preparations. Then the trio sat down to tea and chat. Charlotte's seat rustled as she descended upon it, and rising again she saw a letter there.

"What is the matter, dear?" Mrs. Pettifer asked as her daughter's face grew white.

Charlotte looked up speechless from the piece of paper, her eyes wide as they went first from Mrs. Pettifer to Alex. "It—I—upon my word!"

Alex stood impatiently, removed the letter from her numb hands, and perused it with speed—whereupon his jaw dropped open. Mrs. Pettifer took the disturbing item for herself and snapped it briskly before reading its message. She laughed.

"Why, Judith has gone! Abdicated leadership of the Wicken League and eloped with some man, sailing away to France!"

"Well, that's bleeding massive," Alex murmured in an accent so Irish it was practically colored green and waving a glass of whiskey.

"She says she is bestowing all her authority on you, Lottie dear!" Mrs. Pettifer continued reading. "But I don't understand this part: 'It is a fitting punishment'—for surely this is wonderful news? I certainly don't need a tarot deck to tell me it is the very best news! My dear, you are now leader of the witches!"

"Hurrah," Charlotte said dazedly.

Mrs. Pettifer frowned. "You do not seem very excited. This is what you have been waiting for your entire life, my dear."

"Yes, I am aware. But Mama, how can I marry Alex if I am to head the League? The feud—"

Mrs. Pettifer waved this concern away at once. "Captain O'Riley may be a pirate, but that represents only a small and easily remedied flaw. No one would expect you to give up such an interesting reformation project. And I'm sure his skills will transfer nicely to lawyering or being a member of parliament."

("Excuse me?" Alex said, but was ignored.)

"So long as you don't do something truly scandalous, such as invite a Wisteria Society lady to your wedding, you will be fine."

"Um," Charlotte said, biting her lower lip.

"Oh. Well, I suppose unfortunate things can happen at the seaside. Fear not! So long as you don't invite that scandalous Cecilia Bassingthwaite, you are still fine."

"Um," Charlotte said, and flung herself back onto a sofa.

"Oh," Mrs. Pettifer said once more, at her wit's end. But since it did not take long for her to reach there, it was an easy journey bouncing back again. "Never mind, dear! This shall herald a new age of intersociety enmity. Already I have in mind certain pirate ladies I shall invite to visit so I may serve them weak tea and give lackluster compliments about their hats. Besides, with the amulet in the League's possession, we shall have the upper hand!"

Alex winced. Charlotte closed her eyes, pressing the back of her hand against them.

"I see." Mrs. Pettifer's voice sounded alarmingly Plimmish. She turned on her heel and began furiously pouring tea into a cup.

Alex sat on the sofa next to Charlotte. "I'm proud of you," he said, smiling.

"There's no need to be." She tipped her head to eye him balefully. "I have done nothing special beyond happening to be the recipient of a convenient prophecy."

"What is given to you does not matter so much as how you use it."

Charlotte paused to consider this. "I *have* always thought I'd like to organize the League better. Tidy up our visiting schedule. Make a roster for bank robberies."

Alex's countenance wavered slightly, but he budged it into an encouraging smile. "That's the spirit! Although . . . you told me the other day you wanted to use the amulet's power to make the world beautiful. Even without it, you now have authority over a group of magic-wielding women. You could introduce some really significant changes to England."

"True." Her eyes lit up. "No corsets on weekends!"

Alex nodded, although with his face lowered to hide the expression thereon. "Good. That's, er, good."

"And maybe—just off the top of my head, you understand— diverting aristocrats' resources to help street urchins?"

He looked up through his eyelashes at her. "There's my witchy woman."

She sighed, her expression darkening again. "No, it is hopeless. I shall from now on be bound in London, shrouded with secrets. No more adventures for me—and you, you hate witches. I cannot ask you to tie yourself to the woman who leads England's coven."

"Ah, Lottie." He grasped her hand. "You'd be amazed by what I'm willing to do for you."

Mrs. Pettifer, hearing this, overpoured milk into her tea and flooded the saucer. Charlotte felt the same thing happen in her heart. Tears welled up as she laid a hand to Alex's stubbled jaw, stroking a thumb against its roughness.

"You are a good man, Captain O'Riley."

He scowled, although his eyes glinted with humor. "Have a care for my reputation, madam, if you please."

Straightening, Charlotte brushed the creases from her skirt. "Very well, let's do this. Let's bring in a new era of greatness, as prophesized."

They smiled at each other.

And the drawing room door burst open.

"Darlings, do I have news for you!"

☙ 26 ❧

A NEW ORDER—CHARLOTTE SHINES A LIGHT—THE OLD ORDER—
CHARLOTTE FINALLY SEES THE DARK—ALEX RUINS EVERYTHING—
FEAR AND LONGING—CHARLOTTE HAS THE LAST WORD

We three meet again!" Miss Gloughenbury declared as she sailed into the room. Beneath one arm she carried something that approximated a poodle, although it was bald in some places, singed in others, and one leg had been reattached backward. Seeing Alex sitting on the sofa beside Charlotte, she frowned. "Er, we four, it seems. Charlotte, darling, is this pirate fellow begging for mercy, moments before you have him poisoned or suffocated?"

Before Charlotte could respond, a hurly-burly filled the doorway. Amongst the stripes, spots, chintz, and feathers, three ladies could be perceived, struggling to enter in an order of precedence none could agree upon. Woollery, coming behind them with a laden tea tray, announced belatedly the arrival of not only Miss Gloughenbury but Mrs. Chuke, Mrs. Vickers, and, er, Miss Smith—the latter of whom no one quite recognized, due to the fact she was Bloodhound Bess in disguise, come along for the adventure and to see if these witches had anything worth stealing.

Miss Gloughenbury stated the obvious: "We have returned to London. We caught a ride with a sweet old lady by the name of Miss Monster, and came immediately to give our report. Burning houses! The amulet gone forever! And Charlotte getting up to the most extraordinary—"

The grandfather clock standing behind Miss Gloughenbury began to rock. But before that good lady could meet a timely end, Mrs. Pettifer stepped forward to announce, "Judith has gone!"

The witches gasped with a passable rendition of dismay. The clock settled. Mrs. Pettifer, enjoying something about her sister for the first time in forty-eight years, grinned merrily. "Before she departed, Judith passed her authority on to Charlotte. Ladies, behold your new leader."

With a flourish, she indicated Charlotte, who smiled weakly and waved from the sofa.

If the witches felt horror at this turn of events, one might blink and therefore be entirely unaware of it. They transformed their countenances with impressive speed into happy smiles, and crowding further into the room, proclaimed that it was marvelous news!—Charlotte was an excellent young woman!—the League was in ideal hands!—and other random superlatives that were entirely, wholeheartedly applicable to this situation! Charlotte hurried to her feet before the enthusiasm suffocated her. Alex, following suit, found himself literally bustled to one side.

"What a splendid president you will make, darling," Miss Gloughenbury said, grasping Charlotte's hand and beating it up and down in an aggressive handshake. "And as for Judith, I do not wish to speak ill of the dead—"

"She's only left the country," Mrs. Pettifer interjected.

"Ah." Miss Gloughenbury had the decency to not look too disappointed. "Well, she shall be missed indeed. Hm, ladies?"

"Hm," they agreed through tight lips.

"I say, Charlotte, will you also be taking over your aunt's charitable institutions?"

The smile was full of teeth.

Charlotte took a deep breath. It was all happening so fast. She did not have time to ascertain the most correct response, or the best way to hold her mouth, or even how to rescue her hand from Miss Gloughenbury's grip before nerve damage occurred. Elizabeth Bennet was gone, Anne Elliot was gone; she had only herself to rely upon. The thought terrified her.

Then Alex shifted slightly, clearing his throat, and as she glanced in his direction, Charlotte saw him smiling at her with calm certainty that she would be *strong, fierce, gorgeous, brave.* She realized then that although she could catch herself with her own magic if she ever fell, she had him now—steady beneath his swagger, kindhearted behind all his deadly weapons—so she could make even the most daring leap and be sure.

"Ladies," she said, and yanked her hand away from Miss Gloughenbury so firmly, the elder witch squeaked. "I will not be emulating my aunt's charitable schemes. I intend to run my own philanthropy—and indeed the entire agenda of the Wicken League—on a new model."

The witches exchanged worried glances.

"Rather than deciding ourselves what is right for the world, we will consult with those who would benefit from our witchcraft as to what would be most helpful for their circumstances, and follow that guide."

The worried glances became alarmed stares.

"A fine scheme in principle," Mrs. Chuke murmured. "Unfortunately, dear, people rarely know what is best for them."

"But I—"

"Jolly good to see you trying to be clever," Mrs. Vickers added with a smile so condescending Charlotte felt it knock ten years off her life.

"Your charming little ideas will show just how valuable our League's time-honored conventions are."

"But as your president—"

"It will be reassuring to have another Plim at the helm," Miss Gloughenbury averred. "Tradition is always such a comfort."

"My tarot spread this morning depicted that very thing," Mrs. Vickers said, nodding emphatically.

"And my crystal ball showed me a steady, familiar path for the League into the future," Miss Gloughenbury agreed.

"I see," Charlotte said. And she did, with a clarity so bright it blistered her. She muttered behind the clenched teeth of her smile.

Teacups began rising from the table.

"Good heavens!" Mrs. Pettifer cried out, trying to catch them.

Cushions began rising from the sofas.

"Charlotte, dear," Miss Gloughenbury said, her eyes narrowing. "Are you quite the thing?"

"Of course she is!" Mrs. Pettifer said indignantly, her arms full of saucers. "Remember that Lottie is after all the Prophesized One, true heir of Beryl Black."

"Oh, I haven't forgotten," Miss Gloughenbury said, not taking her stare from Charlotte even for one blink.

Charlotte's stomach dropped. Cups and cushions crashed down along with it. Ignoring her mother's gasp, she stared at the bonfires in Miss Gloughenbury's eyes.

"Despite the shambles of this past week," the lady went on, her smile making cutlass-shaped creases in her taut face, "we can all agree that Charlotte is a good girl."

And there it was—the force that had driven Aunt Judith all these years. Not power but fear. Not authority but obedience.

With bleak irony, Charlotte realized she was indeed heir to the forces that had driven Beryl Black's destiny. She'd be able to keep the

League in check, but only if she kept herself in check also. Show too much power and not enough obedience, too much magic and not enough manners, and the fire would burn for her just as it had for Beryl. Miss Plim might be gone, but Miss Gloughenbury was ready in the wings. And even if she asked Alex to fly the woman off the edge of the world, there would still be Mrs. Chuke, and Cousin Eugenia, and even her mother, well-meaning but having internalized Plimmishness so completely, she could not see beyond her own tea leaves.

Charlotte might rise to League leadership, but the sensitivities that sparked her joy in magic, in life itself, would have to be repressed again and kept that way forever.

Suddenly, Alex stepped forward. "I beg your pardon, ladies," he said.

They turned to frown at him, but before they could speak he took Charlotte around the waist and hoisted her over his shoulder.

"Egads!" Miss Gloughenbury gasped.

"What are you doing, young man?" Mrs. Chuke demanded.

"Be careful of the Fabergé crystal!" Mrs. Pettifer cried.

"I am kidnapping your leader," Alex said, grinning piratically. "If you have a problem with that, I advise you to take it up with the Wisteria Society."

He began to stride toward the door, Charlotte speechless in his grasp.

"You cannot kidnap her!" Mrs. Chuke said. "*She* is the kidnapper in your relationship."

Alex laughed. "She certainly stole me, it's true. Heart and soul, the very moment I saw her. And now I am stealing her from you. Good evening, ladies."

"But this will bring the feud upon us all over again!" Miss Gloughenbury said.

"It will indeed," Alex agreed cheerfully.

A moment of silence followed as the witches processed this.

"You knave!" Miss Gloughenbury shouted, crossing to pour herself a cup of tea.

"Outrageous!" Mrs. Chuke declared, settling comfortably onto a sofa.

"But Lottie," Mrs. Pettifer said in a tremulous voice. "Will there still be a wedding?"

Charlotte's heart, swooping wildly, felt an unexpected, gentle tug of familial love. She looked out through the tumble of her hair to smile at Mrs. Pettifer. "You continue preparations, Mama, and I shall return briefly from being kidnapped to attend it."

The witches fell to murmuring excitedly amongst themselves. From her inverted position, Charlotte heard them say something about Lettice having *actually* pointed at Eugenia Cuttle-Plim's mother when prophesizing Beryl's true heir all those years ago, not Delphine Pettifer, and therefore Eugenia was the *real* Prophesized One.

She would have laughed had that been appropriate for a kidnappee.

Alex carried her from the room, pausing only so she could say good-bye to Woollery (and Alex could steal his pocket watch). As they passed through into the entrance hall, Miss Gloughenbury tapped a teaspoon against a cup peremptorily. "Ladies, ladies, if you will kindly come to order . . ."

A shiver went through Charlotte's blood. That could have been her. She'd been one *Mansfield Park* quote away from corseting her life forever. If not for a week of madness with a wild pirate, she might never have learned what a witch she really was.

"Thank you for rescuing me," she said to Alex.

He laughed. "Just returning the favor."

And so they fled.

Which is to say, they went upstairs, and Charlotte packed several suitcases and wrote a reference for her lady's maid, while Alex complained good-naturedly about just how many books she was bringing . . . then there was a handshake with her father, who accidentally came upon them in the hall and managed to say a gruff word or two about making wise investments . . . then they were almost to the door when Mrs. Pettifer rushed out to ask if they wanted lilies or roses at the wedding reception, and ensure Charlotte had packed a toothbrush, and wish her a most delightful abduction indeed . . . after which they left the house hand in hand and never looked back.

Until three minutes later, when Charlotte realized she had forgotten her favorite teacup, but *after that* they crossed the road to Alex's rumpled little battlehouse and, like proper lovers, flew away into the sunset.

The old stone cottage illuminated the darkening sky like a piratic moon as Bixby steered it one-handedly, a Thackeray novel in his other hand and half an eye on the horizon. He was heading nowhere in particular—"away," Charlotte had told him, and while he did not approve, he obeyed. Meanwhile, in the bedroom, Charlotte and Alex undertook a mature conversation.

"I'm going to exercise you so much you won't be able to walk straight for days," Alex said, tugging on Charlotte's corset ribbons.

"Don't be too sure," she replied, unbuttoning his shirt. "I've become quite fit, this past week."

"Oh darling, you have no idea how much core strength you're going to develop."

The corset clattered to the floor. Her chemise followed soon thereafter.

"On that subject," Charlotte said, trailing a finger across his chest—"when you eventually do ask the question to which you alluded earlier, I will not expect a speech."

"Really?" He pressed her back against the wall and pulled down her drawers, maneuvering them carefully over her boots so as to not cause a premature ejection of darts. "Don't women like such speeches?"

"In principle. But in the actual moment, you should be too overcome with emotion to articulate properly."

"I see." Kneeling before her, he looked up with a feral grin. "I'm sure I can manage to be inarticulate."

He then employed his mouth to render her so thoroughly wordless herself, she could not even recall the witty rejoinder she had intended to make. Her legs trembled to such a degree, he had to hold them steady with his hands. Her voice floated away on a cloud of warm, blissful breath. As she watched the rose-gold sunset shimmer and blur in her dazed vision, she realized he was doing again what he'd done all through their relationship—silencing her with pleasure. Using intimacy like a barrier against the truths neither of them dared to articulate.

"Stop," she gasped.

He obediently abandoned his endeavors and instead kissed his way up her body, as if racing toward her mouth before she could say another thing.

"No, I mean stop altogether, if you please."

He sat back, and both of them took a moment to breathe. Then he stood, all six feet of him moving like a weapon even in his nakedness, casting a heavy shadow against the wall. He cupped a calloused, scarred hand against her face.

"Are you all right?"

But Charlotte found she could not speak again, spellbound by the concern so apparent in his eyes. The house shook on a sudden updraft even as her pulse was shaking, and they stumbled, falling in a tangle on the bed that Charlotte had come to love for its lush, comfortable messiness (although she planned to fumigate the entire room around it). Alex gathered her to him, steadying her softness against all his hard places. For a moment it looked as if he might start kissing her again, so she laid a hand against his heart.

"I want to talk."

"Talk?" he said, as if he did not understand the concept.

"Yes. There is much of importance we should discuss, now that we have eloped." She gathered a list of well-considered topics in her mind, lined them up neatly, and was about to announce the first when suddenly she found her voice tumbling out ahead of her . . .

"I imagine when Cecilia Bassingthwaite ran away with a pirate, *she* was entirely dignified?"

Alex frowned slightly. "Why are we talking about Cecilia in this moment?"

"And she has proper red hair."

"Um?"

"On the other hand, it takes a witch to fly a bicycle."

Alex's mouth twitched as if he was trying to repress a smile. "Charlotte, are you afraid of Cecilia Bassingthwaite?"

Charlotte scoffed. "What a ridiculous question. That's enough talking; let's kiss." She moved toward him, but he leaned back, touching a finger to her lips.

"It is safe to be frightened, you know."

"Ha." She almost bit his finger. "So says the deadly pirate."

"Oh, I am afraid all the time," he answered, and then winced as if immediately regretting the words.

Charlotte looked at him soberly. He was smiling in the wry, sharp manner she recognized as a defense, and she abruptly forgot all her own vulnerability in response to his. "Because of your childhood?" she asked as softly as she could after a lifetime of speaking feral magic.

"I suppose," he said, and his gaze slid from hers into a darkness she realized not even love had yet banished.

She clutched his bare arms, holding him from sliding too far. "Tell me what frightens you, so I can break it into pieces and sweep it away."

He gave a brusque laugh. "Not even you could manage that, Lottie my love."

"Oh?" She hooked a leg over his, the silk of her stocking slipping up and down his skin. "Are you underestimating me, Captain O'Riley?"

His smile trembled as he looked back at her. "Never. And really, it's nothing. Poverty. Love. Memory. God. Go ahead and scoff at me, I deserve it."

Charlotte's eyes filled with a darkness of her own as she returned his gaze. "I would never scoff at that, or deny the courage it takes to live a fierce, fun, piratic life despite such a shadow on the heart. I *am* afraid of Cecilia Bassingthwaite. Not that she will hurt me, but that she might not like me. I am afraid constantly of doing the wrong thing. Saying the wrong thing. Being burned alive for witchcraft. Loneliness. Myself."

"Ouch." He kissed her temple, her brow, the corner of her mouth. "Those are some heavy fears."

"As are yours. And yet still you smuggle food into Ireland to feed the poor, even though you were hurt so badly there, you've repressed your natural accent."

He shrugged. "I admit that I enjoy doing some good with the resources I have. And I'd rather steal food for the poor than get myself an elegant new sofa. But don't tell anyone I said that. I'd be a laughingstock."

"Your secret is safe with me."

He gave her then the true smile she loved so much, crooked and sweet. "And your heart is safe with me, Lottie. You'll never be lonely again, not for as long as I live."

"Oh." She caught her breath. Wicked man. Wicked, fiendish, beloved man.

"*Tá mé i ngrá leat, mavourneen,*" he whispered, his voice like white ocean and loam-scented rain. Charlotte did not need to know Irish to understand what he was saying. His bare heart was in the words, and her wild witch heart heard it.

"I love you," she said in return.

His smile faded into an expression that went unfathomably deeper, and Charlotte felt a reflection of it in her own body. She lay back, and he moved over her with the calm mastery that had first drawn her to him, all those days ago in a St. James's teahouse. As he slowly filled her, body and soul, she prophesized that this was how it would be from now on. Not just exercise, but love in the light. Her magic stirred in response.

"Charlotte!" Alex said with a surprise that would have been outright trepidation in a man less aware of his reputation as calmly masterful.

"I adore you," she answered—but it came out in the ancient language of dreams, lifting them from the bed.

"This is very high-minded of you," he said, shifting to ease his weight from her as they continued to rise.

"I tired of waiting for your proposal, so am elevating our relationship to a new level."

He laughed and kissed the magic on her lips. And then—

"Ow!"

He winced as his head hit the ceiling.

"Sorry, sorry," Charlotte said, but he was laughing again, and as he went back to kissing her she tasted his delight. Her incantation quivered, sending magic and happiness vibrating through her body. Passion flashed against it with each move Alex made. She even felt a small tremor of fear as the air swayed around them, suggesting at any moment they might tip over and fall. It was a beautiful but chaotic moment, and like some kind of pirate she surrendered to it.

Alex shifted onto his knees, setting the palm of his hand against the ceiling to stabilize them. Charlotte spread herself before him, floating, incantating. Her golden bee charms fluttered around her hard-pulsing wrist. Her hair swirled free. She was so content, she did not even notice the cobwebs dangling nearby. She saw only Alex, knowing he saw only her, as he took her with him into their own private heaven.

Afterward, they eased carefully back to earth, and Charlotte cuddled close against the black-inked barbs protecting Alex's heart. "Now this is a perfect happy ending," she sighed.

"You're wrong," he said, brushing the hair (and a grimy strand of cobweb he wisely did not mention) away from her eyes.

"Are you arguing with me in this romantic moment, sir?"

"Yes. And I'll show you why there will be no happy endings for us."

He spoke solemnly, but Charlotte was unafraid. They dressed again, gathering clothes at random from the floor, then Alex led the way through the darkening house, up the attic ladder to the roof. The house was gliding peacefully toward a darkening horizon stranded with the last wistful ribbons of day. The world beneath was indistinct, like the memory of a story but none of the words. Charlotte shivered as she sat on the ridgepole next to her pirate, and he slipped his arm around her.

"I'm not cold," she assured him. A residue of magic or love coursed like warm, sweet tea through her body.

"I know," Alex said, smiling. And she saw in his eyes that he did know—he saw her, and understood who she truly was. The warmth in her flared. "You're in thrall to the sky," he said, and she nodded, loving him, loving him so much.

He pointed to the velvet gray of north, where stars were beginning to appear. "Tomorrow I'm taking you there."

"Where, exactly?" she asked, witch-like.

"Anywhere, darling. Into the forever. Into a life of endless wondrous beginnings."

Her heart rose up, singing, to meet that wild path of stars.

"Well, then," she said, grinning. "Tally ho!"

❖ EPILOGUE ❖

LOVE—HOPE—FAITH

The sight of lovers feeds those in love—as does a substantial wedding buffet. On Cowes Island, the autumnal afternoon was fading into russet colors and sea breezes as the Wisteria Society stood around eating oyster canapés, stealing each other's purses, and admiring the rose garden that hosted the wedding. They awaited the arrival of the bridal couple to lead the first dance on the floor that had been laid at the garden's heart for this purpose. Amongst them was Vicar Dickersley, his hands shaking somewhat as he chatted with Miss Darlington about the contagion rate of stigmata. He had earlier performed the wedding with an eerie sense of déjà vu and several moral qualms that had been appeased by a hefty donation to his church; now, he really just wanted to go home. But the last boat off the island had already left, and the only other ways back to the mainland were by hitching a ride with a pirate or swimming. Vicar Dickersley was glad he had packed his togs.

At last the bride appeared, luminous in white, radiant with joy, hand in hand with her handsome, blushing groom. As they stepped onto the dance floor, the string quartet brought in for this occasion moved their shackles to a more comfortable position and began to play as if, for some reason, their lives depended on it. The groom swept his bride into a waltz.

"She looks so beautiful," Cecilia murmured contentedly to Ned, watching the couple swirl beneath a constellation of paper lanterns.

"Who does, my dear?" he asked. "I have eyes only for you." And grinning, he drew her onto the dance floor.

"He looks so pleased," Charlotte said with a warm sigh to Alex, captivated by the radiant wonder on Tom's face as Constantinopla allowed him to lead.

Alex kissed the top of her head. "What man wouldn't, at his first and only wedding?"

"Hush, you fiend," she whispered, and he laughed. Catching her hand, holding it between both of his, he half-pulled, half-cajoled her to dance with him. He was surprisingly graceful, and as they followed the others in a wide, slow ring, Charlotte found herself relaxing into the sensual rhythm more than any Plim should have done. But then, she was half Pettifer these days, and half something she had not yet worked out. And so she danced.

From across the floor, Cecilia caught her eye and winked. Charlotte smiled in response.

Vicar Dickersley, yawning as he watched the three couples, was suddenly so startled that he almost choked. For before his very eyes they were rising off the ground, their feet gliding on nothing more than glimmering light and rose-scented breezes.

"What witchcraft is this?" the vicar gasped.

Millie the Monster smacked his arm (and stole his cufflink). "Foolish man," she said. "It's just a mad, magnificent dream."

As the magic of Charlotte's wild, uncouth happiness rippled

through the garden, the Wisteria Society paused in their conversations and petty crime-doing to watch the young people dance. Tyrants they might be, lunatics they certainly were, but they also appreciated romance with all their vast and peculiar hearts. As one, they sighed dreamily. It really was a beautiful sight.

At least up until the wedding cake exploded.

Far south, in the British Museum, silence reigned. The doors had closed for the night, and the staff retired. Only two curators crept through the narrow basement corridors. They looked over their shoulders nervously as they went, half-expecting to be ambushed by old ladies or strange police inspectors. But no trouble befell them, and it was with a sigh of relief that they entered the archives room and locked the door behind them.

"Behind the 1802 tax records," one whispered, unshuttering his lantern to provide a dim light.

The other began removing heavy books from a shelf, revealing a small black box tucked almost invisibly in the deep shadows. He drew it out and then paused. Both men looked around, waiting for a woman in an ostrich-feathered hat to leap out, parasol flailing. When this did not happen, they released their breath, and one slowly opened the box.

An ugly glass and gold pendant lay on a bed of velvet.

"Somehow I thought the real thing would be less hideous," he said.

"No, it was an exact replica," his colleague answered.

"How much do you think it's worth?"

"More than your life, if the pirates ever find out we have it. Put it back now, and let's go get a beer. This place gives me chills."

They shut the box, returned it to its hiding place, and left the room, locking the door behind them. Hurrying away, they did not see the glimmering that radiated through gaps in the door frame.

"What was that sound?" asked one. "Almost like the sea on a shore?"

"Nothing," said the other, and pushed his colleague's shoulder to make him move faster. "It was nothing at all."

They hastened from the museum, and went to drink enough beer to make them forget they had ever seen an amulet at all.

And south again, down by the docks, an old woman disembarked from a fishing boat. She hobbled a slow way through grimy little streets lined with taverns and splashed with stains of a thankfully indeterminate nature. She was barefoot, her dress torn and smelling of fish, her gray hair hanging like seaweed down her neck. Stopping outside a pub, she sashayed in front of the first man who came out its door.

"Hey, mister," she said, giving him a crooked smile. "Want to get married?"

He said no, but she didn't let that stop her.

ACKNOWLEDGMENTS

Jane Austen said of her character Emma Woodhouse, "I'm going to take a heroine whom no one but myself will much like." That is how I felt as I wrote Charlotte Pettifer's story. I was concerned many people wouldn't be keen on my bristly, witchy girl, but I couldn't help adoring her. As I faced the daunting landscape of the blank page, Charlotte took it over with calm fearlessness—and ultimately allowed me to reveal her hidden anxieties. For all she is and all she gave me, not to mention all she did for Alex, I thank her.

Kristine Swartz, this book is more magical (literally!) because of you. Thank you so very much for the inspiration and guidance. Taylor Haggerty, I swear, you could soothe even Miss Darlington's nerves! I send you hugs and my warmest gratitude.

Bridget O'Toole, thank you for your encouragement and kindness that uplift me so often, and for filling my e-mail box with wonderful things. Stephanie Felty, I can't tell you how much I appreciate all you do for my books and all the mornings I've started off with a smile because of it. Christine Legon, Stacy Edwards, Mary Baker, Laura Corless, and everyone behind the scenes at Berkley—I'm sincerely grateful. Dawn Cooper and Katie Anderson, you have my endless, effusive thanks for giving me the cover of my dreams, even if I have lost a great deal of productive time just staring at it! And everyone in the Penguin creative team who time and again comes up with gorgeous graphics, videos, and art, thank you!

The Berkletes, including Courtney, Olivia, Freya, Ali, Alanna, Amy, Nekesa, Sarah G, Sarah Z, Eliza, Amanda, Joanna, Lauren, Libby, Lyn, Melissa, Mia, Elizabeth, and Lynn, who have extended to me such a warm hand of camaraderie—socks and BB gifs aside, I don't know what I'd have done without you!

All the romance authors who have been so welcoming, and the fabulous bookstagrammers, bibliophiles, booksellers, and kindred spirits I've gotten to know online—it's a delight to be amongst you! May you always have a good book to read and enough time to do so.

Jane Austen, who is (mis)quoted extensively herein, and William Shakespeare, the only author to surpass Austen in Charlotte Pettifer's literary esteem, all due honor goes to you.

And as always, Amaya, Mum, Simon, Anya, Myla, Dad, Steph—you are my happiness and my heart. I love you.

Keep reading for an excerpt from
India Holton's previous novel . . .

THE WISTERIA SOCIETY
OF LADY SCOUNDRELS

Available in paperback from Berkley Romance!

AN UNEXPECTED CALLER—THE PLIGHT OF THE AUK—
SEMANTICS—THE LEVEL MOON—NOT THE LEVEL MOON—
THE CALLER RETURNS—A DISCUSSION OF CHOLERA—
AN EXPLOSION—LUNCHEON IS SERVED

There was no possibility of walking to the library that day. Morning rain had blanched the air, and Miss Darlington feared that if Cecilia ventured out she would develop a cough and be dead within the week. Therefore Cecilia was at home, sitting with her aunt in a room ten degrees colder than the streets of London, and reading aloud *The Song of Hiawatha* by "that American rogue, Mr. Longfellow," when the strange gentleman knocked at their door.

As the sound barged through the house, interrupting Cecilia's recitation mid-rhyme, she looked inquiringly at her aunt. But Miss Darlington's own gaze went to the mantel clock, which was ticking sedately toward a quarter to one. The old lady frowned.

"It is an abomination the way people these days knock at any wild, unseemly hour," she said in much the same tone the prime minister had used in Parliament recently to decry the London rioters. "I do declare—!"

Cecilia waited, but Miss Darlington's only declaration came in the form of sipping her tea pointedly, by which Cecilia understood that the abominable caller was to be ignored. She returned to *Hiawatha* and had just begun proceeding "toward the land of the Pearl-Feather" when the knocking came again with increased force, silencing her and causing Miss Darlington to set her teacup into its saucer with a *clink*. Tea splashed, and Cecilia hastily laid down the poetry book before things really got out of hand.

"I shall see who it is," she said, smoothing her dress as she rose and touching the red-gold hair at her temples, although there was no crease in the muslin nor a single strand out of place in her coiffure.

"Do be careful, dear," Miss Darlington admonished. "Anyone attempting to visit at this time of day is obviously some kind of hooligan."

"Fear not, Aunty." Cecilia took up a bone-handled letter opener from the small table beside her chair. "They will not trouble me."

Miss Darlington harrumphed. "We are buying no subscriptions today," she called out as Cecilia left the room.

In fact they had never bought subscriptions, so this was an unnecessary injunction, although typical of Miss Darlington, who persisted in seeing her ward as the reckless tomboy who had entered her care ten years before, prone to climbing trees, fashioning cloaks from tablecloths, and making unauthorized doorstep purchases whenever the fancy took her. But a decade's proper education had wrought wonders, and now Cecilia walked the hall quite calmly, her French heels tapping against the polished marble floor, her intentions aimed in no way toward the taking of a subscription. She opened the door.

"Yes?" she asked.

"Good afternoon," said the man on the step. "May I interest you in a brochure on the plight of the endangered North Atlantic auk?"

Cecilia blinked from his pleasant smile to the brochure he was holding out in a black-gloved hand. She noticed at once the scandalous lack of hat upon his blond hair and the embroidery trimming his black frock coat. He wore neither sideburns nor mustache, his boots were tall and buckled, and a silver hoop hung from one ear. She looked again at his smile, which quirked in response.

"No," she said, and closed the door.

And bolted it.

Ned remained for a moment longer with the brochure extended as his brain waited for his body to catch up with events. He considered what he had seen of the woman who had stood so briefly in the shadows of the doorway, but he could not recall the exact color of the sash that waisted her soft white dress, nor whether it had been pearls or stars in her hair, nor even how deeply winter dreamed in her lovely eyes. He held only a general impression of "beauty so rare and face so fair"— and implacability so terrifying in such a young woman.

And then his body made pace, and he grinned.

Miss Darlington was pouring herself another cup of tea when Cecilia returned to the parlor. "Who was it?" she asked without looking up.

"A pirate, I believe," Cecilia said as she sat and, taking the little book of poetry, began sliding a finger down a page to relocate the line at which she'd been interrupted.

Miss Darlington set the teapot down. With a delicate pair of tongs fashioned like a sea monster, she began loading sugar cubes into her cup. "What made you think that?"

Cecilia was quiet a moment as she recollected the man. He had been handsome in a rather dangerous way, despite the ridiculous coat. A light in his eyes had suggested he'd known his brochure would not fool her, but he'd entertained himself with the pose anyway. She predicted his hair would fall over his brow if a breeze went through it, and that the slight bulge in his trousers had been in case she was not happy to see him—a dagger, or perhaps a gun.

"Well?" her aunt prompted, and Cecilia blinked herself back into focus.

"He had a tattoo of an anchor on his wrist," she said. "Part of it was visible from beneath his sleeve. But he did not offer me a secret handshake, nor invite himself in for tea, as anyone of decent piratic society would have done, so I took him for a rogue and shut him out."

"A rogue pirate! At our door!" Miss Darlington made a small, disapproving noise behind pursed lips. "How reprehensible. Think of the germs he might have had. I wonder what he was after."

Cecilia shrugged. Had Hiawatha confronted the magician yet? She could not remember. Her finger, three-quarters of the way down the page, moved up again. "The Scope diamond, perhaps," she said. "Or Lady Askew's necklace."

Miss Darlington clanked a teaspoon around her cup in a manner that made Cecilia wince. "Imagine if you had been out as you planned, Cecilia dear. What would I have done, had he broken in?"

"Shot him?" Cecilia suggested.

Miss Darlington arched two vehemently plucked eyebrows toward the ringlets on her brow. "Good heavens, child, what do you take me for, a maniac? Think of the damage a ricocheting bullet would do in this room."

"Stabbed him, then?"

"And get blood all over the rug? It's a sixteenth-century Persian antique, you know, part of the royal collection. It took a great deal of effort to acquire."

"Steal," Cecilia murmured.

"Obtain by private means."

"Well," Cecilia said, abandoning a losing battle in favor of the original topic of conversation. "It was indeed fortunate I was here. 'The level moon stared at him—'"

"The moon? Is it up already?" Miss Darlington glared at the wall as if she might see through its swarm of framed pictures, its wallpaper and wood, to the celestial orb beyond, and therefore convey her disgust at its diurnal shenanigans.

"No, it stared at Hiawatha," Cecilia explained. "In the poem."

"Oh. Carry on, then."

"'In his face stared pale and haggard—'"

"Repetitive fellow, isn't he?"

"Poets do tend to—"

Miss Darlington waved a hand irritably. "I don't mean the poet, girl. The pirate. Look, he's now trying to climb in the window."

Cecilia glanced up to see the man from the doorstep tugging on the wooden frame of the parlor window. Although his face was obscured by the lace curtain, she fancied she could see him muttering with exasperation. Sighing, she laid down the book once more, rose gracefully, and made her way through a clutter of furniture, statuettes, vases bearing long-stemmed roses from the garden (the neighbor's garden, to be precise), and various priceless (which is to say purloined) goods, to part the curtain, unlatch the window, and slide it up.

"Yes?" she asked in the same tone she had used at the doorstep.

The man seemed rather startled by her appearance. His hair had fallen exactly as she had supposed it would, and his shadowed eyes held a more sober mood than before.

"If you ask again for my interest in the great North Atlantic auk," Cecilia said, "I will be obliged to tell you the bird has in fact been extinct for almost fifty years."

"I could have sworn this window opened to a bedroom," he said, brushing his hair back to reveal a mild frown.

"We are not common rabble, to sleep on the ground floor. I don't know your name, for you have not done us the courtesy of leaving a calling card, but I assume it would in any case be a *nom de pirata*. I am all too aware of your kind."

"No doubt," he replied, "since you are also my kind."

Cecilia gasped. "How dare you, sir!"

"Do you deny that you and your aunt belong to the Wisteria Society and so are amongst the most notorious pirates in England?"

"I don't deny it, but that is my exact point. We are far superior to your kind. Furthermore, these are not appropriate business hours. We are ten minutes away from taking luncheon, and you have inconvenienced us twice now. Please remove yourself from the premises."

"But—"

"I am prepared to use a greater force of persuasion if required." She held up the bone-handled letter opener, and he laughed.

"Oh no, please don't prick me," he said mockingly.

Cecilia flicked a minuscule latch on the letter opener's handle. In an instant, with a hiss of steel, the letter opener extended to the extremely effective length of a rapier.

The man stepped back. "I say, there's no need for such violence. I only wanted to warn you that Lady Armitage has taken out a contract on your life."

From across the room came Miss Darlington's dry, brusque laugh. Cecilia herself merely smiled, and even then with only one side of her mouth.

"That is hardly cause for breaking and entering. Lady Armitage has been trying to kill my aunt for years now."

"Not your aunt," he said. "You."

A delicate flush wafted briefly over Cecilia's face. "I'm flattered. She has actually employed an assassin?"

"Yes," the man said in a dire tone.

"And does this assassin have a name?"

"Eduardo de Luca."

"Italian," Cecilia said, disappointment withering each syllable.

"You need to be a bit older before you can attract a proper assassin, my dear," Miss Darlington advised from the interior.

The man frowned. "Eduardo de Luca is a proper assassin."

"Ha." Miss Darlington sat back in her chair and crossed her ankles in uncharacteristically dissolute fashion. "I venture to guess Signor de Luca has never yet killed any creature greater than a fly."

"And why would you say that, madam?" the man demanded.

She looked down her nose at him, quite a feat considering she was some distance away. "A real assassin would hire a sensible tailor. And a barber. And would not attempt to murder someone five minutes before luncheon. Close the window, Cecilia, you'll catch consumption from that icy draft."

"Wait," the man said, holding out a hand, but Cecilia closed the window, turned the latch, and drew together the heavy velvet drapes.

"Do you think Pleasance might be ready soon with our meal?" she asked as she moved across the room—not to her chair, but to the door leading into the hall.

"Sit down, Cecilia," Miss Darlington ordered. "A lady does not pace in this restless manner."

Cecilia did as she was bidden but upon taking up her book laid it down again without a glance. She brushed at a speck of dust on her sleeve.

"Fidgeting." Miss Darlington snapped out the observation and Cecilia hastily placed both hands together on her lap.

"Maybe there will be chicken today," she said. "Pleasance usually roasts a chicken on Tuesdays."

"Indeed she does," Miss Darlington agreed. "However, today is Thursday. Where are your wits, girl? Surely you are not in such hysterics over a mere contract of assassination?"

"No," Cecilia said. But she bit her lip and dared a glance at Miss Darlington. The old lady looked back at her with a trace of sympathy so faint it might have existed only in Cecilia's imagination, were Cecilia to have such a thing.

"The assassin won't actually be Italian," she assured her niece. "Armitage doesn't have the blunt to employ a foreigner. It will be some jumped-up Johnny from the Tilbury Docks."

This did not improve Cecilia's spirits. She tugged unconsciously on the silver locket that hung from a black ribbon around her neck. Seeing this, Miss Darlington sighed with impatience. Her own locket of similar forlorn aspect rode the gray crinoline swathing her bosom, and she wished for a moment that she might speak once more with the woman whose portrait and lock of golden hair rested within. But then, Cilla would have even less patience for a sulking maiden.

"Lamb," she said with an effort at gentleness. Cecilia blinked, her eyes darkening to a wistful orphan blue. Miss Darlington frowned. "If it's Thursday," she elaborated, "luncheon will be lamb, with mint sauce and boiled potatoes."

"Yes, you're right," Cecilia said, pulling herself together. "Also peas."

Miss Darlington nodded. It was a satisfactory end to the matter, and she could have left it there. After all, one does not want to encourage the younger generation too much, lest they lose sight of their proper place: under one's thumb. She decided, however, to take pity on the girl, having herself once been as high-spirited. "Perhaps tomorrow the weather will be better fit for some perambulation," she said. "You might go to the library, and afterward get a bun from Sally Lunn's."

"But isn't that in Bath?"

"I thought a change of scenery might do us good. Mayfair is becoming altogether too rowdy. We shall fly the house down this afternoon. It will be a chance to give Pleasance a refresher course on the flight incantation's last stanza. Her vowels are still too flat. Approaching the ground with one's front door at a thirty-degree angle is rather more excitement than one likes for an afternoon. And yes, I can see from your expression you still think I shouldn't have shared the incantation's secret with her, but Pleasance can be trusted. Granted, she did fly that bookshop into the Serpentine when they told her they didn't stock any Dickens novels, but that only shows a praiseworthy enthusiasm for literature. She'll get us safely to Bath, and then you can take a nice stroll among the shops. Maybe you can buy some pretty lace ribbons or a new dagger before getting your iced bun."

"Thank you, Aunty," Cecilia answered, just as she was supposed to. In fact she would rather have gone to Oxford, or even just across the park to visit the Natural History Museum, but to suggest either would risk Miss Darlington reversing her decision altogether. So she simply smiled and obeyed. There followed a moment's pleasant quiet.

"Although eat only half the bun, mind you," Miss Darlington said as Cecilia took up *Hiawatha* and tried yet again to find her place among the reeds and water lilies. "We don't want you falling ill with cholera."

"That is a disease of contaminated water, Aunty."

Miss Darlington sniffed, not liking to be corrected. "A baker uses water I'm sure to make his wares. One can never be too careful, dear."

"Yes, Aunty. 'The level moon stared at him, in his face stared pale and haggard, 'til—'"

Crash!

The two women looked over at the window as it shattered. A grenade tumbled onto the carpet.

Cecilia expelled a sigh of tedium. She snapped the book shut, wended her way through the furnishings, pulled back the drapes, and deposited the grenade through the broken windowpane onto the terrace, where it exploded in a flash of burning light, brick shards, and fluttering lavender buds.

"Ahem."

Cecilia turned to see Pleasance standing in the drawing room doorway, plucking a glass splinter from one of the dark curls that habitually escaped her white lace cap.

"Excuse the interruption, misses, but I have news," she declared in the portentous tones of a young woman who spent too much time reading lurid Gothic fiction and consorting with the figments of her melodramatic imagination. "Luncheon is served."

Miss Darlington pushed herself up from the chair. "Please arrange for a glazier to come as soon as possible, Pleasance. We shall have to use the Lilac Drawing Room this afternoon, although I prefer to keep it for entertaining guests. The risk from that broken window is simply too great to bear. My own dear cousin nearly died of pneumonia under similar circumstances, as you know."

Cecilia murmured an agreement, although she recalled that Cousin Alathea's illness, contracted while attempting to fly a cottage in a hurricane, had little real consequence other than the loss of a chimney (and five crew members)—Alathea continuing on in robust health to maraud the coastline for several more years before losing a skirmish with Lord Vesbry's pet alligator while holidaying in the South of France.

Miss Darlington tapped a path across the room with her mahogany cane, but Cecilia paused, twitching the drapes slightly so as to peer through jagged glass and smoke at the garden. The assassin was leaning back against the iron railings of the house across the street. He noticed Cecilia and touched one finger to his temple in salutation. Cecilia frowned.

"Don't dawdle, girl," Miss Darlington chastised. Cecilia lowered the curtain, adjusting it slightly so it hung straight, and then followed her aunt toward the dining room and their Thursday lamb roast.

Photo courtesy of the author

INDIA HOLTON lives in New Zealand, where she has enjoyed the typical Kiwi lifestyle of wandering around forests, living barefoot on islands, and messing about in boats. Now she lives in a cottage near the sea, writing books about unconventional women and charming rogues, and drinking far too much tea.